Cross-eyed Dragon Troubles

Gloria Oliver

DEDICATION

This book is dedicated to my husband, John. It was his creativity and vision, which made this wonderful adventure possible.

CONTENTS

Also by Gloria Oliver

Novels:
Cross-eyed Dragon Troubles (YA Fantasy)
In the Service of Samurai (YA Fantasy))
Inner Demons (Urban Fantasy)
Jewel of the Gods (Fantasy)
The Price of Mercy (Fantasy)
Vassal of El (Fantasy)
Willing Sacrifice (YA Fantasy)

Coming in 2019:
Alien Redemption (SF)

Novelettes:
Charity and Sacrifice

Has Short Stories in the following Anthologies:
Tales From a Lone Star
A Lone Star in the Sky
Ladies of Trade Town
A Time To … Volume 2
Ripple Effect
The Four Bubbas of the Apocalypse
Houston: We've Got Bubbas
The Best of the Bubbas of the Apocalypse
Flush Fiction

Chapter One

IT JUST WASN'T fair. Talia scuffed at the soft ground with her foot. A hawk's cry echoed in the air, resonating with her own inner turmoil.

She sighed. It was just too early. She wasn't ready to be apprenticed yet.

With a frown, she looked up from where she sat on the front steps of her home and scanned the tilled fields and small buildings comprising the only world she knew. She scuffed angrily at the ground again then punched the bag at her side for good measure. She was only fifteen—she wasn't ready!

Only three days ago her parents calmly informed her they'd apprenticed her to the Dragon Knight's Guild. She'd ranted and raged at them, and they'd listened to her arguments, but they all knew it would change nothing. It was just the way things were done.

Was it so grievous a thing that she didn't want to leave her home? She would have a better life, more opportunities, by being apprenticed, they told her. But what if she didn't want those things? She was perfectly happy here!

Though their town was small, there were several people she could apprentice with here rather than go so far away. None of their crafts were all that interesting, but she would get to stay here. Yet her parents told her it was too late for that—money had changed hands.

A soft breeze caressed her cheek as if trying to comfort her troubled face. Talia breathed deeply, calmed a little by the scent of turned earth and evergreens—all pieces of what she thought of as home.

She knew her parents gave up a lot to get her apprenticed, and with the Dragon's Knight Guild no less. She would do her duty because it would make them happy, but she couldn't pretend to like it.

Not when they were coming for her today.

Her few possessions didn't take long to pack. Three sets of clothes and undergarments. The brush and mirror set Uncle Shay brought as a gift from his last visit to the capital two years ago. A dress, a present from her mother, made from fabric bought with the last of their savings. Last, the strange rock she and Lir found in the river when they were little and which she'd kept all these years.

Talia took out the mirror and studied her reflection and that of the whitewashed porch behind her on its surface. She stared at her short, brown, curly hair, her triangular face, and dark brown eyes. How would she look once her apprenticeship was over? Would her parents even recognize her? Would her years away change her until her home meant little to nothing to her anymore?

She put the mirror back in her bag, shying away from such thoughts. All her worldly possessions were in this small bag. She was sure others owned more to show for their lives than she did, but material things weren't so important to her. Other things she couldn't take she would miss more—her room in the loft, her mom's special winter porridge, the smell of freshly tilled fields. Watching the sunsets and the rising stars from the roof. Lir's teasing and playing tag after school. Helping her father with his wood projects and working the fields. All the things she could only take with her as memories. A pang of coming loss poured through her. It was all she could do not to cry. She didn't want to go.

A large shadow crossed the yard. Talia glanced up and used her hand to shade her eyes. She didn't recognize the strange silhouette. Blinking rapidly, she saw a shape zoom past the morning sun. Its wings weren't in the familiar figure of a falcon's or a hawk's; they were more angular, wider. The tail, it was all wrong. It was long and thin. She doubted it was made of feathers. Then the strange shape twisted in the air and dropped, spiraling down.

"Mom! Dad!" Talia raced out from beneath the porch, trying to keep the odd, falling figure in sight. She heard the door of the house open behind her but didn't look back as her parents hurried outside. "Look up there!"

She pointed upwards and watched the shape grow larger and larger as it fell. It twisted and spiraled at reckless speeds. Her breath caught as she made out the creature's long neck and big head, its colossal body colored dark green with purple flowing from the scaled ridges on its back.

Goosebumps flowed up her arms—she was seeing an actual dragon!

Talia's eyes grew even wider as she spotted something glinting on the dragon's back and realized it was an armored figure. Someone was on the thing.

The dragon and rider continued to plummet. Talia took a step back, her chest tight as they came closer.

Something was wrong. They were coming down too fast. Just when she thought they would crash to their deaths, the dragon pulled up his body and instead plowed sideways into the ground. Dirt and plants were thrown everywhere. Its large body came to a stop in the middle of the cornfield.

"No!" Talia rushed forward in a half-panic, as she saw the rider go under the dragon's massive bulk. Her hurried breaths filled with the smell of earth and something more profound, foreign. She gave the beast a wide berth as she ran around it looking for signs of the rider. She hesitated as the dragon rocked once against the plowed ground then righted itself.

She stared in dumbfounded amazement as a moment later the rider who'd been pinned beneath the monstrous mass slowly sat up and staggered to his feet. Seemingly unhurt, he reached up and removed a dirt-covered helmet whose large red plume had seen better days.

"Are you all right?" Talia stared, not sure how he could possibly be standing after what she just saw.

The young man shook out his sweat-matted, sandy-blond hair and glanced over at her. His intense blue gaze locked with her own. A small smile tugged at his lips, brightening his flushed face. "I'm quite all right. Thank you for asking." He took off one of his gauntlets and ran a hand through his wet hair.

Talia frowned, for though her mind insisted it should be different, other than looking as if he'd been at work in the fields for hours without rest, the armored man seemed to be just as he claimed.

"Do you have any water?" he asked her softly.

It took her a moment to realize he was speaking to her.

"Oh. Yes, we have a well on the other side of the

house. I'll, I'll get some for you."

"No, it's okay. I'll get it." The young man waved her off and staggered toward the residence.

Talia followed him with her gaze, still not sure whether or not she believed him. It was then she noticed her parents standing on the porch staring at her, their faces filled with fear and shock. She felt a cold shiver travel down her back as she remembered she wasn't alone. Even as her eyes moved of their own volition to glance to her right, the dragon's head swiveled on its long neck to take a look at her with one, large, purple eye.

Talia heard her mother gasp, even as she felt her own knees lock, the rest of her going terribly still.

The strange smell she noticed as she approached them earlier was definitely coming from him.

Small, dark green scales with just a touch of purple covered the dragon's long face. Its eye was a deeper purple, almost black, and it stared at her with keen intelligence. It was only when it tilted its head to the side to look at her with both eyes that she realized they were crossed.

Hello.

She heard her own in-drawn breath of surprise echoed by her parents as the soft voice rang in their heads. Was there a touch of amusement in the greeting? Talia didn't know and at the moment was too terrified to care. "H— hello?"

The massive, scaled body moved and shook the ground as the dragon twisted to take an even better look at her. A long, snake-like tongue darted out of the dragon's large mouth; she could see sharp, wicked teeth glinting at her. She gulped as it occurred to her the dragon might be hungry.

Before the thought could go much further, the

dragon's rider came back from around the house carrying a filled bucket with water. "Here you go, Clarence." As if the large creature before him were nothing to fear, he set the water before it.

Talia stared at the bucket. It looked like a thimble compared to the size of the giant snout. The dragon's tongue reached down, dipped into the water and rapidly flicked it up into the gaping mouth.

"Do you have any other buckets?" the young man asked. "It would really help me out. He's likely to want to go through at least ten of those." He gave her a friendly look.

Talia tore her gaze away from the drinking dragon so she could find a voice to answer him with. "Su—sure. I'll go get them." Feeling abruptly free, she took off and headed to the shed at the back of the house. She glanced back behind her once, not totally able to discard the fear the dragon might come after her.

Breathing hard, she quickly searched the shed for the buckets and found three. She grabbed them and rushed to the well where she found the young rider waiting for her.

"Here."

"Thanks!" He took the buckets and dropped the line to bring up more water. "By the way, my name is Kel, and my friend over there is Clarence."

She could only nod, trying hard not to look in the dragon's direction.

"Your name is Talia, right?" She could only nod again.

As Kel worked to pull up the water, she studied him carefully for the first time. It wasn't often she got a chance to meet strangers, and this pair was stranger than most. In these parts, blue eyes were rare, especially bright ones like his. Kel's features were rounded, not as sharp as those of the people around her village. His hair was also lighter than tended to be the norm. She rather favored it.

She'd also noticed in his voice a slight accent she'd not heard before. She was sure he must be from somewhere far away.

"He'll need to rest for a few minutes before we can start back," Kel explained. "I hope it's all right."

Talia quickly nodded, then looked away as she realized he'd caught her staring. "No, no, that's fine."

After the buckets were filled, she volunteered to help him carry them over to where the dragon still lounged in the field, though she made sure not to get too close. Only after three more sets of buckets were brought over did Kel finally sit down and take a long drink for himself. Once he was done, he leaned back on the ground, his armor creaking, and sighed with relief. Talia jumped as Clarence slowly stretched out and laid himself out in the sun as well, his eyes closed.

She stared at them as they lay there and rested, as it slowly dawned on her that this man was a Dragon Knight— that these were the people she was apprenticed to. It also made her think of her parents. Glancing behind her, she saw they'd come off the porch but were sticking quite close to one another. Her mother spotted her looking at them and, after making sure Kel and the dragon weren't paying them any attention, waved for her to come over.

Talia did and noticed her father staring sadly at his ruined fields then with disbelief at the cause of the destruction of some of this year's crop. She turned to look that way herself.

Almost as if he sensed he was the object of scrutiny, Clarence opened his eyes and swiveled his massive head to stare at them. Talia suddenly found herself hugged hard from behind by her mother, who pulled her a few more steps back.

With a long, rippling movement, the dragon rose to his feet. He shook the dirt off himself as would a dog throwing off water after a swim, then lumbered in a drunken walk to the edge of the fields and squatted. Before long, a large pile of dark excrement accumulated on the ground. Talia and her parents all curled their noses at the pungent smell.

You can take this and sell it to your local alchemist. The three of them stared at the dragon as his words whispered themselves into their minds. *Dragon refuse always brings in a good price. This will hopefully make up for the unfortunate mess I've made of your fields.*

None of them said anything; they just stared at the dragon in amazement.

After a few minutes, Kel stretched and yawned before he sat up and quickly rubbed his face. Standing up, he brushed off some of the dirt Clarence inadvertently rained on him earlier and approached Talia and her stunned parents. "I almost forgot," he said, "I'm supposed to give you this." He took a small pouch from his belt and handed it to her father.

Her father opened the pouch then looked up, confused. Talia was released from her mother's hold as she, too, turned to see what was inside. As her father poured the contents out onto his hand, Talia was able to see what Kel had given them. Her eyes grew wide. In her father's palm, glinting in the sun, were three beautiful rubies. Her father stared at them, his mouth moving but no sound coming out. She'd never seen her father speechless before. "We, we don't understand..."

Kel's answering shrug was mostly dispelled in his armor. "It's just payment for the trouble and the fact your daughter is being taken so far from home."

Talia frowned, sure the damage and the inconvenience weren't worth a small fortune. Why would the knights pay them so much more than her parents paid to get her into the guild? It didn't make any sense to her. Was this really a standard practice of the dragon knights?

"If you'll get your things, I think Clarence is about ready to go." Talia found herself once more the recipient of Kel's shy smile.

"Ah, sure." She turned away as a bolt of excited fear shot through her. It was true—she was really going. It was happening. Sudden mixed feelings rose inside her, but not all of them were made of the unhappiness she felt over the last few days.

Picking up her bag from where she'd left it on the porch steps, she suddenly found herself surrounded by her parents. The tears she saw gathering in her mother's eyes told her more than anything that this was real.

"Talia." Her mother took her in her arms and hugged her hard. She felt tears rising to her own eyes. Her mother eventually let go.

"Be good, won't you? I know you'll make us proud." Her father hugged her fiercely. Tears shone in his eyes as well.

She almost sobbed then. How was she going to go on without them?

"Be strong, my daughter." He slipped one of the rubies into her hand. "Write us if you can."

Her mother wiped away at her eyes. "Don't forget us. Always remember that we love you." The sorrow in her mother's eyes brought home to her that it was as difficult for them to let her go as it was for her to leave. Yet they still wanted her to do this.

She felt her throat grow tight. "I will. And I'll try really hard. I love you." She hugged them both at once. She was going; she was really going.

When she finally let them go, all their eyes were filled with tears. Talia turned away and wiped at her wet face, then searched for where she had dropped her bag. It was gone. Glancing around her, she spotted Kel with it, as he secured it to the battered two-person saddle strapped to the dragon's back. She hesitated a moment, then walked over to join them.

Almost there, she turned around to take a last look at her parents and her home. As hard as she could, she tried to engrave into her memory the view of the whitewashed house with its sloping porch, the plowed fields with their earthy smell and swaying stalks of wheat and corn, the barn with all the sheep, cows, and horses. It would be years before she saw any of it again. But she would be back. Of this she was sure. She would make her parents proud even if she possessed no idea of what it was she would be doing.

Her eyes stinging, Talia turned away and forced herself to approach the dragon. She hurriedly rubbed her eyes again as she caught Kel studying her.

"I'll need to show you a couple of things before we get started," he said.

She noticed his light, amused smile as she still hesitated to get too near to Clarence. She made herself step closer.

"See these?" Kel pointed to some long, leather straps hanging from the saddle. "I'll help you tie them on once we get you up. They'll make sure you stay on your seat in case anything happens. The Administrator frowns on us losing any new students." His expression was serious, but his eyes were full of mirth. Clarence snorted behind them.

Talia wasn't sure she wanted to know just how exactly they went about losing a student.

"There's a place here you can use to hold on to." He pointed to a grip on the front of the second seat of the leather saddle. "If you feel you're slipping at all though, you might want to hold onto one of Clarence's scales instead." Gently he lifted one of the dragon's green, oval-shaped scales from where it lay flat against its brothers. "It's attached to his skin here, and it takes a lot to make one of them come off. It won't hurt him, so don't worry about it. He's also worm-free, so you don't have to be concerned on that account, either."

Her brows drew together, not knowing about half of the things he just mentioned or what they meant. Why would a dragon have worms?

"Here, I'll help you up." Kel cupped his gauntleted hands together to give her a boost up Clarence's broad side.

Still tense and apprehensive, she put her foot in his cupped hands and, with a tentative hold on one of Clarence's scales, pulled herself up onto the back seat of the large saddle. Now that she was on board, the scent of oil and possibly jasmine mixed with the strange, animal scent she smelled before.

The leather saddle felt comfortable and warm and looked to have seen heavy use. Its surface was smooth, though not as smooth as Clarence's scale.

Once she settled herself in, Kel climbed up with the ease of long practice, using the scales as foot and handholds to climb up. He sat down in the saddle backward so he would be facing her.

Going slowly and explaining as he went, Kel showed her how to take each of the saddle's straps and where to loop them to safely secure herself in her seat. Once he tested their handiwork to make sure it was tight, he turned around and strapped himself in as well. When he was done, he took his helmet off the pommel before him and put it on.

Talia grabbed hold of the groove before her with a yelp as Clarence rose to his feet. She could feel his muscles moving beneath her, bringing her higher into the air than a horse ever could.

"The trip is going to be long and a little bumpy, I'm afraid." Kel turned his head in her direction. "You might not have noticed it, but Clarence is cross-eyed, and he has an inner ear problem, too. It tends to make our trips a little interesting."

"But—" The word had barely left her lips when Clarence swept open his long wings with a snap. Realizing what it meant, she grabbed hold of the saddle even tighter. Clarence's legs churned the ground, and he went into a snaking run, then leaped into the air.

Talia was jerked back as the dragon moved. She held on for dear life. The wind whipped past her, smacking her as if it were angry. She turned to look down and watched in horrid fascination as all she knew shrunk below her. As Clarence pumped with his vast wings and spiraled upwards, roads became thin lines and fields took on the look of squares on a quilt. A thick dark blue line below them she was sure must be the Morrass River. Beside it, the small town of Queegam was turned into dozens of miniature dollhouses with ants crawling all about.

The wonder of the view was just beginning to imprint itself in her mind when Clarence stopped his climb and leveled out.

One of his wings dipped too far to the right and suddenly tilted them sideways.

The saddle shifted, and with a scream clamoring in her throat, Talia released the saddle's groove and grabbed hold of two of Clarence's scales. The scales were almost cool to the touch, but this was pretty much lost to her as Clarence overcompensated for his original error and threw them all sailing in the opposite direction.

The ride at no time grew steady. Without fail, every few seconds Clarence would invariably dip too far one way or the other. It was all she could do just to hold on. She kept wishing the saddle held more straps, that it was nailed to Clarence's back, or better still that she'd never left the ground to begin with. A strong gust of wind caught Clarence's wings like sails and pushed them all back. Talia's scream was lost in the wind as Clarence tilted backward and over.

When the dragon twisted back to the right direction things got worse as he somehow got them turned upside down. Clarence dropped like a rock and took them with him. Talia tried to scream again but shut her mouth as her stomach rose to her throat. Any sound she might have made was stolen by the wind as if it were rejoicing in her misery. She clung on, her heart hammering in her chest, as Clarence was finally able to right himself.

Sorry. Clarence's tone seemed shy yet at the same time amused.

She felt a metal-shod hand on her shoulder but wasn't willing to open her eyes. Was this what it was to be a Dragon Knight? She wanted nothing to do with it. She wanted to go home.

The dizzying ride continued for what seemed like forever. They dipped, they dropped, they rolled. Hardly was there a moment it could be said they went in a straight line. She just held on knowing she had no choice but to endure it. But how did Kel do it? He had willingly got back on after the horrid landing at her house and with the dragon falling on top of him, too. Was he mad, then?

We're almost there. Clarence's voice came clearly into her mind. *If you look, you can see the school.*

Despite her stomach's vigorous protests, Talia opened her eyes to see where she would soon be living.

A large mesa rose before them snuggled amidst tall mountains. Nestled in the middle of this mesa was the largest building she'd ever seen. Instinctively, she knew what it was. It could be nothing else—and it was grander and more massive than she ever imagined from the stories told by the bards who occasionally traveled through town. It was a castle.

Clarence circled the mesa, almost as if he were giving her a chance to get a good look. His circling pattern brought them closer and closer. The structure grew before them the nearer they came. On top of the castle, at a steep angle, was a flat white dish with numbers. After a moment, Talia realized it was a clock—and it was huge! The one which was such a source of pride and joy to Queegam was nothing in comparison.

Balconies protruded from the castle on every side. Gigantic flying buttresses held the whole structure together, making it look even more extensive and grander than it already was.

Close to the stone castle was another building. It was almost as large as the former but made of wood rather than stone. The exterior was virtually identical in design but held long slit windows instead of balconies. A wooden castle? It was something she'd not heard of before.

Surrounding the castles were cultivated fields and a small forest. On one side of the grounds was a large strip of land which ran from one end of the mesa to the other, lined by bushes and trees. Once they came close enough, Clarence dived for it.

Talia lost all feeling in her hands, her knuckles turning

white, as the ground seemed to rush up toward them. The castle and mesa expanded rapidly around them as they headed straight down. She couldn't tear her gaze away from the approaching doom. Her mind screamed at her that she was about to die!

Clarence shifted up as the ground blurred before them like a wall and plowed into the strip of land, claws first. Talia's teeth clacked together from the impact, which made her already tight jaw hurt. The dragon slipped, his legs going out from under him, and he slid across the ground on his stomach. His body tilted sideways, throwing dirt up everywhere even as he continued to slide.

Talia ducked down onto the saddle, trying to avoid the flying clumps of earth. She held on with everything she possessed and watched the rolling dirt as Clarence dipped slightly more to one side, shifting her even closer to the moving ground. With cold terror, she recalled his landing on her father's fields. While Kel might somehow miraculously survive being landed on by a dragon, she doubted she would be as lucky. As fast as she could, she sent out quick prayers to as many of the twenty gods who watched over her land as she could recall.

Clarence's body plowed into a thick line of bushes which appeared as if they received this kind of treatment regularly. Talia felt her heart rise into her throat as she saw the lip of a cliff not ten arm lengths beyond them.

Both of Clarence's claws reached out, grabbed like anchors onto the dirt, and brought them to a rough stop before they could go over the side.

Talia made her lungs breathe again, until that moment absolutely sure they wouldn't make it. Her gaze was locked to the cliff's edge not five paces from them; she was sure they were still about to fall.

"Talia, are you all right?"

She heard Kel turn around before her, his concern evident in his voice. Not trusting herself to do anything but scream if she opened her mouth, she forced herself to nod instead. He quickly undid his straps then turned fully in the saddle to work on hers.

Once they were all loosened, she found she still couldn't move. Her numbed fingers were wrapped tightly about Clarence's scales and didn't seem in any mood to let go.

Kel didn't say anything, but slipped out of the saddle to the ground and removed his helmet, shaking his damp hair. Clarence lay quietly, craning his neck to look at them, and waited for them both to get off.

Talia tried again to make her fingers move, but they were having nothing to do with it. She felt stupid and self-conscious half-hanging as she was from the saddle, but couldn't bring herself to attract attention to her present predicament. Even as she tried fervently to think of what she could do, she noticed Clarence's eyes focus in her direction. Kel suddenly turned from where he was retrieving her bag as if someone were speaking to him.

"Oh, you're right." Kel let go of the straps and pulled the gauntlets off his hands, letting them drop to the ground. He half-climbed back on the dragon, an apologetic look on his face. "Here, let me help you."

Talia glanced away as his hands touched her fingers and carefully worked to pry them off Clarence's scales one by one. She flinched as the blood flowed back into them again and they tingled with pain.

"Don't worry, they'll be as good as new in a minute." Gently, he put her right hand between his and rubbed the feeling back into it.

She tried not to cringe as the pain in her hand got

worse before it got better. After about a minute or so, he let go of her right hand and took up the other. As she experimentally flexed her fingers, he reached up to help her down. "Thanks."

Once on the ground, Talia found her knees feeling weak, but they held. She was very grateful. She was sure she'd already made enough of a fool of herself for one day.

After studying her for a moment to make sure she was all right, Kel turned back to Clarence and retrieved her bag. He gave it to her then picked up his gauntlets and helmet. "I'll meet you at your place once I've taken her inside. All right?" He glanced over at the dragon. The boy nodded as if he received an answer though Talia didn't hear anything.

The dragon waited patiently until they stepped away then rolled up to his feet. He shook himself, sending dirt and pieces of bush flying everywhere.

Talia used her arms to cover her face against the assault. When it seemed to be over, she peeked out only to find Clarence looking in her direction.

It was a pleasure to meet you, Talia.

"Y—yes, the same here." Though she definitely hoped she'd never have the pleasure of ever having to ride on him again. If all dragons flew the same as he did, she wasn't sure why anyone would ever want to become a Dragon Knight in the first place.

Clarence inclined his head, almost as if he guessed her thoughts. He then lumbered along the long dirt track they'd used for the landing over to a spacious, cobbled path between the cultivated fields. Kel turned to follow in the same direction and waved for her to come along. Taking a deep breath, hoping her legs were steadier than before, she started after him.

Once her confidence grew and she became positive the ground would stay beneath her feet, Talia looked ahead at what lay down the road. The stone castle she'd seen from the air towered over her, imperious and foreboding. Three rows of balconies crowded the upper floors of the four-storied structure. Her mind boggled as she tried to count them and guessed they numbered around a hundred per level.

Between each balcony and descending all the way to the ground flying buttresses supported the massive walls. As she studied them, it felt as if she were gazing at a many-legged spider, lazily waiting for its next meal. She shuddered, feeling more and more insignificant in comparison to the mighty building. She glanced at Kel, who just kept walking as if the oppressive, towering structure before them were nothing at all. It was difficult to fathom how she might ever think of such a place as home.

The cobbled road split off to the right, and Clarence wove off in that direction. Kel kept on the main course and headed toward a set of dark double-doors. The doors were a full story tall and at least as wide as the length of two horses. The door on the right was slightly ajar, and he stepped through it to the inside. Talia reached out to touch the dark wood and found it amazingly smooth. The doors were as thick as her forearm was long.

Kel's footsteps echoed in the still air as he walked on the polished green marble floor within. The light was muted inside though still bright enough to see by. The entryway was large with cushioned benches on the far side facing the doors. Colorful paintings of knights astride ferocious-looking dragons decorated the walls. A carved column rose to the tall ceiling every ten feet or so, shaped to represent knights in armor. The air smelled clean and the floor shined, yet all of it still seemed imbued with a deep sense of antiquity.

"Nice, don't you think?" Kel was smiling at her openmouthed amazement. She was only able to nod, not having seen anything so splendid in her life.

"This way." He led her down a broad hallway on the right.

They'd not gone far before he stopped in front of a closed door. He knocked on it twice then opened it, but didn't go in. "This is where I leave you. Tammer is inside. He'll get you your room assignment." He gave her a shy smile and set her bad on the floor. "Maybe I'll see you again later."

"Thank you." It was all she could think of to say. She was here. This was all really happening. The fact the only person she'd met was about to leave her only made her heart beat faster.

"Take care." Kel took his leave.

Talia watched him go as she stood not quite in the new room's open doorway until he disappeared from sight.

"Come on in, would you please? I haven't got all day."

She turned around, grabbed her bag, and stepped into the room at the impatient voice. "Sorry, sir."

The office she found herself in was small but comfortable. Several deep chairs sat before a long oak desk, which was bare except for an inkwell and quill as well as a lone folder.

"Sit. Sit."

She did as she was told and tried not to look directly at the desk's occupant. The man there seemed to be about thirty. His hair was even lighter than Kel's, but his eyes were a deep brown. His squared features were bland and unexcited. Without ado, he opened the folder before him.

"You're Talia from the village of Queegam, is that correct?"

"Yes, sir." She felt butterflies swash madly in her stomach.

Tammer made a notation on the papers before him. "You've been assigned to the Rimorn room," he said without much emotion. "You'll find it up the right corner stairs on the next level, the one with the red marble floor. Just follow the hallway. Your room will be the twenty-fifth on the right." He made another notation on the papers.

"Your appointment with the Administrator is tomorrow morning at nine," he continued. "You'll find her office behind the gold door on the fourth level." He glanced up, for the first time making eye contact. His brow arched high as he looked at her. "You do know how to read a clock face, don't you?"

"Y—yes." Pendrora, Queegam's schoolteacher, made sure they all learned how. The village owned a leaky water clock in the center of town, but it didn't keep good time. On many occasions, she'd wondered why her teacher bothered. The sun was more than good enough to tell time by. Plus, they didn't own a clock at home. Now she mentally thanked Pendrora for having made them learn it anyway.

"Good." Tammer scribbled something else on the papers. "I guess that's it then." He set the quill down. "Go ahead and find your room. Don't forget about your appointment in the morning." He closed the folder and dropped it into a drawer.

Talia stood up, clear on the dismissal, yet feeling there surely needed to be more. "But—"

Tammer stood up and led her outside into the hall, closing the office door behind them. "The stairs are over there. I suggest you get moving." He pointed off to the right to a stairwell in the far corner.

"But—"

Without another word, he turned away from her and headed off in the opposite direction. She stared after him, totally uncomprehending. This was all he felt she needed to know?

For hours the night before Kel came for her, she'd wondered what it'd be like to be here. Yet, though the building itself seemed more than anything she might have expected, her introduction to the guild was less than she'd thought possible. Was this how they did things in the outside world? How could they just bring in total strangers and tell them nothing at all then leave them on their own? How was she supposed to know what she could and couldn't do?

Abruptly uncertain and lost, Talia felt conspicuous standing there in the vast hallway alone. Realizing there was nothing else she could do, she headed for the stairs Tammer had pointed out to her.

The staircase leading up to her room at home was barely wide enough for a grown adult. The stairs before her now could have easily handled at least ten people standing side by side. The hard stone was worn down from use. Her mind boggled at the number of feet which would have needed to walk on it to make it that way. Even the dark, wood banister was large, the same as everything else she'd seen of this place. She felt dwarfed and alone. Was such a vast place really necessary? She remembered her guess at the number of balconies she'd spotted on the outside of the castle and she was stunned by how many apprentices it would take to fill them all. Most large guilds held ten to thirty apprentices at a time, and those were only located in major cities. This place held many, many more, and they were all to be Dragon Knights? Were there that many dragons in the world?

The stairs reached a landing then continued up. The second floor, as she'd been told, was covered in red marble. Doors were set only on the wall closest to the outside, while on the opposite side were chest-high banisters facing the middle of the building, making the hallway a sort of indoor balcony. Other than for her, the hall was totally empty.

Talia started down the passage, counting doors, and tried to ignore her rising uneasiness. As she went along, she thought she heard low voices coming from the other side of the banister. Curious, and at the same time eager to prove this place held other living beings, she stepped over to take a look.

Beyond the railing, a vast expanse spread out before her all the way to the other side of the building. Looking up, she could see two more stories like this one. All three made a full rectangle and were open in the middle.

Beyond the top floor, she could see the angled ceiling for the roof, which in the center displayed huge round holes covered in what appeared to be glass, which allowed the sunshine to filter inside.

Looking down, she found all those she'd not seen so far. The area below her was split into roofless rooms by flimsy, movable wooden walls. Children who appeared to be grouped by age sat in desks in clusters of twelve or so, listening raptly to a teacher. Their voices rose and mingled together so she couldn't make out what was being said. Soon she, too, would be there with them.

Talia watched them for a few minutes, her previous unease settling a bit at the normal looking activity. The children and young people she spotted below looked to be of all races and colors. She'd not realized so many existed. Back home, Pendrora used some simple maps to show them other places but they'd never really meant much to her. Now she saw the world might just be a lot bigger than she'd ever thought.

Finally pulling herself away from the balustrade, she resumed her count and searched for her room. Beside each door was a small plaque bearing a name. The twenty-fifth door, the one which was supposed to be hers, stood slightly ajar. The plaque beside it was inscribed with the name Rimorn, just as she'd been told it would. Taking a deep breath, she ventured inside.

To say the room was large was an understatement. It was at least the size of the main floor of her house, if not bigger. To the left, nestled in its own nook in the wall, was a massive set of bunk beds made of mahogany. Its thick supports were carved yet were almost worn smooth by the thousands of students who'd slept on them over the years. On the far wall were two full doors with glass, an extravagant expense, which opened out onto a large balcony. With each door came a set of shutters and a thick bar that would fit in the hooks behind them. Offsetting this were thick curtains, which at the moment were pulled back.

To her right, Talia spotted a majestic stone tub filled almost to the brim with steaming water. She frowned, wondering if someone finished filling it right before she arrived, for she could see no signs of a fire.

Two dressers sat against the wall by the door and perpendicular to them was a generous desk with a stack of unmarked books, several quills, and an inkwell. In a niche close to the balcony doors stood a gorgeous arrangement of flowers. The slot on the opposite side held a miniature water clock and pendulum. Talia stared at the latter in total fascination, not ever having dreamed one could be made so small. If she stood close and listened hard, she could even hear the water as it flowed inside it.

A small, utilitarian vanity sat not far from the beds and held a water-filled basin. Beside it were two buckets stacked inside each other. Next to them was a regular sized door. Opening it, she found a small closet filled with linens, two more buckets, and cleaning implements.

As she looked around, Talia noticed not all the light in the room was coming from outside. High in the walls, she spotted several globes, which seemed to be glowing. She raised her hand toward one but felt no heat emanating from it. Her brow furrowed not knowing such a thing was possible.

Shaking her head, she turned and decided to put her things away. Her meager possessions barely took up two of the available drawers on the first dresser. With the two beds and the extra dresser, she wondered if she'd be sharing the room with someone. As far as she could tell, however, there was no indication this would be the case.

After she finished, she noticed a bronze plaque set into the back of the room's door as well as a place for another wooden bar. Embossed on the sign were the times for the serving of breakfast, lunch, and dinner, which were at seven, noon, and six. It seemed cold and impersonal.

A pang of longing for her parents and home cut through her. Everything seemed to be so different from what she was used to. Nothing felt familiar anymore. She sighed, suddenly tired. Moving toward the balcony to glance at the sun outside, she made herself stop and look at the clock beside her instead. It was only three o'clock. That was three hours before dinner, three hours on her own. Her stomach took this as its cue to remind her she'd not eaten lunch. With another sigh, she lay down on the lower bed and was almost swallowed by the soft, thick mattress.

She glanced up and didn't see the familiar sight of her room's low rafters or the gentle inside slope of the roof. Instead, she found the carved and scarred surface of the bottom of the bed above her.

Someone had scratched in rough sketches of the school's floor plan in the wood. Each floor was there, even the location of the Administrator's office. It also showed her other essential things like the location of the kitchens and the dining hall. Other students looked to have added other bits of information—class names and times, information she wasn't sure applied to her. Others seemed to have been content just to add their own names or initials almost as if to make sure those who came after would know they'd been there. As her eyes closed on their own, she wondered where they all were now.

Chapter Two

THE CHIRPING SINGSONG of a bird startled Talia awake. Realizing she'd inadvertently fell asleep, she scampered out of bed in a panic. What time was it? Did she miss dinner? She glanced at the clock, once she remembered it was there, and saw it was only a quarter past five. Her speeding heart slowed as she realized she hadn't missed another meal after all.

Without slipping back into the bed, lest it lull her back to sleep, she leaned over it and looked up to study the map scrawled there again. Having time, she decided it might not hurt to make sure of where the Administrator's office was as well as where she'd have to go for dinner.

After she made sure their locations were set in her mind, she braved herself to leave.

The hallway outside was as deserted as it'd been hours ago. If she listened, though, she could still hear the soft hum of voices below her. With quiet steps, she turned right and moved to the stairwell at the far end of the hall. According to the map, a major stairway filled up each of the building's four corners. This one was only slightly smaller than the one she'd used earlier to come up. On the landing to the third floor, she saw the tiles there were of black marble. When she reached the landing for the fourth and final floor, she saw those were colored a sparkling white.

Heading off to the right again, Talia spotted the Administrator's golden door long before she reached it. The door was tall, almost as high as the ceiling. When she got there, she stared up at it. The feeling of being small and insignificant washed over her again. She shivered. Did her parents feel this way when they went for their apprenticeships? She mentally kicked herself, realizing she should have spent her time before coming here asking questions rather than brooding on her unfair fate. Two other doors filled the hallway where the Administrator's office was located. They stood as tall as the Administrator's, but one was made of silver and the other of bronze. As she wondered what they meant, she decided she'd been there long enough and retreated down the nearest set of stairs.

Not far from there, on the first floor, she found the dining hall. The room was huge, extending almost half the length of one of the building's shorter sides. Massive tables filled the room, each lined with heavy benches. Only one table in the room possessed actual chairs, and it was slightly set apart from the others. The chair at the far end of that table was also somewhat larger than the rest, with gold trim along the top.

As Talia stepped inside, she found the room currently empty, yet muffled sounds echoed inside it from four doors set close at the far end. Trying to remember the map over her bed, she was pretty sure that must be the kitchens. Suddenly, she itched to go over there, to look at the people who worked and lived here up close but didn't dare. Walking between the tables, she picked a place to sit along the back. She wasn't there long before a group of kids about her own age stormed into the room.

She watched as fifteen boys and girls talked animatedly to one another and chose a table somewhere in the middle. She stared somewhat longingly at them but with no real idea of how to approach them. She didn't consider herself to be shy, and many of the people back at Queegam often said she didn't know what the word meant, yet for the first time in her life, she found herself hesitant to introduce herself to strangers. These people were foreign to her in a way none had ever been. She didn't know what she should say or do with them.

As she watched, full of indecision, one of the boys at the table spotted her and pointed her out to a number of the others. Feeling suddenly conspicuous, she looked away, hoping they didn't know she'd been staring.

Next thing she knew, one of the girls was making her way over to her table.

"Hi! My name is Mandee." The light-skinned girl gave her a bright smile. "You're new, aren't you?"

"Y-Yes." She couldn't help but gawk, not having seen such curly, red hair before. "My, my name's Talia."

"Pleased to meet you." Mandee gave her a light curtsey. "Did you just come in this afternoon?"

Talia nodded. "Yes, with Kel and Clarence."

Mandee made a face. "Oh, yeah, Clarence. I'm still not over that ride, and it was over six months ago." She laughed. It was an easy sound. "I'll tell you now other dragons don't fly like him. I was actually worried about it for a while." She laughed again. "Say, why don't you come join us? We normally get here a little early, and we've already collected some of the other kids who'll be in your class."

Talia nodded, welcoming the invitation as well as Mandee's friendly demeanor. "Thanks."

At the other table, introductions passed quickly around. Of the fifteen kids there, she learned three of them were new, the same as her. She found out that each of them had experience as one of Clarence's victims. Mandee shoved over a couple of the others and got Talia to sit in the middle with her.

"Is Kel a Dragon Knight?" Talia asked.

A couple of the boys laughed out loud.

"No," Mandee answered, "he's a squire. And he's been one for a long time."

Someone else snickered.

Talia frowned. "Is that a bad thing?"

"Well, once you've got a dragon you're supposed to pass a test together to become an official knight," a girl with dark brown skin and a serious expression explained. "He just can't seem to pass it. So they made him a squire and all he gets to do is run errands on Clarence."

Talia's stomach knotted inside her. She tried to imagine going through the horrid ride she'd been on day after day; it made her feel ill. She was sure she'd rather be dead. It must be incredibly frustrating for Kel.

More students entered the dining hall. They sat down randomly, some staying as a group with their classmates while others dispersed to mingle with different friends. The room ended up only about half full, but Talia still felt a little overwhelmed. Even during the harvest festivals back home, she'd never seen so many people in one place at one time before.

Men and women from a few years older than the students to too old to tell poured out of the doors from the kitchens, armed with full trays. In droves, they hit each of the tables and deposited dishes, utensils, and large containers of food. The students at each table passed the dishes and utensils along even as the servers came down the table and filled each of their plates with food.

The noise level rose as voices and clanging plates mingled together into a confused din. A rich aroma grew thick in the air.

"You'll need to eat it all," Mandee told her. "Especially the vegetables. If you don't, the watchers will get on you and make you do it anyway. And you won't get any dessert. Which would be bad, because you learn to live for those desserts." She giggled. "They say they do it because eating vegetables is good for us. Back home, it didn't matter how much of this or that you ate, but it sure does here. As long as you eat all of what they serve you the first time, then you're allowed to have seconds if you want. If you can stand it, you can even have *thirds*."

Talia stared at her overflowing plate, not sure she'd be able to eat what she'd been given let alone more. But it did smell and look good. The roast she recognized for what it was, as well as the potatoes and carrots. A couple of the other vegetables on her plate, though, she was pretty sure she'd not seen before. She took small bites of everything to sample them all. A couple of the strange vegetables tasted a little weird to her, but not bad. What she knew, she found thoroughly delicious.

In the end, she surprised herself by eating it all.

She noticed those whom Mandee called watchers walking quietly between the tables and scrutinizing the students as they ate. Occasionally, she heard a groan or two as one of the watchers would tap a plate with a long wooden spoon, but otherwise, everyone seemed happy and mostly ignored the grown-ups.

"Have you met with the Administrator yet?" Mandee didn't look at her as she spoke, too busy soaking up her roast's juices with a piece of bread.

"Not yet," Talia replied. "I have an appointment in the morning." The sense of insignificance she'd felt when standing before the Administrator's golden door returned. "What, what is he like?" She hoped the Administrator wouldn't be as overwhelming as his door.

"He's a she." Mandee's eyes were dancing. "And she's like no one you've ever met before."

The comment didn't make her feel much better. She let her gaze travel across the room to the table on the far side, but couldn't see well enough past the other tables to see if the Administrator was there. When Mandee added no more information about her, Talia decided to change the subject. "I understand why one might want a bar for the shutters, but why would we need one for the door?"

Yllin, the long-faced, dark-skinned girl sitting to Talia's right, answered the question before Mandee got a chance to swallow her latest bite. "It's to protect yourself from the peepers."

"Peepers?" Talia stared at the girl beside her in confusion.

Yllin glanced at the boys in their group with distrustful dark eyes before inching a little closer to her, keeping her voice low. "Yes. They're all over the school. They're continually trying to sneak into our rooms, to get a peep at us while we're bathing. You have to be very careful." Her expression was direly serious.

"But, but why would anyone want to do that?" Talia asked in confusion.

"Beats me, but they do. It's a boy thing." Yllin stated it as if it explained everything.

Mandee leaned over to whisper in Talia's ear. "Some say the old lecher at the cave is the worst one of them all." Her voice held a tone of amusement.

"Some say the old lecher at the cave is the worst one of them all," Yllin said. Mandee giggled quietly as her words were repeated exactly. "So if you end up having to buy anything from him, watch out."

"Thanks." She didn't know what to make of the information at all.

"Uh oh, they're opening the doors. It's time for our walkies." One of the boys pointed to a set of large doors on the other side of the dining hall. A few of the others who'd eaten too many tarts for dessert groaned out loud.

"Walkies?" Talia asked.

"The watchers make us walk through the garden after every meal." Mandee stood up, stretching as she did so. "It's another one of those things they say are good for us."

"It's a total waste of time if you ask me," Yllin said this softly as she looked around to make sure none of the watchers would overhear.

"Well, I enjoy it. It helps my food settle down so I can have more at the next meal." Mandee grinned. "Especially dessert."

The bunch of them followed the other students as they moved toward the set of doors leading outside. A cobbled walkway wound from there into a lush flower garden filled with trees and bushes. Short stone columns ringed the area, most claimed by roses or vines. About halfway around, Talia noticed the path branched off and seemed to head in the direction of a distant hill.

"The lecher's place is that way. He's got a cave on a cleft in the hill," Yllin said. "If you ever need anything, he's the store master. But if I were you, I'd really make sure I needed it before I went over there to get it." Her deep frown easily conveyed that she'd find very little to be that necessary.

As the path exited the garden, Talia got her first close look at the second large building on the grounds. In many ways, it appeared to be a smaller version of the school but made of wood instead of stone and without the balconies. Two massive doors, currently open, faced the path. Looking to see what she could of the inside, she spotted what appeared to be huge open stalls. A thick covering of straw was strewn everywhere. The barn, for that's what the interior made her think of, looked much too large to hold horses or cattle.

"What is that building for?"

"Oh, that's where the dragons stay," Mandee said. "Clarence is the only one who actually lives there, but it has plenty of room to house any visitors we might get." She pointed off toward the other end of the building. "There's another set of doors on the front. It has a road that winds around to the landing area. There's also a small lake with a natural spring on the other side of the building and a giant pit for their refuse. How they've gotten it not to stink up the area when the wind changes, I just don't know." She smiled as she added the last. "Hey, if you're free, we could show you around. After dinner, our time is our own until lights out at ten."

"Free time after we're done studying you mean. If there's any left before lights out."

"Yllin." Mandee reprovingly shoved the serious girl's shoulder. "Be nice. You've already got her half scared out of her mind, and she's only been here less than a day."

"Oh, sorry, Talia." The other girl sent her an apologetic look.

"I, I don't want to be a bother." Did they really give the students so much work to do? While she didn't want to get the two of them in trouble, she relished even less the thought being alone.

Mandee waved a hand to dismiss her words. "Don't worry about it. You're no such thing. I know this place seems different and maybe even a little weird, if not downright scary, until you get used to it. So if we can do anything to get you acquainted with it, so it's not all quite so awkward, and get you to love it as much as we do, then it's no bother at all." Mandee sent a sly look in Talia's direction. "Despite whatever Yllin may say." The serious girl humphed in indignation.

Mandee laughed with delight.

"So, what do we study here?" Talia asked.

"Well, to be honest," Yllin confided, "so far it's nothing all that exciting—history, politics, geography, mathematics— mundane stuff. Though you do get to learn a lot about guilds and the choices you can make. And some about dragons, all the different types of dragons."

Most of it seemed to be the same as what they were typically taught back home. It definitely didn't tell her what it was she'd been apprenticed for. "Are there many kinds of dragons?"

"Loads," Yllin answered. "Red, green, blue, black, small, big, some talk, some use their thoughts to speak. It's almost mind-numbing, really."

Talia caught Mandee looking at her excited friend, a small grin on her face.

The path ended at another set of doors, which led back into the school. The watchers who'd come through with them didn't follow much farther.

"Yes! Freedom." Mandee grabbed Talia's hand and pulled her forward. "Come on, it's time for your tour."

"Hey, wait up!" Yllin came running after them.

First Mandee showed her where her room was on the far side of the second floor, then Yllin's on the third.

They both explained that as far as they could tell, room assignments were random. Teachers and watchers, however, were interspersed on each floor as well. At the moment, many of the rooms were empty, the school currently at about half capacity. All offices were on the first floor except for the Administrator's, the Treasurer's, and the Taskmaster's. Their offices and bedrooms were adjoining and located on the fourth floor.

Though Talia learned both Mandee and Yllin had only been at the school for six months, they seemed to know a lot about the place. They took her outside to the grounds and showed her the planted fields she'd caught a glimpse of before. Since this time she wasn't clinging onto a dragon for dear life, she was able to study them more critically. This was something she knew a little about. Each square field grew something different, giving Talia the impression the farmers rotated their crops. Corn, wheat, lettuce, and others she easily recognized, though some vegetables she didn't. Each of the fields looked incredibly healthy and abundant—almost amazingly so. She wondered how they did it, and knew her father would give almost anything to find out.

The forest bordering the fields was lush and thick. She saw patches where it appeared some of the trees had been cut down and later replaced with rows of saplings. Her curiosity was piqued as she spotted a couple of trees near the dragon's landing area. These showed torn limbs, and some were cracked, one of them almost in half. Yet it didn't look as if lightning was responsible. "What happened to those trees?"

"Clarence, that's what happened to them." Yllin snorted. "He's a menace. It's a miracle nobody's been killed riding him."

Talia stared at the two trees and could only too easily

imagine the dragon careening into them. Was Kel riding him at the time? That was harder to picture. How in the world could he have survived it? She still didn't have any idea how he came out unharmed when the two of them landed at her home. "Why would they make him ride such a dangerous dragon?"

"They don't."

She stared at Mandee in surprise.

For once, the red headed-girl looked somber. "From what I understand, he wants to do it. He wants to pass the test so he can become a full knight, and he wants to do it with Clarence. He practices with him constantly. You can see them flying around all day and half the night when he's not off running errands."

"I bet he's crazy," Yllin added. "Half the older students say so. Clarence probably landed on him one too many times and snapped something loose in here." She tapped the side of her head.

So Kel willingly went through this agony day after day? She shook her head, not able to understand it.

"Come on, we've got more to show you!" Mandee waved them on.

Briskly, they followed the road from the dragon landing area and went around the right side of the school to the back. Talia spotted the small, bubbling lake the girls mentioned to her earlier and the tiny river winding away from it, which turned into a waterfall at the end of the mesa. A short distance away was a large pit filled partway with the same dark excrement Clarence left for her parents. Two men were there, scooping some of it onto wheelbarrows. Later, she saw the two men head off back toward the fields. She wondered if it made good fertilizer. She remembered how Clarence told her parents it was worth a lot of money to alchemists. Could excrement have so many uses? She did notice, just as Mandee mentioned, that there didn't seem to be much of a smell, unlike when he used her father's field.

Several poles lined the far edge of the area with globes similar to those in her room. At the moment, however, they weren't lit.

They walked on past the dragon's domicile to the hilly area beyond the garden. Though they didn't get too close, mostly at Yllin's insistence, Mandee pointed out to Talia where the store master's cave was. They didn't linger there long and soon made their way back into the school building.

Inside, they walked around the first floor, and her new friends showed Talia the offices they knew as well as where they went to class. The last thing they went to visit was the immense library on the opposite side of the building from where the dining hall was—and it was almost as big. She stared as they walked past row upon row of books. "Will we have to read them all?" A tone of both wonder and trepidation filled her voice.

Mandee laughed. "Thankfully, no, we won't. Though I'm sure we will need to read some of them. Not all of them are for study anyway." She pointed off to the far back. "The section over there is all legends and stories."

From what she could see of them, Talia noticed those books looked more worn than the rest of the ones in the library. Even now, it seemed to be the area with the most students gathered about.

When they were done there, Yllin and Mandee both asked to see her room. Once they stepped inside, Yllin slipped the bar across the door. If the danger from these "peepers," as she called them, really existed, would it really matter right now since they were fully clothed? Talia decided not to comment on it.

Mandee deftly climbed up onto the higher bunk bed and bounced on the thick mattress. "Aren't all these rooms great?"

"Definitely bigger than what I had at home," Talia replied. She stared at the ample room around her, still not quite able to believe all this space was hers alone.

"It does have some drawbacks..." Yllin walked over to the tub. "Every week we have to empty the water and fill it up again." She glanced over at Talia. "Not that it ever gets dirty or really gets low." She pointed to the buckets by the water basin. "It's what those are for."

"Yeah, it wouldn't be so bad if we didn't have to drag them all the way from the lake." Mandee sighed. "At least we get to just throw the old water out the balcony." She jumped off the bed.

"But how does the water stay hot?" Talia asked. She noticed wisps of steam still rising from the surface.

Mandee shrugged. "It's magic. They use it a lot around here. So a lot of stuff doesn't work like we're used to."

"I'm pretty sure the whole water thing is just to keep us busy, too," Yllin said glumly, "Because if their magic can keep the water clean and warm, it could keep itself full."

"Oh." Magic—it would explain the lights in her room as well. As with dragons, it was something Talia knew existed, but she'd not been exposed to any of it before. Magic was something for the rich and powerful. Was the guild so well off they could use it on such trivial things?

"We'd better be going," Mandee said. "I have a feeling Yllin and I have filled you with way too much to think about already." She smiled. "See you at breakfast tomorrow?"

Talia nodded. "Yes, that'd be great. Thanks for showing me around." She walked them to the door. Yllin took off the bar.

"No problem. Good night." Mandee and Yllin stepped outside and waved as they moved on down the hall.

"Good night." Talia watched them then slowly closed her door.

The room suddenly seemed incredibly quiet except for the barely audible trickling of water from the clock. Though she'd seen earlier the rooms to either side of her were occupied, she could hear nothing through the thick stone walls. At home, though she had her own room, she could typically hear anyone moving about downstairs or the wood of the house creak during a strong wind. It seemed much too quiet here.

Sighing, she walked to the balcony doors and opened them wide. She stepped out, sighed again, then let herself be embraced by the calm darkness there. The moon shone brightly above. Looking to either side, she noticed others were also out on their balconies. It eased her heart a little to see them there.

Unexpectedly, something caught at her attention from the corner of her eye. Talia looked up just in time to see a large shadow cross over the moon. She followed it with her gaze and noticed how it wove up and down in no constant pattern.

Not sure what it was, she leaned over the rail as the object came closer. Trying to look up past the balconies above her as it flew overhead, she jerked back with a gasp as it suddenly dropped past hers toward the ground.

A light scent of oil rushed by with the wind. She recognized the smell as the shadow rose again, zooming past. Light shone on dark green scales and a figure made of metal. It was Clarence and Kel. Were they both mad? What if Clarence careened into one of the balconies? It was dangerous enough flying a cross-eyed dragon during the day. It was lunacy to do it at night.

As if to accentuate her point, all the lights in the students' rooms went out at the same time. Faint, voiced protests reached her ears as bedtime arrived. Talia forced herself to take deep breaths, her heart still at a gallop in her chest. From what Mandee and Yllin said, Kel's and Clarence's practice was a regular occurrence, and from the disappointed sounds of the students so was the dousing of the lights.

Giving the dragon and the squire one last glance, she went back inside and closed the balcony doors behind her. She changed clothes with what moonlight filtered in from the outside then crawled into the strange bed.

Sleep was a long time coming.

Chapter Three

TALIA WOKE TO the call of birds again. The lilting chirps were high and loud, nothing like the familiar whistles of the red speckled Talerns or even the noisy cacophony of the rooster in the hen house. The call came again and this time was answered by one closer still. She slowly sat up in her bed, glanced out toward the balcony doors, and spotted a bright blue and green bird eyeing her from the rail. It dipped its head as if bidding her good morning then left with a flurry of wings.

She smiled at the greeting but soon sobered. The sun was out, and she had an appointment. In a half panic, she scrambled out of bed to glance at the clock in its niche in the wall. She felt suddenly foolish, as she saw it was only ten minutes to six. By this time, her mother would already be up, busy preparing breakfast, while her father would be out looking over the fields making his plans for the day.

She wiped at her face as she felt a warm tear trickle down her cheek. She was being silly and she knew it. She'd never thought of herself as the sentimental type before. Just as all the other children in Queegam, she'd known her whole life that sooner or later she would be apprenticed. She just never thought it would be so hard ... Or that she'd miss home so much...

Shaking herself out of her growing sadness, she made the bed then took a bath. Once she'd gotten dressed, it was twelve after six. She wanted to go down to breakfast, but this was too early. She eyed the blank papers and quills at her desk and thought of starting a letter to her parents then put the idea aside, not wanting to run the risk of calling up more tears, especially since she was supposed to attend a meeting with the Administrator this morning.

At six thirty, the globes in her room turned on. Already slightly startled by the unexpected event, she started when someone knocked hard on her door. "Time to rise!"

Talia rushed to her door, but when she opened it no one was there. She looked down the hall and spotted a watcher knocking on a door three down from hers and calling out it was time to rise. The watcher then moved on to the next one.

Since the whole school was being awakened, she decided it would be all right for her to go downstairs. Stepping out into the hall and closing the door to her room, she headed for the nearest flight of steps. She got a couple of surprised looks from some of the watchers she passed along the way, but they said nothing, so she went on.

The dining hall was empty when she arrived, but the sounds of voices and the rattle of pots and pans echoed softly through the room from an open kitchen door. The smell of baking bread teased her nostrils.

She glanced around then drifted closer to the

Administrator's table. She decided on the one closest to it, hoping this time she might be able to catch a glimpse of the woman before she met her later this morning. The strange way in which Mandee spoke of her had made Talia a bit more nervous about the coming meeting than she might have been otherwise.

As she waited for Mandee and the others to appear, a lone person came into the room from the door leading out into the garden. As she wondered what they'd been doing out there so early in the morning, she realized she knew this person—it was Kel. The squire spotted her at about the same time and waved a greeting to her as he walked toward the open kitchen door. She tentatively waved back.

People were pouring into the dining hall in earnest by the time she saw him come back out of the kitchen. He held a large basket of fruit in one hand and a filled plate in the other. She was a little surprised as she saw him walk over to the Administrator's table and take a seat at the far end. Kel set his things down and started eating, seemingly paying attention to nothing or anyone. She frowned.

"What are you looking at?"

She almost jumped out of her seat at Mandee's soft question. She'd been paying so much attention to Kel she didn't hear her come up. "Ah, nothing." She looked away at the slight lie. "Good morning."

"Morning." Mandee sat down next to her. "You sure got here early. I way overslept on my first day." She grinned.

"I—I guess I'm just used to it. We got up early at home every day."

"Not me. At least, not when I could get away with it." Her grin grew into a mischievous smile.

Yllin and a few of the others Talia met the day before

joined them. Greetings were passed all around.

As the watchers started serving breakfast, she noticed Kel finishing his. Though some teachers now populated the table, he didn't speak to them other than to trade pleasantries. As soon as he was done, he got up, picked up his basket of fruit and left the dining hall the same way he came in.

"There goes the useless one."

Talia snapped to look behind her. The table next to theirs was filled with mostly older-looking students. A couple of them were chuckling as they stared in Kel's direction, but she couldn't tell who'd voiced the comment. Was this how people really felt about him? Just how long had he been trying to pass his test?

The Administrator's table was soon full, but her chair remained empty. Talia wondered if this was a good thing or not.

As before, the watchers maintained an unobtrusive vigil over the students as they ate. Talia found it hard to put away all she'd been served, though everything was delicious. She felt stuffed as time ran out and they all stood to go for their walk through the garden. She admitted she did feel better by the time they were through.

"We'll see you at lunch, okay?" Mandee said, "We've got to go to class now."

Talia looked at her in surprise as they reached the hallway inside. "Oh." She stared at the two girls as they prepared to go, realizing she'd forgotten they'd be leaving her. It meant she'd have to spend the rest of her time alone before going upstairs for her appointment with the Administrator.

"You'll do fine at your meeting," Mandee said, as if reading her mind. "Yllin here made it through, so how bad could it be?" Mandee put Talia between her and the grim-faced girl as she spoke, her eyes filled with mirth.

"Hey!" Yllin threw the redhead a dirty look. Then she glanced at Talia. "You can't do any worse than Mandee, and they kept her, too." Yllin looked glum, yet a small grin was trying to tug the edge of her mouth.

Mandee laughed at her attempt to get her back. "You'll have to tell us all about it when we see you again." She grabbed Yllin's arm. "Come on, sourpuss, or we'll be late."

Talia stepped to the side of the hall, out of the way, and watched them and the other students go past. Once almost everyone was gone, she made her way back to her room. After pacing there for a while, she sat down on her desk and began a letter to her parents. At the moment, she was distracted enough by the coming event that she felt sufficiently disassociated to do it. She felt extraordinarily nervous and skittish. Her stomach knotted inside her, making her wish she'd not eaten breakfast. Still, how bad could this interview be? They wouldn't send her back if she failed, would they?

She set the quill down, unable to write anymore.

She'd heard of such things. It was rare, but it happened on occasion. Once rejected by a guild, it became doubly hard to get accepted by another. Some found they were unable to ever get any training at all. It was people of this sort who became beggars, bandits, and worse. She wouldn't be one of them.

Five minutes before the hour, she left her room and made her way upstairs to the fourth floor. As if she were a condemned criminal on the way to the block, she slowly approached the golden door at the end of the passage. The door towered higher the closer she came, making her feel smaller with each step.

Staring up at it, she finally came to stand before it. Talia took a deep breath, trying to calm herself even as her hand came up to knock on the door. Before she got a chance to do it, however, a soft voice whispered out to her from within.

"Come in. It's not locked."

Her brow furrowed, wondering how in the world the Administrator knew she was there. With a different kind of worry now gnawing at her stomach, she pushed on the door. It gave way to her touch and opened silently before her. She stepped inside.

The room beyond was deep but not wide. A large blue and gold rug covered the cold marble floor, the scent of incense wafting through the air. Three doorways led from the long room, one on the right and two on the left.

"Come on over. I'm back here." The sweet voice came from the second door on the left.

Feeling uneasy, Talia headed in that direction.

The room the second doorway opened into was large. Columns similar to those she'd seen bordering the garden were set along the walls, a shimmering, sheer azure cloth strung between them. In the center of the room was a big oval tub, with what looked to be the remains of an unusual amount of bubbles. Beyond it, sitting on a long settee, was the woman she'd come to find.

The Administrator looked over at her, reclining comfortably in the settee, a long thick robe covering her from neck to ankles. "Come in, come in. Take a seat. I'm running a little late this morning, but it won't interfere with what you need to do."

She waved Talia over to a chair on the other side of the room.

Tearing her gaze away from the woman, she took a seat. So this was the Administrator. As far as Talia was concerned, she was one of the most beautiful women she'd ever seen. A far cry from what she'd half expected. The Administrator's skin was light with a hint of a tan. Her face was round, with a small nose and full lips. Black, wavy hair was piled on her head to keep it above the soapy water and it accentuated her deep blue eyes. Talia couldn't believe her interview was to be conducted in a bathroom. Surely this wasn't how ordinary people held meetings in the outside world? Then she remembered her encounter with Tammer, and how it didn't go exactly as expected, either.

"My name is Lareen," the Administrator said in the same soft voice Talia heard from the outside the office. "I'm this school's administrator." Lareen changed position, turning on her side to get a better look at her. "Welcome to Dragon's Peak." She gave Talia a warm smile. "I love my job. It has many benefits. For example, no early morning wake-up calls. Unfortunately, though, sometimes I do have a tendency to oversleep." Her smile turned sly.

Talia felt embarrassed for her. Though from the look of her the Administrator seemed less than bothered by it. Not exactly what she expected from someone in such a high position. Surely she took her job seriously?

"Welcome to my school, Talia. How have you liked it so far?" Lareen's intense blue stare seemed to bore into her.

"Fine, ma'am. It's very nice." She tried her best not to fidget.

"Don't worry," Lareen waved her hand lightly, "you'll get used to everything. Your homesickness will pass before you know it."

Talia stared, wondering how she knew about this. She'd never mentioned it to anyone.

The Administrator moved to sit back as she'd been before. "Our guild is rather extensive. This school is but one of many. Though it's also one of the best." Her tone turned serious. "You'll be here with us for four years then you can either decide to stay for more general training or go to a more specialized school. Unlike most guilds, you have choices on what you want to become. Almost anything is possible here." Her intense stare locked with Talia's own. "Do you have any thoughts on what it is you would prefer to be?"

Talia looked away, caught off guard by the question. She possessed no idea what she wanted to do before her parents took the decision from her and knew no better now. The stories she'd heard didn't really speak of what jobs this guild offered. She assumed the only one they had was to be a Dragon Knight. Wasn't that all they trained for here? "A knight?"

Lareen smiled again. "You have no restrictions here. You can be anything. We require more than just knights. Since our guild is self-sufficient and a government unto ourselves, we need people with skills in all walks of life— farmers, weavers, cooks, even administrators." Her eyes were bright. "We don't have enough dragons for everyone and there exist more challenging roles for some than being a knight."

Talia stared at the floor, more surprised by this than she wanted to admit. So she would still have to make a choice sometime after all. She wasn't sure whether she was relieved by this revelation or not.

"Don't worry, though. If a Dragon Knight is what you want to be, you'll get your chance. Everyone can play the lottery. Until the time comes, you'll learn all manner of things and perhaps see what else is out there which might interest you."

Talia nodded, trying to absorb all she was being told, even as dozens of questions sprang to her mind. She could be anything? How massive was this guild? What was the lottery?

"If you wouldn't mind, would you be a dear and go into the room to the right of this one and bring in the cart that's there?"

"Yes, ma'am." Talia rose immediately and went in search of the cart. She quickly found it, but upon seeing its contents, a whole new slew of questions intruded in her mind.

The cart she pushed back held three tiers. Each of them was full, and their contents were not anything she'd have expected to find in them.

"Ah, yes, that's the one." Lareen waved her closer. "If you would, please go through what's on the top and pick out the best five you can find."

Talia's mouth opened, but it still took her a second to be able to respond. "Y—yes, ma'am." She turned to look at the contents of the cart's first tier and swallowed hard as she again stared with disbelief at the sparkling gems that filled the shelf to the brim. Never in her life did she think she'd see so many, let alone be asked to pick five of them. Worse, she didn't know anything about precious stones. She hadn't even seen any of any real worth until Kel bestowed some to her parents.

"Take as long as you need to pick them," Lareen said. "There's no hurry."

Talia couldn't quite bring herself to even touch them.

"Maybe you should dump them out on the floor," the Administrator suggested. "It might make it easier to look through them. You can use the corner over there." She pointed off to the right.

Talia nodded, swallowing hard, then touched the

gems. They felt strange to the touch, slick and cool. She handled them gingerly as she set them out on the floor, a little horrified she was being allowed to treat them this way. The gems before her were of every size and color. She didn't even know what half of them were. She was only too aware she didn't have a basis on which to make her choices either. The Administrator wanted her to pick the best five, but she didn't know how to make that determination.

She stared at the treasure before her and tried to think of everything she'd ever heard about precious stones or other valuable things and how they were customarily valued. Talia knew a little about cloth, how the finer the weave, the more expensive it was, but couldn't quite figure out how she could apply the knowledge here.

Her father, as a hobby, worked with wood. He'd made a lot of the furniture in their home himself and occasionally made a piece or two to sell in town. She'd always thought he was good at it. Every time, before he ever started a project, he carefully checked the wood for rotting, consistency, and cracks. Maybe those criteria would work here as well.

She shrugged her shoulders, not able to think of anything else, and got to work.

Picking up each gem and looking at it carefully, she set aside any which were cracked, chipped, or weren't consistent in color. Of the forty jewels before her, she was able to get rid of ten.

After he gathered the wood, her father would take painstaking care to measure out the lengths he'd need and make sure all the parts would be even when he got done. Keeping this in mind, she looked through the remaining gems and took out any which were cut unevenly or which weren't symmetrical. That got rid of twelve more.

Softly biting her lip, she stared at the gems left before her, trying to find some other way to narrow her choices further.

When her father worked on his projects, she recalled that the ones he took the longest to make or that were made up of the most components usually looked better than those he just speedily threw together. If she remembered right, he got paid more for those, too. Not sure if the same could be said of precious stones, she still set out to separate them with the same idea in mind. She divided the eighteen remaining gems by the number and shape of their cuts.

Of the eight most intricate of the lot, she picked out five whose colors she liked best.

"Are you done?"

Talia looked up surprised, long ago having forgotten about the Administrator. She quickly nodded. "Yes, ma'am."

"Let me see." Lareen sounded suddenly eager.

Gathering up her choices, she brought them over to her.

Lareen critically studied the gems in her hands.

"Very well done," she finally remarked. "They're yours to keep."

Talia felt her eyes grow wide. Lareen couldn't be serious. This was a small fortune.

"You'll find some small bags lining the bottom of the top shelf of the cart. Pick one to keep them in."

She hesitated. She just couldn't believe the woman was serious.

The Administrator insisted, waving her on. "Go on."

"Y—yes, ma'am." Talia retreated with her prizes. She was still utterly confused. How could they let her keep these? Everyone knew apprentices were not usually given money of their own. Even if they were, this was just too much.

Almost in a half daze, she studied the small bags that lined the first shelf of the cart. After looking them over, she realized they were all the same size, but their colors were as varied as a field of flowers. She picked a dark blue one to call her own and dropped her prizes inside. Tying the bag shut and latching it on to her belt, she picked up the other gems off the floor and put them back in the cart.

"Let's move over to my bedroom so I can get dressed while you start in on the next shelf." The Administrator stood up from the settee and released her bound hair, combing it as she left the room barefoot. Talia grabbed hold of the cart and set out to follow her. Lareen strolled to the room across the way.

The Administrator's bedroom was twice as large as her bathroom. A spacious, canopied bed dominated the far side, yet the room still didn't look crowded. Two sets of doors led out to separate balconies. As Talia watched, Lareen sauntered over to a marble-topped vanity and sat down before the large mirror. She set down the comb, picked up a brush, and gently stroked it through her cascading hair.

"You'll find some papers on the second shelf of the cart. I want you to read through them then tell me which of them would be the most useful." Lareen glanced at her in the mirror's reflection.

"Yes, ma'am."

"Why don't you make yourself comfortable and use the chair back there?" Lareen pointed toward the corner of the room closest to the door where a bulky but well-padded chair and a small table sat nestled.

Talia steered the cart in that direction and sat down.

Gingerly, she pulled out the four sets of parchments in the cart and set them on the table. Noticing the Administrator was paying her no attention whatsoever, she pushed herself farther back on the comfortable chair and opened the first parchment.

Within, she found what looked to be a list of everyday items—rope, hoses, eggs, chickens. It also listed their weights, quantities, and prices. The list was quite extensive, almost ten pages worth. She read through all the items, unsure whether something important might be hidden within.

She didn't find anything.

After looking through the list a second time, she rolled it back up, set it aside, and moved on to the next.

The new parchment contained a long poem. It was simple, the rhymes not well thought out, but it was amusing. The poem told of how the sun learned of the beautiful moon by the gossip of the clouds. He then went on to spend his every waking moment trying to see her for himself. This could not be, of course, since the moon would only show herself once he'd gone from the sky. The sun, however, kept on, and on, oblivious.

Talia was forced to put her hand over her mouth several times as she read through the poem to keep from laughing out loud.

"Say, which one of these do you think I should wear today?"

She glanced up and found Lareen standing before a long dresser holding up four brightly colored and strangely cut clothes. Talia frowned, not having seen the like before.

"Uh, ah, I'm not really sure, ma'am."

"Oh well, never mind." Lareen put the clothes back then pulled out others which looked even stranger than the first.

Wondering what that was about, Talia rolled up the poem and reached for the third parchment.

The next one was sixteen pages long. Though it was written in a somewhat winded and dry style, she still found herself instantly fascinated. The contents went into some detail about the proper daily maintenance of dragons. A section was even devoted to the likes and dislikes of the different colored types. She was surprised at the number of distinct varieties. The paper only listed eight but suggested there were more.

A point of interest, common to all types, was their almost compulsive love of cherries. If the pits were left in them, the fruit even tended to have an intoxicating effect. Bold lettering strongly proclaimed though that if they were given too many pits, it could prove dangerous for the dragon. While small quantities were inebriating, large amounts were poisonous.

Cherries were poisonous?

The last section of the parchment dealt with a common vermin to dragons called worms. From what the paper said, it seemed these worms worked to get underneath a dragon's scales and latch on to the skin beneath. While the parasite was mostly an annoyance to the dragon, the parchment said they could be dangerous to a rider. It didn't tell how, although it did go to some length to explain the steps for their proper removal. Talia never heard of such a creature before, though now one of Kel's references when he first picked her up made sense. She wasn't sure she wanted to know more, though.

Talia glanced up to see what Lareen was doing before going on to the last parchment in the cart. She spotted the Administrator looking in her direction. The robe was gone, replaced by a frilly red dress of gossamer material, which accentuated certain parts of her and didn't look overtly utilitarian. This was how the top person in a school dressed?

"Do you like it?" Lareen came closer and twirled before her so she could see all of it. Talia was hard-pressed to say anything, though Lareen did look beautiful in it.

"Hmm." Lareen pouted lightly. "Maybe it's not quite right for today. Oh, well. Carry on." The Administrator went back across the room and pulled out other dresses as thoroughly inappropriate and strange as the first before disappearing behind a high set of screens to change.

Talia forced herself to stop watching her and grabbed the last of the parchments.

This was the thickest of all—over thirty pages long. Unlike the previous one, however, it was written simply and was easy to read. It was a story of a Dragon Knight.

The whole tale was fun and exciting, though it seemed to be lacking in substance. The knight in the story was very busy—he was off saving princesses, slaying monsters, and doing other courageous deeds. Yet the descriptions in the story were vague and didn't impart much of anything. It did have a good ending though—he married the most beautiful princess he'd rescued and got his own kingdom. She doubted anyone could ask for more.

When she finished with the last and set it down, she found Lareen sitting quietly on her bed staring at her. "Finished?"

"Yes, ma'am." Talia noticed, with some amusement, that the Administrator was wearing the same red dress she'd initially put on.

"Which of them do you choose?" Lareen asked. "Or do you need more time?" She lay down on her side on the bed, in no way appearing as if she was in a hurry.

"No, I ... I've made my decision." Talia took the parchment on dragon maintenance.

Lareen's brow rose on her lovely face. "That one? Why not the first?"

The Administrator's seeming amazement at her choice surprised Talia. Her mind stumbled to come up with an explanation even as a small part of her now doubted her decision. "The, the list is nice and is made up of useful things, but other than to maybe be used for figuring out the general weight of things, you can't really use it. Though it has prices on it, there's no way to tell whose prices they are so the information is worthless." She hoped she didn't sound as unsure as she felt.

Lareen nodded. "And the poem?"

"It was funny. But other than possibly cheering someone up it has no real use." Her stomach knotted as the notion occurred to her that Lareen might have written it.

"Hmm, and the story?"

Talia forced herself to take a breath and plunged on.

"Entertaining, but lacks any real information."

"All right, then why did you pick the one you did?" Lareen asked, her eyes bright.

She looked away from the woman's suddenly intense stare. "Well, it has good, practical information. Things which as a guild member I could use." She tried to come up with more to say, but her brain wasn't cooperating. She hoped it would be enough.

"Keep it then. I think you'll definitely find it helpful."

Lareen rose from the bed. "Let's go on over to my office. Bring the cart, won't you?" Her colorful skirt rustled as she crossed the room. Talia picked up the other parchments, dumped them into the cart and, tucking the one she was to keep inside her vest, rushed to follow.

The Administrator's office was the door closest to the golden door. A large, abused looking desk sat prominently in the back. Papers lay in neat stacks on one side of it. Lareen waved her toward the three padded chairs facing it.

Talia rolled the cart to the closest one and sat down.

"If you'll look at the last shelf on the cart, you'll find a nice assortment of knives there. Look through them and find one you like. Sheaths for them are in the drawer beneath it." As she spoke, Lareen sat down and picked up one of the stacks of papers.

"Yes, ma'am."

The last shelf of the cart held thirty-two knives in all.

Some were made of silver, others of bone, some even of gold. Some held long blades; others were curved like snakes. Just as she'd done with the gems, she took all of them out of the cart and spread them before her. At least this was something she knew a little about.

Without much thought, she set aside the strangely curved blades and those made of precious metals. The curved knives would be too awkward for her to handle and the others were either made of a metal which would be too soft to prove useful for anything but decoration or would tarnish too easily. The blacksmith's son, Lir, taught her these things even as he learned them. Unlike her, Lir knew all along what he wanted to be. He, too, would be apprenticed to a guild soon.

She wished he were here with her now.

Telling herself she had no right to think such things, Talia studied the eleven blades left. One by one, she picked them up and tested their balance and weight as well as how they felt in her hand. She put three of these swiftly off on the rejected pile. After several more minutes, she finally settled on a thin, double-edged knife with a leather grip. She very much enjoyed the comfortable fit of the grip in her hand. The blade was also light, possessed good balance, and appeared to be able to take some amount of abuse.

She placed all the other knives back in the cart, then opened the drawer beneath and sifted through the sheaths there until she found one that would handle her blade.

Once done, she stood up and glanced at Lareen, wondering what the Administrator would want her to do next. The fact she was being tested was obvious, but what the results of the tests would be used for she wasn't so sure. Lareen was still at her desk, busily writing, her eyes moving over other papers set before her. Her round face was set and focused, almost as if she were a different person from the carefree one Talia met not long before.

Before she could decide if she should interrupt her, the Administrator looked up as if sensing her stare. "All done?" she asked.

"Yes, ma'am."

Lareen beckoned her over. "Let me see what you picked."

Talia brought over the sheathed blade and handed it to her. Her eyes glanced down at the papers on Lareen's desk and she noticed the neat handwriting on the documents. One of them contained her name at the top. She was about to try and see what it said about her when Lareen spoke. "Very nice choice. You've done quite well." The Administrator's smile was warm.

Talia guiltily looked away from the papers. "Thank you." A knock reverberated into the room from the hallway. Lareen glanced in that direction. "Ah, lunch is here. Perfect timing." She gave her back her knife.

"Would you mind getting the door?"

Talia nodded, amazed so much time had gone by. To her surprise, she saw the overwhelming door wasn't gold on the inside but a dark wood with steel reinforced supports. She went ahead and opened it.

A severe-faced, middle-aged woman nodded at her as she wheeled in a cart full of food. Her hair was cut very short and was colored black and gray. The woman immediately headed toward the Administrator's office. Talia closed the door and followed.

"Ah, thank you, Tula. Your timing is as impeccable as ever." Lareen rose from her desk.

The scent of roasted pork and a tangy sauce swirled in the air making Talia's stomach rumble in expectation.

"Tula, meet Talia, our newest recruit," Lareen said.

"Pleased to meet you." The newcomer's accent was thick.

"Tula is our head cook. She rules the kitchen with an iron fist." Lareen smiled as she spoke. "She has many talents."

"Don't listen to her, child. She's just trying to flatter me to get more dessert." Tula's blue-gray eyes suddenly twinkled, brightening her face perceptively.

"Pleased to meet you, too, ma'am," Talia said.

"None of that, please. I'm nobody's ma'am, just Tula." The head cook started uncovering the dishes on the cart.

Lareen brought over a small table and lifted two wings on its sides to make it larger. Talia jumped in to help and brought over a couple of chairs for them to sit on.

Tula served them both, making sure both their plates held plenty of vegetables and meat before taking her leave.

Lareen poured them cups of watered wine. "This is to celebrate your addition to the guild." She raised her cup high. After a moment, Talia rushed to follow suit. "Congratulations and welcome." Lareen beamed. Talia tried her best to return her smile, feeling suddenly a little overwhelmed and awkward.

"The rest of your class will be arriving over the next week. Until then, your time will be your own," Lareen said. "Since you have money now, you might want to visit Nertak's store. It's located in a cave in the back of the grounds. I'm not sure how much you actually brought with you, but if you need anything, you should be able to find it there. If he doesn't have it, he can order it for you."

Talia nodded. She wondered if the Administrator knew what rumors were being spread about this man.

"He can also take care of any mail you might need to send." Lareen stared at her knowingly. Talia honestly didn't know what to make of her.

"Your group's teacher will be Helyn. She will probably introduce herself to you sometime before your classes officially begin."

As they ate, Lareen added little pieces of information to the meal. The building and the school it housed had stood for over eight hundred years. Over time, the rooms were given the names of knights who'd studied there and gone on to gain great fame. Lareen told her she was only one of a long line of administrators at Dragon's Peak and had cared for the school for the last five years. The school was one of six teaching general, rudimentary skills. Specific schools for particular lines of work were seeded throughout the world.

"School is six days a week. The seventh day is your own, but part of it is to go toward the changing of the water in your tub and the linen on the beds," Lareen told her. "There's a bag in your closet for laundry. You just put what needs to be cleaned in there and set it out in the hallway on the way to breakfast. You should find it returned by the next day." Talia tried to commit all this to memory.

"Do you have any questions?"

Talia sat back and seriously considered if she should ask anything. Yet one of her many questions from earlier came up to the fore. "What is the lottery?"

"Ah." Lareen appeared intrigued by her choice of question. "It's a process we use to assign a knight to a dragon. Every year we have more people than there are dragons available. With the lottery, those who want to participate choose the color dragon best suited to their personality then numbers are drawn to see who actually will be paired."

"Is it how Kel got Clarence?" She inhaled quickly, not sure if she'd stepped out of line in asking this. She saw Lareen's brow rise.

"Well, as you've seen, Clarence does have a certain flying disability. Though he's spent quite a long time with the guild, he wasn't normally included as part of the lottery—this was his choice. After Kel won his draw, he specifically requested Clarence. Since Clarence agreed to it, it was done." Lareen sighed, a wistful look crossing her face.

"Unfortunately, to become a full knight, the rider and dragon must pass a final test once they've bonded. Though expectations were high some of Clarence's deficiencies would be overcome once he and Kel joined, it wasn't the case—and so the final test proved beyond them."

Talia nodded, Lareen's words explaining a lot. She now understood where some of the jeers came from. But why would Kel have chosen Clarence in the first place?

Surely both of them were aware there'd be a chance the idea wouldn't work. How would Clarence's deficiencies have been overcome by this anyway? Was there more to the bonding than just getting to know each other?

"You'll learn more about all this in your classes," Lareen went on. "But there is one point I need to make. Dragons are not beasts of burden or just mounts, though I'm sure at times they might seem that way." The Administrator's gaze caught her own. "They're our *partners*. Their time with us is a kind of apprenticeship for them. They are as smart if not smarter than humans and have the wisdom of long lives. Our partnerships are beneficial to both sides. Don't ever make the mistake of thinking of them as nothing more than winged horses. They care, they think, they feel. Their bodies are different, but inside we're very much alike."

At Lareen's words, Talia found herself feeling guilty. She'd already committed the mistake. Though Clarence spoke to her when they first met, she had still just thought of him as Kel's mount—she'd thought Kel was the only one who was miserable. How much worse was it actually for Clarence? He was the one with the deficiency; he was the one who wasn't thought of as a real dragon in the first place.

"Any other questions?"

She couldn't bring herself to ask another.

"Well," Lareen said, "if you come up with anything else, just ask any watcher or teacher. They'll be happy to help. And I'm always available, of course." The Administrator gave her a warm smile. "One more thing though—I would appreciate it if you kept all details about this meeting to yourself where any of the other new students are concerned.

"It wouldn't be fair to you or the others if they came

to see me knowing what to expect." Her eyes held a mischievous glint.

"Yes, ma'am." Talia nodded, not entirely understanding.

Lareen stood up and came around to her side.

"Unfortunately, I've got work to do, so I'm going to have to shoo you out now." She led her to the main door. "Enjoy your time off before the work begins in earnest. I think you'll make a nice addition to the guild." Lareen gave her a big smile before shutting the golden door and leaving her alone in the hallway.

Chapter Four

TALIA WALKED SLOWLY back to her room, her mind still having problems reconciling the strange facets of the school's leader. Mandee's earlier description of her seemed to fit quite well. The Administrator was like no one she ever met before. She was just relieved it was over.

Once back in her room, she finished the letter she'd started for her parents. She tried her best to sound excited without showing any of her fears or trepidations. She hoped they were well.

When she was done, she folded it and left her room. With a determined stride, she made her way downstairs. As she stepped outside though, she slowed as she spotted the hill containing Nertak's store. Perverts were a new concept for her, but though Mandee, and even more so, Yllin, were concerned by this man, Lareen didn't seem to have any problems with him at all. She was sure it meant he was all right. Nevertheless, she made sure her new knife was in easy reach as she stepped onto the path which would lead her there.

As she drew closer, Talia spotted a man outside the

cave. He was short and fair of skin, with a mop of glaring white hair and a nicely trimmed beard. At the moment, he was sitting in a chair that leaned back against the rock wall beside the entrance, whittling on a piece of wood. It wasn't exactly the way she thought a pervert would look.

"Good afternoon, sir," she said.

"Good afternoon." The old man leaned eagerly forward, righting his chair. A piercing green gaze met Talia's own.

"You're new here, aren't you?"

"Yes, sir, I am." She tried not to let it bother her as he looked her up and down.

"Well, go on in and take a look around. If you want anything or need any help, give me a shout. Name's Nertak." The old man winked at her.

She wasn't sure what to make of it. "Thank you. I'm Talia."

"Well, you just make yourself at home then, Talia." He gave her a big, friendly grin.

"Thanks."

Nertak gave her one last probing look then returned to his whittling. She went inside.

The entrance to the cave was dark and led down a short corridor. After less than a dozen steps, it widened out into a large cavern lit up by globes, the same as those in her room. Supported shelves stood in every direction, making the cave into a giant maze. Talia stared, amazed at the number of goods she glimpsed before her.

As she walked around and gawked at all she saw, she slowly realized the distribution of goods wasn't as disorganized as the placement of the shelves made it appear. Close to the entrance, she found all manner of fruits, vegetables, and grains as well as pickled and preserved foods. The section after contained clothes of all shapes and sizes, from simple underwear and outer garments to things as frilly and strange as what she'd seen the Administrator wear.

Papers, books, inks, and quills came next—any and all supplies necessary for school. Beyond them, she found leather goods such as saddles, belts, gloves, scabbards, and others she wasn't sure about. This then led to weapons and tools for anything and everything. All of this couldn't be just for the students of the school?

The temperature inside was pleasant, the air smelling of moisture and oils.

At the end of the maze on the cave's far side was a large counter. Behind it, she noticed another passage leading off to somewhere she couldn't see. She stared at the space beyond in confusion not having thought the cave could possibly be as large as it was from what she'd seen of it from the outside.

Her gaze was distracted from this quandary by a set of small bookshelves behind the counter holding old and worn books. Written across the spine of each was a person's name. In the shelf beneath them were identical looking books, but these looked new and the spines were blank.

"They're a jewel each if you want one."

"Oh!" Talia jumped at the voice so close to her side. She'd not heard anyone coming up beside her.

Nertak smiled at her palpable surprise. "Those are old diaries of previous students. Some are of their time here in the school, others after they'd gone. Could make for some interesting reading."

She said nothing, still working at slowing down her speeding heart. How could this old man have sneaked up on her so quietly?

"Find anything you want to buy?" He moved to go

around the counter.

Talia went back through everything she'd seen and, though a number of them were tempting, she didn't really need any of them at the moment. "No, thank you, not today."

He shrugged. "Inventory changes all the time, so don't be shy about coming to visit. Also, please keep in mind if you agree to model for me, I'll happily give you a discount." He looked her up and down again, a leering look in his eyes.

She felt her skin go cold as she abruptly realized she was there alone with the old man. The fact he'd been able to sneak up on her so quietly just made her feel more uneasy. She resisted the urge to reach for her knife. "I'll, I'll keep it in mind. Thank you." She tried hard to smile in a friendly manner.

The old man's eyes seemed to gleam.

It was then she remembered one of the reasons she'd come there in the first place. "There ... there is something you can do for me though. The Administrator said you could mail this for me?" She reached into her pocket and brought out the letter for her parents. "How much will it cost?"

"Oh! Well! Aren't you the dutiful daughter?" The old man seemed incredibly pleased.

She didn't understand it at all. She wasn't sure she could get used to these people. The old man, just like the Administrator, seemed to be able to change from giving one impression to another at will. It was very confusing.

"That service is free. So write to your parents all you want. I'm sure they'll be happy to hear from you." He gave her a broad smile.

She stared at him, wondering if everyone in this place would be the same as this. "Yes ... Thank you." She got out of there soon after, confused enough for one day.

Not having anything better to do, and deep inside knowing she'd gotten more excitement than she wanted already, she dawdled in her room until it was close to dinner.

When she entered the dining hall, it was still early, the scent of baking bread drifting lightly in the air. One student was there already though, sitting in the back, far away from everything, his eyes wide and staring, looking pale though he had sun-browned skin. Talia realized immediately he must be new. Did she look so lost and scared just yesterday? Her heart went out to him; she knew exactly how he felt. She decided to try and help him out. Nonchalantly, she made her way over toward his table.

As she came close, the boy appeared about to bolt. She decided to plunge right in. "Hi! My name is Talia. What's yours?" She tried to give him the friendliest smile she could come up with.

The boy's dark gaze locked with her's for a moment then glanced away, trying to look at everything but her. "I'm, I'm Daltan."

"Please to meet you," she said as cheerily as she could. "Did you just get in today?"

He nodded slowly, still not looking at her.

"I just arrived yesterday, myself. Overwhelming place, isn't it?"

The boy's gaze stopped roaming and actually focused on her once more. "Just a little."

Talia smiled again. Daltan made a halfhearted attempt to return her smile.

"You came in on Clarence, right?" she asked.

The boy's color turned a little green. It was answer enough. She was sure it was this way for almost everyone who came here. Between the horrifying ride, the immensity of the place, and lack of information from Tammer, no one would feel at ease right away.

"Have they told you much?"

Daltan looked away again. "No."

"I'm no expert, but I'll share what I know if you want," she offered. "The others will be here soon and I'm sure they'd love to help as well."

"Others?" His voice rose in panic.

She sat down, realizing she'd just made things worse. "New students like us," she added quickly. "And just a few who have been here a little longer. They're all very nice." His panic seemed to recede a little.

She started talking in the hopes it would calm him even more. She told him what little history she'd learned of the place as well as what she knew of their schedule and chores. He looked slightly more relaxed when other students started to trickle into the hall. As some of her soon-to-be classmates came in, she waved them over and introduced them. By the time Mandee and Yllin made it in, Daltan was busy fending off questions from the other boys.

"Hi, Talia." Mandee plopped down next to her. "I see we've got a new student for our group." She flashed a big smile. "And he's cute, too."

Daltan glanced over and away, his cheeks blushing.

"We need more girls," Yllin commented sourly. She barely spared Daltan a glance.

"You're not thinking about this in the right way, Yllin," Mandee replied. "Fewer girls means more boys and less competition."

The dark girl rolled her eyes but otherwise ignored the comment. "So, Talia, how did your meeting go?"

Mandee's eyes lit up. "Yes, yes, tell us all about it!"

"Well..." Talia glanced around to make sure Daltan was busy, remembering the Administrator's request she not discuss this with any new students who'd yet to see her. At the moment, the dark-haired boy was being grilled about his home and wasn't paying her any attention. Whispering, she quickly told her two friends about the three tests she'd taken.

"Aren't they just bizarre?" Mandee commented. "And it's so hard to tell if you did well or not." She frowned slightly. "The dagger test seems to be pretty consistent though not done every time. For me, the other two were to pick the best cloth from a set of samples and to explain a weird story she told me to read. When I picked the cloth, she gave me five jewels to keep."

"They just don't make much sense," Yllin said. "I still haven't been able to figure out what the tests are for." Mandee nodded. "But they have to be for something, otherwise why would they make everyone go through them?"

"Nobody knows what goes through the Administrator's mind."

Talia nodded at Yllin's comment, sure it was probably right.

After dinner was over and the students went through the garden, she hung around Mandee and Yllin for a while before returning to her room for the night.

Heavily in thought, she stepped out onto her room's balcony, still pondering all the things that happened to her this day.

As she relaxed in the cool evening air, her attention was drawn up to the sky as she noticed a weaving presence not far away. It was Kel and Clarence, practicing. They dove, spun, and dipped, a mockery of precision and skill. Unlike the time before, however, she knew what they were trying to do.

The part she just couldn't understand was how Kel expected Clarence to overcome his handicap once they became partners. No matter how hard they practiced, a cross-eyed dragon could never fly straight. Right? Still, so many things in this place didn't make sense. It was hard to tell what would and wouldn't work. Home wasn't this complicated.

Suddenly tired, Talia walked back inside, closed the balcony doors and let the drapes fall across them. She changed clothes, and looking at the doors again, opened one of then slightly to let in the night air. As soon as the globes in her room turned dark, she slipped into her bed and rapidly fell into a deep sleep.

The night passed by uneventfully, except for a brief moment when she was startled awake by a strange noise. When she couldn't identify it and it wasn't repeated, she fell back asleep and was not disturbed again.

The next morning, she rose early and went down to the dining hall as she'd done the day before. To her surprise, she found a haggard-looking Daltan already there. From the bags underneath his eyes, she guessed he hadn't slept well. "Good morning, Daltan."

"Morning." He didn't sound as if he thought anything was good about it.

"Is your meeting with the Administrator today?" She saw him stiffen. This was her just the day before.

"I have an appointment at eleven," he told her.

Talia sat down. "She's quite nice. You really don't have anything to worry about." She decided to keep the fact the Administrator was somewhat strange to herself. It seemed the boy was worried enough already.

The door that led out to the garden opened, and Kel walked in. It grabbed her attention immediately. She watched the squire as he crossed the room and headed for the kitchen. When he returned with his food, he spotted her across the room and to her surprise, waved to her like the day before. She waved back. Did Kel's cheeks just redden? From this distance, it was hard to tell. She decided she must have imagined it.

She talked distractedly with Daltan, watching Kel unobtrusively from the corner of her eye as he gulped down his breakfast. He was about finished by the time people started filling up the hall. He traded pleasantries with the teachers who arrived at his table but still didn't appear to actually engage any of them in conversation. Pretty soon the room got too full for her to be able to see that far anymore.

After breakfast, she spoke to a couple of the other people who would be in her class, and they all gathered about Daltan to keep him occupied. The boy said little, even as they all went as a group and toured the grounds. He grew a little paler with each passing hour. Talia was sure he'd soon be ill. She wished she could tell him just a bit of what would go on in his meeting to ease his mind, but didn't dare.

As the hour neared eleven, they were all in his room. Daltan was pacing, looking as if he would bolt at the slightest provocation and never come back. His eyes were wide and staring as the time on the clock slowly ran out.

"Daltan?" She watched him, genuinely starting to worry for him.

"Y—yes?" His eyes didn't leave the clock face.

"Would you—" She hesitated, trying to make sure she chose her words carefully. "Do you want some company on the way? It's time."

Daltan looked away from the clock, the room suddenly growing quiet. His eyes flashed like those of a hunted animal.

"I—"

"No, I don't mind at all. Really." Before he could protest, she gave him a small smile and headed for the door. Jarel and Sonsan got up as well. Daltan stared at her, his expression uncertain.

"Come on, you don't want to be late." Jarel beckoned to him encouragingly. Hesitantly, the boy followed.

As if being led by his peers to a fate worse than death, Daltan woodenly walked up the stairs with them. Talia hung close to him, concerned. As his gaze lighted on the gold door at the end of the hallway, she saw his eyes fill with utter despair. She didn't feel this badly yesterday, did she?

She tried to ignore the uneasiness the large, imposing door still instilled in her though she knew what was behind it. She leaned in close to whisper in Daltan's ear. "It's going to be all right. Really it is." She tried to put as much conviction into her voice as possible. She thought she saw his expression clear just a little.

"Thanks." He tried hard to smile then pulled away so he could approach the door alone.

Before he could knock, Lareen's soft voice rang out from within. "Please come in."

Daltan jerked back startled and looked back at Talia one last time before he forced himself to move forward and open the door. It shut softly behind him as he stepped inside, cutting him from view.

"How does she do that?" Sonsan's almond-shaped eyes stared hard at the gold door as if she could pry the answer from it. Her voice was no louder than a whisper.

Not exactly of their own volition, all their eyes then turned to the door. Quietly, the three of them backed away. Surely the Administrator couldn't see through walls.

Could she?

Once out of the fourth floor, they all rushed down to the dining hall together to wait for lunch. Talia knew if Daltan's experience were similar to hers, he would be locked away for several hours.

After the meal, she strolled outside on her own. Walking by the cultivated fields near the dragon runway, she spotted men and women working on the crops. She watched them with a dull ache, their labors reminding her of her father and of home. She thought of asking if they wouldn't mind some help, just to get the feeling of home that much clearer, but couldn't quite bring herself to do it. She missed her parents, and she loved and respected them. Yet the idea of becoming a farmer was something which definitely didn't appeal to her at all.

A large shadow crossed over her and she looked up. A winged form was slowly circling in an erratic pattern with wings spread wide—Clarence. Talia turned where she stood and followed the dragon's weaving form as it dipped and dived ever closer to the ground. With bated breath, she watched him approach the landing area. Everyone else in the fields totally ignored the sight.

She spotted Kel astride the dragon, his armor gleaming in the sunlight. Behind him, she could make out a cowering figure holding on for dear life.

Clarence came in for a landing. His legs dipped down to touch the dirt. He tripped and fell hard on his belly, his wings going everywhere. His body bounced, then bounced again then he slid on the runway, sending dirt every which way.

Her throat grew tight as she saw Clarence's body head for the edge of the cliff, giving the definite impression he wouldn't be able to stop in time. Not sure what she could possibly do, she ran in their direction, praying they wouldn't go over. Just when she thought nothing would stop them, Clarence's claws reached out and buried themselves in the dirt, becoming unmovable weights. His body stopped mere inches from the precipice.

"Are you all right?" Breathless, she reached them, her sides on fire and her heart racing.

Both dragon and squire turned to look at her in surprise.

"Talia?" Kel removed his helmet, revealing his sweaty hair.

She doubled over a moment to catch her breath. The smell of turned earth was sticky in the air.

We are somewhat dirtier for the experience, perhaps, but otherwise, all are in good health. Clarence's crooked gaze met her own even as his lips peeled back to show his teeth. She felt a small shiver course through her, for if it weren't for the amused tone in Clarence's thoughts, the sight of his teeth would have been enough to send many a man scurrying in fear of his life.

"You shouldn't have worried. This is normal for us." Kel gave her a warm smile while at the same time looking embarrassed at having made her ask the question at all.

She could only stare. This was normal? She couldn't understand how they could both go through this day after day.

A soft moan drew her attention to Clarence's back. A thin boy about her age was leaning forward, his eyes closed and his face pale. His fingers were wrapped in a death grip about the leather harness that held him to the saddle. Clarence moved slowly to right himself properly. At the movement, the boy moaned again.

Kel quickly undid his straps then turned around to work on the boy's. Talia stepped up a little closer, ready to lend a hand, though she wasn't sure what she could do.

After Kel unwound his straps, the boy still didn't open his eyes.

"Hey, it's all right now. You've reached the school. You're safe." She hoped hearing her voice would help him realize they'd landed safely, but he made no move to let go. "You're on the ground."

His eyes screwed shut even tighter. He moaned again.

"She's telling you the truth, Dyl," Kel said. "You can let go now."

Moaning yet again, as if expecting this to be a trick, the new boy hesitantly dared to open one eye. After he took a long, careful look about, he opened the other.

Talia tried to give him her best smile when he looked in her direction. "Hi! I'm Talia. I'm a new student here, the same as you."

"Hi." The smile he tried to give in return was a little shaky.

This time, Dyl didn't resist when Kel helped him pry his fingers from the harness. She watched as the squire then helped him down, and made sure the boy would be able to stand on his own. At least Dyl's face now held a little more color.

Kel retrieved Dyl's bag from Clarence's back then climbed down. "I'll see you in a bit, Clarence." He picked up his helmet and gauntlets.

"If you want, I'll take Dyl in for you," Talia offered. "It's the same office as before, right?"

"Ah, yes." Kel sounded a little surprised. She wondered why. "You wouldn't mind?"

"Not at all."

His blue eyes were bright. "Thanks." He then gave her a grateful smile. "It'd be a big help."

Yes, thank you. Clarence's voice rang in her mind.

Wondering if she'd ever get used to voices in her head,

she blushed a little, not having thought nearly as much of the favor as the two of them were making it out to be.

"Come on, Dyl. Let's go get your room assignment." She took Dyl's bag from a still smiling Kel then waited for the boy to join her. She kept them off to the side of the path so Clarence could pass once he'd risen to his feet and showered the area with the loose dirt on his back. Kel waved down at them from his high perch as they sauntered past.

"All dragons don't fly like him, do they?" Dyl's voice was low as his wide eyes followed the departing dragon.

Talia almost smiled at the question. His reaction seemed to be so close to her own. "No. At least, that's what I've been told." As she led him toward the main building, it suddenly occurred to her to wonder if perhaps the ride on Clarence served a purpose. If riding on him was the worst experience one could ever have on a dragon, all else would be a joy in comparison regardless of the weather or circumstances. As Clarence disappeared from view, she pondered again how the two of them could willingly go through this again and again.

She shoved all thoughts of Kel and Clarence aside as they reached the school's main doors. "Dyl, welcome to Dragon's Peak." She pushed aside one of the massive doors and led him inside. She suddenly understood Kel's amusement as the boy gasped beside her at the sight of the opulent interior.

As she continued forward, she also realized at that moment, she'd not thought of herself as an outsider but rather as someone who belonged. She enjoyed the feeling.

Maybe she would get used to all this after all.

Feeling a little strange at the revelation, she led Dyl to the room she'd first been taken to by Kel on her arrival. She knocked on the door then stepped to the side.

"Go on in. I'll wait for you out here."

With a slightly worried glance in her direction, he opened the door and went inside.

Talia leaned back against the wall and contemplated the area around her, questioning how a place such as this, so different from everything she'd ever known, could start to already feel familiar and commonplace. In the stories the traveling bards shared with the village, the heroes of old often were not in control of their destinies, having been set on a number of roads by fate. Was this how she ended up here as well? Because she was meant to come here? Was that why she was starting to feel comfortable? Maybe it also meant someday she'd actually be able to pick something to be.

For the next few minutes, she explored the strange line of questioning, but she'd come no closer to an answer by the time the office door opened again. Dyl stepped out into the hallway looking lost even as a somber-faced Tammer followed him out. She could well understand Dyl's expression.

As Tammer closed the door behind him, he noticed her standing there. His serious expression faltered, his brow rising in surprise. He didn't question her presence, however, and left them without a word.

Talia waited until he disappeared from sight before saying anything. "So, should we go take a look at your room?" she asked.

Dyl nodded slowly, still staring the way Tammer had gone.

"He didn't tell you much, did he?" She led the way to the stairs.

"No," the boy answered. "Is it normal?"

She grinned. "Around here, yes. It's as if they want to see if you can find things out on your own." Even as she said it, she wondered how true this might just be.

They found Dyl's room easily on the second floor. After helping him get settled, she spent the rest of the afternoon showing him around the building and filling him in on what little she knew.

At dinner, she introduced him to the others. She was pleased to see Daltan looking a lot more relaxed. She also found out from Dyl his appointment with the Administrator would be at the same time as Daltan's but the next day. From what some of the others mentioned during dinner, it seemed girls met the Administrator at nine while boys met her at eleven. Talia would have found that curious except for the Administrator's apparent habit of sleeping late. It wouldn't do to have young boys see her in her robe. Though according to Yllin, most of them would like nothing better.

When she returned to her room to turn in for the night, she spent a few minutes on her balcony watching Clarence and Kel practice maneuvers in the sky while batting other strange lines of thought about.

The same as the night before, a strange noise woke her, but when it didn't repeat itself, she sleepily dismissed it and went back to sleep.

In the morning, she went down to the dining hall early, as was becoming her custom, and she spotted Kel as he came in. He waved at her as he'd done on previous mornings and she did the same. This time she could swear she saw him blush. She just didn't understand it.

Once breakfast was over, those students who would belong to her class stayed together and helped Dyl pass the time until his meeting with the Administrator arrived. Unlike Daltan, whose nervousness made him quiet and withdrawn, Dyl talked in hurried bursts and couldn't sit still for longer than a minute. He almost ran to the meeting when it was time to go.

After lunch, Talia ventured outside to watch the farmers at work, though in reality, it was more to distract herself as she waited for Clarence and Kel to arrive with another student.

Witnessing another painful crash, she rushed to their final landing-place, then took charge of the new arrival. By bringing them to Tammer and waiting for them afterward, she did her best to ease their transition to what she knew to them would be a strange, foreign place. It also gave her something worthwhile to do.

Observing Clarence's landings didn't get easier. Once she watched, to her utter horror, as dragon and riders actually slipped past the edge of the cliff and fell. With her heart hammering inside her chest, it was a few breathless moments before she spotted Clarence's large green form rise back into the air to attempt another landing. The second was much more successful.

As she did every time she saw them, she wondered how the dragon and squire could stand to go through this day after day. That they went and retrieved new students for the school made things bad enough, but every evening the two of them were out there practicing as well.

Early on her seventh day at the school, Talia was up and dressed and was only waiting for the morning knocks from the watchers before heading downstairs to breakfast. She frowned, as she glanced at her clock, realizing they were late. Making her way downstairs, she noticed a lot fewer people showed for the meal, though Kel, as usual, came in early, ate his breakfast in a blur and left. There were fewer watchers than usual, and even those there seemed to be keeping not quite as sharp an eye on everyone as usual. She worried about the strangeness for a while, until it dawned on her today was the day students kept for their own.

When Mandee and Yllin finally made their way in, Talia's suspicions were confirmed.

"Oh, yeah. It's bucket day..." Mandee's tone hinted at horrible things. "The day we have to change the water and clean our rooms." Her eyes narrowed with a sly look and she leaned close. "But after all that—then the day is ours!"

Changing the bed's linen and cleaning up her room proved easy enough. Talia found these tasks a breeze compared to the pile of chores she'd been responsible for at home on a daily basis. The changing of the tub water, however, proved to be another matter altogether.

Getting rid of the water currently in the tub itself was simple. Mandee and Yllin told her all she needed to do was fill the buckets and dump the old water out the balcony. She made a mental note to never be out and about the grounds in the morning on this day.

Once she'd emptied the tub, however, she needed to take her two buckets and make the long trek to the mesa's lake behind the school. Getting there wasn't much of a problem, but coming back with two filled buckets, navigating around everyone else doing the same chore, then trekking up the stairs without spilling it, was not.

The first two buckets barely seemed to make a difference to the amount of water she'd have to bring to fill the tub. By her fifth trip to the lake and back, her arms shook from the strain. As she sat down on the bottom of the stairs to take a short rest, she saw many of the other students weren't doing much better. Everyone was getting water—students, teachers, watchers. Massaging her arms, she watched the people go back and forth giving the impression of a long column of ants.

When she finally dragged her way back upstairs, Talia

saw her tub was only half full. Steam was rising from the water. She frowned. The tub was obviously magical. She'd been unable to figure out another way the water could stay warm with no seeming source of heat. The lights in her room also must be as well—they came on and off precisely at the same time every day. The basin water never lowered or even got dirty. So why couldn't they have used the same kind of magic on the tub? The basin even refilled itself very slowly, but the tub did not. Could things only be made to do one or two things, or did they just not feel like doing it so everyone would have to torture their arms out of their sockets?

She could almost hear her father's laughter.

Talia had occasionally pointed out to him the futility of some of her chores, especially the weeding in the garden. For no matter how hard one worked and pulled, the weeds perpetually came back. She was sure if she asked him about this, his answer would be the same as it was then. This definitely appeared to be a chore he would have approved of—it would breed patience and improve her character and strength. But what about her poor arms? She was suddenly intensely grateful her room wasn't on the fourth floor.

Glancing over at the tub with disdain, she wondered if she couldn't live with only a half-filled one. She reached out to touch the water then pulled her hand back, her fingertips throbbing with pain. It was hot! She sucked on her abused digits and stared at the liquid. It wasn't this hot before. She wouldn't be able to take a bath in that. She pouted a moment as she realized this, too, was probably done on purpose. It'd definitely stop anyone from being tempted to only do half a job. Her father's robust laugh rang through her mind again.

With a heavy sigh, she picked up her buckets and

headed for the door.

Taking frequent breaks to ease the strain on her arms, it was almost noon before she was able to reach her floor with the last set of buckets. As she came to her door, she found someone there waiting for her.

"Hello. Are you Talia?"

She nodded, not sure if she'd ever seen the longhaired, sweet-faced woman before. "Yes, ma'am, that's me."

"My name is Helyn. I will be your teacher for your first year." The tall woman took a step toward her. "Here, let me help you with those."

Talia gratefully let the teacher take one of her buckets, and they both stepped into the room. With deft expertise, Helyn tipped her bucket over the side of the tub and poured the water in with a minimum of splashing.

"Three more students will be arriving this week, so five days from now, we'll be starting classes." She smiled. It was a pretty smile. "I wanted to make sure I got to meet all of you before then. And if it would be all right, I thought those of us who're here might meet after lunch so I can show you where our classroom will be and what you'll need to bring to class."

The prospect of classes beginning appealed to Talia. She'd gotten a little restless the last day or so, with nothing definite to do. "That would be fine."

Helyn's smile grew even wider. It made her face glow.

"Wonderful! After lunch then, I'll wait for all of you at the garden's exit." She moved toward the door. "I'm really looking forward to our class. See you." She left, giving Talia a delicate wave as she did so.

Lunch was as informal as breakfast and consisted of different types of bread, smoked meats, cheeses, and fruit. As she sat with Mandee and Yllin, Talia took her time as she ate, not wanting to antagonize her aching arm muscles more than she'd done already. They would never be the same again.

"So, did you get your tub filled yet?" A hint of amusement danced in Mandee's eyes.

She glanced at her friend, wondering if her discomfort was so obvious. "Yes, I just finished a little while ago."

"Bet your arms are sore," Yllin commented between bites.

Mandee smiled in sympathy. "We overdid it our first time, too. Yllin here thought her arms were going to fall off."

"Did not," Yllin replied indignantly.

"I'll bring by some salve later that will help. I won't be needing it since we finally came up with a system that works without killing us. It does take longer, but..."

Talia noticed the amused look was back in Mandee's eyes, and though she was doing precisely what the girl wanted her to do, she didn't care as long as it'd be able to help her from straining her arms like this again. "What do you do?"

"It's quite simple really," Mandee watched her intently as she spoke. "We just make sure to only make one trip an hour. It makes all the difference."

"Oh." She felt like an idiot. It never occurred to her, yet it made perfect sense. Mandee and Yllin both laughed at the dumbfounded expression on her face.

"It sounds simple, and you want to kick yourself once you realize you can do it this way, but you'd be amazed at the number of people who've not thought of it," Mandee said. "Everyone just wants to do it all at once and get it over with."

"Especially the boys." Yllin rolled her eyes as if this said it all.

"One day though, the two of us realized since the

whole day was ours, it wouldn't matter how long it took us to do it as long as it got done before lights out," Mandee gave her a smug smile.

Talia nodded thoughtfully. She wasn't sure how long it would have taken her to come to the same conclusion, but the idea was a good one. Her arms would definitely be grateful. If only she could do something to help them feel better now.

Yllin interrupted her thoughts. "They won't really start to bother you until later. We'll get you the salve long before then."

"Will it really help?" She didn't want to get her hopes too high.

"Oh, sure. The stuff is excellent. I think it's one of the more popular items around here," Mandee said.

She didn't doubt it. "Thanks, I'd really appreciate it." The thought of actually having some relief brought an easy smile to her face.

By the time lunch was over, Talia found herself getting a little excited as the time to meet with Helyn drew near. Having already told her friends about the meeting, she parted company with them when they came out of the garden back into the building proper.

As promised, Helyn was waiting for the new students not far from the door. She was the third to join her. It wasn't long before the rest of the students arrived. Talia was somewhat impressed as Helyn greeted each of them by name.

"I'm glad you could all make it," she said. "Come, let me show you our classroom." Helyn led the way down the hall.

All the classrooms were set in the middle area of the first floor. The walls, unlike all the other ones in the school, were made of a dark wood rather than stone. As they went through the small mazelike hallways between them, Helyn explained how the walls in this area were not permanent but were made so they could stand alone or be moved to create different sized rooms depending on the need. Talia stared at the solid walls around her, finding it difficult to believe they could be moved. The only thing that gave credence to Helyn's statement was the fact neither the hallways nor the rooms possessed a ceiling and could be looked down into from the floors above.

Their own room was close to the center of the maze. Twelve large desks were arranged inside it in two rows bent in a large semicircle, the desks staggered so none would impede another's view. The chairs behind the desks were large and padded, but also short to accommodate their nonadult-sized legs. She couldn't help but smile, thinking these desks and chairs extremely luxurious compared to the stiff wooden benches they all shared at school back home. She wondered fleetingly what her old friends would make of all this.

A tall, full desk faced all the others, and a massive blackboard was hooked to the wall behind it. Giant rolls of paper lay stacked on the large desk. Talia was curious as to what they could be for.

"This will be your classroom for the next year," Helyn told them. "I'm very much looking forward to getting started." The teacher's face almost glowed as she looked at each of them. For several minutes, Helyn encouraged them to look around and try the desks and chairs, before she led them back out and promised to meet them after breakfast four days from then.

As she returned to her room, Talia found herself more excited by the prospect of school than she would have thought. Her eagerness surprised her, not ever having felt this way about being taught before. Still, she thought she would be able to learn things here she'd never imagined knowing. Something about it held a lot of appeal.

After she made sure to write another letter to her parents, despite the deep ache settling into her arms, she took an early bath and soaked her unhappy appendages in the liquid they'd labored so hard to bring up. Once she got out, she felt heavy and slow. She got dressed then decided to lie down on her bed for a minute. Before she realized it, she fell asleep.

A knock at her door startled her awake. Momentarily disoriented, she scrambled out of bed, almost smacking her head against the upper frame. Her arms and shoulders twinged in displeasure at the sudden movement. She grimaced in discomfort as she stumbled over to open the door.

"Hi!" Mandee's bright smile greeted Talia. Yllin stood beside her. "We're not disturbing you, are we?"

"No, please come in." She opened the door wide. "I—I accidentally fell asleep." She hurriedly ran her hand through her curling hair and hoped it wasn't too out of order.

The two girls came in. "Sorry to wake you, but we did bring a gift." Mandee pointed dramatically at Yllin and the other held up a small, earthen jar. "Yes, we know you can't believe it, but it's true. Salve for your aching arms and shoulders—delivered to your very door as promised!"

Talia's arms and shoulders throbbed as if the prospect of relief meant they needed to complain more. "Thank you very much."

"Sit down and let me put it on," Mandee offered. "You look like you could really use it." Her friend steered her to sit on the bed while Yllin opened the jar. A strange, pungent odor filled the room.

As Mandee smeared the greenish concoction on her

skin, it began to tingle.

"Where'd you get this?" she asked.

"The old pervert." Yllin looked away. "When I first came here, one of the other students told me about it."

"Yeah, she was hurting so bad the first time even the threat of the old man leering at her didn't make her hesitate." Yllin threw her friend a dirty look. Mandee laughed.

Late that same evening, Talia woke up in the middle of the night but wasn't sure why. As she lay in the darkness, not really sleepy anymore, she frowned as she recalled this happened before. Even as she sat there and thought about it, she heard a small, barely perceptible sound coming from the direction of her balcony.

Not sure what it could be, or why it'd be at her window, she slowly rose out of bed, a chill of mixed fear and curiosity moving down her back. As she stared at her balcony doors, she thought she could make out a large shadow through them, but couldn't really be sure if it was something she was seeing or just a trick of the night. She drew closer.

Before she could get to them, however, her foot accidentally knocked over one of the buckets she'd forgotten to put away after her earlier efforts. As the sound of the wood hitting stone echoed softly around her, the dark shadow outside seemed to swell then it abruptly disappeared. Rushing forward, she brushed aside the curtain over the balcony doors and peered out the glass. Nothing was there.

Frowning, she went back to bed but lay awake a long time listening for the odd sound to return. It didn't. Sometime during her vigil, she was dragged back into sleep.

Chapter Five

A BANGING SOUND reverberated through the room. Talia gasped, the noise startling her, her heart rising into her throat.

"Time to get up!"

As she heard the muffled cry through her door, she realized her lights were on. Slipping out of bed, she glanced at the clock in its niche and saw it was already six thirty. She'd overslept.

Her arms ached only a little as she washed her face in the basin then got dressed. In her mind, she profusely thanked Yllin and Mandee for the salve, even as she applied some more, knowing the slight discomfort she felt now was but a taste of what would have been hers without it.

By the time she made it down to breakfast, the dining hall was filling fast. As was the case every morning since she arrived, the Administrator's chair was empty. When she continued glancing down the table, she also realized Kel had already come and gone. It felt a little strange not to see him first thing in the morning.

By late afternoon, the aches in her arms and shoulders were gone. It significantly brightened her mood as she went outside to get ready for yet another of her classmates to arrive. Both Clarence and Kel seemed quite happy to see her.

She was just glad they didn't mind her help.

For the next three days, she followed the pattern she'd started the week before. Tammer no longer appeared surprised to find her outside his office. He even gave her a slight smile on the last day. On the fourth, the last student went to meet with the Administrator for the first time. The following morning, classes would begin.

As she ate breakfast on that fifth day, Talia felt anticipation grow inside her. This was why she'd been brought here; this was where the rest of her life would begin. Looking at the other four girls and seven boys comprising her class, she saw many of them felt the same way as well. Dyl literally leaped from his seat when the door to the garden was opened and they were all dismissed.

For the first time, Talia was able to walk with Mandee and Yllin farther than the garden's far end. This would be the first time since she'd arrived she would be the same as everyone else—a student of the Dragon Knight Guild.

"Have fun." Mandee grinned at her as she and Yllin reached their classroom. Talia waved back at them, then went on with her classmates to their own room.

Helyn was already there when they arrived and greeted them all with a bright smile. "Good morning, everyone."

Each of them took a seat. Talia ended up in one near the center. She took a quick glance at the others and saw expressions ranging from barely restrained excitement to nervous fear. She found herself vacillating between the two.

Helyn stood before her desk, her face still smiling. "Today, all we'll do is get you a little more acquainted with the guild and the school, what we do, and why we are," she said. "But first, let me show you where we are."

As Helyn went around the desk, Talia noticed one of the rolled parchments she'd seen on their previous visit to the classroom was hooked up to the top of the blackboard. With a long pole Helyn took from a hook on the wall, she reached up to the parchment and undid the string which still held it coiled. The paper rolled open for all of them to see.

Talia leaned forward as she realized it was a map. It was the biggest she'd ever seen, and it was wonderful. She stared at it, looking at the dark and light browns, yellows, and greens, which were colored in such a way as to make it easy to tell what were valleys, mountains, and forests. The oceans, seas, and rivers were each done in unique shades of blue. It appeared more a work of art than a real map, yet more detailed than any she'd seen before.

"Our world, as you know, has seven continents—Amara, Tulain, Carsock, Bolamia, Tusees, Sparmat, and Minas. Our school is located here, on Minas, in the Achron Mountain Range." Helyn used the stick she'd used to lower the map as a pointer and indicated a mid-sized continent in the Southern Hemisphere. "Now let's see where you all come from."

One by one Helyn asked each of them their area of origin then pointed the place out on the map. Talia's home sat in the continent of Amara, which was even farther south than Minas. She was a little disappointed to find hers to be one of the smallest of the lot. She also felt a pang of loss as she realized how far from home she actually was.

"Ours is but one of the numerous schools belonging

to the Dragon Knight Guild," Helyn explained. "Many schools are specialized, while others, like ours, are more general, created to build a knowledge base for the students to grow from before they go on to the specialized schools." She pointed out some of the locations of the schools that were the same as theirs. All looked to be in large mountain ranges. "Over the seven continents, are spread hundreds of kingdoms. Our guild's job is to keep all these places in peace, to be arbitrators in disputes, to help guard the innocent, and protect the populace from attacks by rogues or maeloon."

Talia shivered. Maeloon—savage creatures who inhabited desolate areas of land. She'd heard many stories about the maeloon. It was said they were cursed long ago by the gods for having had the tenacity to bite one of them. Because of it, it was their lot to be born insane—and they were. They attacked any living thing without provocation. They slaughtered for pleasure, not for food. Some said intelligence and cunning hid behind the madness, for they recognized their own kind and it was rumored on occasion they'd actually gather in packs and go in search of human settlements to terrorize for no other reason than they could. She hadn't seen a maeloon and never wanted to. The tales told about them were bad enough they'd given her nightmares.

"And we do more," Helyn continued. "We help kingdoms during times of famine. We help find cures for the sick. We educate. Our highest goals are to help people in any way we can.

"It is this purpose which united our ancestors with the dragons and has made the guild what it is today. Now each of you will become part of this legacy as well." She stared at each of them in turn, her expression serious.

The girl named Sonsan raised her hand. Helyn

motioned for her to go ahead and speak.

"Some of my, some of my friends back home said the Dragon Knights were nothing but bullies and that all they want is money and power." The almond-eyed girl held a defiant stance but spoke quickly as if just wanting to get the awkward statement out of the way.

Talia didn't think she'd have the nerve to say such a thing herself. Though she'd heard something along the same vein once or twice back home.

Helyn didn't seem bothered by the comment in the least. "You'll find people think of the guild as monsters as well as saviors. It all depends on whom you ask. However, in the end, it's best if you keep an open mind and judge for yourselves. During our time together you'll learn much about the history of the guild and the things it has done, both right and wrong."

Helyn went on and informed them the Dragon Knight Guild was over eight hundred years old. It came into creation during one of the most bloodthirsty periods of man's history. At the time there'd been thousands of small kingdoms, and almost all of them were at war with one another. Just like a number of other intelligent races, the dragons found themselves caught in the middle of the human explosion and later became targets of violence as they were seen only as dangerous creatures which needed to be destroyed. Mostly loners by nature, the dragons found themselves outnumbered and outmatched despite their vast resources of strength and magic.

As their numbers dwindled, the eldest of the dragons gathered together and tried to plan how best to save themselves and if possible, save man from himself as well.

Using their pooled skills, they devised a means of locating humans who wanted the conflict to end as badly as they did. With these people, they forged a contract then bonded with them so together they could work to stop the conflict one kingdom at a time.

The contract was still being honored to this day.

Talia tried hard to picture the things Helyn told them, but couldn't. Stories of war and strife were things in tales, nothing she'd actually experienced, and so it was difficult to truly grasp. Men murdering each other? Trying to drive themselves and dragons into extinction? It just seemed more akin to a fantastical tale than reality.

Lunch brought a much-needed break so they could all attempt to absorb what they'd been told. Afterward, Helyn told them more about the guild.

"Over the centuries, the guild has grown, but a lot of the structure has remained the way it was set up in the beginning," she said. "At the head of the guild is the Council of Elders. It's comprised of the twelve most respected and capable of the dragon/human pairs as well as the oldest and wisest of dragons. To them are left the highest decisions, those which affect the guild and humanity as a whole.

"Beneath the Council of Elders are the Judges. These are human/dragon pairs who hold sway over disputes between the different groups in the guild as well as between the guild and the countries it protects. Due to the nature of the job, and the guild's high standards for the position, their numbers have invariably been few. Currently, we only have twenty-three of them. The guild is constantly looking for more."

Talia's gaze moved to the map still hanging from the wall. Twenty-three men and dragon pairs to cover all of that? The arbitrator in their small village had more than his hands full doing his job, and he only took care of a small area. How could only twenty-three pairs do all which would need to be done in seven continents?

"Beneath the Judges are both the Regional Overseers and the Inspector Generals," Helyn continued. "The Regional Overseers' duties are mostly administrative. They keep track of guild members in their area and make sure all is well with the small outposts and supply depots. Each of these, in turn, has a leader who reports to the Overseer.

"As for the Inspector Generals, their role is to inspect any location, whether a school, outpost, or supply depot, and make sure the upkeep, functionality, and interests of the guild are being maintained. Their utmost goal is to make sure those belonging to the guild are being properly taken care of."

Talia frowned at the last, wondering why such would be a concern.

"The many schools belonging to the guild are in themselves semi-independent and self-ruling. They fall under the jurisdiction of the Inspector Generals rather than under an Overseer. The schools available to those of the guild are wide and varied. As your skills and talents are discovered, you will have opportunities to choose to go to more specialized schools."

DINNER WAS FILLED with talk about what kinds of specialty schools the guild might have and also what each of them thought they might want to have schooling in. Talia didn't say much in the last regard, still having no real idea of what being a Dragon Knight entailed, let alone anything else. A few of the others already knew what direction they wanted to take. She felt a tinge of jealousy that they could already be so sure of what they wanted to be.

Yllin declared in her usual severe expression that of late she'd been considering becoming a healer. Talia saw Mandee choke back a giggle, but at least the somber-faced girl's friend had the sense for once not to tease. Looking away lest she give something away, Talia admitted it was hard to picture Yllin as a figure of comfort and care.

As they went through the garden after dinner, she suddenly wondered what it was Kel might want to be if he and Clarence were ever able to pass their test. Surely he didn't intend to pick up students forever, did he?

The following day, Helyn took the class around the school and showed them the facilities available to them. They spent a couple of hours at the library alone, learning how to use magical devices to help locate books.

Helyn told them to gather about a tall, thin box sitting outside the history section of the library. "This is what you will use when you need to find a book. You should stand before the sloped end then speak evenly at it. Tell it the subject type, then the actual information you are looking for. Like this." She turned to face the box. "History. Minas. The Hundred Year Feud."

Talia gasped as a three-dimensional picture of the stacks of the history section grew from the top of the box. In the image, two rows down and three shelves up, one of the books was lit in blue. Realizing that it was a map, most of the students scurried to go where it pointed. They all skidded to a halt as they could plainly see, on the third shelf, a hefty, bound tome glowing a light blue. The light remained around the book until Helyn removed it from the shelf.

"As you can see, this is very easy. If the book is not in the section of the library you are at, the image will expand to show you where you need to go and the location of the box for that section. If a book is currently unavailable, the image will show you its usual place, but it will be colored in red." She placed the book back on the shelf. "Now who would like to try it?"

Twelve hands raised simultaneously in the air. Talia thought this the most marvelous thing she'd ever seen.

After lunch, they spent a large part of the afternoon at Nertak's cave. The old man stared intently at each of them as they were introduced, once or twice winking at the girls. Having been there before, Talia only paid half attention to Helyn's instructions, instead watching Nertak as he tagged noiselessly along. Aside from the strange, lewd looks he flashed toward them on occasion, he seemed to be absorbing everything any of them did or said. She wondered if he just didn't get many visitors and was lonely, or if it was something else.

In the following days, Helyn flooded them with even more information, though a lot of it was more mundane and things Talia could have been taught at home. Helyn also gave them small tests to try to find out how much each of them already knew about history, mathematics, and geography. Almost as if to give them a treat, however, as soon as the testing was done, she spent some time talking to them about dragons. Talia found herself fascinated by her class more than before.

"Dragons come in a variety of shapes and sizes. They range from the size of a household cat to as large as a midsized barn. You'll see that some are long and thin, while others tend to be short and squat. They even come in all sorts of colors."

Sonsan snickered. Talia grinned, picturing a shop full of them where you could buy them and take them home to put on your bed.

"Only seven colors of dragons exist, though every once in a long while one with a different hue might appear, but these are very rare. The seven main colors are red, green, gold, purple, blue, silver, and black. The color tends to determine body style as well as whether they can speak vocally or through thoughts. Though as with all things, there have been exceptions."

She unrolled a pinned chart on the blackboard showing the main body types.

"Dragons are as intelligent as us, if not more so. You might not think so due to their lack of mechanical inventions, but that would be an error. Dragons focused more on developing their minds than in making things. And many are born with magical aptitude. They've been great contributors to the field."

Tyr's eyes grew wide. "So dragons can do magic?"

"Some of them, yes, and very well at that. Others though prefer to spend their time preserving and teaching the lore of ages past, theirs and ours. They have an amazing capacity for retention of information. They hand it down from generation to generation through songs and poetry in their own common tongue."

In the end, Talia came to realize that dragons were as diverse as their human partners.

That night, she slept deep and hard, dreaming of colorful dragons making rainbows as they flew overhead.

Chapter Six

THE NEXT WEEK passed by quickly. Talia's class learned about each of the seven continents, the oceans, the plants and animals of each. With so much information, and parts of it so strange and at times wondrous, she could barely think when she went to bed at night. The world was proving to be an incredibly complex place—things could be done in so many different ways. It was so much more than she would have ever found in Queegam.

Mandee and Yllin both laughed when she confided this.

"It's a shock, isn't it?" Mandee grinned, thoroughly amused. "And you've barely even started."

Talia questioned whether her poor brain could possibly take more.

One day, after returning to class after lunch, she and the others grew restless when Helyn did not appear. They'd started discussing amongst themselves whether or not they should send someone to try and find her when she finally arrived. The teacher's eyes looked troubled, and her usually cheerful face seemed subdued. Talia wondered what was wrong.

"I'm sorry I'm so late." She looked at each of them, an apologetic smile touching her lips. The troubled look didn't leave her eyes, however. "There's been a change in plans for today. You see, there appears to be a worm infestation at the dragon dormitory—so you will all need to be fitted with armor."

Talia frowned, the pronouncement sounding ominous yet making no sense. What did armor and worms have to do with each other?

With everyone else looking as confused as she felt, she left the room as Helyn shooed them all out. The teacher then led them toward the back of the school to a broad set of stairs leading down.

When Mandee and Yllin took her on her tour of the school, they'd not shown her this almost hidden way to go underground. Talia would have customarily have assumed the stairs led to some sort of cellar but at the moment she wasn't so sure.

As the students followed Helyn down, their footsteps echoed all around them. The air turned slightly cooler as they continued the long descent, and they could see water condensing on some of the stones. A moldy scent tainted the air. Talia and her classmates walked closer together.

At the bottom of the stairs, Helyn turned to the right down a long, dark corridor, leading them to a room with a sturdy, oak door. After she stopped and glanced back at them with a solemn air, she opened the door and escorted them inside.

The room within was small and unadorned except for a set of old benches at each wall. At the room's far end was an undersized door, and the first thing they all noticed was the thunderous booming sound coming from its other side.

"Go ahead and take a seat." Helyn almost yelled to be heard over the din.

Wondering why they couldn't hear the noise out in the hallway when in here it was so loud she almost couldn't think, Talia did as she'd been told. Everyone else also sat down, half of them covering their ears, trying unsuccessfully to hold back the racket.

After they all sat, Helyn looked satisfied then left through the small door. Several minutes later, the pounding from the other side stopped.

Talia sat with the others, nervous, not sure what to expect next.

The small door suddenly opened. One of the students gasped as they caught sight of who was there. The man was big, huge. He ducked through the narrow opening into the room. Muscles rippled over his body as if they possessed a mind of their own. His skin was tanned, like old leather. The man was bald, and a thin sheen of sweat covered his head. A large, ragged scar cut through the middle of his massive face. What trapped her gaze, however, was the large stump where his right arm should have been.

Despite his missing limb, the giant looked strong enough to snap any of them in two with just his left arm. The hammer he carried appeared capable of bringing down walls. The stranger's dark eyes raked over them one by one and finally came to rest on Tull, who was the biggest amongst them. "You there." The man's voice boomed across the room as he pointed the hammer in Tull's direction. Those sitting next to the boy speedily scooted away from him.

"Sir?" Tull's face went white, his voice a high squeak.

"You'll be first." The armorer, for she assumed that's

who he must be, slowly licked his dry lips then smiled. It didn't look friendly. "Come on inside."

Talia quickly looked from one to the other, the only thought in her head being that she was glad she wouldn't be first.

Tull didn't move.

"I don't have all day, boy." The armorer glared at him with impatience.

Tull swallowed hard then stood up. Hesitantly, he moved forward. As soon as he'd gone through the small doorway, the armorer raked the rest of them once more with his dark eyes then laughed before ducking out the way he'd come. Talia felt a chill weave down her back as his cold laughter echoed through the room.

"What is going on?" Narilla's eyes were wide with barely controlled fear.

"That's the armorer?" Mari asked. "He looks more like something from a nightmare." She hugged herself as if spooked by her own words.

Talia shuddered, agreeing with her only too well. "Surely he's not as bad as he looks, don't you think? This is a school after all." She hoped her words sounded more confident than they felt.

They all jumped as a loud yelp echoed from the other side of the small door. A high, cackled laugh, belonging to who knew what, followed after.

Everyone in the room froze, not sure what to make of what they'd heard. A number of them looked even paler than before.

Talia kept her gaze on the door. None of this made any sense. Still, she couldn't stop her heart from hammering in her chest.

A squeal came through the door trailed by more cackling. This was soon followed by another yelp, which was abruptly cut off. The creepy cackling came again, this time from multiple voices. Talia felt the hair rising up on the back of her neck.

Less than a minute later, they all jumped in their seats as the door through which Tull was taken through started to inch open. Talia heard someone in their group gasp and scurry to the back, but didn't see who it was. Her gaze was riveted to the opening door.

Standing only about the height of her own shoulder was the oldest person she'd ever seen. The woman was hunched over as if carrying a great weight, and she leaned on a thick cane. Her face was puckered as if it was fruit left out in the sun too long. The old woman smiled a secret smile at them, revealing a gap filled mouth. "Who's next?" Her voice sounded like loose gravel.

When none of them volunteered, the old woman shuffled a few steps closer and eyed each one of them. "You," she said, pointing at Narilla with a crooked, aged finger. "You'll be next. You look good and healthy." Something about the way she said it Talia didn't take pleasure in at all.

Narilla let out a small squeak of fear. The old woman laughed. They all now knew where the cackling came from.

"Ma'am, where is our teacher?" Talia didn't realize she was going to speak until the words left her mouth.

The old woman turned yellowed eyes in her direction. "Don't you worry yourself about her, sweetness. Your turn will come soon enough." She cackled with glee, her laugh echoing harshly in the small room. She shuffled forward again and yanked Narilla by the wrist. Fear pouring off her in waves, the young girl hesitantly followed the old woman through the door.

It slammed shut with resounding finality. After a

moment, they heard a bar being placed across it from the other side.

"Maybe you shouldn't have said anything, Talia." A quiet voice spoke up from beside her.

She glanced over at Daltan's worried face, quite sure he was probably right.

The boy looked as if he might say something else when a frightened scream ripped in from the other room. The cackling which soon followed sounded even more dreadful than before.

"This is wrong." Willer shot to his feet, panic written all over his face. He ran to the door they'd come in through and tried to pull it open. It didn't budge. "We're trapped in here."

Talia felt a touch of alarm rising inside her and hurriedly tried to quench it. Things weren't supposed to be this way. None of this was right. "Let's stay calm. We really don't know what's going on. This is a school. They wouldn't hurt us."

A couple of the others nodded in agreement, albeit slowly, but the rest looked unsure. Willer still kept trying to open the door.

No additional sounds came through the door from the other room as the minutes ticked by. Talia stared at it, uselessly trying to guess at what was going on behind it while at the same time attempting to hang on to her resolve that whatever it was it was harmless.

The rest turned to face the door as it opened again. The old woman came forth, but before she could say anything, Talia sprang to her feet. "I'm next!"

Someone gasped behind her, but she didn't dare check to see who it was. She knew if she saw the fear she already felt reflected in any of their faces, she wouldn't be able to go through with this. She'd already decided going would at least let her know what was happening, which was preferable to just sitting there, allowing her fears to be fed by her own overactive imagination.

The old woman's bushy brow rose high at her declaration then came down as she started to laugh. It was a natural sound, nothing like the high cackling they'd heard before. "All right then, if that's what you want. Come along."

Talia stepped forward and went through the door, not once glancing back. She heard the old woman close it behind her then bolt it.

No one else was in the small room she now found herself in. A stool sat near the door, and shelves covered the wall on the right. The one closest to the bottom held a pile of cream-colored clothes folded in neat piles. On some of the higher shelves, she spotted two other bundles of clothes. She tried to wrack her brain to recall what Narilla and Tull had been wearing. Straight before her was a thickly curtained doorway.

"Where are—"

"Shshsh. No talking." The old woman kept her voice low, bringing a gnarled finger to her lips.

"Yes, but—ow!" Talia jumped back, her shin throbbing where the old woman whacked it with her cane.

"Shshsh." The old woman put her gnarled finger to her lips again. "Grab one of those from the bottom shelf and change into it. You can leave your clothes there on the shelf. I think one of the ones from the second pile should fit you quite nicely." She was still keeping her voice very low.

Talia didn't move, looking from the shelf to the old woman and back until the old woman took another swing at her shins. She jumped out of the way.

"Come on, get going. The others are waiting their turn."

With some trepidation, she turned her back to the old woman and picked up the clothes from the second pile as she'd been told. The fabric felt soft and comfortable in her hands, but it didn't feel familiar. She unfolded them to see what they were.

One was a loose shift and the other pants—both close to her size. The pants came with a string at the waist which could be pulled tight. What were these for?

Not willing to ask for fear of getting hit in the shins again, she took off her vest and shirt and pulled the shift over her head. She folded her top clothes neatly and set them on one of the shelves, before taking off her shoes.

Glancing around, Talia found the old woman settling herself on the stool by the door as she watched Talia with a toothy grin. Not liking it, Talia turned her back to the old woman again and pulled down her pants. She was in the process of pulling her right foot out of them when she was pinched hard on the rump from behind. With a yelp, she tried to move away and ended up tripping over herself and falling hard on the floor. Evil cackling rose up loudly beside her.

"Why did—"

"Shshsh!" The old woman came close a grin on her face. "Quiet, now. Get dressed."

Annoyed and embarrassed more than hurt, she rose back to her feet and finished changing, this time keeping her eyes on the woman. When she was done, the old crone got up from the stool and motioned Talia to go before her through the curtained doorway.

Still trying to keep her eyes on the old woman, who was grinning again, she didn't pay much attention as she moved the curtain aside and stepped through.

Hands fell on her arms and suddenly yanked her to the other side. A startled yelp left her lips but was abruptly cut off as a hand was placed over her mouth. Mad cackling laughter rang up all around her. As cold fear ran through her, Talia struggled to turn around and see who held her but was released before she'd tried very hard.

Trying to catch her breath and still her speeding heart, she looked up and stared, startled, as she caught sight of who'd been holding her.

Helyn met Talia's gaze for a moment then looked away, her cheeks coloring slightly. Beside her stood the Administrator, who was grinning from ear to ear. Both of them were wearing the same type of cream-colored garments Talia wore. Theirs, unlike hers, looked to have been made specifically for them. Lareen's fit very close to her body, revealing her curves, and was cut low at the throat.

Talia opened her mouth to say she knew not what, when Lareen, in a perfect imitation of the old woman, brought a finger to her lips asking for silence.

Confused by everything that had gone on so far, she took a look at her surroundings for the first time. The room they were in was spacious with large shelves covering most of the walls. The shelves were mostly full, all types of armor and leather pieces stacked on them. In the center of the room sat a raised dais and on it stood a baffled Narilla as the giant armorer placed piece after piece of armor around her body. Talia spotted Tull not far from there, standing very still in simple, light, full body armor. The visor on his helmet was up, and she saw his gaze move to look over at her, but the rest of him remained as still as stone.

"Now be a good little student, Talia, and stand over there until Seren is ready for you." Lareen's voice was barely above a whisper. "Isn't this fun?"

Talia said nothing, not sure how to answer the question. Frowning, she moved to stand where she'd been told. She wasn't there long before a frightened yelp followed by cackling laughter came in from beyond the curtained doorway. She shook her head, still not sure at all of what was going on.

Before the fourth victim was brought into the room, Seren finished with Narilla, and after helping her off the dais, he beckoned at Talia to come over.

"Hmm," he said softly. "You're a small one, aren't you?"

She said nothing, amazed by the difference in the man from when she'd seen him before. His voice was no longer harsh and loud, but soft and strangely gentle. The hungry look in his eyes was gone, replaced with one of light amusement.

From the stack of armor pieces set next to the dais, Seren took several back and front plates and set them before her.

"Turn around please, and hold out your arms for me."

She did so. Seren held up a few back pieces against her for fit, and once he'd found one which satisfied him, he speedily found a matching front. Having her turn around to face him again, he set the two pieces together and hinged them on the left side.

As she watched, he gently put the two pieces around her and clicked them shut. "To get this off is easy, but only if you know how," he told her. He gave her a half smile. "Just reach down with your finger to this spot, rub it twice, then run it upwards." Seren demonstrated this as he spoke, using his callused finger to rub at a small indentation at the waist then ran it up the side. With an audible click, the two halves swung apart.

Talia stared in amazement, realizing this, too, must be more magic. It seemed here, unlike everywhere else she'd ever heard of, it was used in just about everything.

Seren shut the two pieces together and asked her to try it. Once she did, he closed them again then started adding strips of leather and armor to the shoulders and arms. The more he added, the more weighed down she felt, but not terribly so, which confused her. It was hard to say if the weight was dispersed more by the ingenuity of the design or by magic. She possessed no real way to tell the difference. By the time Seren finished, he'd covered her from head to toe in metal. When he set the helmet on her head, it felt as she was being buried in it. The air inside got hot and close. She could barely see out through the eye slits. She felt her breathing grow faster until Seren lifted the visor and exposed her face to the outside once more.

"Are we doing okay in there?" His dark eyes studied her critically.

She gave him a quick nod, not really sure.

"Good. Now I want you to step down. Take it slow. This will take a little getting used to."

Talia wasn't sure she'd be able to budge at all. Gingerly, she made her leg move and took a hesitant step. She gave a little sigh, finding it easier than she'd expected. Gaining courage from it, she took another. She took a third and a fourth until she reached the end of the dais. She looked downward, trying to recall how Narilla got down. She couldn't remember. The distance to the ground wasn't far, but she'd not done it wearing pounds of metal before, either.

Seren was right at her side, his hand half held out as if prepared for the worst. "Just bend your knees and step out, but keep your upper half straight. There's nothing to it."

She nodded, not entirely sure how she would manage it. She felt wobbly after her knees bent and she reached out, but still made it down. Concentrating on her every step, she walked slowly to join Narilla and Tull. When she stood beside them, it felt as though she'd just run up a long flight of stairs. She could feel the perspiration gathering at her armpits and neck.

One by one, each of the other students was brought in and fitted. The Administrator stood by the curtained doorway looking happy and content. Only when Willer's panicked screams echoed in from the other room did a dark shadow momentarily cross her face. Helyn left to go help the old woman as Willer's shrieks grew even shriller.

Minutes later, a shame-faced Willer stepped into the room. He wore the same cream clothes as the rest of them. As he spotted them across the room staring at him, his face turned crimson and he quickly looked away. It was clear he'd allowed his imagined fears to run too far. If this was some kind of test, Talia was sure he'd not passed.

Lareen patted him gently on the shoulder, speaking softly to him, and personally took him over to the dais.

Once they'd all been fitted, Helyn and Lareen disappeared for several minutes before returning wearing suits of armor of their own. They approached the group of waiting students.

"Thank you, Seren, LaSeren," Lareen gave the armorer and the old woman a half bow. She then turned to face the twelve of them. "Come, the dragon dormitory awaits."

Talia clanked carefully along with the others, realizing that, up until this moment, she'd totally forgotten why they'd come to be fitted for armor in the first place. Could making them forget have been the actual intention of the strange pranks that went on before? She wanted to ponder this, perhaps even ask the others what they thought of it, but it wasn't to be. Lareen set a fast pace though they barely knew what they were doing, and it took all of her concentration just to keep putting one foot in front of the other. Soft groans cascaded down the line as they reached the stairs leading up.

Helyn instructed them on how to go about it, and she and Lareen stood attentively by, making sure none of them got into trouble. Going up was even worse than just walking. The whole process seemed to take forever. Eventually, though, they all made it to the top of the stairs.

As they all breathlessly crowded there to rest a moment, Talia sidled over to stand by Willer. "Are you okay?"

The boy glanced over at her, his face growing red. "Yeah."

"They're just trying to keep us from thinking about the worms." It was the first thing she could think of saying. She was surprised a moment later when she found out she was actually right.

Willer nodded without looking at her. "I know. It's what they told me." His features grew determined. "I won't fall for it again."

Not long after, Lareen led the bunch of them outside toward the immense building which served as the dragons' dormitory. As they approached, Talia noticed a huge bonfire raging about a stone's throw from the dormitory's open doors. Crackling in the flames were what looked to be arm sized tubes. Thick black smoke rose from the fire and its strange contents, filling the air with a fetid smell.

Not slowing, Lareen led the group to a pile of odd,

triple-pronged tools, which sat beside the dormitory entrance. There, she turned to face them, armored hands on hips. "So," she said. "Here we are." Her eyes were bright. "Today you're about to help clean out this habitat of one of the worst pests to plague dragons—the dreaded scale worms."

Talia waited for her to go on, not at all liking the fact she'd used the word dreaded.

Lareen's keen gaze swept across them. "The worms enjoy attaching themselves to the soft flesh beneath a dragon's scales. They're parasites and an annoyance. Though not normally a major problem, we seem to have at present a rather large infestation."

Talia glanced back at the burning pyre. She shuddered as she suddenly realized what it was that was burning in it.

"The older classes have already swept through, so we are only looking for stragglers. Seeing as this is not a normal part of the curriculum, however, you shall each be paid five small gems for your trouble."

Talia brow furrowed. Five gems for just looking for straggler worms? Either these people really possessed no idea about what money was, or they were being paid a small fortune for something which wasn't as easy as it sounded. She got an uneasy feeling about the whole thing.

Lareen picked up one of the long-handled, pronged tools.

Helyn grabbed several and passed them out.

"The worms have teeth and can be pretty nasty," Lareen said. "This is the reason why you have been fitted with armor. If you happen to see one, stab it with one of these." She demonstrated how they were to be used in a downward stabbing motion. "For every kill, there'll be an extra gem as a reward."

Talia held her tool tight, having to verify by sight that

she actually held it since she couldn't feel it through the gauntlets. Three evenly spaced prongs shot out from a central bar, all three with flared, pointed ends. With a shiver, she got the distinct feeling the tool had already been heavily used, for a thin coating of yellow ooze still covered the ends. She liked the idea of doing this exercise less and less. She was convinced that all the strangeness from before was meant as a distraction so they wouldn't consider getting away until it was much too late.

"Please line up in two rows of six." Lareen stepped toward the opening into the dormitory. "As you move on through, stomp and poke the ground to startle any remaining worms and flush them out. As soon as you spear one, switch places with the person behind you. Remember, at least four other groups have come through here already. There shouldn't be much if anything left for you to find."

Helyn lined them up, and as luck would have it, Talia ended up in the front. Mar stood to her left and Lana on her right. They were one arm's length away from each other, three from the second row.

"Lower your visors," Lareen commanded, her voice taking on a tone brooking no argument.

Talia reached up and brought hers down. Unlike before, in the face of meeting a foe she knew little to nothing about, she felt comforted rather than shut away inside her armor.

"All right, step inside."

Holding her tool tight in her hand, she stepped forward with the others.

The dragon dormitory was a vast, open room with incredibly large stalls set along the sides. Pillars as thick as trees fortified the roof and walls, arranged at wide intervals. The floor was made of stone, strewn heavily with hay, but looked to have seen better days. Cracks ran along its surface everywhere, the straw sticking to it with dried yellow muck, all giving evidence to a previous brutal hunt.

The stalls they passed looked to be empty, except for one at the end, which sported a riding harness over the door. Not having seen any dragons but Clarence since she'd arrived here, she could only assume it was his. Still, if only one dragon lived here, how could they have as severe an infestation as the Administrator was implying? Kel had assured her Clarence was worm free.

Gingerly, the group moved forward, stomping their armored feet hard on the ground and stabbing at the muck-covered hay, while trying to stay balanced on their feet and ignoring the weird stench wafting up from the dried yellowish goo. About halfway into the dormitory, when Lana tried to pull her tool back up from stabbing the straw, it scurried forward instead. A gray worm, almost as big as Seren's large arm, wriggled out from beneath the hay and tried to squirm away with the girl's weapon.

Lana was pulled down to her knees by the writhing creature. The worm twisted back around, showing a mouth that was all teeth.

Revulsion screaming through her, Talia didn't think, but brought her own tool forward and stabbed down. Yellow goo sprayed out as she impaled the worm, and it let out an awful screech. It abruptly stopped moving.

Her heart stomping at a gallop inside her chest, she helped Lana to her feet, and they both moved back to the second line. With great distaste, she was forced to step on the worm's body to get it off the tool. More goo oozed onto the floor. The smell coming off the fresh muck was even worse than the stench of their burning bodies. She was even more grateful for the armor as it kept her from direct contact.

Moving lumps wove through the hay. Two of the others speared a couple of worms and shuffled back. One of the girls screamed as a worm landed on her shoulder from a rafter above. Daltan and Tull swiftly knocked it off and killed it, while one of the others helped the startled student back to her feet.

A loud screech issued from the other end of the dormitory.

The lumps of movement in the hay suddenly intensified.

"There's too many. This isn't right."

Talia half turned to look behind her where Helyn and the Administrator stood. When Lareen spoke again, her voice was loud enough for all of them to hear. "All right, that's enough! We're going to back up slowly now. Keep facing forward and keep sharp!"

Three or four loud screeches followed the first. Helyn moved up to the front line and so did Lareen. They set themselves several paces in front of the students then motioned them all to start moving back. Lareen glanced momentarily over her shoulder and called out in a booming voice. "Clarence."

Talia felt the floor vibrate beneath her as the dragon entered the dormitory from behind them. The hay-filled ground writhed like a living thing.

Lareen looked back only for a moment at the rest of them.

"When I say the word, fall to the ground. Now!"

With rising fear, not at all sure how she'd get up again, Talia dropped down to the floor with a clang. A great whooshing sound rushed over them, followed by an intense wave of heat. Fire poured out like a stream of water from Clarence's mouth and fell on the hay.

Screeching, pain-filled screams clogged the air even as hot air and a sickening numbing odor choked their lungs.

"Out, everyone out!" Lareen's voice rose over the sound of the screeching and boomed at them to get moving.

Even as she struggled to her feet, Talia dared take a look at the chaos before her. The worms were everywhere, thrashing, biting, screaming in the fire, even as they were burned alive. Bile rose in her throat as some of the worms fell to attacking one another madly in their pain. Though her body was sweating profusely from the heat and exertion, her blood ran cold.

"Don't just stand there! Go, get out!" Helyn pulled on her arm, bringing her fully upright, then turned her away from the carnage. Talia ran after the others, not thinking, just doing, and didn't look back. As she passed him, Clarence once more released fire into the room. She frowned as a part of her noticed he didn't seem to be fumbling this maneuver at all.

When she made it outside, she collapsed on the ground with a number of the others. As she tried to catch her breath, she looked back toward the dormitory and spotted Lareen standing close to the entrance, watching intently at what still transpired within.

"Mistress Helyn, should we not go get water for the fire?" Sonsan was half sitting and pointed over to the small lake not so far away. Her accent was thicker than usual.

"No, it's all right," Helyn said. "The dormitory won't burn, only the hay. When it was first built, it was made immune to this type of thing."

Black smoke tinged with yellow rose from the dormitory's thin windows. Talia rose gingerly to her feet and actually made it on her third attempt. She was standing up, her visor raised to get better air when Kel came running from around the corner of the main building. Though he was unarmored, he sprinted to where the Administrator still stood watching the raging fire inside. The two spoke briefly, though both only had eyes for what was going on within.

Talia wondered what would happen now when Kel made as if to go into the building after Clarence. Lareen held him back and spoke to him some more. He stood quietly beside her and didn't try to enter again.

After another ten minutes or so, it all looked to be over. Clarence sidled out from within the dormitory. His crossed eyes roamed over all of them. *They are dead*, he said. *The danger is past.*

"Thank you, Clarence." Lareen lifted her visor and beamed at him. She then patted Kel on the shoulder, saying something Talia couldn't hear, before moving to join the rest of them. She saw Kel rapidly check Clarence over before the two of them headed off toward the lake.

"You did very well today. All of you." Lareen's gaze rested momentarily on each and every one of them. "And as I promised, here is your reward."

Seemingly out of nowhere, the Administrator brought forth several small, tied bags. "Since things didn't go exactly as I expected, you'll find a little more in there than I originally promised." She gave them a small grin. "Also, the armor you're wearing is now yours. With your new bounty, you can go see Nertak and get a stand for your armor as well as the proper cleaning materials to maintain it." She handed each of them one of the small bags.

Talia just held onto hers, not trying to see what was inside, knowing with her gauntlets on she didn't have a prayer of being able to open it.

"You may return to your classes now, with my thanks." Lareen half bowed in their direction.

Helyn got the bunch of them moving back toward the main building. As they arrived, Kel was coming out followed by a bunch of unhappy looking students carrying buckets and mops.

She didn't envy them their coming task at all. All she wanted to do at the moment was collapse and they'd not even been really involved in all of this. Once they reached their classroom, Helyn removed her helmet and gauntlets— revealing her hair, which was gathered up in a bun to keep it out of the way. "Take your seats, please. "

After looking doubtfully at her chair, Talia shoved herself inside it, despite the tight fit. She then looked around and noticed the rest of her classmates appeared as ragged and dirty as she felt.

Helyn picked up her long pointer and clicked it against the desk calling for their attention. "Though most scale worms you'll encounter won't be of the same number and size as those we saw today, you should never make the mistake of taking them lightly.

"For though dragons are their preferred source of sustenance, humans and other animals will also do in a pinch." Helyn took some chalk and drew on the board a picture of a standard worm. This one, unlike the ones they'd seen, was about as large as the size of a grown man's hand. Talia puzzled over this but was too tired to ask any questions.

"The worms are attracted to large-body heat sources and sneak beneath a dragon's scales when they're asleep. Attaching themselves to their skin, they live off their blood. They're similar to ticks."

Helyn then went on to explain exactly how the worms reproduced and propagated from host to host. Though usually Talia would have found the information interesting, if not a bit scary, she was just too drained to feel much enthusiasm today. She was delighted they'd not been told any of this before they went through the exercise, however. She doubted any of them would have dared set foot inside the dormitory otherwise.

Mercifully, once the lecture on the worms was over, Helyn released them early so they could go clean up before dinner.

After clanging upstairs to her room, leaning heavily on the well-worn banister all the way, she ran into a little trouble removing her armor, but not too much. Dried yellow goo, soot, and hay clung all over the metal surface, and she wasn't looking forward to having to clean it at all. Pushing the thought aside, she got undressed and climbed into the bathtub. As she scoured herself clean, the warmth poured into her and was welcomed by every bone in her body. She relaxed in it once she was through, but didn't notice her eyes growing heavy. Before she was aware of it, she fell asleep.

Talia awoke a while later with a jerk and sat up too fast, spilling water over the edge of the tub as she realized what'd happened. She glanced over at the clock and jumped out of the tub in panic as she took in that dinner was already half over.

Grabbing the first clothes she came across, she got dressed then pelted from the room.

She ran all the way to the first floor and only slowed once she came close to the dining hall. The loud hum of hundreds of voices raised in conversation drifted through the doors as she came near. Hoping not to be too conspicuous, she inched one of them open and sneaked inside.

Her gaze roamed left and right as she walked between

the nearest set of tables looking for her friends. Snatches of conversations thrust themselves at her as she quietly walked by. From what some of the other students were saying, they'd all gotten a go at the dormitory today. More than once, she heard exclamations of disbelief at what they'd found there.

"They weren't natural," said a high, lilting voice. "I'm telling you, she arranged it."

Talia slowed, wanting to hear more despite herself.

"She does this every time. If it's quiet for too long, boom! She comes up with some crazy thing to get everyone stirred up." Many murmurs of agreement followed the pronouncement. "It's as if she can't handle peace and quiet. Hell, why do you think the silver and bronze seats are empty? Who in their right mind would want to deal with her crazy schemes!"

She was tempted to turn and see who was speaking but didn't dare.

"Have you eaten?"

She suddenly found her path blocked by a watcher. "Ah, no, no, ma'am."

"Talia!" She spotted Mandee waving from one table over.

"I was just looking for my friends. They're over there." She quickly pointed over to the other table, thanking Mandee mentally for having spotted her.

"All right then, get on and have some supper. Time's almost up."

She nodded and hurriedly moved to join her friends.

"Where have you been?" Yllin asked reprovingly. "You almost missed dinner."

Out of nowhere, a watcher put a plate in front of Talia.

Mandee started scooping meat and vegetables onto the

plate for her. Talia felt her cheeks grow warm. "I—I fell asleep in the tub."

Mandee giggled. Yllin frowned. "That's dangerous," she said. "As if we didn't put our lives at risk enough today. You could have drowned! How embarrassing."

Mandee suddenly roared with laughter, though Yllin was obviously quite serious.

Talia decided it was time to change the subject. For once Yllin appeared as if she might give in and throttle her best friend. "Say, I—I heard someone say Lareen arranged for the worms to be in the dormitory. Could it be true?" Her question caught the interest of a number of the others sitting at their table.

Yllin was the first to answer, her expression even more grave than before. "I wouldn't be surprised. There's talk she's been behind a lot more things than people suspect."

"It makes no sense. How could she even do it?" This came from the usually subdued Daltan.

"Magic," Yllin whispered the word as if it contained all the mysteries of the universe. She now held everyone's attention. "She is the head of this school after all. She'd have access to that kind of power."

Several nodded in agreement.

Sonsan spoke up. "The guild does seem to be pretty liberal with it. I'd seen a little magic in the city, most of it fake, and all of it incredibly expensive. Yet here they treat it as if it's nothing special." More nods made the rounds around the table.

Talia ate and listened, though their animated discussions didn't really get them anywhere. Still, she found the whole question intriguing. Why would the Administrator do something like this? What did she hope to gain? Was it just to add a little spice to their lives as someone suggested? It seemed to be an awful lot of trouble merely for that.

She walked the garden route with the others once they were released from dinner, but excused herself once they reached the end. Mandee and Yllin seemed reluctant to let her go until she told them where she was going. Yllin gave her a hard look. "Just watch yourself."

Talia almost smiled. "I will."

She returned to her room just long enough to retrieve the small bag of gems Lareen gave them, as well as a letter she needed to mail to her parents, then headed back downstairs.

She made her way to the store master's cave.

The large cavern looked even more full than the last time. She was a little surprised when as she walked down the first aisle she immediately found what she came there to buy. Almost as if he expected it, Nertak had filled the lower shelves with armor stands of all shapes and sizes. Above them sat materials for cleaning and maintaining the armor as well.

"Come to make a purchase?"

Talia snapped around, not having heard anyone come up behind her. How did he do that? She felt a nervous shudder course down her spine. "Y—yes, Master Nertak, I have."

"Hmm, needing anything in particular?" His old eyes seemed to dance before her.

She swallowed hard. "Yes, I need an armor stand and cleaning materials for armor. I—I'm not exactly sure what it is I really need though. Would you have any suggestions?"

His face broke out into a wicked grin. "Yes, of course! I would be delighted to help." He actually looked like he meant it. "Now, were you looking for a decorative or more of a utilitarian stand?" He pointed to a number of them on display. Studying them more closely, she noticed they were more varied than she expected. One of them even contained inlays done in gold and jewels.

"I'd prefer something strong and durable," she decided.

"Well, then you probably want to pick one of these." Nertak indicated the set of stands farthest away from the entrance.

After looking them over, she chose one of the smaller stands available—the pieces of the apparatus were fitted rather than nailed together and were composed of a dark, almost black wood. "I'll take this one, please."

"Nice choice." Nertak nodded slowly in approval. "Now for your cleaning materials. Do you wish for the full range? Would you prefer low or high-quality materials?"

She hesitated a moment, not really sure what would be best. She looked down at her small bag of jewels then thought about the grimy state of her armor. "All of it, and the best, please?"

"Now you're my kind of customer." The old man gave her a big grin and a wink. Talia hoped she hadn't just got in over her head.

Nertak walked down the aisle and grabbed several brushes, three kinds of oil, two types of polish, assorted cloths, and four or five other things she wasn't sure about. Carrying the bundle in his arms, the old man took the lot to his counter in the back of the cave. He then disappeared behind it for a moment and came back with a large sack. "Would there be anything else you'd care to purchase today?" His eyes shone like polished brass. "I have some special options which could come in handy for your armor. For a favor, I'll let them go at a discount."

Talia felt suddenly nervous. She didn't like the old

man's expression; it had something seedy about it. "N-no, that's all right. This will do for now, thank you."

Nertak shrugged, his previous expression vanishing as if it'd never been. "Okay then. That'll be two gems, please."

She fished out the required amount, surprised it wasn't more, but not willing to say so. To be honest, she wasn't sure what to expect, since all she priced before were the diaries. Perhaps the reason they gave them gems was because things here were so expensive? Still, if the books were one a piece, wouldn't what she was buying be more?

"Ah, thank you kindly," Nertak said as she laid the gems on the counter. "And to show my appreciation for your being such a good customer, I'll throw in some instructions on proper armor care for free."

She flushed with gratitude, already troubled by how she was going to figure out how to use half the things he'd picked for her. "Thank you, thank you very much."

"No problem." The old man smiled. "Any mail today?"

"Oh!" She'd almost forgotten. She rapidly retrieved the letter for her parents from her vest. "Yes, here."

"I'll take care if it for you," he said. "Come back soon." Talia grabbed the sack, the stand, then nodded. "Thanks. Goodbye." She made her way out, struggling with her burden as she tried not to let the stand knock into things.

By the time she got her purchases up to her room, she wanted to do nothing more than collapse. Despite her weariness though, she opened the balcony doors and slowly dragged the armor, the stand, and the cleaning supplies out into the early evening air.

The instructions Nertak gave her on the care and cleaning of armor were written simply, in a step-by-step process, and looked to be very thorough. She followed each one even as the last of the sun dipped slowly out of sight in the horizon.

Hours later, she sighed as she leaned against the balcony's rail. Her arms and hands ached from all the scrubbing and rubbing—she didn't realize how many pieces Seren had fitted together on her—but she was finally done. The moon was high in the sky, almost full, with stars twinkling brightly around it in a veil. She stared at them, thinking of nothing, not yet able to gather the compunction and strength to get herself and her items back inside. After a moment, she blinked, not sure if she'd just seen a shadow cross the moon. Her gaze searched the skies and finally found the silhouette that caused it. As it passed before the light of the moon again, she realized what it was—a dragon. A moment later she knew which dragon it was. She'd seen the dizzying pattern of flight too many times to be mistaken. It was Clarence. As he flew nearer, she realized Kel was with him as well.

She studied them as they wove through the sky and pondered once more why they put themselves through this. They both tried so hard, but it was obvious they were getting nowhere. She then recalled Clarence's unexpected and smartly executed rescue earlier in the day—could it mean they were making progress after all?

Talia sat and watched them until it was almost time for the lights to go out. With a small groan, she forced herself to her feet and grudgingly brought her possessions indoors. With tired pride, she smiled a little as she gazed at her armor gleaming clean and bright. As she closed the balcony doors and prepared for bed, she only hoped she wouldn't have to clean it again any time soon.

TALIA'S EYES SNAPPED open. She was awake but didn't immediately know why. As she lay as still as possible, she heard the strange noise of a few nights before echo minutely through her room. She sat up slowly then crawled from the bed to the floor as quietly as she could manage. Frowning in the darkness, she snaked in the direction of the balcony doors. She would find out what this was about.

She made it to the doors and was about to lift the curtain to take a peek when a flurry of movement rang out outside. The light from the moon was cut off momentarily as whatever was outside her doors rose upwards. She pulled the curtain aside with a yank, but nothing was there. Damn.

This was a mystery she didn't enjoy. Yet sooner or later she'd find out what was going on. Whatever it was didn't try to come in before, but she'd rather dissuade it than wait until it decided to do so. Yllin's mention of peepers drifted in her thoughts. Could it be what this was about? Just to be on the safe side, she placed one of her buckets a hand's span from the balcony doors so if anyone opened them, she would hear it.

It took her a long time to go back to sleep.

Chapter Seven

YAWNING SLEEPILY, TALIA made her way downstairs for breakfast. Her mind was a little muddled from lack of sleep compounded by the mental and physical exertions of the day before. She became a lot more alert, however, as she made the turn in the final hallway and saw the dining hall doors were closed. More unusual was the fact two watchers were standing before the doors as if guarding them.

Puzzled, she slowed her pace as she approached. She felt both women's gazes latch on to her as they spotted her and they didn't look away. She felt her apprehension rise.

"Mornin', Miss," the younger of the two said.

Before she got a chance to return the greeting she was cut off by the other.

"The Administrator has ordered all students to wear their armor today. No one is to get in without it."

She frowned at the news, wondering why Lareen would give such a command.

"I would suggest you get yourself upstairs and put it

on." The older woman's stare was hard.

"We'd also appreciate it if you'd mention this to anyone you passed along the way?" The younger watcher gave her a small, apologetic smile.

"I'd, I'd be happy to, ma'am." Talia turned away, the frown still on her face. What was this about? Even with the rumors about her involvement with the worms, why would the Administrator order this, and before breakfast at that?

She only met two other students on her way back to her room. She informed each one of what she'd been told and while the younger of the two turned back around to get his armor, the older one stared at her as if she'd gone insane and continued on his way.

Shaking her head, she entered her room and glanced at the armor in the corner. It looked clean and maintained, and suddenly she was delighted she'd taken the time to do so last night. She wondered how many of the others decided to wait and would regret the decision before too much longer.

Putting the armor back on turned out to be a long and tedious process. How was she supposed to do this on her own? The back and front breastplates were easy enough but after those... She struggled with the rest of it and needed to get a little inventive to get it all on. Lifting the visor of her helmet, she sighed heavily when she was finally done.

Her stomach grumbled, pointedly reminding her she'd yet to give it breakfast. With any luck, she would be satisfying it soon.

Going down the stairs felt more awkward and dangerous than it was going up them the day before. She clung to the banister on her way down, keeping her eyes solely on the steps before her.

Older students passed by wearing their armor and taking the stairs with no trouble whatsoever. She gritted her teeth at the sight and kept on.

Once she came near to the dining hall, she spotted those dressed in armor being admitted through the doors. Against one side of the wall, however, were two students who were having problems getting parts of their armor on. They looked so miserable as they struggled with them she contemplated helping them—even though she wasn't sure how much aid she'd really be. Luckily, one of the older students decided to give them a hand before she got there.

"No, you can't come inside." The older watcher was glaring at a student whose armor was covered in grime and dried worm goo.

"But I have my armor on," the girl whined.

"That's true," quipped in the other. "But it's filthy, and this is breakfast. Do you think those sitting around you would enjoy their food with you smelling and looking like that?"

Now that she mentioned it, Talia did notice an undercurrent of nose-curdling odor in the air.

"But—"

"Be off with you!" The older watcher took a menacing step forward. "If you put your back to it, you should be able to get it clean in an hour or two."

The other added with a grin, "There might be food left if you hurry."

Talia saw the girl's helmeted head droop in defeat. "Yes, ma'am." She turned away and trundled back the way she'd come. Talia wondered how many others got turned away in the same way.

Once her own turn came, the two women gave her no trouble, immediately opening the door so she could go in.

Inside, all she could see was a sea of metal. She stared at the armored crowd searching for her friends, but was hard pressed to recognize anyone in their metal-encased bodies. "Talia!"

She turned to look to her right and saw an armored arm waving for her attention. Recognizing Mandee from what she could see of her face through her open visor, she gratefully headed in her direction. She wondered how the other girl was able to recognize her from so far off.

"Is this a mess or what?" Mandee was grinning from ear to ear, obviously enjoying the strange chaos.

"It's something bad, that's what it is." Yllin turned in her seat and nodded a greeting.

"Have they said what this is all about yet?" Talia sat down, trying to hide her disappointment as she noticed breakfast hadn't been served yet.

Yllin's expression turned sour. "Of course not."

"Have they done something similar to this before?" She tried to get more comfortable on the wooden chair but already knew it was going to be a lost battle.

"No, I don't think so," Mandee answered. "At least not while we've been here. Which since it's been less than a year..." She shrugged, leaving the rest unsaid.

"Just as long as it doesn't have anything to do with worms."

Talia shivered at Yllin's words. She hoped so, too. "Would you mind if I asked a stupid question?"

Mandee grinned. "Can't be any worse than some I've heard." She threw a look at Yllin. Her friend scowled.

"Money here doesn't seem to work the same as it did back at home. Yesterday, the Administrator gave each of us what would amount to a small fortune, and the prices don't seem to make sense at the store. Do you know why?"

"We asked our teacher once," Mandee told her. "I'll tell you what he told us, though it's a little strange. He said things are done this way to get us used to it. They want us to use gems or large coins and give us enough so we don't worry about it. What they're hoping for is to get us to be this way once we're out in other countries. That way ... Yllin, how did he put it?"

"We'd make people happy arbitrarily and help the country's economic something or other, too." Yllin snorted. "It's weird, but strangely makes sense. Though if the guild ever runs into money problems, no one will know how to deal with it."

"Oh." Talia would have to think on this a while.

After another fifteen minutes or more, the flow of those entering the dining hall trickled to only a few. Breakfast was then served, and even the watchers wore armor. Still, no information was forthcoming on the reason for the strange change.

Eating with her armor on proved to be awkward and cumbersome. Some of her friends appeared to wear more of their food than they were able to eat. She did notice for the newer students, the type and shape of armors were pretty much the same. But for those who'd been there longer, she saw this wasn't the case at all.

Some of the ones she spotted were bulkier, ganglier than her own. Others were made of even more pieces than hers and fit their owners almost like a second skin. Colors went from gold and bronze to a shiny metallic black. Many were engraved and sported patterns which ranged from simple to extremely complex.

One thing which seemed to prevail amongst them though was the fact they all showed at least three gems somewhere on the armor. She wondered if it was some kind of fetish having to do with the school.

A couple of students dragged themselves into the dining hall even as the outer doors were opened for their after breakfast walk. Nothing had yet been said on why they were going through all this.

At the end of the path, Talia bid goodbye to Yllin and Mandee and headed with Daltan and Sonsan to their class. As her classmates arrived, she noticed none of them looked happy. She knew exactly how they felt.

They'd been in class, waiting for about ten minutes when Helyn finally appeared. Like them, she wore her armor, but it wasn't the same one they'd seen on her the day before. The new armor fitted more closely to her figure than the first and looked to be of better quality. Three roses stood engraved in the shiny metal, one at each shoulder and a third at the waist. All three held a different colored jewel set in the middle.

"Good morning, everyone," Helyn said brightly.

"Good morning." None of them, including Talia, sounded as if they really thought so.

Their teacher stood before her desk and studied each of them then sighed softly. It was at that time that Talia realized Helyn's previous cheeriness was only for their benefit. "The Administrator has ordered everyone to stay in armor for the rest of the day."

Several groans followed this pronouncement.

"I realize this won't make for the most comfortable of days for you, but we must try to make the best of it." Helyn waited until they'd all quieted down. "Also, she has stipulated no one is to go anywhere alone, not even to relieve themselves."

"That makes no sense! What is all this about?" Sonsan was half out of her chair with indignation.

"I realize all this is awkward, but those are still the Administrator's orders and they're to be followed." Her tone softened. "Lareen wouldn't give orders, no matter how strange, unless she has a good reason. Regardless of how it looks." Her gaze scanned the room again. "So let's get started. We've already lost enough time these last two days."

The longer the class went, the more uncomfortable Talia felt. The Administrator's orders spun round and round in her head as she tried to make some sense out of them, and it made it very difficult to concentrate on the lessons. Even worse, parts of her body itched and she couldn't scratch them. The more she tried not to think about them the worse they got.

Lunch was a welcomed reprieve, despite the difficulties. Everything didn't look to be going well with her other friends, either. Yllin looked even more morose than usual and Mandee's previous excitement was definitely ebbing. No one possessed a hint about what the Administrator's orders were about.

The afternoon class session felt as if it would never end.

When they were finally released for dinner, Talia cheered up knowing the uncomfortable day would soon be over. After dinner, she planned to go to her room, take a long, well-earned bath, and luxuriate in not having to wear her armor anymore.

"Listen up, everyone." Lareen's voice boomed across the dining hall. The sound of metal rang across the room as the entire assembly turned to look in the direction of the Administrator's table. She stood atop the table, commanding all eyes to her.

Talia stared. The armor the Administrator wore wasn't the same she'd worn yesterday, either. While Helyn's conformed to her form, Lareen's looked to have been poured over her body. It moved fluidly as she walked over the table, which should have been impossible, but it did nonetheless. Lareen's armor was engraved almost from top to bottom, jewels at each shoulder as well as other places. Her helmet was as showy: twelve red plumes arranged like an open fan. "We will be having a special treat tonight," the Administrator informed them. "We're going to camp outside in our armor."

Her cheery announcement rang through the hall even as dozens of groans echoed after it.

"Hmm, I guess for those of you not quite feeling the correct excitement, this is a mandatory exercise," she added a moment later. "Once you go outside, meet up with your respective teachers. It's not as if this is something we do every day. It'll be fun." With that said, she waved to her audience and hopped off the table.

Talia didn't feel hungry anymore. They were going to sleep outside? In their armor?

"She's crazy," Yllin stated seriously. At the moment, Talia couldn't agree more. It was going to be a very long night for all of them.

Tired and worn, she followed her friends as they were herded outside. Rather than let them complete the circuit back into the building, however, they were sent out of the garden to the east side of the grounds. As they moved past, she noticed all the doors leading into the building were closed. The Administrator was really serious about this. Once more it seemed to her as if things were happening which didn't make sense or that in any way added up to what little they'd been told.

Every last student, teacher, worker, and watcher spread out across the lawn on the east side of the plateau. Even Kel and Clarence lumbered not far behind. The dragon was to be made to sleep outside as well? She watched as Clarence picked a spot close to the tilled fields and lay down. After a moment, Kel sat down beside him and leaned back against him as if the dragon were a giant cushion. As he raised his arms to set his hands behind his head, Talia blinked, noticing for the first time that jewels were hidden under there, where they wouldn't be seen when his arms were down. Why would you get gems for your armor then place them out of sight? Could they be more than just mere decoration? She shook her head slowly, not sure what to make of it.

With a lot of ado, each teacher stood at particular spots with a large pole and flag. Students drifted from one to another until they found the one they belonged to. She was lucky as Helyn set up not far from where she'd been already standing. The rest trickled in.

Night crawled in but Talia felt too uncomfortable to attempt to sleep yet. She tried sitting on the hard ground five or six different ways but her armor would still chafe or a part of her body would fall asleep. Though most of the other young students seemed as uncomfortable as she was, she noticed most of the older ones, as well as the teachers and others, did not. Irritated by this, she studied them as some sat on the ground with seeming ease and others just curled up and went to sleep. Everyone who looked comfortable seemed to have one thing in common—their armor had jewels affixed to them. Not only that, but she also noticed none of them seemed to have more' than one of the same color gem on them, yet many of them seemed to have the same as each other. It was odd. Again she got the itching feeling the jewels were more than just decoration. Suddenly, she remembered Nertak mentioning something about armor options the day before. Surely the gems couldn't have been what he meant. Could they?

Talia wished Mandee and Yllin were part of her group

so she could discuss her suspicions with them. That's when she caught sight of the Administrator sauntering down the row of teachers toward the front of the school building. Her eyes grew wide as she realized Lareen's armor was glowing softly. She also noticed the Administrator wasn't walking like someone carrying the weight of many pounds of metal. While the construction of the armor did make it easier to wear such weight, it was as if Lareen didn't have one on. Those jewels must be magic.

The Administrator walked on by at an unhurried pace waving at people here and there. As soon as she reached the edge of the crowd, she stopped and stared expectantly at the main doors to the school.

Talia jerked back, surprised, as three men abruptly appeared before the Administrator. All three wore long, dark, hooded robes with long sleeves which covered their hands.

"Zeth, look over there." An older student of the group beside Talia's banged on the helmet of one of his fellows. "Wizards."

A ripple effect coursed through the students. More and more of them turned to look in the Administrator's direction. The same question echoed from person to person—why were there wizards here?

Talia was suddenly sure they had been ordered outside and in armor for an actual purpose. If only she could figure out what it was.

Lareen spoke quietly to the three mysterious figures for several minutes, then they disappeared as miraculously as they appeared. She remained where she was a moment longer then turned around and went back the way she came as if nothing unusual had occurred.

Trying to shift into yet another not so uncomfortable

position, Talia let her questions circle around in her head until she was finally able to fall asleep.

A strange ululating sound brought her awake a few hours later. Opening her eyes, she gasped. The school, something was wrong with the school.

Not believing what she was seeing, she sat up and stared. Every door of the balconies on this side of the building were open, and a thick fog rolled from each one like a giant, multi-tiered waterfall. Strange lights twinkled within the fog with bright yellows, blues, greens, and reds. A queer, low-toned keening wailed through the air almost beyond hearing. The fog rolled onto the ground and headed outwards.

Talia stood up with a jolt as the cascading fog rolled over the students. A cold shiver crawled through her at the thought of being asleep under the thick, glowing blanket. She got a second shiver as she wondered what it was the wizards were doing which necessitated this strange phenomenon.

No longer feeling the least bit sleepy, she decided to take a walk and get away from the creepy fog. As she left, gingerly watching her footing so she wouldn't step on any of her classmates, she spotted one or two others who were awakened by the strange spectacle and seemed as spooked as she was. Everyone else remained asleep, invisible beneath the increasing fog. Her brow furrowed with worry, wondering if they really would be all right under it. But surely Lareen wouldn't have let the wizards do this if it would harm them. Right? In the dark, with this creepy fog, it was hard to be sure. She suddenly wished she'd paid more attention to where Yllin and Mandee went.

"Can't sleep?"

Talia jumped, startled by a voice on her left. She'd just

reached the edge of the fog and was looking back, still feeling uneasy.

"It does look eerie doesn't it?" Kel glanced up at her from where he still leaned against Clarence. He gave her a small smile.

Talia found she couldn't speak, her heart thumping inside her at the unexpected intrusion. When she first approached the edge of the fog, she'd thought both the squire and dragon were sleeping.

"I have a feeling it's just for effect," Kel said. "Lareen does enjoy putting on a show."

She finally found her voice again. "But—but why are the wizards here?"

Kel smiled in amusement as if at a private joke. "They're here to get rid of the worms."

"The worms?" But didn't the students and Clarence do so already?

Kel's blue eyes danced. "Yep. The little exercise in the dragon quarters went a little beyond the Administrator's expectations."

Talia asked another question before she could think better of it. "How do you know all this?" Surely it was just conjecture on his part. Yet he seemed so sure.

He grinned, the expression made strange as it was washed over by the fog's strange bright lights. "Who do you think got to carry the message to ask for help from the wizards in the first place?"

"Oh." It was stupid, but it was all she could find to say.

"One of the cooks found two worms getting into the supplies in the cellars beneath the kitchen. Others were trying to burrow into the walls," he added. "It's why everyone was asked to wear their armor. They weren't sure how far the infestation went, so it was the safest thing to do."

This confused her. "Then why didn't they just tell everyone this in the first place?"

Kel shrugged. "It's frequently hard to tell what's going on. Nothing has been what it seems ever since Lareen became Administrator. I think she prefers it that way." He smiled again. "It also means things don't get boring around here, either."

Talia couldn't help but agree. Still...

A frightened yelp cut through the night from the center of the sleeping students. She spotted an armored figure jump up out of the fog, followed by more and more of them as students awoke to find themselves covered by the eerie lights. It wasn't long before most of the assembly was on its feet staring about.

For the first time, it dawned on her that Clarence and Kel were well out of the way of things, yet at the same time close enough to the group for them not to miss anything which might go on. She glanced back at Kel, a strange suspicion rising in her mind. "You expected all this, didn't you?"

He turned away from the semi-panicked student body to look up at her. She knew she'd asked the right question, for even Clarence opened an eye to glance in her direction. "Lareen is not one to let an opportunity go by. So, sure, we expected her to do something to rile people up. She always does." His blue eyes seemed to stare at her more intently than before. "She told me once that keeping the students off balance would teach them not to lose their heads in real panic situations. After having gone through all her fabrications, she figures almost nothing would faze them out in the real world."

Talia blinked several times, trying to mentally digest what he just told her. After a few moments of thinking about it, she could see how it might make a certain amount of twisted sense. It definitely explained the strange behavior of the armorer and everyone else when her class got fitted for their armor.

I believe you might want to consider returning to your class. She glanced at the dragon in surprise. *If I hear it correctly, your classmates have noticed your absence, and several are under the impression you've been consumed by the fog.* His thoughts seemed filled with barely controlled amusement.

She didn't find the thought at all laughable. "I will, thank you." As quickly as she could, she made her way back to her group. Helyn's hands were full keeping down the panic by the time she arrived.

"Talia! You're alive!" Narilla's relieved voice caught everyone's attention. More than just their group turned to look in her direction.

She abruptly found herself surrounded from all sides. "Did it drag you off?" "How did you escape?" "Did it mesmerize you with the lights?" "Did it hurt you?" "Are you all right?" The questions rang out around her, merging into one jumbled sound until she couldn't tell one apart from the next.

"Come on, all of you, that's enough." Helyn shoved herself into the group holding a lamp aloft. "She'll never be able to answer any of your questions if you don't stop asking them all at once."

Talia felt grateful and embarrassed to be the cause of so much fuss. "I'm-I'm sorry, everyone. I just went for a walk. The fog..." She left the rest unsaid, feeling foolish she'd ever been frightened by it.

"Oh." Jarel seemed actually disappointed the fog didn't eat or ensorcell her after all.

"As I explained to all of you, the fog is nothing to be alarmed about," Helyn said. "It's most likely just a side-effect of whatever the wizards are doing inside. That or they're having some fun at our expense." Her tone told them she believed it was the second reason more than the first. "We do have classes tomorrow, so fog or no fog, it'd be best if you all tried to go back to sleep now. No more wandering off for anyone."

Protests rang out at this.

"I'm sorry, but no exceptions," she insisted. "Back to sleep."

Talia was no longer afraid of the fog, but getting down into it still made her shudder as it embraced her again. She closed her eyes, the strange lights glowing past her eyelids. The area grew quiet. Eventually, she succumbed to sleep again.

When she next awoke, the sun was just peeking up past the horizon. She sat up with a small groan, her body feeling achy and stiff. She shifted her right leg, which was asleep, then grimaced as pain flooded through as the circulation got running again. The balcony doors above them were closed, and all traces of the mysterious fog were gone.

She hadn't been up long when the Administrator sauntered by smiling. She looked as refreshed and rested as if she'd gotten a wonderful night's sleep. Surely it was an act, wasn't it? How could she possibly look so rested sleeping out here? Talia followed her with her gaze, feeling incredibly put out. She forgot all about it, however, when she spotted the three wizards waiting for Lareen where they'd met the night before. Unlike the first time she saw them, the three men's cowls were thrown back, revealing young and thoroughly exhausted faces.

She watched, fascinated, as Lareen spoke to them and gave each one a small, filled bag. Half bowing in her direction, the three young men promptly disappeared.

Lareen stood there a moment longer then turned around with a smile to face the field of sleeping students. "All right, everyone, it's time to get up!" Her voice boomed across the area like thunder.

Yelps and groans followed her command, as everyone was startled out of their sleep. Lareen briskly walked down the front and singled out some of the older classes. "You will go inside, please. Cleaning duty."

Heavy groans echoed through the yard.

Talia wondered what would happen next. She didn't have long to wait. Members of the kitchen staff, aided by watchers, came down the line and dropped off small cauldrons at each teacher's station along with a stack of bowls and long wooden spoons.

Everyone served themselves. The porridge was nice and thick and smelled faintly of cinnamon. Talia could see small pieces of apple floating in it as well. She took her time, savoring it, trying her best not to spill it on her armor.

About the time most of them were through with breakfast, the Administrator's voice boomed once again across the field. "This now concludes our exercise. Thank you for your participation and patience. You may return to your rooms to clean up, but you will be expected to return to your regular schedule in an hour." She waved cheerily at them all. "That is all!"

Talia sighed with relief and heard her sentiments echoed by many of others. Whatever the wizards accomplished must have done the trick. Life could return to normal.

"You heard her," whispered Helyn. "Now run before she has a chance to change her mind."

Tired as she was, Talia didn't have to be told twice. Even though she knew the threat was over, from what she learned of late, the Administrator might just take it into her head to make them wear the cumbersome things another day. She had absolutely no desire to do that. From the way a number of the other students were shuffling off for the open doors, she could tell they felt the same way as well.

Once she got upstairs, Talia shed her armor and immediately got into her bathtub. The warmth of the water seeped into her body, relaxing her battered muscles. She wished she could wallow in it forever. With regret though, she forced herself to get out as it started to make her relax too much and her eyes grew heavy. Falling asleep was the worst thing she could do—no matter how tempting it seemed. She got dressed, but not before she gave some of her still aching muscles a thick application of the healing salve she'd gotten from Mandee and Yllin. She then speedily cleaned the worst of the grass and dirt stains off her armor, planning to give it a more thorough cleaning later. As she worked on it, she remembered her conclusions about the jewels many of the others used to decorate their armor. She decided she would have to pay a visit to Nertak as soon as she got the chance.

She wanted to learn more about his options.

Talia was the first to make it to class. Slowly the rest of them dragged themselves in. Helyn then started in on their lessons as if nothing had disturbed their usual routine.

At lunch, the dining hall was filled with the roar of loud conversation, friends getting together to discuss the strange events of the night before.

Word came down from the older students that clean-up duty entailed the carting off of hundreds of large worm bodies. Speculation, gossip, and innuendoes flowed with incredible speed across the room. The theories ranged from mutant worm mating to the beginnings of the end of the world. She listened to it all, mostly amused, yet at times astounded people could come up with such things. But, though she now knew all Kel mentioned to her was accurate, she found herself not sharing it with the others.

As she ate, she tried to figure out why she didn't share her information, why she felt she shouldn't. All Talia could come up with was that she'd reduce the effect of Lareen's strange lessons if she did. Besides, she wasn't so sure anyone would believe her.

Once everyone got up to go through the garden, things quieted a little, so she decided to take the time to speak to Yllin and Mandee about the one conclusion she did want to share.

"You really think they're magical?" Mandee asked her after she'd told them of her deductions.

"I do," Talia answered. "If we go talk to Nertak we can find out for sure and maybe get some of our own."

Yllin grimaced, as Talia figured she would loathe as she was to deal with the old man.

"Just think of the possible benefits. It'll make it worthwhile," she pressed.

"All right. I guess if we all go together..." Yllin said grudgingly. "Let's get it over with after dinner." The other two agreed.

At the evening meal, gossip still ran rampant, the stories even more outlandish than at lunch. As she did only at dinner, Lareen appeared at the head table for supper. She wore her usual eccentric, revealing clothes, which looked to be her trademark, and laughed and joked with the teachers as usual, totally oblivious to the raging buzz around her.

Once the dinner routine was over, Talia, Yllin, Mandee

and a couple of others who'd overheard their conversation in the garden drifted together to go to Nertak's place.

The old man was sitting back in a rickety chair at the cave's entrance, busily whittling away at a piece of wood. When he spotted them coming up the walkway, his face broke out into a broad grin. "Ah, customers!" He stood up to greet them.

Talia saw Yllin frown from the corner of her eye.

"What can I do for you young ones today?" Nertak asked eagerly.

When none of them spoke up, Talia forced herself to take a step forward since it was her idea. "We're interested in seeing the armor options you mentioned before."

The old man's eyes shone. "Oh? Is that so? You didn't enjoy your night out in heavy armor last night I take it?"

"Not especially," Yllin said gruffly. "Not that it's any business of yours."

"Yllin!" Mandee stared at her friend, looking shocked.

Nertak seemed to take no offense whatsoever at her tone or words. "Come on inside then. I'll show you what I have." He led the group through the cave to the counter at the back. "Wait here just one moment." He disappeared behind the area beyond the counter. Not for the first time, Talia wondered just how massive the place was.

"Yllin, look, I know he's a pervert, but could you just behave yourself, please?" Mandee hurriedly whispered this to her friend while the old man was out of sight. "He's likely to raise the prices if you keep being mean to him."

The dark girl frowned unhappily but finally nodded.

"Do you think he'd really do it?" This came from Daltan, who was one of the other two of their group who'd decided to tag along.

Yllin turned a hard eye on him. "Yes."

None dared ask how it was she knew.

"Here we are." Nertak returned, carrying with him a covered case. He set the case down on the counter then took off the black velvet covering hiding the contents from view.

"Talia, you were right." This came from Lana, their second tagalong.

Before them, nestled in a bed of velvet, were ten rows of different colored gems. All were round, ranging in color from clear to black, and were cut flat at both the top and bottom.

"So, which of these would you prefer?" Nertak asked. Before any of them could reply, he went on. "Though perhaps you really don't want them." He put the cover back over the case. "Some factions of the guild don't believe in the use of magical comforts for their warriors. They deem such things make them too soft."

Yllin grabbed the cover and pulled it off roughly. "Why don't you just tell us what they do? If they do anything other than just look pretty, that is."

Talia flinched at the other girl's impatient tone. Mandee sighed deeply beside her. "Yllin..."

The girl grimaced at the reminder and put the black cover back on the counter. "Please..." She said the last through gritted teeth.

"Of course." Nertak smiled at her as if she'd spoken to him as sweetly as honey. "I'll warn you though since they're magical, they are a little expensive. How about I just show you the more popular ones?"

"That'd be great," Talia said quickly, hoping to forestall Yllin in case she took offense at the suggestion. With any luck, her friend wouldn't get into an even fouler mood than the one she was in already. Talia hadn't realized how badly her friend didn't like this man. What had he done?

"Well then, let's see..." Nertak stared down at the rows of gems, deep in thought. "One of our most popular is this one." He pointed to a light blue gem. "It allows one to fly." The five of them glanced at one another, not sure whether or not they should believe him. "It does take a lot of practice, but can be a great consolation if one does poorly in the lottery." He grinned.

Next, he pointed at a row of light amethyst-colored stones. "These are indispensable if riding on our famed Clarence. It makes one immune to being crushed."

Talia's eyes grew wide, remembering Kel's miraculous lack of injuries at some of Clarence's worst landings. No wonder he'd been all right; he'd taken precautions.

"These diamonds over here have been specially magicked to make armor comfortable. It keeps the wearer cool and dry, as well as making them feel as if they aren't wearing any armor at all." The old man smiled. "Indispensable for those long nights spent outside. They've been selling very well today for some reason." His smile turned into a mischievous grin. "These shiny white ones over here, the opals, are also popular. Though I can't really explain in detail how they work, they're supposed to make it easier to use the facilities while in armor, if you get my meaning." Nertak winked.

He showed them a gem for helping the wearer move silently and another which gave the wearer greater strength. One gave the wearer the ability to blend with his surroundings, while another one let him run faster. Talia felt a little dizzy as she listened to the possibilities. Was there nothing these gems couldn't help them with?

"Okay, how much are they then?" Yllin cut Nertak off,

her eyes narrowed as she stared at the jewels, an unhappy look on her face as if she'd just eaten something sour.

"Well, I did warn you they'd be expensive." The old man's voice grew low. "They're five a piece." All of them grimaced.

"However," Nertak added, "I could give you a discount... If you would agree to model something for me. Then they'd only be three gems a piece."

"Why you!"

Mandee stepped forward and covered Yllin's mouth before her friend could say any more. She staunchly dragged her back toward one of the aisles, signaling with her head for the others to come, too.

When Mandee finally let go of Yllin and freed her mouth, her friend cursed at her with several expletives. Lana's face turned red at some of the more colorful terms Yllin used.

Mandee only raised a brow under the barrage, looking unusually grave. "And you say I don't know how to behave."

Yllin stopped cursing, and suddenly looked embarrassed as she glanced at the rest of them and their open mouths. "It's just that it's so easy to see what the pervert is after. He's taking advantage of his position. He's such a letch!"

"But it is a good discount," Mandee countered. "Plus there's five of us. It's not as if he can try to pull anything."

"You're not actually serious, are you?" Yllin stared at her friend as if she'd just grown wings.

"She's right, though." Talia felt nervous about where they were going with this, but it made sense no matter how embarrassing it might be—anything to avoid a night the same as the last one.

"But, but he's—" Yllin stuttered, her face turning a

deep red.

"I'll do it. It's a good discount." Lana's voice was barely audible.

Daltan stood in the back, his cheeks crimson and his gaze on the floor.

"So, do we do this or not?" Mandee asked. "It might just be fun, you know." Her eyes sparkled.

"Mandee!" Yllin stared at her as though not believing her ears.

"I'm in, too." Talia still didn't feel better about the whole thing, but if they all went into it together...

"I'm in." Daltan still wouldn't look at any of them.

"So, Yllin, what do you say?" Mandee grinned at her. "It is a big discount."

The somber girl studied each of them, swallowed hard then finally nodded.

As a group, they returned to the counter where Nertak patiently waited for them.

"We'll do it," Mandee stated for them.

At her proclamation, Nertak grinned and pulled four wrapped packages out from behind the counter. He gave one to each of the four girls. "There's a place over there where you can put these on." He pointed off to a small curtained area to the right. He glanced over at Daltan. "This offer though doesn't extend to you. While we wait for them, you and I can discuss how you can earn your discount." Something about the old man's grin turned nasty.

As the rest of them headed off to the curtained area, Talia was suddenly loath to leave Daltan alone. She went on after a moment, wondering fervently about what the old man held in mind for the shy, dark-haired boy.

Once behind the curtains, the girls all opened their packages. Yllin snorted in disgust at what they found.

Each of them held a long, silken shift in a bright color. Talia's was deep red.

She held up the garment by the thin shoulder straps and gawked at it in disbelief. This looked like something Lareen would wear!

"I'm not doing it." Yllin threw her shift down in disgust. "I'm not changing for him."

Mandee held her own forest green shift up against her body. "They are a little brazen." Her tone didn't indicate she actually thought this to be a bad thing.

Lana stared at her, her face crimson. "Are we really going to wear these?"

Talia frowned, not too enthused herself though the shift really was pretty. The material felt cool and slick, much better than the usual cotton nightgown she slept in. Her eyes lit up as she got an idea. "You know, he didn't say how we were to model these."

Yllin's gaze locked with her own as if sensing where her idea might be going. "What do you mean?"

"Well, since he never did stipulate how these were to be worn," Talia continued, "nothing could be said against us if we just slipped these over our clothes." She shyly looked at the rest of them to see what they made of this.

Yllin actually smiled. "You're brilliant." Mandee chuckled.

"But won't it make him angry?" Lana tugged nervously at one of her golden curls.

"If it does, it would serve him right," Yllin countered. "It's not as if we won't be doing as he asked. Besides, the worst that could happen is we don't get the discount. He's already stated his price." Her smile turned nasty. "If he changes it, we can go to the Administrator or one of the watchers. I bet it'd get him in a little trouble."

Mandee grinned from ear to ear. "The old goat won't

be expecting this."

Nodding their agreement, all four girls donned the shifts over their clothes. Mandee wasn't kidding when she'd called them brazen. Talia's cheeks colored just thinking about putting it on without clothes. Her mother would have tanned her hide if she'd ever heard of it. As one, the four of them left the curtained area and walked back to the counter.

"Oh, my! Don't you all look lovely," Nertak crooned. He looked them up and down, obviously tickled by their current state of dress. Even though she was fully clothed, Talia felt herself blushing at his hungry stare.

Daltan was standing with his back to them, but at Nertak's words, he took a quick peek over his shoulder. Talia noticed his cheeks were flushed and he seemed upset. When he saw what they'd done, though, he gawked at them in surprise, seemingly forgetting whatever it was which went on between him and the old man.

"So, ladies, gentleman, which of these beauties will you be purchasing then?" Nertak seemed in no way put off by the trick the girls pulled on him. Yllin looked disappointed by his lack of reaction. It surprised Talia a little as well.

All five of them asked for the diamonds. Talia also picked up an amethyst and an opal, anything to make her life less miserable in armor. She honestly wasn't sure how anyone would want to do without them if they got a choice. A few others tempted her as well, but not knowing when or how she'd get more money or what other expenses she might incur, she decided to keep the last of her gems untouched.

When Daltan paid for his purchase, she couldn't help but notice that, unlike the rest of them, he paid full price. Just what had the old man asked of him?

"You'll notice there's a small paper on this side of the gems," Nertak said. "When you've decided where you want to put them on your armor, just peel it away and press the gem onto the surface.

"There's a way to get them off if you make a mistake, but that's extra." He grinned. He then pulled out some small rolled up scrolls tied with strings matching the colors of the gems they'd purchased. "These will tell you a little more about what you've bought and how to use them properly."

Talia thanked him then pulled the borrowed shift over her head and tried to return it to him.

"No, no, keep them," he said. "They're yours. On the house." He winked.

"What's the catch?" Yllin asked, suspicious of the strange generosity.

The old man gave her a shocked look. "You wound me, miss. There's no catch." His eyes lit up. "Though if you want me to put one on it..." He stared her up and down in that undressing way of his.

Yllin humphed and turned away, not deigning to give him a response. Barely able to control a sudden fit of laughter, Mandee hurried after her.

As soon as they'd left the cave, Talia's curiosity got the best of her. She dropped back until she was walking beside Daltan and asked, "I noticed you didn't get the discount. What happened?"

The dark-haired boy glanced over at her then looked away, his cheeks red. "It just didn't work out. That's all." He started walking faster, pulling away.

She didn't try to keep up, seeing her question troubled him. Just what did the old man ask him to do?

In the evening, she cleaned and polished her armor until it shined. Handling her new purchases carefully, she peeled the paper off the back of the gems and placed them in a triangle just below the breastplate's collar. She wouldn't be caught unprepared next time. She laughed as she found herself aching for an excuse to try them out.

As she set her armor back on its stand, she glanced out the balcony into the night's sky, where she could barely see Clarence and Kel practicing. As they looped lopsidedly then went into a dead dive, she shuddered realizing Kel probably tested his gems more times than she would ever want to.

Eyes drooping, she bathed then crawled into bed where she was swiftly dragged down into a deep sleep.

Chapter Eight

TALIA JUMPED AS a harsh pounding echoed off her door. Heart hammering, she glanced at her clock and realized she'd actually slept until the watchers started their rounds. Feeling entirely too awake, she sighed and made herself get out of bed. She did feel more rested than yesterday, but she wouldn't have minded if the watchers let them sleep the day away.

The buzzing conversation in the dining hall was still hashing over the events from two days before, but by evening everything pretty much returned to normal. Conversations turned back to more mundane matters, to lessons, rumors on teachers and students, as well as upcoming tests.

That evening, she opened her balcony doors wide, and occasionally took a break from her homework to watch Clarence and Kel practice. As they twisted and turned, often with little control, she wondered yet again why they did this. Lareen, she knew, used the pair as couriers and errand boys. She'd heard others say Kel was also continuing with his studies though he'd finished the standard course load sometime back. As if it weren't enough to occupy his time, every evening he and Clarence practiced. Practiced toward a goal which seemed impossible. Talia shook her head, not understanding it at all.

The dragon and squire were still practicing when she finally turned in for the night.

ᚱᛇᚱᛇᚱᛇ

KEEPING PERFECTLY STILL, she heard the odd sound once more, the one which had awakened her a number of times before. With everything going on lately, she'd almost forgotten about it. Since it was back, her curiosity burned more than ever to find out what it was once and for all.

As quietly as possible, she rose from her bed and inched slowly forward along the wall to approach the balcony doors from the side. As she sneaked along, she felt more excitement than fear, sure whatever was out there meant her no harm, for if it did, it had plenty of opportunities before now to try and hurt her.

The strange sound whispered clearly across the room every few minutes or so. She tried to figure out what it might be even as she carefully made her way to the doors.

After what seemed akin to forever, she finally reached the balcony entrance. Moving even slower than before, she turned and gingerly shifted the heavy curtain just enough to take a peek outside. There wasn't much light to see by, but she could barely make out a large figure just beyond her balcony's edge. It fluttered quietly, blocking most of the space beyond it. Then it suddenly tipped to the side. The strange sound she'd heard before reached her ears as the figure tried hurriedly to right itself.

It wasn't long before it overcompensated and listed to the opposite side.

Talia frowned. Was it a dragon? If it were, what in the world was it doing outside her window?

A muted sound rang from above and unexpectedly the dark figure was gone. Swiftly moving the curtain aside, she studied the sky, hoping for a better look. She eventually spotted a swaying figure dip back into her field of vision. Shaking her head, she recognized the silhouette, having studied it just that evening. It was Clarence and Kel. But why?

All of Yllin's warnings about lechers and peepers whispered rapidly and loudly through her mind. She shook her head again, this time trying to dispel her words. Yet now that the idea was there, it wouldn't go away. But it didn't make sense. Why would they be outside her room? Kel could have easily gotten off the dragon onto the balcony, if peeping was his intention, but didn't do so. The curtains were so thick he wouldn't have been able to see anything anyway. So what else could he and Clarence be trying to do? Could this somehow be some kind of exercise?

It was a long time before Talia was able to go back to sleep.

⚶⚶⚶

THE STRANGE VISITATION still weighing heavily on her mind, Talia made her way down to the dining hall early as usual. She walked to her regular table and spotted Kel coming out of the kitchen with his breakfast.

She took her seat, suddenly uncomfortable. She watched him as he ate, trying not to be obvious about it.

Kel finished his meal and returned to the kitchen. As was his want, he came out carrying a handful of fruits for Clarence. She felt her face go red as he waved at her on his way out. She made herself wave back even as a kernel of anger ignited inside her. How dare he act as if he'd done nothing? How dare he treat her in the same aloof, friendly manner he always did before?

She stewed, not sure what she wanted to do about it. In truth, she wasn't one hundred percent sure it'd been Kel and Clarence at her balcony. But if it wasn't them, then who? No other dragons were staying at the school that she was aware of. Still...

Though she considered it, Talia decided not to mention her strange discovery to the others. She held the sneaking suspicion Mandee would find the whole thing way too exciting and Yllin would only fill her head with more lecherous horror stories until it wouldn't feel safe to sleep at night.

As she ate her breakfast, brooding, she knew she must do something. On this she grew more and more determined by the moment. Just what to do though was proving hard to decide on. She'd come no closer to a decision as she bid her friends goodbye to make her way to class.

"Talia, could I talk to you for a minute?"

She turned to find Daltan at her elbow. His dark eyes wouldn't meet her own. "Sure, what do you want to talk about?"

The boy shyly pulled on her sleeve to get them closer to the wall and out of the way of traffic. He stared at the tiled floor. His expression seemed troubled, which drew her out of her previous distraction. "Is something wrong?" she asked him.

He still wouldn't look at her. "I—" He sighed and after

a moment tried to speak again. "My room... it's on the third floor."

She nodded at this, it being something she already knew.

"Well," he continued, "it's right over yours actually."

Talia nodded again, finding the fact interesting and one she'd not put together herself. But what was he trying to get at?

"I occasionally have trouble sleeping." Daltan glanced up at her for a moment before looking away again.

She felt herself go cold. Did Daltan see something? Could he clear up her doubts once and for all? She got the sudden urge to grab him and force him to blurt out what he wanted to tell her but held herself back.

"I wasn't sure the first couple of times," Daltan said quietly. "You see, since it was beneath me and all, and, then I wasn't sure how to tell you..."

She thought she might scream. Say it already! "What did you see?" She sounded calmer than she felt.

Daltan swallowed hard. His words rushed out all at once. "The squire, the squire and his dragon—they've been hovering by your window every night."

So it really was them. She felt her earlier anger return. "You're sure that's who it was?"

He met her gaze, his expression somber, and nodded.

"Thank you for telling me." Her mind rushed to figure out what she should do now that her suspicions were confirmed.

"Should we tell Helyn?" Daltan asked sheepishly. "Maybe she could tell the Administrator and find out why he's doing it and make him stop."

Looking at him, she finally got the stirrings of an idea. "No, it's all right. I think I'll deal with this on my own." She smiled. "I really appreciate you telling me this though.

Honest."

Daltan glanced away, his cheeks coloring.

"Just don't tell anyone else about this. Please?"

He nodded.

She smiled at him again, already forming plans for the evening, as they headed off to class.

༄ ༄ ༄

BY THE TIME dinner was over, the details of Talia's plot were worked out. Peepers or not, when she was through, the dragon and squire would think twice about hanging around her balcony in the middle of the night and disturbing her sleep.

The hours ticked by slowly as she sat awake, fully clothed in bed, and waited for the faint and familiar sound which would announce the arrival of her quarry. Before she closed the balcony doors, she'd made sure the two of them were out practicing as usual. She grinned to herself in the dark, knowing the two of them wouldn't know what hit them.

Too excited to feel sleepy despite the late hour but feeling bored and restless, she thought they might not come after all, when she noticed what little light seeped through the curtains darken even further. After a moment or two more, she heard the sound announcing beyond a shadow of a doubt those she was waiting for had arrived. Sneaking out of bed, she grabbed the half-filled bucket she prepared hours ago. Making not a sound, she tiptoed with it hugging the walls until she reached the balcony doors.

Grabbing the bucket carefully by the bottom and the

handle, she gathered her resolve and stoked her anger. Counting to ten, she kicked the doors outwards, instantly rushing after them out onto the balcony.

"Peepers!" Talia swung the bucket with all her might and sent the cooled water from the tub sailing through the air. The dark mass before her reacted and a barely visible dragon's head snapped up. She heard a loud whack as Clarence's head smacked into the overhang of the balcony above. Dragon and rider dropped like a stone, followed by the water.

"Oh, no!" She rushed up to the end of the balcony and peered down, her previous anger and righteousness snuffed by a wave of worry. She hadn't mean to hurt them. All she'd wanted was to humiliate them a bit and make them stop.

What had she done?

Her desperate gaze searched the dark ground below, but she could see nothing. She was just about to rush out of the room and go down to look for them when a lilting laugh floated down to her from above. Startled, she looked up and saw Lareen drifting down through the air, wearing what looked to be sheer blue and green scarves sewn together into a dress.

"My, but that was delightful," Lareen said as she came level with her balcony. "Who would have thought he had it in him?"

Talia thought the whole episode anything but delightful but was having a hard time finding the words to say so between her astonishment at Lareen's entrance and her fear she might have inadvertently harmed Clarence and Kel.

Lareen looked down toward the ground as if reading her thoughts. "Don't worry, they're all right," she said. "Clarence may end up with a nice headache, and both will have a wounded pride, but that's as it should be." She looked over at her and winked. "Though I have to say, it's nice to see Kel showing interest in someone—even if his methods leave much to be desired." She gave Talia a dazzling smile. "I do tend to worry about him now and then."

Talia nodded, still unable to say anything, not sure what she would say if she could. Kel was interested in *her?* They didn't even know each other. Not that he seemed like a bad sort, at least not until she realized he'd been hanging out at her balcony every night. He did have a sweet smile. Yet, why would any of it be of interest to the Administrator? She felt her cheeks grow warm.

"I trust you will be discreet about this?" Lareen asked her quietly. "I doubt he will ever do such a thing again."

Talia wasn't so sure, but she nodded anyway. The whole situation and its unexpected results were too embarrassing for her to want to share with anyone. Already enough rumors existed about Clarence and Kel that she didn't want to add to them, especially since she would then become a part of them.

"Don't think too harshly of them. I've been watching them, and I'm sure they didn't mean any harm. If I needed to guess, I would say Kel was using you as a focus to concentrate on, to see if it would help him and Clarence fly in place. Not that they've been very successful." Lareen's voice still rang with laughter. "Good night, Talia."

The Administrator drifted slowly up and out of sight. Talia could only stare after her.

Almost in a daze, she retrieved her bucket and stepped back inside her room. The Administrator knew her name. With all the hundreds of students here, she'd remembered her name. She'd also known what Clarence and Kel had been doing. She shivered, realizing after this, Lareen wasn't likely to ever forget her name. She wasn't sure it was a good thing at all.

Worse, if she had known the two of them were doing this, why didn't she stop them? Surely she didn't believe Kel thinking about her would actually help their current problems, did she?

What did it all mean?

Not bothering to change, she crawled into bed. Sleep took a while in coming.

THE NEXT MORNING, Talia was up early, though she felt tired and drained. She hurried downstairs and spotted Kel at his customary place. She watched him as she approached her table, worried, angry, embarrassed, all at the same time. At least the worry eased a bit as he seemed to be alright.

She sat down on the opposite side of the table she normally did, with her back to him. She didn't look his way again.

When he joined her later, Daltan said nothing about the ruckus from the night before. She hoped it meant he knew nothing of it, but doubted it. He perpetually kept to himself, so surely her secret would be safe with him?

Talia found herself listening to the gossip around her more sharply than usual. As far as she could tell, no one seemed aware anything strange happened the night before. She was only too glad of it, though she understood it was still too early to tell. Yet news of this sort would have spread like wildfire. By lunchtime, she'd know if she were in the clear for sure.

When the group separated in the evening, she still hadn't heard anything. Only then did she feel she might be able to put this behind her. Just in case, though, she partially filled her bucket again in the event a certain pair came calling on her once more.

Setting the bucket close to the balcony doors, she was about to undress when she was startled by a soft knock at the door. Frowning, wondering who'd come to see her this close to curfew, she went to the door. When she opened it, no one was there.

Her frown deepened as she glanced down both sides of the hallway and spotted no one. At her feet, however, were a small red box and a glass vase with a strange set of flowers. Looking both ways down the hall again and still seeing no one, she picked them up took them inside.

Gingerly, she set the vase on top of her dresser and just stared at the flowers. The back of the arrangement was a wall of ferns ranging from a deep green color to almost white. The flowers set before them were the most dazzling orange she'd ever seen. Each flower possessed six pointed petals with a black stripe running down the middle of them. The aroma was sweet, reminding her of tangerines. She was sure her mother would have loved them. She wondered if they would grow in the soil back home.

The small red box was bound with a pink ribbon, which she carefully untied. Inside, she found chocolates and candies nestled in delicate paper. A small envelope sat over them, her name written on it. Nervous, though not entirely sure why, she opened the envelope and took out the card inside.

The card held but one word on it, in the same neat handwriting as the envelope. The word was "Sorry."

Talia stared at the card in her hand, the one word telling her from whom the gifts came. Maybe Lareen was right after all. The gesture was definitely sweet, and at least he was trying to apologize; though this in no way made up for everything. Still, with a small smile tugging at her lips, she reached for one of the dark chocolates. She bit into it, the flavors of cocoa and sweet fruit tickling her tongue. It was definitely a good start though.

So the next day when she went down to breakfast, she didn't sit with her back to Kel as the day before, but neither did she wave a greeting to him.

That evening, she slipped into her bath feeling more relaxed than in the last few days. No rumors about Kel and Clarence's activities at her balcony were circulating at all. She was still pondering why the two of them had bothered trying to hover at her window. It's not as if either of them could see anything with her curtains drawn. Plus the way Clarence invariably swayed from side to side trying to keep his balance would have prevented them from seeing anything clearly even if the curtains were pulled back. So, the question remained—what were they really trying to do? Was trying to hover in place all there was to it? Surely the Administrator's supposition insinuating Kel was interested in her was wrong. She couldn't hold back a sigh. In the end, she might never know. She wasn't going to ask, and she doubted Kel would tell her. Besides, the whole thing was just too embarrassing.

Talia shifted her legs along the bottom of the tub, creating gentle waves in the water. She was still bouncing ideas along in her head when one of her toes touched something sharp. Startled, she sat up and looked into the water but could see nothing. She reached out with her feet until she felt the gentle sting again. It moved when she touched it. Sitting up, she hunted for it not with her eyes but with her hands.

After a couple of minutes, she found the prickly object and fished it out. She looked at her find. It was a light, almost transparent blue. The gem was cut in a multifaceted diamond shape. It looked expensive. But what was it doing in her tub?

Scowling, she looked critically around her room.

Everything seemed all right, but hadn't she left the bucket by her bed this morning? Someone had been in her room. To plant this? Confusion and annoyance swirled inside her. With the jewel in her hand, she got out of the tub. Dripping, she grabbed a towel and walked to her dresser and set the gem there beside her beautiful bouquet of flowers. Her gaze lifted to the bright orange blooms, and her scowl deepened.

Surely it couldn't have been Kel. He'd already apologized. Didn't he think his original gifts enough? Plus, why would he break into her room and put it in her tub of all places? What was wrong with him?

She finished drying off and put on her nightgown still staring at the gem. Enough was enough. This would have to stop. Maybe Kel was mad. Clarence must have crushed him one too many times, just like Yllin said. She couldn't let it continue.

Sighing, she crawled into bed and thought about what she'd have to do in the morning.

Chapter Nine

TALIA RUSHED TO get dressed, wanting to make her way downstairs and get things over with. She wasn't looking forward to this, so the sooner it was done with the better.

People just didn't do things like this at home.

She grabbed the light blue gem and stuffed it in her pocket on the way out.

The dining hall was deserted when she stepped inside. As she stood there, Kel came out of the kitchen with a loaded tray and headed for the Administrator's table. She felt her stomach tighten as she spotted him, but made herself start walking in his direction. Her mind was set—she would go through with this.

Going the long way around, she passed the kitchen doors and found her nostrils teased with the scents of freshly baked bread and sizzling bacon. Walking on, she reached into her pocket and held on tightly to the gem as she came up beside Kel. Though she hadn't noticed it before, this morning he'd brought a book with him, and he looked to be reading it as he ate. She took a long, deep breath. "Excuse me."

Kel looked up, a surprised expression on his face. "Talia?" He almost fell in his hurry to stand.

She would have thought his bumbling humorous if she didn't feel so nervous. She knew she must do this, but it was just so hard to believe anything bad about him when she was so near. But, if he wasn't crazy, then... It didn't matter. "Look, I—I appreciated the apology even though I really don't understand what that was all about," she said. "The flowers and candy were sweet, but now you've gone too far." She tried to rush the words out and stared at Kel's shoulder instead of his face. "Leaving things outside my door is one thing, but breaking into my room to leave gifts, no matter how extravagant, is just too much. I have to insist you stop."

"What?"

Talia's gaze moved of its own volition to Kel's face at his tone of utter confusion. She felt a bolt of uncertainty course through her at the perplexed look on his face but didn't let it diminish her resolve. Calculatedly, she reached for his hand and dropped the large gem into it.

Kel's eyes grew wide as they spotted the jewel. Talia held her breath as she then saw them abruptly go dark. Was this a mistake?

Kel's hand curled over the gem until his knuckles turned white. Tight lines filled his face, making him look cold and empty, even as his eyes suddenly blazed. "Damn him!"

Talia gasped at the abrupt change, not having expected this kind of reaction. Without realizing it, she took a step back. "Kel?"

As if he hadn't hear her, he jerked away from her and stomped off toward the exit, leaving his book and unfinished breakfast behind.

Talia stood there and stared after him, having no idea what had just happened. He looked so angry, but the anger wasn't aimed at her. Why would a gem cause such a reaction? Why would it throw Kel into a murderous rage?

She shivered at the thought. A murderous rage—it was exactly what it looked like, and she brought it about. Now he'd stormed off to vent it, to do something horrible to someone.

Not thinking, only acting, she ran to follow him.

Once out in the garden, she hurried down the path leading to the closest exit. She reached the edge of the garden just in time to see the dragons' dormitory doors burst wide open.

Nostrils flaring, Clarence leaped out with Kel on his back.

Though she was too far to hear, she could see Kel was yelling at the dragon and pointing in her general direction. Clarence glanced back at his rider, Talia presumed so he could argue, but then abruptly took off to the air. He didn't go far before he turned in the direction Kel wanted and streamed down.

She watched, her heart racing, as the two of them flew past in a perfectly straight line and landed just before the entrance to Nertak's cave. Clarence reared back on his hind legs, taking a deep breath then let go. Whoosh—a gush of liquid flame ejected from his mouth into the opening.

"No!" She screamed, horrified as Clarence breathed into the opening again and again. She knew from the things Mandee and Yllin previously told her the old letch not only ran the store but used the cave as his home as well. They would kill him. "No..." Her knees turned to water and she dropped to the ground. All this over an expensive gem?

A bright flash caught her attention as it flared several lengths to Clarence's left. Singed and smoking in places, Nertak appeared, wearing only a long smock and nightcap.

He fell to the ground coughing.

Kel spotted him. The hatred on his face burned hotter than the fire in the cave. "You *bastard*."

The old man stood up uneasily, staring in confusion at the squire's vehemence. "Kel? What in Vargen's name...?"

Nertak disappeared as a burst of flame hit where he'd been standing. The heat of it washed all the way to where Talia sat. The old man reappeared fifteen to twenty lengths away. He took one look at Kel's fuming rage and ran.

"Go after him!" Kel yelled this at Clarence, pointing after the spindly old man. The dragon shook where he stood but didn't move. "I told you what he did," he argued, his voice filled with impatience. "He has to pay for it. Now go." He slapped Clarence on the side. It was as if a set of invisible chains were torn away by it—the dragon charged with incredible speed after the old man.

Her chest tight, Talia stumbled to her feet and ran after them. This was all her fault. She had to stop them before they killed Nertak.

Clarence shot more fire after the old man, but as before, Nertak disappeared before it could hit him, reappearing farther ahead. Small fires dotted the yard, making thin tendrils of acrid black smoke, and had already laid claim some of the bushes outlining the garden as trophies.

Students started appearing at the balconies, drawn by the noise, the heat, and the smoke.

Nertak continued to run, trying to maneuver himself over to the main building to escape inside it. Kel and

Clarence kept cutting him off. More and more of the yard caught on fire, leaving the old man less and less room to escape.

Talia slowed, shaking, not able to get closer due to the liquid flame burning the area. Unlike Nertak, she couldn't dodge the fire, and the dragon and his quarry's movements were so erratic, she wasn't sure which direction they were going to go from one moment to the next.

Out of nowhere, Lareen appeared on the scene wearing something closely resembling the scarf dress she wore the other night except this time it was yellow and orange. "Kel! Stop this at once!"

Nertak ran right for the Administrator, Clarence and the squire at his heels. Lareen shifted to get between them, her arms outstretched. "Stop!"

Clarence jumped over her in a perfectly graceful arc.

As he realized Lareen hadn't slowed his pursuers, Nertak yelped and ran faster.

Students started pouring out from the doors and through the garden. Nertak headed right for them. People screamed and scrambled out of the way as they saw what was barreling behind him.

A towering, one-armed, armored figure stepped out of the doorway even as Nertak zoomed inside.

Clarence skidded to a halt, the door too small for him, as Kel yelled at him to keep going. The dragon was about to take another deep breath to expel more flame when the armored man crossed the distance between them in a blur and, with a mighty fist, punched Clarence in the face.

Dragon and rider whipped back as if they'd been struck by a cannon. Kel lost his hold on his seat and fell to the hard, ground stunned. Clarence shook the yard as he landed backward, almost crushing Kel's unprotected body.

Seren ignored the dragon. He walked past Clarence, bent down to pick up a dazed Kel and threw the squire over his shoulder. As if this were no more than the usual routine, he turned around with his burden and strode back inside.

"All right, everyone,c Lareen's voice boomed across the yard, "the excitement is over. Go back inside. Now please." She stood with hands on hips watching them until the grumbling audience finally started to comply. Without another word, she followed in the same direction as Seren.

Watchers came out in droves to put out the fires in the yard.

Talia stared and watched all this, her whole body numb. She'd done this. Though she had no idea how or why—she was responsible for this. It was only through a miracle no one was dead—a miracle.

Her chest feeling tighter than ever, she stepped out of sight behind one of the pillars bordering the garden. Her strength suddenly left her and she collapsed to the ground. Her whole body shook as a sob racked through her. She threw her hands over her mouth trying to hold it in to no avail. Hot tears rolled down her face as she wept bitterly into her hands.

Less than an hour later, she raised her head from the ground as loud voices filtered to her from somewhere in the garden. With a panicked gasp, she realized breakfast was over and everyone was on their way to class. That she'd missed the meal made no difference to her—she honestly didn't know if she ever cared to eat again—but with everyone going to class she would be missed. She was sure Mandee and Yllin would be wondering where she'd been this morning. If she didn't show up for class,

Helyn would worry and send people out to look for her. Once they found her, the questions would begin. She couldn't go through that.

Shaky and exhausted, she forced herself to her feet. She wasn't ready for questions; she wasn't ready to admit her guilt. The time would come, sooner or later, she knew, but she didn't want it to happen in such a way everyone would find out. She didn't want to become the latest piece of gossip in school.

She wiped at her face with shaking hands then brushed the grass and soot off her clothes. Whether or not she could make it through class without breaking down or confessing she wasn't sure, but she needed to try. Then later, when she got a chance, she'd go see the Administrator and tell her everything.

Her stomach knotted in pain at the thought. Even if they sent her home in disgrace for what she'd done, she just couldn't let Kel take the blame for all this. She couldn't. She still possessed no idea how everything could have gone so wrong, but at least in this, her thoughts were clear.

As soon as the main tide of students died down, she pushed through the garden out into the path. She followed the last of the breakfast crowd back into the building then headed off to her class.

She was the last of her group to arrive. She cringed inside as the buzz going on inside the room hushed at her entrance. She didn't look at any of her classmates as she headed for her seat. Did they already know? Did someone see her? She felt her lips quiver as she sat down.

"Talia?" Helyn was suddenly before her.

It was all she could do not to break down right there and then and confess.

"Are you all right?" the teacher asked her. "You don't

look well. Should I take you to the healer?"

She shook her head, not trusting herself to speak.

"You look very pale," Helyn insisted. "How do you feel?"

She didn't look at her teacher as she forced herself to answer. "I-I think something didn't agree with me from dinner last night," she said. "I'm doing better now." She felt her eyes mist over at the lie. What was she doing?

"Are you sure?" Helyn pressed.

The teacher's concern only made her feel worse. Talia nodded slowly.

"Well, all right, if you're sure. But if you start feeling worse, tell me right away."

Talia nodded, trying to reassure her, though she knew nothing would ever be all right again. It proved to be one of the longest mornings of her life.

The tears attempted to come back off and on throughout the morning. Though she tried, she found she couldn't pay attention to Helyn's lessons—her thoughts drifting off of their own volition to what she knew she needed to do. She couldn't help imagining the horrors being inflicted on Kel and Clarence as she sat there safe and sound.

As soon as they were released for lunch, she rushed out of the room and headed for the stairs instead of the dining hall. Since the Administrator didn't usually join the students for lunch, she hoped this meant she might find her in her office.

To her surprise, once she came within sight of the golden door, she saw five or more students already gathered there, while four watchers guarded the entrance. The students were bombarding the two men and two women with questions even as the latter stalwartly ignored them.

Talia slowed, even as the taller of the two men appeared to have more than enough of it. "We're not tellin' the bunch of you nothin'. Get out of here before we put you down and give ya a real reason to come here." His tone was gruff.

Cowed, most of the students left in disappointment. One passed Talia and pointed back at the watchers. "Don't bother. You won't get anything out of them."

She stayed where she was until they'd gone.

One of the women grabbed one of the remaining two students by the ear as he said something rude.

"Ow! Let go!"

She didn't, giving him a hard look instead.

"He's a menace, I tell you! He needs to be expelled." The boy was trying hard to look dignified even as he stood on tiptoe to minimize the pain to his ear.

The watcher yanked on it again. "You'll get your say, I'm sure, but not here and not now. Out!"

The tall man who'd spoken to the others stared at the culprit while rolling up his sleeves. A small smile of anticipation lighted on his lips.

"All right, all right! We'll leave." The other of the two boys came forward and grabbed his friend's arm. The watcher let go of the first boy's ear and allowed the second to drag him away even as he protested.

Totally unsure how to proceed at this point, Talia slowly stepped closer to the obviously annoyed adults. "Excuse me."

"Miss, you have no business being up here. Please go back downstairs." This came from the second of the two women. She was plumper than the other and had a kind looking face.

"Please, I—I need to speak to the Administrator." Her voice shook.

The woman frowned. "I'm sorry, but we're under orders. No one is to disturb her right now."

"But I have information," she insisted. "Information on what happened this morning and why." This raised several eyebrows.

"Child, it may be so, but there are to be no exceptions," the woman said gently. "If you'll leave your name and your teacher's, I'll make sure to tell her."

Talia stared hard at the white-tiled floor. If she told them her name, word would surely get out. But what else could she do? Everyone would learn about it eventually anyway. "T—Talia. My name is Talia. My teacher's name is Helyn."

"She'll get your message." This came from the shorter of the two men.

Without looking at them, she turned around and walked back the way she came. As she reached the stairs and started down, she was half tempted to run to her room and bar the door and never come out again. She sighed, looking down the hallway as she reached her floor, the idea truly tempting her. Her parents would be so ashamed of her if they knew. Facing up to one's responsibilities was something they both firmly believed in. She did, too. But she'd never thought it would be so hard.

With another sigh, she resumed going down.

As she opened the door into the dining hall, she was almost deafened by the roar of conversation going on inside. Every few seconds, she heard Kel's name mentioned from one direction or another. Some of the discussions were reserved, but most of the ones she heard were pretty heated. Several watchers were even forced to stop a fight that broke out at one of the tables, something she'd never seen happen before.

For once, she didn't look for her friends but instead sought somewhere a little out of the way, hoping for some quiet and solitude. It was not to be. Mandee spotted her from across the room and rushed to her side.

"Talia! Where have you been?" the red-haired girl asked with some worry. "What happened to you this morning? Daltan said you looked ill in class."

She opened her mouth during the deluge of questions, but nothing came out. In the end, she just nodded.

"Well, come on. We're over here. You probably should try to eat something." Mandee grabbed her arm and dragged her over to where the others were waiting.

When they got there, Yllin was in a hot argument with one of the other girls. "He deserved it and you know it! This has been coming for a long time. It would have served him right to have fried."

Talia grimaced, not having to guess what they were talking about.

"Yeah," chimed in one of the others, "but what could Kel have against the old man? I heard they got along, maybe were even friends."

Yllin snorted. "I don't know and I don't care. I just hope whatever it was, this has taught the letch a lesson."

"Ah, Yllin, not this again." Mandee made a face. "It's all you talked about at breakfast." Talia sat down, not looking at any of them.

"I heard one of the other classes is taking bets on what will happen to the squire." This came from one of the boys in Yllin's class. "They're giving ten to one odds Kel will be declared insane."

One of the others jumped in. "The third-year class is giving three to one this whole mess has something to do with a girl."

Talia stared only at her plate.

"It's too bad you were sick this morning, Talia," Yllin said. "Since you normally get here early, you might have gotten a good view as the old letch ran for his life."

"Hey, that's right!" Sonsan's eyes it up. "We could have gotten the news straight from an eyewitness."

Talia wished she could make herself disappear.

"Are you okay?" Daltan's query whispered to her from across the table.

She looked up into her classmate's dark eyes and saw genuine concern there. She didn't deserve it. She figured he recalled those nights he'd seen Kel outside her balcony. "Yeah." She tried hard to smile. She wasn't sure how well she succeeded.

Lunch was filled with rumors and innuendoes, but no one seemed to have any real facts. She listened to them all as they were laid out before her, her stomach in knots.

"Do you think they'll execute him?" Sonsan's voice seemed filled with fear and awe at the same time.

"No way," Mandee protested. "He didn't kill anyone, so why should they?"

"But he did try," another argued. "He would have done it if not for the old man's magic bracelet. I heard one of the teachers say so."

The words were blows to her soul. The Administrator wouldn't have Kel killed, would she? Her stomach cramped hard; she doubled over in pain.

"Talia!" Mandee paled beside her.

She tried to say something but couldn't. It would be her fault. If he were killed, it would be her fault. Her friends' concerned faces quickly surrounded her but were then pushed back by a couple of watchers.

"Child, what's wrong?" The smaller of the two put her hand on her shoulder and tried to peer into her face.

Talia tried to speak again, yet all that came out was a

sob. Two or three of the others answered for her instead. "She didn't come down to breakfast." "She was sick this morning."

"She hasn't looked good all day."

"All right, all right." The other watcher held up her hands as they all spoke at once. "We'll take her to the healer. Don't worry, we'll make sure she's all right."

Talia knew they were wrong.

"Come, child, the healer will fix everything." The woman who'd been checking on her gently tugged on her to get up.

Though she didn't want to go, though she wanted to tell them nothing was wrong with her which she hadn't brought on herself, she also knew she couldn't stay. More and more students were turning in her direction to see what the commotion was about. It was the last thing she desired.

She tried to stand but immediately doubled over as her stomach cramped harder than before. "Ughn."

"Mala, help me!" The watcher held onto her, keeping her from falling to the floor.

Talia didn't resist as she felt herself being picked up by the other watcher. The two women rushed her out of the room. She closed her eyes to concentrate on keeping the shooting pain at bay.

The noise and scents of the dining hall were left behind as the women exited out into the hallway. Without slowing, they headed for a nearby set of stairs leading down.

Talia opened her eyes, but could barely see, tears clouding her vision. She tried to make the tears stop, but the more she did the faster they came. The whole situation scared her. She'd not reacted to anything in this way before. But then again, she'd never almost been responsible for the death of someone, either.

The watchers set her down on a soft bed in a small, cozy room. A cool cloth touched her face and wiped away her tears. "Just relax, the healer will be here soon."

Talia looked away, knowing the healer would be able to do nothing to help her. Desperate, she studied the room, trying to distract herself.

Shelves covered all the walls and were filled with all manner and size of jars and bottles. Each was clearly labeled, though she didn't recognize most of the names. A plain desk, containing a large assortment of bowls and glasses, stood in one corner of the room. It reminded her a little of her village's own healer. All the kids loved him, especially for the sweets he always set aside to give them when they visited.

When she'd been very young, she remembered stretching her illness a time or two just so her mother would take her back to him again for more jokes and sweets. Thinking of Hale, his kindness, and how he normally was able to make her feel better, she actually relaxed a little. The cramping in her stomach eased a bit but didn't go away.

"My, my, what have we here?"

The watcher stood up, even as Talia's gaze shifted toward the doorway. Her eyes grew wide as she noticed the small, gnarled form standing there—it was the cackling old woman from the armory.

LaSeren stepped inside with the help of her cane, followed closely by a handsome young man in green. Grinning her gap-toothed smile, the old woman made her way to the bed. "Ah, I know you," she said as she got a good look at Talia's face, "you're the gutsy girl from Helyn's class." Her eyes were bright. "What seems to be the problem?"

Talia looked away from her penetrating gaze. She forced herself to speak. "It's just a stomach ache. I—I'm all right. Really."

"Her friends told us she's been sick since this morning," one of the two watchers interjected. Talia really wished she hadn't. "She doubled over in pain at the dining hall before we brought her here."

"Is that so?" LaSeren said. "Come, dear, show me where it hurts."

Talia hesitantly pointed at her stomach, not thrilled at the attention she was getting. She wasn't sick.

The old woman nodded. "Lift up your shirt please."

"Really, this isn't—"

LaSeren poked her in the side with her cane.

Talia gasped in pain and moved to comply before the old woman could do it again.

"Now tell me when it hurts," LaSeren instructed her.

Talia closed her eyes as the healer's gnarled, wrinkled fingers moved to touch her. Her touch was gentler than she expected, as LaSeren probed over her stomach and abdomen. She occasionally grimaced as the muscles cramped beneath the healer's touch but said nothing.

"Did you eat lunch?" LaSeren asked her.

Talia opened her eyes at the unexpected question. "A—a little."

"Any breakfast?"

She looked away. "No." She wondered what it had to do with anything.

"Mala, Leen, I think I can take it from here." LaSeren gave the watchers a gap-toothed smile. "But, if you wouldn't mind, could you ask Tula to send some broth? Maybe a little mild cheese, too, and cut fruit."

"We'll bring it right away." Both women gave Talia a reassuring smile before leaving.

The young man in green stayed, but stood in the back of the room out of the way, observing them. Yet though they weren't alone, Talia still felt uneasy having the old woman so close. After the pranks she and her son had played on them at the armory, she wasn't entirely sure what she could expect.

"Have you ever had these types of pains before?" LaSeren's yellow-tinted dark eyes watched her expectantly.

"I—I don't think so, ma'am."

The old woman cackled, though the sound seemed one of true amusement and definitely more natural than those she made at the armory. "Did you hear this, Wulan? You could learn something from her." She threw a look at the young man, who just shrugged. LaSeren smiled broadly looking back at a confused Talia. "There's no need to be so formal, child, just call me La." The old woman chuckled. "Wulan, mix me some Beltia root and Sorum for me, won't you?"

"Yes, La." The youth took up one of the many bowls on the desk then reached up to the shelves on the wall searching for the things LaSeren had requested.

"Now tell the truth. You're very worried about something, are you not?"

Talia stared into her shrewd eyes and gasped. How could she know?

LaSeren smiled. "That's what I thought." Her face softened. "It must be pretty serious, too. Or at least more serious than thinking you're about to be eaten by a crone and her giant son." She cackled again.

Talia didn't dare say anything and so looked away. She almost jumped when the old woman patted her unexpectedly on the shoulder.

"Don't worry. I won't pry," she told her. "But do drink

this down for me." LaSeren held out the bowl Wulan picked up earlier from the desk.

Talia didn't reach for it, struggling to sit up. "Wh—what is it?"

"Some herbs to help settle your stomach enough so you can eat." Talia stared at it suspiciously. "It will help you relax," LaSeren insisted. "No harm will come of it."

Hesitating only a moment longer, she finally reached out for the offered bowl. Not expecting it to taste pleasant, which it didn't, she gulped the contents down.

"Slow down," LaSeren cautioned. "I know it's not delicious, but don't forget your insides are already unhappy. We don't want to antagonize them any more than they are already, do we?"

Talia made a face, not really wanting to taste the foul concoction any longer than necessary, but complied with LaSeren's instructions. The liquid felt very heavy inside her.

The old woman tapped the side of the bed with her cane. "You just sit and relax and let the medicine do its work. When the food comes, I want you to eat as much of it as you can." She gave her a hard look. "I have a meeting I have to go back to, but I'll check back on you in a little while. I'll send Wulan here to Helyn to let her know you're all right and you're to be excused from classes for the rest of the day."

Talia tensed. "I don't really think I need—"

"Ah!" LaSeren raised her cane and pointed it at her. "I'm the healer here. Just be a nice girl and do as you're told."

She sighed, actually relieved she wasn't going to have to go back. Though she felt a little better, she wasn't ready to face the others again. She'd worry about having to catch up on her studies later. "Yes, ma'am."

The old woman cackled. "Me, a ma'am! Who'd a thought it." She cackled some more as Wulan opened the door for her, a fond smile on his face. "Now don't forget what I told you—eat and rest."

Talia nodded and watched them go. Over the next several minutes, the pain inside her stomach lessened until it was almost gone. Her body, which previously felt so tight and coiled, finally started to relax. She pondered over the old woman's words and wondered if worry was really what was causing her to be ill. She didn't know it could do such a thing.

There was guilt to add to it as well. She sighed again.

The door to the room opened, and she looked up. Mala was back, holding a tray with lunch. The young watcher smiled as she came in. "Feeling any better?"

"Yes, thank you. I'm sorry for all the trouble." She wouldn't meet the watcher's eyes, knowing the fault was all her own and not from an illness.

"Don't worry about it." Her smile was friendly. "Just do what LaSeren says and you'll be fine." Mala set the tray on the desk then unfolded a small table from where it was hidden beneath the bed. She moved the food close enough for Talia to reach them.

"Would you like some company while you eat?" Mala asked kindly.

Talia still wouldn't meet her gaze. "I'm all right, thank you. I've already inconvenienced everybody enough."

"Are you sure? I'm a good listener," Mala insisted.

She tried hard to smile, "Yes, thank you."

After Mala reluctantly left, she tried her best to eat though she didn't feel hungry. She ate slowly, giving the broth, cheese, and fruit plenty of time to settle in her stomach. When she was finished, she was feeling better than she had most of the day. She lay back to rest for a moment, and almost immediately fell asleep.

⁂

"TALIA."

Her eyes snapped open at the unfamiliar voice. She found herself staring up into the face of LaSeren's handsome assistant.

"Sorry to wake you," he said. "But I was sent to fetch you."

She sat up slowly, her mind muddled from sleep. "Fetch me?"

"Yes," he answered. "The Administrator wants to see you."

Her heart jumped into her throat. "Oh." She could feel her insides trying to tense up again.

"Are you up to it?"

"Y—yes, I want to see her." This would be her chance. She'd be able to confess her part in all of this and maybe help Kel and Clarence.

Wulan nodded. "This way then."

The young assistant led her out of the room and down the passage on the right. Talia followed, feeling her nervousness rising with every step. As they took a set of stairs and reached the fourth landing, she hurriedly ran her hands through her short curly hair and straightened her slept-in clothes. She tried to keep her mind clear, even as she almost shook as they approached the golden door. To her surprise, besides the four watchers from before, a fifth had been added, one who waited quietly with a boy about her age. She was sure she'd seen him before. He was one of the boys in Mandee and Yllin's class. What was he doing here?

As soon as she and Wulan came close, the watchers

opened the gold door and let them through. The boy and the waiting watcher followed in after them. Once they'd gone in, the door closed behind them with a resonating clang.

Wulan led them all down to the Administrator's office on the right.

As they entered, Talia immediately noticed it had changed from when she saw it last. Lareen's desk was pushed almost to the wall, and ten or so extra chairs had been added. Two sat on either side of the desk facing out. The rest were scattered about the room, all facing forward toward the desk.

Lareen was not sitting, but stood, looking and acting in no way like her usual self. Instead of the provocative dresses which were her habitual attire, she wore a formal black robe without adornment. Her normally bright face looked grim and deadly serious.

Two others were wearing black robes identical to the Administrator's. To her surprise, one of them was Nertak, who sat on the right side of the desk. To make her astonishment grow even more, she found the other to be LaSeren, who sat to the left of the desk.

Still, her surprise and notice of these details was fleeting, for as soon as she spotted him, only Kel occupied all of her attention.

The squire sat on a chair set off to the side and was facing the Administrator's desk. He wore a simple tan tunic and pants. His feet were bare on the cold marble floor. Weighing down his wrists and ankles were large iron manacles connected to one another by large heavy chains. He didn't glance toward the door as they came in, but faced forward, his expression sad yet at the same time almost serene, as if he'd already accepted his fate whatever it might be.

Talia's heart pounded in her chest as she studied him. Wulan steered her to one of the chairs in the back of the room.

Lareen spoke up when she spotted them. "Thank you for joining us." She nodded in their direction. "I'll try to keep you no longer than necessary." She stepped away from the desk. "As you have no doubt heard by now, we had a major altercation take place this morning. This council has been convened to review the matter and pass judgment." Her hard gaze stabbed at Talia for a moment then at the boy who came in with her. "You've been called here to give statements which will help shed light on this matter. It would be in the best interest of everyone concerned if you tell us all you know."

Lareen returned to the desk before slowly turning around to face them again. Her gaze locked with Talia's own. "We will begin with you—Talia."

Her gaze snapped from Lareen to Kel as she saw him react to the mention of her name. He stiffened in his chair and his head half turned to look back before he abruptly stopped himself and forced his face to stare forward as before. Talia felt her stomach cramp as she went cold all over. She hoped the old woman's medicine would hold out until this was done.

Lareen's gaze homed in on her again. "It is my understanding you tend to arrive in the dining hall early every morning. Did you happen to do so today?"

"Y—yes, I did," she answered.

Lareen nodded in acknowledgment then continued.

"Did you happen to see Kel there today?"

She swallowed hard. "Yes, I did." She then plunged on, not waiting for the next question before her courage might desert her. "But, but what happened wasn't his fault. It was mine."

Kel once more moved as if he would glance back at her, but stopped before he did so. Though the boy beside her gasped at her revelation, no one else in the room seemed surprised. Talia felt her stomach cramp again.

Lareen leaned back against the desk. "I see," she said. "Why don't you tell us about it?"

Feeling their eyes riveted on her, she looked down to stare at her hands. "I found a gem in my room, a large one. I thought it was Kel's, so when I went to breakfast this morning, I returned it to him." She didn't and hoped she wouldn't have to tell them why she'd thought it was his. Lareen already knew about Kel's other strange activities, but the others didn't. It wouldn't help Kel to bring them up; if anything it might make things worse. She hoped they wouldn't be.

"Go on."

Talia took a deep breath before doing so. "Kel seemed to recognize the gem when I gave it to him. He—he was furious, but not at me. He then left the dining hall."

"What did you do then?" Lareen asked.

She bit her lip, not wanting to lie, yet knew if she told of what came next, she wouldn't be helping his case.

"Talia?" Lareen prompted.

She decided to go ahead, knowing they would have heard or already figured out most of this on their own. "I-I realized Kel was going to go see the owner of the jewel, so I went after him to try and stop him." Out of the corner of her eye, she saw Kel start to turn again as if he would finally look back, but he didn't. "I didn't make it in time."

"I see."

Talia could make nothing of Lareen's neutral tone.

Stumblingly, she then told them what she'd seen of the chase.

She tried to recount it as simply and as rapidly as she could. When she was finished, she realized her stomach was no longer hurting. Come what may, she'd stated her blame, though she wasn't sure what difference it would make in Kel's defense.

"Thank you," Lareen said once she was through. "I do believe this clears up a few things." She gave her a quick smile. "Now it's your turn, Elar."

The boy visibly shrank in his chair. Despite everything, Talia found herself feeling curious as to why he'd been called.

Lareen walked over to him. "Do you recognize this?" She pulled out the light blue gem Talia had given Kel.

Elar's eyes grew wide, his gaze snapping to the back of Kel's chair before he quickly nodded.

"Is it yours?" Lareen asked.

"N—no!" His eyes rolled in panic between the chained squire and the gem. Then for the first time, he glanced over at Nertak before he stared only at the floor.

"Don't be afraid. Nothing will happen to you," Lareen reassured him. "We all know who this gem actually belongs to." She waved her hand in Nertak's direction, then stepped back to give the boy room. "You held this gem in your possession for a time, did you not?"

"Yes." The boy's voice shook almost uncontrollably.

"And it was given to you by Nertak, was it not?"

"Yes."

"Why would he do such a thing?" Lareen asked quietly.

Talia noticed both Nertak and LaSeren were staring at the boy with detached interest.

"We—we," Elar stumbled, still staring only at the floor. "We'd made a deal."

"A deal?" Lareen asked. "What kind of deal?"

Talia noticed movement coming from Kel's chair and saw his right fist clenching and unclenching at his side. How was all this connected?

Elar's cheeks colored. "I would get a discount on armor magics if ... if I'd plant the gem somewhere in... in her room." He pointed at Talia without actually looking at her.

"Did Nertak tell you why he wanted you to do so?" Lareen made the question sound trivial, though Talia was suddenly sure it was the pivotal question, the one which would answer everything about this ordeal.

Elar hesitated a long time before answering. As it was, once he did, Talia was forced to strain to hear his words—and she was sitting next to him. "Yes. It, it was supposed to take an inventory of her room. I was supposed to put it there then pick it up the next day and bring it back."

She stared at Elar in disbelief. The gem would take inventory? What did that mean?

Lareen spoke, almost as if she'd read her mind. "Yes, take inventory. How exactly does it do this, Nertak?"

The old man sat back, reflecting, and pulled at his short beard. "Once activated it starts recording. When it sits somewhere for about an hour or so, it starts cataloging anything and everything in the room. The process normally takes a few hours, so overnight usually does the trick."

Talia stared, still not understanding.

"Please, demonstrate its use for us," Lareen said. She walked over to the old man and handed him the gem.

With a sudden mischievous smile, fitting more with what she knew of him, Nertak rose to his feet. She noticed Kel stiffen again, but he didn't move.

"The first few images alone will do just fine," Lareen

purred.

Nertak's smile suddenly soured. "As you wish." Stepping out near the center of the room, he waved his hand over the gem and murmured a few words too low for any of them to hear clearly. He set the jewel on the floor and miraculously, Talia's room appeared around it.

She gasped, recognizing it at once, not sure how this was possible.

The view changed and was seen through the clasped fingers of Elar's hand as he stepped into the room. He tripped over a bucket, then he picked it back up and placed it in a different spot from where it came from.

"He's sure got a lot to learn." This came from the old man. He sounded slightly disgusted. Talia didn't know what to make of it. It seemed as if the gem was able to do more than just take "inventory."

After putting the bucket down, Elar walked across the room over to the bathtub and dropped the gem inside it. The view changed and showed only the confines of the tub as seen from inside it.

The image grayed for a minute or so then cleared again. As she watched, Talia saw pictures of the things in her room appear in sequence. One door, two dressers, a brush, a comb, a mirror, four pairs of socks, three nightgowns—two cotton, one silk. She felt her cheeks warm as the picture of the shift she received from Nertak flashed for all to see. They felt even warmer when it showed her underwear, clean and dirty.

"That's enough, Nertak. I think we've seen how it works now," Lareen said.

The old man stared wistfully at the gem for a moment before he bent to pick it up and murmured more unintelligible words. The images disappeared.

"I'll take it back now, thank you." Lareen held her

hand out. The old man grudgingly gave it back. "Now if you would explain why you got Elar to deliver this?" She sent the old man a knowing look.

Nertak gave her a half pout. "Telling takes all the mystery out of everything."

"Nevertheless," Lareen insisted.

The old man sighed then went on. "I have two reasons for having students place inventory gems in a room. First, it catalogs the students' belongings and lets me anticipate what goods might be needed at the store. Second, it allows me to see if the student placing the gem has potential in other possible lines of work." He dismissed the whole topic with a wave of his hand and returned to his chair by the desk.

Talia stared at her lap. The potential for other lines of work? This was tested by breaking into another's room? What kind of profession could he possibly have in mind? Did the guild actually train people to be thieves?

Several things though fell into place. She now understood why Daltan wouldn't tell her what Nertak wanted him to do in exchange for a discount and why he behaved so strangely afterward. It could also be the main reason for the rumors of peepers Yllin told her about.

Still, the one thing all of this didn't explain was why Kel's reaction was so violent. At the moment she wanted to murder the old man herself for what he'd done, but why would it have mattered to Kel? He knew what the gem was, and the old man admitted he'd gotten others to do this before. Kel might have even done it to someone else for a discount at some point. So why did he get so angry? She stared at his back, at his stiff posture, but got no answers from there.

"You brought this on yourself, you old fool," LaSeren said. "Head of your guild or not, there are better ways to test for prospective members."

Nertak glared at the healer. "That may be so, old hag, but it wouldn't be anywhere near as rewarding." He suddenly smiled. "Besides, it puts a little extra spice in life."

LaSeren snorted in disgust. "I'm sure life has enough *spice* without needing you to add any."

"Enough, you two." Lareen turned a stern eye on them. "Your individual methods for recruitment are not why we're here today. Though it may become a topic very soon."

Nertak sat back, scowling.

Talia stared from one to the other of them, trying to understand. The lecher was the head of a guild? So there were guilds inside the guild? Plus, why would the leader of a guild be testing people by having them break into others' rooms and give discounts to girls for modeling clothes? Might the latter be some kind of test as well? It made her head ache.

"Well, thank you two for your assistance in this matter." Lareen was looking at both Talia and Elar. "You may return to your classes now. Though it would be greatly appreciated if you would keep everything you've learned here today to yourselves."

Elar's head moved up and down so fast it made her think it might fly off. She didn't say or do anything, too stunned to know what to do.

Wulan and the watcher who'd come with them led the two of them out. As they reached the office door, Talia glanced one last time at Kel. He sat just as when she first saw him, his hands on his lap and his eyes forward.

Once they were led out into the main hallway past the golden door, Elar hurried away, not once looking back. She watched him go, her mind numb.

"Are you all right?" Wulan's soft voice brought her out of her distraction.

She made herself look at him. "Yes."

"How's your stomach?" he asked.

She stared at him for a long moment before she realized what he meant. It was only then she became conscious that her previous discomfort was gone. "Much better...?"

"Good." Wulan smiled. The act made him look even younger than he did already. "You can go back to class then if you want. You should be fine now."

She nodded slowly. After a moment, Wulan left her to go back into the Administrator's quarters. She watched until the golden door closed behind him before taking her leave. With slow, unhurried steps, she made her way back to her class. All the events she just witnessed kept playing over and over in her mind.

She didn't realize she'd reached her destination until Helyn spotted her standing at the doorway and called out her name.

"Talia, you're back."

Startled, she only stood there.

"Come on in," Helyn said. The teacher came to her side and guided her into the room. "The others told me what happened. Are you feeling better?"

Eager eyes across the room stared at her, all waiting for an answer. "Y—yes. The healer gave me some medicine. I'm much better now."

Helyn smiled and let her take her seat. Some of the others welcomed her back quietly as Helyn picked up their lesson where she left off moments before.

Talia's reception once they were released for dinner, however, was much more vocal.

"Talia!" Mandee ran up to her and hugged her so hard

she could barely breathe. "We've been so worried about you." The red-headed girl let her go so she could look at her face. "Are you all right?"

She felt a little guilty over all the attention. "I'm much better." She tried to smile. "Sorry to have caused you trouble." The two of them walked to the table and sat down.

Mandee and Yllin sat protectively on either side of her.

"No trouble," Yllin said. "We're just glad you're all right." She squeezed her shoulder lightly.

Talia realized they'd honestly been worried about her. She felt even guiltier about putting them through all this than before. "Thanks."

"Say, is the healer's assistant as cute as they say?" Mandee's eyes were bright with interest.

Talia was caught off guard by the question. "I... I guess so."

"Then maybe I could be the one who's sick next," she chirped.

"Mandee!"

"It was just a thought, Yllin." The girl pouted. "You're only jealous because I said it first."

"Do you see what I have to put up with?" Yllin asked.

"Yllin!"

Talia couldn't stop the grin spreading on her face.

Unlike that morning, she found herself feeling famished. She also noticed Mala keeping an eye on her. The watcher winked at her when she saw her looking.

They'd not been eating long when she braved to ask one of the questions which had clung to her mind all afternoon. "Are there any other rumors about Nertak other than he's a lecher?" She hoped the query came across as nonchalantly as she intended.

"Hah," one of the boys eating with them said, "there

are almost as many rumors about him as go around about the squire."

Talia felt a tinge of pain at the mention of Kel. As of yet, no word had come as to what would happen to him.

"That he's a lecher is actually a fact rather than a rumor. Even you've seen the proof," Yllin informed them smugly.

"Well, I've heard he's the man to see if you want anything. It may cost you, but if you want it, he can get it." This came from the boy who spoke before.

"I've heard he'll do the same with information, too," piped in another. "One of the older students said Nertak used to be a spy for the guild."

Talia was also told a sorceress supposedly turned Nertak into a toad once. He'd also allegedly won a kingdom on a bet in a whittling contest.

"Are there guilds within the Dragon Knight guild?" She threw the question in before the rumors degenerated further.

"I've heard it's true," Mandee said. "Since not everyone can become a Dragon Knight, they made guilds within the guild for almost everything else so they can use all of the people's skills."

"Waste not, want not," Sonsan chimed in.

Talia recalled the Administrator saying something of the sort to her on their first meeting. It just didn't occur to her that meant there was more than one guild. The rumors the others shared about Nertak didn't say whether he was a part or even a head of a guild or not. Having boys sneaking around into girls' rooms had nothing to do with the sale of goods—or did it? If he'd really been a spy... Yet would the guild need those sorts of skills? The more she learned, the less she felt she knew.

"Your attention, please." Lareen's voice boomed

across the dining hall, surprising them all. With a bright flash, the Administrator appeared on top of her table, startling a number of the teachers right out of their chairs. Lareen still wore the black robe from before. Talia's skin went cold.

"I presume you are all aware of the events which transpired this morning?" Lareen didn't wait for an answer. "Violence was committed against one of the guild's members, as well as the destruction of school property." Her grave expression scoured the room. "The tribunal convened earlier today. Upon hearing all the evidence, we've finally reached a judgment."

Lareen paused as if to let the almost palpable tension build before revealing the decision. Talia hardly dared breathe as she waited for what the Administrator would say next. The entire room was silent with anticipation.

"Both Clarence and Kel have been fined a thousand gems each to pay for damages to both the store and the school grounds. What they cannot pay, they will make up for in labor."

A faint murmur of disbelief rippled through the assembly at the high sum. Kingdoms could be bought for less.

"This is not everything, however," Lareen told them. "For the next four weeks, both have been placed under house arrest and are restricted to their quarters. Their meals will be nothing more than what is served in the Bolamian Imperial Dungeons. That is all." With another sudden bright flash, the Administrator was gone.

The noise level of the dining hall immediately rose to three times its standard volume. Talia didn't notice, relieved Kel and Clarence's punishment wouldn't be worse than it was. The fact Nertak, the crime's victim, was part of the tribunal had nagged at her in the back of her mind. She'd not been sure what kind of satisfaction the strange old man would vie for. She'd dreaded that Kel would be whipped, or tortured, or worse because of it.

By the time they were dismissed from dinner, wild speculation ran rampant on the punishment chosen and whether it was just or not. Even after the mandatory walk, students milled around discussing it. Talia excused herself, not caring to hear any more of it, saying she was tired and wanted to turn in early.

In truth, she felt exhausted. The day's strange events and the pure relief that Kel and Clarence's fate wouldn't be a disastrous one claimed all of her energy and more.

Not even bothering to change, she crept into bed and fell almost instantly asleep. She didn't wake once throughout the night.

Chapter Ten

WHEN TALIA WALKED into the dining hall, the place was empty. With a pang, she realized it would be some time before she would see Kel rushing through his breakfast before picking up fruit from the kitchen to take to Clarence.

A touch of guilt colored her feelings. Though in the end, the incident wasn't directly her doing, she still couldn't help but believe she was at least partially responsible for what happened. No one else seemed to think she had anything to do with it—yet she just couldn't get rid of the certainty that if not for her actions, Clarence and Kel wouldn't have done what they did.

She found her group's usual table and sat down to wait for the others. In ones and twos they trickled in, this being their free day. She didn't really say much once they arrived, and found she didn't have much of an appetite. She ate less than usual even with the watchers' gentle prompting.

"Talia, are you still not feeling well?" Daltan's shy, dark eyes studied her from across the table.

"You do seem awfully quiet today," Mandee added.

"I'm a lot better actually." She tried hard to give them a sincere smile. "I guess I've just been a little distracted this morning. Sorry."

"There's been an awful lot to be distracted with lately," Sonsan said.

She could only agree.

After breakfast, she and a number of her classmates got together in the library to study. This was mostly to pass the time before they would all have to cave in and lug their weekly water upstairs. It was well past midmorning when they were interrupted.

"Excuse me." A watcher came up to them. "Is one of you Talia? The Administrator wants to meet with her."

Talia tensed, even as all her classmates turned to stare at her in surprise. What could this be about? Did Lareen finally decide she should be punished for her part in Kel's attack? Strangely, the thought of punishment didn't upset her as much as she thought it might. She rose to her feet. "I'm Talia."

The watcher smiled kindly at her and without another word led her away as her friends watched. She followed, walking a couple of steps behind the woman, saying nothing as they climbed the stairs. They passed a number of people already intent on bringing in their water, but no one paid her much attention.

She tried to think of any other possible reasons why Lareen might be summoning her and could come up with nothing except her original thought. Would her own punishment have to be decided by the tribunal as in Kel's case or would Lareen decide it on her own?

Once they reached the golden door leading into the Administrator's rooms, the watcher opened it for her yet didn't follow her in. Talia glanced back as the door closed behind her, then strolled down the small foyer-styled hallway to Lareen's office. She hesitated a second, listening when she found the door to the office slightly ajar. Hearing no voices issuing from within, she knocked then went on in.

"Ah, you're here."

Talia heard the Administrator's voice yet didn't see her. The room was once more arranged the way she saw it on her first visit, but no one was there.

"Come on out here," Lareen said.

It was only then Talia realized the room's balcony doors were open. She walked over to them and peeked outside.

Lareen was spread out on a long settee, her eyes closed as the sun's warm rays washed over her body. Though her eyes didn't open, she signaled to Talia to join her as if she knew she was there. "Sit, sit, let's enjoy this for a minute."

Not totally understanding, Talia stepped out onto the balcony and headed for the second settee. She sat down, still feeling tense, and tried to relax as she looked out at the tranquil, far off view of the mountains. Her gaze wandered after a few minutes, and she studi+ed the fast progress of some of the clouds across the sky. Despite what she expected from this meeting, she soon found herself growing slightly more at ease.

"Are you feeling better today?" Lareen asked. "I heard you weren't doing well yesterday." The Administrator still lay with her eyes closed.

Talia forced herself to answer. "Yes, much better, thank you."

"I'm glad to hear it." Lareen turned her head and looked at her for the first time. "If you're feeling up to it, there's a job I'd like you to do for me."

Talia frowned. This didn't seem to be going where she

expected.

"I'll pay you two jewels a week if you take the job and I'll also add a note to your record," Lareen said.

Her frown deepened. "I don't understand." This all sounded as if it were more a reward than a punishment.

Lareen smiled lightly and sat up. Talia quickly did the same.

"As you know, two of our people are currently under house arrest. Since they can't leave their quarters, it makes it a little difficult for them to get things to eat," she explained. "So I'm currently looking for a volunteer to take their meals to them."

Talia stared at the Administrator still not understanding. The job itself was simple enough, but why have a student take care of it? Why pay them? More confusing still; why ask her if she wanted it?

"You have to understand, this is an important job, and I have to be careful as to who is chosen," Lareen said solemnly. "If the wrong person were picked, and they decided not to feed them, we might not find out for days, if not longer." Her eyes shone.

Talia stared at the Administrator in shock. Was she serious? Did she really think someone would let Clarence and Kel starve? Would they? Or was she actually insinuating she was giving her this task so she could take revenge on them if she wished? The thought sent a shiver down her arms.

"To be honest, I believe you're uniquely qualified for this task," Lareen went on. "Not only are you already intimately acquainted with the case, and so won't be too curious, but you'll also keep anything else you might discover to yourself."

Talia looked away, feeling more lost and confused than ever. Was she saying she trusted her? It was almost as if the Administrator knew she hadn't told a soul about what happened. But how could she? Not for the first time, she was sure the school's administrator was more than she seemed.

"Will you take the job?" Lareen stared at her hopefully.

Talia found she couldn't meet her stare for long. "I—" She hesitated, not sure what she should say. Still, dare she take the chance someone else might be given the job, and they might let Clarence or Kel starve for fun? Over the last day, it'd become increasingly obvious not everyone was fond of them. Maybe, by taking the job, she might find a way to make all this up to them. "Yes, I'll do it."

"Great!" Lareen gave her a bright smile.

"But the pay isn't necessary."

"Nonsense." The Administrator waved the comment aside. "You'll need the money later. Besides..." her voice lowered to a mere whisper, "it's the very least I can do after what you've been inadvertently put through."

Talia's eyes widened. "Excuse me?"

Lareen stood up and stepped up to the balcony's wide banister, her silken dress flowing around her legs. "Kel pushes himself very hard, but I push him even harder. Perhaps too hard..." She glanced back at Talia, her eyes troubled, before looking out toward the mountains. "Despite what you may have heard, I know Clarence and Kel have great potential. I believe they could be Judges."

Talia felt her pulse rise. Kel and Clarence judges? Helyn had told them that in the guild, Judges stood second only to the Council of Elders, though in some ways they held even more power. The Judges roamed the land and were the final decision-makers on cases of the highest magnitude or those involving locations of the guild or foreign countries. Their impartiality was their greatest asset and equally as rare. To become one was a long and arduous process.

"As you now know," Lareen continued, "Nertak's methods may be crude, but they do serve a purpose. Kel has been well aware of this for some time. His reaction to what was done to you is, therefore, more than puzzling, to say the least. It may be a sign I've pushed him too close to the breaking point." She sighed.

Talia could hear the guilt and worry in Lareen's voice.

"There are so many things we don't know about him..." Lareen turned around and leaned against the banister. "In many ways, Kel is a special case. You see, unlike most of our students, we know almost nothing of his past. From what I've learned over the years, he recalls little to nothing of it himself." She paused for a moment before going on. "He was found at the age of eight by a group of knights after he made his escape from a local orphanage. He'd been there three years, given to the orphanage by a merchant who found him walking down a road alone in a daze. Seemingly, Kel owns no recollection of how he got there or any memories from before that time except his name."

Lareen stared at her with sudden intensity. "He's always been a loner. Other than for the adversarial relationship he's developed with Clarence, I dare say he has no real friends, just many acquaintances. Though before this I would have said Nertak was closer than some. It makes it very difficult to tell when something is wrong."

Talia found herself asking a question before she could stop herself. "But wouldn't Clarence know? Wouldn't he tell you?"

Lareen smiled, but it was a sad smile. "He might find out, but he wouldn't tell me. Those two are in a class by themselves. Clarence's past is even more of a mystery than Kel's, and he's as stubborn and as much a loner as his partner. It's part of the reason I thought they might get along well together." Her eyes softened. "Well, enough musings. If you'll go see Tula in the kitchen after you're through with lunch, she'll show you where Clarence's food will be set for you as well as Kel's."

Talia nodded.

"Clarence will be in the dragons' dormitory," Lareen told her. "Kel's room is on the roof and can be reached by a set of stairs Tula will show you." She reached down into a pocket which wasn't obvious before. "Here." She handed her two gems. "Now go on, I'm sure your friends are waiting for you."

Talia nodded again, half-bowed, then left. Only once she reached the hallway leading to the golden door, she stopped and glanced back the way she came, suddenly unsure about everything which just went on.

The lunch bell echoed in the room, startling her. Without further hesitation, she went out the door and headed for the nearest stairwell. By the time she made it to the dining hall, her friends were already there.

"Talia, is it true?" Narilla scooted over, making a place for her to sit.

"Is what true?" She threw her an askew glance, noticing how everyone seemed to be staring at her.

"Sonsan said you got called to go see the Administrator."

She bit her lip, not sure how to respond. "Uh, yeah, it's true."

"Well, don't just sit there," Sonsan cut in, "tell us what happened!" Yllin and several of the others nodded in agreement.

Talia stared at the table before her. "She just, she just wanted to tell me I'd been picked for some extra chores."

Please, don't ask what they are. Don't ask.

"What chores?" Yllin stared at her intently.

It took all she possessed not to groan out loud. "I have to take food to the squire and the dragon."

"Really?" Sonsan leaned across the table, her surprise making her eyes wide. A number of the others looked just as amazed.

"Is it safe?" Daltan's dark eyes gazed at her with worry.

She abruptly realized some of the things which might be going through his mind. "Yes, of course. There's nothing to worry about." She tried to give him a reassuring smile.

The boy didn't look too convinced but said nothing else.

As soon as lunch was served, she dug in, using her need to hurry as an excuse to avoid any other questions. When she finished her meal, she excused herself and made her way toward one of the kitchen's doors. As she got there, she was almost run down by a woman carrying out a heavy-laden tray.

"Sorry." Talia opened the door, making sure to stay out of the way in case anyone else was exiting.

A wave of heat flashed out at her from the inside, even as her eyes drank in the hive of activity within. Perspiration broke over her brow as she took a tentative step inside. The room was large, fully one-third the size of the dining hall. Long tables took up the central portion of the room, each seeming to serve specific functions. Along the walls, cupboards covered every inch. Half were standing open as kitchen staff took things in and out of them.

After staring about for a half minute, she finally found someone who wasn't rushing off somewhere. "Excuse me."

The short, wrinkled woman looked up from where she was filling bowls full of soup from a large cauldron beside her. Looking her up and down, the old woman glowered. "Are you supposed to be here?" she asked her with a thick accent.

Talia nodded, feeling more and more uncomfortable in the humid heat. "Yes, I'm supposed to report to Tula?" she asked hopefully.

"Ah," the woman said, "she should be somewhere down in that direction." She pointed off to the far end of the room where large wood-burning stoves covered the back wall. "She'll be the one standing on the stool glaring at everyone."

"Thank you." Nodding in thanks, Talia left her and gingerly made her way deeper into the kitchen, trying not to be trodden on or in the path of those shuffling about. The farther she went, the higher the temperature rose. Though the room was filled with the mouthwatering scents of bread and cooking meats, the air itself felt heavy in her lungs and felt stifling.

As she came closer, she spotted the back of a small woman with short-cropped hair standing on top of a stool calling out orders like a general. When she turned to point with a wooden spoon at one of the scullions rushing past, Talia realized she'd met her before. She was the woman who'd brought her and Lareen their meal during her test. Noticing how Tula and the others seemed totally unhampered by the raging heat, Talia stepped forward.

"Ma'am?" She was forced to dodge as two men rushed past holding pots full of boiling sauce.

Tula turned on her stool to look down at her. "Ah, I've been expecting you." The harsh expression on her face softened a little, welcoming her. "Everything's been prepared. Come, I'll show you where everything is." She jumped off the stool, her movements spry. "Teere, take over. I'll be back in a few."

"This way." Tula walked forward, making no move to dodge those hurtling past her. Cooks and servers parted before her as if an external yet invisible force were moving them out of the way. Talia gratefully followed in her wake. Tula strode out a side door in the back of the kitchen.

Stepping outside was the difference between summer and winter. Talia felt suddenly woozy as the relatively cold air fell around her. She leaned against the wall for a moment to steady herself. Tula walked on as if not noticing the radical change. Luckily, she didn't go far.

"These two barrels are for Clarence. You can use the dolly there to take them to the dormitory." She looked at the barrels then at Talia's small frame. "Do you think you can handle them okay?"

Talia stepped away from the wall to take a look, feeling a little steadier. One barrel was filled to the top with dried corn while the other was filled with oats. Each was almost as tall as she was and three times as wide. She eyed them, suddenly unsure. "I should be able to."

Tula nodded. "Here, I'll help you load the first one." The head cook grabbed the dolly as if it were nothing, and swiftly showed her the finer points of loading, unloading, and tipping back the cargo for transport. "The ground's uneven, so take it slow. When you're finished, come find me and I'll show you where to pick up Kel's meal."

"Thank you."

Tula gave her a small smile then went back indoors. Once she was gone, Talia studied the terrain before her and started off, pulling the dolly behind her. The uneven ground soon made her perspire from something other than heat. A couple of times on the way, the barrel threatened to topple, sending her into a panic to stop it each time. After what felt close to an eternity, she finally made her way across the yard to the entrance of the dragons' dormitory. Only then did a wave of nervousness sweep through her as she realized she was about to meet someone whose punishment she was at least partially responsible for. Taking a deep, steadying breath, she went inside.

The interior of the dormitory looked much as it did when she first saw it. Fresh hay covered the floor, and the thick wooden pillars holding the roof aloft looked clean. She could see no signs that worms at one time infested the place or that a fire hungrily licked all around it. Magic was an astounding thing.

Glancing down the row of stalls, she didn't see the green dragon. Remembering from her first visit that she'd seen a riding harness on the one at the end, she dragged her burden in that direction. When she reached it, she could see Clarence curled inside it through the slats of the gate, his head tucked beneath a spread wing.

"Excuse me. Lunch is here." She struggled to drag the dolly out from beneath the barrel.

Clarence's wing pulled back, and his head rose so his crossed eyes could take a look at her. *Oh. It's you.*

She felt her face grow hot at his tone, not sure how to take his words. She tried not to make eye contact. "I, I have another barrel for you. I'll bring it right over."

Yes. More corn, surely. Goodie. He didn't sound impressed at all.

She almost ran in her hurry to leave. By the time she returned with the second barrel, the first was empty. Without a word, she set the second one down next to the first.

Oh, I see it's even better than I expected. Oats instead of corn. The dragon's disgust was only too evident.

Talia felt more ashamed than ever. "I'm really sorry." She tried to find something more to say but nothing came.

Clarence's large head turned away from looking at the barrel. *You shouldn't be. It wasn't your fault. It was Kel's.* He snorted with the last, sending out two light puffs of smoke through his nostrils.

"But didn't you help him?" She remembered Kel arguing with the dragon, as if Clarence were resisting him, but still, it'd been the dragon who shot the flames into the cave. It didn't quite make sense.

Oh, yes, those without the proper knowledge would see it that way, wouldn't they? Clarence picked up the barrel of oats with his two forelegs then leaned back in the hay with it, looking thoughtful. *You haven't covered the specifics on the bonding, have you?*

"The bonding?" she asked.

One of Clarence's eyes riveted itself to her. *Yes, the bonding. It's what happens when a rider and dragon are paired. A strong link formed between them through a ritual.*

It's supposed to help them act as one.

"I'm sorry, but I still don't see—" She stopped, unsure whether she might be pushing too far.

Clarence tipped up the barrel and swallowed a third of the oats. His words flowed undisturbed into her mind. *Though ours may not be a true or whole bonding, still, emotions flow from one to the other. They can be quite overwhelming at times. I was caught off guard by Kel's murderous rage. I wasn't able to reassert full control until after it was over.*

"Oh." Caught unawares by Kel's murderous rage—she shivered. "Do you, do you know why he was so angry?"

She was surprised the dragon was explaining himself to her. It didn't seem to fit with what Lareen said of him. Perhaps it was because he felt as embarrassed and guilty about all this as she did.

Clarence finished the rest of the oats and set the barrel back on her side. His scales rolled along his shoulders, as he seemed to give her the dragon equivalent of a shrug. *It was just the final stroke which broke the dam.*

Talia frowned, the statement not making much sense to her.

He hasn't eaten in a while. You might want to hurry so he won't starve to death. Clarence lay back down, his long tail coiling about him as he made himself more comfortable.

"Oh." Realizing what he said was true and that Kel wouldn't eat until she took food to him, Talia picked up the first of the two barrels with the dolly and went back the way she'd come. She pushed the barrel as fast as she dared back toward the kitchen though her arms were already unhappy about the heavy loads from before. She then rushed back to the dormitory to get the second one and noticed Clarence was back to the tucked position she'd initially found him in. Trying to be as quiet as possible, she picked up the second barrel with the dolly and left.

Gasping by the time she made it back to where the barrels were kept, she propped her cargo beside the first barrel then set the dolly up against the wall. With a small grimace, she walked over to the door leading back into the kitchen. She opened the door and immersed herself once more in the waves of heat coming from inside. It felt worse than before.

"Ah, there you are!"

Talia glanced to her left and spotted Tula looking over at her.

"Come, his lunch is getting cold and I don't believe he's eaten since yesterday," Tula said, and waved for her to follow.

Talia nodded and let the head cook lead the way, too tired for anything else. Tula took her to a small table set beside the doors leading out into the dining hall.

"Did you manage okay?" Tula picked up the tray as she spoke, and handed it to her.

She only nodded again.

Tula grinned. "You won't be short on time today, so it should help. I'm sure you'll get used to it all soon enough."

Talia doubted it. The tray in her hands already felt like dead weight to her tired arms.

With precise directions, Tula then told her how she could make her way to the roof and Kel's quarters. Talia thanked her, finally getting enough of her strength back to speak.

Making her way out into the dining hall, she saw most of those who'd been there had already cleared out and were taking their walk around the garden. She picked up her pace and headed for the door leading out of the hall and toward the stairs Tula had told her of.

Following the head cook's directions, she climbed to the fourth floor then opened the small door at the top of the landing which hid the narrow stairs leading to the roof.

The roof of the school was a huge space. From it, she could see all of the surrounding mountains and the wide-open sky.

It was also one of the tallest things Talia had ever stood on. She stepped close to the edge and looked down. After getting a glimpse of the far-off ground and the way it seemed to be calling her down to it, she backed off, no longer curious.

The middle area of the roof sloped upwards in the shape of a giant triangle and held the large, round glass windows she'd seen on her first day. On her right rose the strangely shaped structure holding the school's tilted clock face. A small door faced her from the side. It was the only door she could see up there.

Suddenly remembering why she was there, she felt her stomach tighten. She forced herself to go on up to the door, and trying not to think on who was on the other side, she knocked on it with her foot and waited for it to be answered.

No one came.

Frowning, she balanced the laden tray precariously on one hand and reached out with the other to try the door. It was unlocked. She went ahead and opened it.

The room which greeted her was about the size of her own, if not a little larger. The roof sloped strangely from one end to the other and the walls had no windows. A lone globe illuminated the place, keeping the room covered in half-shadows, though she spotted two others unlit in the room. A small bed was set against the shortest wall. A tub sat against a corner, as did a dresser and a desk. This left the middle of the room bare, except for a large, dark colored carpet and a low table with thick cushions set around it. Stacked books filled over half the table, and also packed four or five shelves set about the room.

Tubes and gears were visible through the tallest wall, a part of it carved out and replaced with glass so one could look into the clock's inner workings. A ledge was set before the window, which adjoined a small, stooped door on the right side. It was there where she spotted Kel. His back was to her.

"Just set it down anywhere." He didn't glance away from the gears as he spoke. A soft ticking thrum filled the room from the direction of the machinery.

Talia ventured further into the room and walked to the short table. Now that she was closer, she noticed Kel was dressed much the same as he'd been the day before. As far as she could tell his hands were no longer in chains. His ankles, however, were. They would make walking quite uncomfortable.

"If it's all right, I'll, I'll pick up the dishes when I come back tonight." She took an involuntary step back as Kel snapped around at the sound of her voice.

"It's you!" His eyes grew wide as he stared at her. Then as he seemed to realize he'd spoken, his cheeks turned crimson. They both looked simultaneously away, even as she felt heat rising to cover her own cheeks.

"I've got to go," she mumbled. "I'm going to be late for class." Without looking at him, realizing he'd know she'd just told him a barefaced lie, she turned around and hurried out the way she came, closing the door firmly behind her.

Her insides in even bigger knots than before, she rushed down the stairs and headed back to her room. She closed the door and barred it, though she couldn't quite explain to herself why.

Talia knew her friends would soon be looking for her, but she didn't think she could face them just then. Instead, she made herself clean her room and worked on some of the class's future reading assignments. She also made the dreaded rounds with her buckets to replace the water in her tub. Her arms protested the abuse quite loudly.

Eventually, though, she left to go down to dinner. She soon found herself surrounded by her classmates on the way and bombarded with questions about Kel. The news of her new chores had made the rounds. She'd ended up attracting attention to herself, whether she wanted it or not.

As deftly as she could, she avoided their questions or made as little comments as possible as they herded her along to the dining hall. When she joined her other friends at the table, the questions started all over again.

"I'm telling you, there's nothing *to tell*." Talia felt her frustrations trying to get the better of her.

"You can't just keep this kind of thing to yourself. At least tell us if he was surrounded by guards, or was chained to the wall, or anything!" Sonsan's eyes were twinkling hungrily.

Talia sighed. "He's just in his room. Where he's supposed to be. He's alone, by himself."

"Yes, yes, but was he fuming?" Sonsan insisted. "Was he vowing revenge? Did he try to kill you when you came in?"

A number of those around her leaned forward eager to hear the answer.

"No, of course not! Why would you think such a thing?" Talia felt her anger rising. "He's never hurt anyone before."

"Come on, all of you, leave her alone." Mandee, to her amazement, rose to her defense. "It's not as if she asked for this job."

Those around them mumbled in displeasure but backed off. Talia felt her anger fade, grateful for her friend's interference. After devouring her dinner, she got up to go. As she made her way toward the kitchen, she couldn't help but notice how many of the students seemed to turn to follow her with their eyes. Did the whole school know? Why did they care? She found herself walking faster. She sighed with relief once she was hidden on the other side of the kitchen door.

Trying to ignore the heat washing over her, she made her way quietly through the busy kitchen to its back door.

"Talia, hold up a moment."

Her hand stopped on the door. As she looked back over her shoulder, she spotted Tula rapidly converging on her location.

"Before you go, take a few of these. Just shove them down in the oats so no one will see them," she said. "I know how the old grouch hates oats." Tula handed her a small sack. "Let's just keep this between us, okay? Most of us agree Clarence deserves a little something for bringing the old windbag's ego down a notch or two." She winked.

Talia stared at her, surprised.

The chief cook noticed the look and smiled. "At no time was he in any real danger, you know. The old windbag is a cautious one, and Kel knew about his amulet. So though the boy went a might overboard in showing his displeasure, deep down he knew he wouldn't kill him."

Talia nodded, trying to absorb this new information, and took the bag with her outside. Making sure no one else was around, she opened it. Inside, she found seven ripe apples. Quickly, she took them out one by one and shoved them deep into the oat-filled barrel. Putting the small empty sack by the door, she grabbed the dolly and hooked it to the corn barrel.

Struggling with her load, she dragged her burden to the dormitory. She found Clarence in his stall, curled up much the same as how she saw him hours earlier. "Good evening," she said softly. "I've brought your dinner." She set the barrel in front of the stall door and pried the dolly out from beneath it.

Clarence said nothing, reacting in no way other than to give a light snort, which sent a small trail of smoke rising into the air.

Not wanting to push him, Talia left to go retrieve the other barrel. By the time she made it back, she was breathing hard and her arms hurt. She set the barrel down next to the first, then rubbed her arms fervently trying to get some blood back into them.

Unobtrusively, Clarence's claw reached over the stall door and grabbed the barrel full of oats. The other was already empty.

She fitted the dolly to the empty barrel, not at all relishing the task of having to take it back when Clarence's surprised exclamation filtered through her mind. *What's this?*

Talia looked up and saw the dragon's green snout peering into the partially empty barrel with bright eyes. His long tongue moved around inside it until it came back out wrapped about its prize.

Apples! His skewed eyes turned to look at her. *Is this your doing?*

She hurriedly shook her head. "They're a present from Tula."

Ah, a wise, mysterious, and wonderful woman.

Talia smiled at his evident pleasure then left to take the first barrel back. When she returned, she found the second barrel already empty and waiting for her. Clarence was sitting back, rolling the last of the apples around in his mouth with his long tongue.

She set the barrel on the dolly and turned to go back out. "Good night."

Good night, he replied. *By the way, he also did it because he likes you. I think I might like you as well.*

Talia glanced back, startled by his words, but Clarence

had turned away. Not knowing what to say, she said nothing and went on her way, her thoughts heavy. She barely remembered her aching arms as she reached the kitchen's outside wall and set the barrel down.

She felt suddenly tense about seeing Kel again. There were too many things she honestly didn't understand. Yet he'd go hungry if she didn't meet with him, and she still wasn't so sure she was blameless in all of this. With a deep sigh, she rubbed absently at her arms again then opened the door leading into the kitchen.

Trying not to pay heed to the radiating heat, she made her way to the front of the kitchen to pick up Kel's tray. The dishes on it were covered, but something about the meaty scent wafting lightly from it made her think Clarence wasn't the only one being thanked for his actions. She wondered what it was the kitchen staff held against the old man. Looked like a lot more people than just Yllin held a dislike of him.

Gearing herself up to the inevitable, she took command of the tray and left the kitchen. The dining hall was almost empty, so she had no trouble making her way across to the exit on the other side. She followed the stairs to the fourth floor, ignoring the stares from those who'd already made their way around the garden and come back inside. They made her feel more nervous than she already was.

The sun lay low on the far horizon as she reached the roof. Talia studied the spreading streaks of orange and gray, her steps slowing. It was a dazzling sight. The mountains of green and brown made a startling contrast with the fading light. Forcing herself to take a few deep breaths, she let the serene view wash over her.

As she'd done earlier in the day, she used her foot to knock on the door. She almost dropped the tray when the moment she did so the door was yanked open startling her.

"Hi!" Kel's bright gaze met hers for a moment then looked away. "Please come in." He moved out of the way, holding the door open for her.

Talia felt her heart racing inside her but wasn't totally sure of the reason. She gingerly stepped inside.

She heard the door close behind her and felt her shoulders grow a little tighter. Kel's chains rattled as he followed after her.

"I'm sorry if I was rude to you earlier." His tone sounded hesitant and unsure.

She tried not to think about it. "You have nothing to apologize for. I-I wouldn't be too happy, either, about having to stay in my room for four weeks, especially wearing those." She dared to glance over her shoulder at him as she set his tray down.

Kel shrugged. "It's not so bad. Really. At least now I've got plenty of time to study." He gave her a shy grin.

She frowned. "I thought you already graduated. That it was why you were able to put your name in the lottery."

Kel sat down on one of the cushions and scratched gently at where one of the chains was chafing his right ankle. "There are a million other things to learn about. And Lareen thinks it helps keep me out of trouble." He smiled brightly. "Though I guess maybe it hasn't worked too well so far."

The smile lightened his face. Talia found it almost contagious. A grin tugged at her own lips. "She really worries a lot about you." The words were out of her mouth before she realized she was going to say them.

Kel glanced up at her. "Who does?"

She looked away, wondering what made her bring this up. "The Administrator. I-I got the impression she cares about you and Clarence very much."

Now it was his turn to look away. He didn't say anything.

She didn't like the way the light went from his face. "She thinks she's been pushing you too hard."

Kel slowly shook his head from side to side. "She didn't have anything to do with this." His gaze locked with hers. "And neither did you."

She stared at him, astounded. Did he somehow guess at her own feelings of guilt? She suddenly decided she didn't want to know. "I—I'd better get going. I've got to take these back." Without looking at him, she grabbed the emptied tray from lunch then headed toward the door.

Once she got there, she hesitated a moment and glanced back. Kel was where she left him, a troubled look on his face. When he said nothing, she opened the door and left.

As unsure of how to feel about this meeting as she was about everything else, she took one quick look at the darkening sky then headed for the narrow stairs.

She was half rushing down the steps when she realized someone was standing in her way about three-quarters of the way down. She slowed, not recognizing the thin, older student, and wondered what he was doing there. From his confident bearing and the expression on his face when he spotted her, she was sure he was waiting for her.

Talia didn't look at him as she drew near and tried to go past. "Excuse me."

He sidestepped to block her path. "Hold up. I want to talk to you." He didn't really give her much choice.

She felt a kernel of fear bloom deep inside her. "Yes?" She tried hard not to let her trepidation show.

"You're the one feeding the prisoner, right?"

Talia brow furrowed. The fact she was the one should

have been obvious. Who else would be using these stairs carrying a tray? "I am."

"Good." The student smiled, which widened his narrow face, but the action didn't make her feel any better. He reached inside his vest and pulled out a small, filled bag. "How'd you like to earn these?" He opened the string on the bag and let her see the gems nestled inside.

"What do you want?" She liked this less and less.

The student's smile widened, his voice lowering to a bare whisper. "I'll give them to you for a small favor." He shook the bag so she could hear the gems rattle inside. "It'll be worth your while."

She opened her mouth, but he went on before she got a chance to say anything. "It's no big thing. And no one need ever know. All I want is for you to forget to take the prisoner his food for a few days. No big deal."

Talia stared at him with disbelief. He wanted her to do what? "I-I can't do that." She took a step back on the stairs. Lareen's words when she'd initially offered her the job whispered to her again in the back of her mind.

The student stepped up, not willing to let her go so easily. "Sure you can," he purred. "All you have to do is dump the food out somewhere then take the dishes back. No one would be the wiser."

She stared hard into the thin face and brown eyes before her and saw he was earnest about this. "Why? Why would you want me to do this?" She firmly kept the tray between them, not sure what he would do.

"The prisoner needs to be taught a lesson," he told her reasonably. "Since he's no longer the perfect pupil, it's an excellent time." The student sneered. "He thinks he's too good for us. Only consorts with teachers if anyone at all. And that's just because he's got a dragon, as if that beast could be considered one anyway. He's a disgrace, is what he is.

"And now, he's gone off and attacked Master Nertak and destroyed all our stores in the bargain. As if it was his place to determine how things should be done." He snorted. "The misfit needs to be shown his proper place."

"You want to do that by starving him?" The words were out of her mouth before she could stop them.

The student's grin turned cold. "It's a start."

"I'll-I'll have to think about it. Now please, I have things to do." She tried to cut past him again and this time he let her.

"You do that. Think about it hard."

Talia felt the hair on the back of her neck rise.

"And I wouldn't be telling anyone about this if I were you." Amused laughter followed her down the stairs. "I'll be seeing you soon."

She didn't look back.

By the time she reached the bottom of the stairs and turned into the hallway, her heart was hammering. Was the boy mad? Was she as well? She'd resolved nothing, only put it off. What was she going to do?

The regular uproar in the kitchen had died down by the time she made it back, the staff shutting things down for the night. Weighed down by her troubled thoughts, she put the empty tray in its regular slot then left without looking at or speaking to anyone.

She just couldn't believe it. She'd honestly thought Lareen's words were about her taking revenge on Kel if she wanted it. But maybe she heard it wrong—maybe Lareen really was talking about someone else wanting to do the squire and the dragon harm. Or could she have meant both at once? With a heavy spirit, she rose up the stairs toward her room.

To her chagrin and dismay, she found several of her

classmates and a few others she didn't know milling about her doorway. Sonsan spotted her first. "There she is!"

Daltan was there, hanging in the back as usual, and so were Yllin and Mandee. Why were they here?

"So, what happened?" Sonsan asked eagerly. "Surely something did this time." She was almost jumping with her excitement.

The eagerness she saw in most of their faces and the fact something did happen combined to make Talia feel ill. "Nothing. Nothing happened. Nothing is going to happen. Now leave me alone!" Roughly, she cut past them, ignoring their shocked expressions, and opened the door to her room. She slammed the door behind her and slipped the bar across it so they couldn't get inside. "Good night!"

Tears rose in her eyes as she flung herself on her bed, so she roughly wiped them away. Things were supposed to be getting better, not worse. What was she going to do?

No answers presented themselves to her. When the tears came again, she let them fall. After a while, she got up, cleaned her face and rubbed ointment on her aching arms. She opened the balcony doors to let in some air then tried to write another letter to her parents. The words became jumbled in her mind and she didn't know how to fix them. It wasn't long before she gave up and did nothing at all.

She was seriously thinking of just taking a bath and going to bed when a soft knock at her door bid for her attention. With dread coursing through her, she walked over to answer it. Removing the bar, she opened the door just a crack only to find a solemn-faced Mandee and Yllin standing there.

"Hi." She didn't look at them directly, recalling her

earlier behavior toward them.

"Hi," Mandee said quietly. "May we come in?"

She opened the door further. "Sure." She stepped out of the way so they could do so, keeping her gaze on the floor.

"Talia, are you all right? We were concerned about you." Mandee sounded unnaturally subdued.

"You haven't been acting like yourself." This came from Yllin. The anxiety on her face actually softened her usually severe features.

"I'm okay," she said. "I really didn't mean to be so rude to everyone. I've no excuse." She looked up at them and saw them trading glances.

"You know you can confide in us if something's wrong, don't you?" Mandee came up close. "Unlike some of the others, we don't think everything is everybody's business."

Talia saw the sincerity in Mandee's face and it made her want to cry. "I-I know that. I appreciate it, I really do." She looked down at the floor again. Should she tell them? Maybe they could help her figure out what to do. But if she did confide in them, how much should she tell them? How much was she willing to let anyone know? "I'm just not used to people wanting things from me this way. I don't understand why everyone is so obsessed with Kel. Can't they just leave him alone?"

"Sonsan and some of the others, they come from big cities," Yllin said. "Things are happening there all the time. Spectacles are a way of life," she added with a touch of disgust. "And at the moment, the squire is the biggest spectacle around."

"I guess we're all just looking for some excitement," Mandee admitted. "Studying all the time does get somewhat boring. And none of us were really thinking about what others felt."

Looking at it that way, she figured they were both right. Anything or anyone new back home was big news. The village would soak up anything the strangers said or did, the same as a dry cloth on water, and at times it was as if they could never get enough. Though she didn't like it, this was the same. Except for this time, she was in the thick of it. "But it still wouldn't explain why someone would want to starve him."

"What?"

Startled by the double exclamation, her head snapped up as she realized she inadvertently spoke her thoughts aloud.

"Talia, what aren't you telling us?" Mandee sat on the edge of the bed, looking grave.

She turned away, not sure how she would get out of this. A part of her insisted it'd be best if she at least told them some of what was going on. "The Administrator joked with me about the job being important because the wrong person might decide not to feed Kel for a few days—it never occurred to me someone might actually want to."

"Are you saying somebody asked you to do that?" Mandee actually appeared horrified.

Strangely, it made Talia feel a little better to see it. "Yes."

"Who?" Yllin sounded and looked angry, but kept her voice low.

"I don't know. I've not seen this student before." She hoped she never would again, but she knew better.

"Maybe the old fart put him up to it." Yllin's eyes closed to narrow slits.

Talia shook her head. "I don't think so. He just didn't..." Nertak just didn't look upset during Kel's trial.

He didn't even have the decency to look embarrassed at what he'd done, let alone look like someone who wanted revenge. If he'd pushed the point, she was sure he could have easily made Kel's punishment more severe than it ended up.

"Maybe you should tell someone in authority about this," Mandee suggested.

Talia tried hard to smile. "I'm sure I'm worrying over nothing. It was just strange, that's all." She had no proof. It would be her word against the student's. If the news of this got out, how much worse would things become?

"Well, if it happens again, you should go find a watcher immediately. I'm sure the Administrator wouldn't be happy about this at all." Yllin's expression showed it didn't sit well with her, either.

"I'm really sorry about before," Talia told them.

Mandee smiled. "Don't worry about it. I'd been way crankier myself. But do let us know if you need any help."

"Thanks. I will. But nothing will happen." She smiled back realizing for the first time how much these two very different girls were coming to mean to her. "You two are great."

"Yeah, and don't you forget it, either." Mandee stood up.

"Not that we'd ever let you," Yllin added as she headed toward the door.

Talia returned their smiles, more at ease than before. She thanked them for coming then bid them goodnight. With a lighter heart, she bathed, lathered her arms with salve then went to bed for the night.

Chapter Eleven

TRYING TO GET a jump on things, Talia rushed to get downstairs to do her morning errands. She entered the empty dining hall, then headed straight for the kitchen. The heavy scent of fresh baked muffins coiled about her as she opened the door and dived into the stifling heat. Some of the kitchen staff acknowledged her presence as she went by and she even traded a few good mornings.

She reached the back door and gratefully stepped outside, sweat already gathering at her armpits. Shivering at the sudden change in temperature, she found the barrels were already filled as she'd hoped they would be.

"All right, let's do this." She stepped forward and reached for the dolly to get started. The sun was just peeking up over the horizon as she struggled to get the dolly over the dew covered grass and make her way to the dragons' dormitory. Unlike before, the large doors to the habitat were closed. Not sure she was strong enough to open them, she pulled on the closest one, and to her amazement, it moved easily. More magic, she was sure.

With that done, she retook command of the dolly and dragged it and its cargo inside.

A solitary globe shone close to the ceiling of the dormitory, lighting the inside just enough to let her see by. Padding down the center of the broad aisle, she made her way to Clarence's stall. She peeked through the slats of his door and saw he was curled in upon himself, his eyes closed. She set down the barrel with care, trying not to wake him.

Good morning.

"Oh!" Talia glanced up, but Clarence's eyes were still closed. "Good morning."

Clarence said nothing else. She removed the dolly from beneath the barrel and left to get the rest of his breakfast.

When she returned, she found him exactly as she'd left him, but the first barrel was empty. She saw him open one crooked eye as she set the second barrel down. As she switched the dolly to the first one, he stood up and stretched, making the walls of his stall creak with strain. By the time she took the first empty barrel back and came for the second, the dragon was up and looking alert. As she set up the second barrel on the dolly, Clarence swung open his stall gate.

I must go make fertilizer now, he said. *I'll see you at lunchtime. Thank you for your efforts. I do appreciate them.*

Talia nodded, plastering herself and the dolly against the opposite stall's door as Clarence lumbered past. She watched him go, still surprised by the fact she'd held a conversation with a dragon. His immense size was enough of a marvel, but that he was also intelligent...

Pulling the dolly behind her once Clarence went out of sight, she passed a sleepy looking older man wearing a leather apron as he shuffled on in. The man returned her softly voiced greeting with a yawn. She assumed he must be the dormitory's keeper.

She ditched the dolly and the barrel in their niche by the kitchen door, then braved the heat and made her way out into the dining hall. She searched over the crowded room for her friends, hoping to catch sight of them before one of the watchers made her sit down. Yllin spotted her and waved her over.

Talia happily sat down. "Morning!"

Yllin and Mandee eagerly returned her greeting as did Daltan and a few of the others, though Sonsan seemed somewhat more subdued than usual. Talia also noticed she wasn't bombarded by questions, either, for which she was very grateful. She smiled, glancing at Yllin and Mandee, knowing they were likely responsible for the reprieve.

She rushed through her breakfast, listening to the conversations around her but not adding much herself. When she finished, she excused herself and headed for the kitchen to pick up Kel's tray. She figured she might just be able to get it delivered and make it back before everyone else was dismissed to go to class.

Leaving the drone of voices behind her, she headed for the stairs with the tray and followed the way to the roof. Once she reached Kel's door, she used her foot to knock as she'd done before. She was startled again when Kel opened the door almost immediately, as if he'd been waiting for her arrival just like the night before.

"Good morning." Kel gave her a bright smile and stepped aside so she could come in.

"Morning." She walked inside, questioning again why anyone would want him to go hungry. The rattle of Kel's chains echoed in the room as he followed behind her. She set his food on the table then took up the tray from the night before.

Talia hesitated as she turned to go, glancing at him from the corner of her eye, wondering what he'd say if she told him about what happened yesterday.

"Is something wrong?" Kel frowned lightly, studying her, a touch of apprehension in his voice.

She realized he'd caught her staring. "Ah, no. Sorry, just thinking about some lessons we're going to cover this morning. Nothing much."

His expression cleared. "I'd be happy to help you with any you might find difficult if you want. It's the least I could do."

She looked away, suddenly feeling guilty about having lied to him. "Thanks. I'll keep it in mind." She started toward the door. "I'll see you at lunch."

Kel followed her to the door and opened it for her. "I'll be here."

She felt his gaze on her as she headed for the stairs. She wasn't sure whether she should be flattered by the attention or worried. It could just be that Kel felt lonely, that it had nothing to do with her. He was probably just grateful to see a friendly face.

As she reached the stairs, however, all her previous thoughts evaporated. Dread filled her as she looked down, trying to see if anyone was waiting for her. She chided herself as she found the stairwell empty. She hoped it would remain that way.

Hurrying back, she actually made it to the dining hall before everyone was released for their walk through the garden. Happy she'd timed this well, she was even more so when she was able to find Mandee and Yllin and joined them for their daily walk.

Though Talia was on time to class, their teacher wasn't. After several minutes, a low buzz filled the room as everyone wondered where she was. Luckily, they didn't have to wait too long to find out.

"Sorry, class." Helyn rushed in, apologizing to them. "We had an impromptu meeting just after breakfast." She glanced over at them. "Most of the classes have been drafted into a project, ours included. Luckily, the first shift is going to be handled by one of the more advanced classes. Unfortunately, all the first year students get to take the second. It will be at ten."

Mar raised his hand. "What are we going to be doing?" A number of the other students held unhappy expressions on their faces, the last project they'd been assigned to weighing heavily on their minds. They all hoped this new project wouldn't involve worms.

"Well," Helyn replied, "for the next week or so, we'll be helping to clean out the burned store."

The cave! Talia had forgotten all about it. Clarence had breathed his strange liquid fire into it and caught everything inside ablaze. She remembered the huge number of goods she'd seen in there and felt a pang of responsibility at the fact all of it was destroyed.

"Everyone will be doing their part, so this shouldn't be too hard on anyone." Helyn smiled at them. "Now are there any questions regarding yesterday's reading assignment?"

THEIR CLASS'S TURN to go to the cave came upon them before long. Helyn herded the students outside and there they merged with a couple of other classes, including the one Mandee and Yllin belonged to.

Talia studied the cave entrance with apprehension as

they approached it. It was here Kel attempted to kill a man. Only Nertak's magic saved Kel from completing the crime. She secretly hoped Kel honestly did know about the old man's tricks, just as she was told, and expected him to escape his attacks. If it were true, maybe Kel didn't really try to murder the old man in his sleep after all.

Mops, brushes, and buckets filled with water lined the entrance of the cave. As each student got there, they were given one of each and told to go inside. Older students were coming out of the cave, carting off what was left of the shelves and goods once housed within. The stench of smoke and wet wood drifted to the line. Nertak stood off to the side watching them, looking depressed.

"Ugh, yuck!"

Talia took her bucket, mop, and brush and stepped forward in the line, not sure she really wanted to see what'd brought out such an unenthusiastic exclamation from those ahead of her.

The stench grew worse, invading her nostrils as she walked inside. Globes lit the interior of the cave, making it look enormous since it was empty. The walls, the ceiling, everything was covered in dark soot and grime. She was sure she'd not seen a more pitiful sight.

"We'll never get this cleaned," Yllin commented with a frown.

Mandee grinned at her. "It did get us out of geography though."

"I'm not sure this is better," Yllin mumbled back.

The teachers split the students into groups of three and sent them to different areas of the cave so they could start cleaning. For the first time, Talia got a good look at the room beyond where the counter used to sit. About a third as large as the main chamber, it opened up before her. A tub stod at one end, seemingly undisturbed by the fire. On the side by the entrance was something else not touched by the flames—two giant, concentric circles with strange runes carved into the floor between them, their indentations filled with a silvery looking metal. Talia and her friends were cleaning around it even as she pondered what it might be for. It wasn't long before the water in their buckets turned as dark as the rest of the burned-out cave.

After a couple of hours of cleaning, the teachers let them go so they could get themselves cleaned up for lunch. Her knees and arms hurt from scrubbing the floor and most everyone else didn't look any better. She glanced back as they left and sighed, as she realized they'd barely made a dent in the amount of work still needing to be done.

"That squire should be doing this, not us." This came from a husky boy in one of the other first-year classes. His clothes were covered in grime, the same as the rest of them. "It's his fault all this got burned." Though his tone was angry, he kept his voice low so none of the teachers would hear as they entered the school building.

"Yeah, it should be his punishment, not ours," piped in one of the other boys. "We had nothing to do with it." A number of the others nodded in quiet agreement. "They should have chained him in there."

Talia made herself climb the stairs faster despite her knees' protests. Now even more people would be angry with Kel. It didn't seem to matter to them that there was no way he could clean the mess on his own. Though couldn't the Administrator use magic to clean it? She didn't know much about the subject, but if it could keep water clean and warm, put light into dark rooms, and make a man disappear from where he's standing, surely it could be used to clean? Why make them all go through the trouble?

Nothing ever went around here as expected. You'd think she would be used to it by now.

Reaching her room, Talia bathed and redressed, but not before she put some salve on her aching knees. When she finally entered the dining hall, she found all her friends in a glum mood. Without much enthusiasm, she heard them grumble about the work they'd been tasked with even as she hurried through her meal so she could go on to complete her extra set of chores.

She barely paused in her efforts to deliver Clarence and Kel's food to say a word to either of them, but even doing so, she was still late for class.

Helyn took pity on them and didn't start any challenging subjects in the afternoon. Everyone was grateful.

At dinner, she didn't rush through her meal knowing she had more time, but still left before everyone else was dismissed. She fought with the dolly as she pulled it along for Clarence's feeding. The dragon was awake when she came in, one of his eyes staring right at her. She nodded a greeting to him when she saw him and set the barrel down. She promptly left to go get the next one. She returned with it not long after.

I take it the Thieves Guild's Master is having his cave cleaned? There seems to be a heavy scent of soot in the air today. Clarence arched a brow in her direction as he picked up the second barrel and grimaced as he swallowed its contents.

"Thieves Guild's Master?" Talia stared at the dragon in confusion. Did he mean the old man?

Yes. I believe the name he is currently going by is Nertak. It's the man Kel tried to punish, Clarence stated.

"Y—yes," she stuttered trying madly to fit all the pieces together. "We had a shift to clean the cave this morning. But you say the old man is a thief?"

Clarence finished his meal and lay down with a long stretch. *That is correct. And he's very good at it. Though aside from thievery, his skills range into spying, analysis, all the usual requirements for a master.* The dragon used one of his claws to pick at something stuck in his long teeth. *He gathers quite a large amount of information,; at times too much. That and his unusual hobbies got him sent out here rather than the capital. Though from the way he does business, you'd never know the difference. He is as much in control of his sources here as anywhere.*

Talia shook her head not sure if she should believe what she was hearing.

The little trick which almost got him killed and the extra entertainment he tries to gain for himself with his discounts are some of the many ways he tests students to find likely candidates for his guild. Clarence sounded almost bored as if he were speaking of something elementary. *I'm sure you've already been told not everyone will become a Dragon Knight. Sometimes, the younger they can be trained for other things, the better. All guilds have their uses.*

She nodded, only half listening to the rest of his words. Nertak really was a guild master, as LaSeren had said. Did others know? Somehow she doubted it. Then another thought occurred to her. "Clarence, is it okay for you to be telling me all this?"

The dragon shrugged his massive shoulders. *I'm telling you nothing which is not already there to be learned.*

She said nothing, not entirely sure what to make of his answer. She forced the dolly under the first barrel and took it away. Clarence was quiet when she came to retrieve the second.

As she retrieved Kel's meal, her conversation with Clarence was very prominent in her mind. Once she reached the roof, she knocked on the door with her foot but wasn't surprised this time when Kel almost immediately opened the door.

"Hi," he said brightly. "Come on in."

As she followed him into the room, she wondered if he ever took any of Nertak's tests and how he'd fared. She felt her cheeks grow warm as she realized if he had succeeded in them, then Nertak probably would have ended up with a total inventory of someone's underwear and more. She was sure if the female population of the school ever found out what the old man was up to, what Kel tried to do to him would be merciful compared to what they would do.

Without looking at him, she stepped up to the table and set his tray down then picked up the one she brought earlier.

"Talia?"

She stopped in mid-turn, hearing a strange note of uncertainty in Kel's voice.

"Could I ask a couple of favors of you?" He didn't look at her directly.

"I—I guess so," she responded. She felt her curiosity rise at what he might need her for.

"Wait here a moment, please?" He didn't wait for her to answer but shuffled off down a small passage she hadn't noticed before.

As she waited for him, she turned to watch the moving mechanism behind the glass at the far wall. The ticking sounds, which seemed muted and barely noticeable when she'd come before, were more distinct and clear this time and resonated in the silence. How could Kel stand them, day after day, hour after hour? Did the Administrator consider this before meting out his punishment? It would drive Talia mad if she had to put up with it.

She swiftly shoved those thoughts aside as Kel reentered the room. He'd brought back a small pouch with him. She was sure it held gems inside. She felt a chill course down her back remembering another favor which was recently asked of her with the same type of reward.

"I know it's a lot to ask," Kel looked away as he spoke, hesitating. "But, I'd really appreciate it if you would oil Clarence's skin beneath the scales for me once a week. I'll pay you whatever you want for the trouble." He sent a furtive glance in her direction. "His skin gets very dry, and it itches him badly, but he's too proud to ask anyone else to do it for him since it's my job." His words picked up speed as if it was hard for him to say. "I'd hate to add neglect to all the other things I've put him through lately. I think he trusts you, so he'd allow it." Kel held the pouch out to her expectantly. "It would mean a lot to me." His blue-eyed gaze sought her own.

Why did people think they continuously needed to pay her to get her to do things? Didn't anyone believe in just asking around here? She tried not to let her thoughts show on her face. "I'll do it." She made no move to reach for the bag. "Where do I get the oil?"

Kel's face broke into a bright, relieved smile which made him look younger than his years. He took a step toward her, his chains' rattle echoing in the room. "Everything you'll need is already in his stall. He'll show you where. It'll take a few hours, but you don't have to do it all at once." He looked away. "I really do appreciate this." He set the pouch on the tray she was carrying.

"It really isn't necessary," Talia said.

"I have plenty," he insisted, "and I know I'm putting you out. You're kinder to me than I probably deserve." His expression was earnest.

She looked away. All this time, she'd felt more as if she

owed him, not the other way around. Plus how could he afford it? Didn't Lareen already charge him a ridiculous amount of gems for the damage he'd caused? "All right, if it's what you want. I'll help Clarence tomorrow." She turned to go.

He didn't stop her. "Thank you."

She hesitated before reaching the door. "What was the other favor?" she asked.

"Ah," Kel hesitated again, "would you mind delivering this for me as well?"

Talia turned around and saw him pull a letter from a shelf.

"If it's too awkward, I'll understand." He held out the letter to her and she saw Nertak's name scrawled on the outside of it.

She couldn't help but be curious as to what it said. "No, I'll do it."

He set it on the tray beside the bag. "Thanks. I don't expect a reply."

She nodded in acknowledgment then left. She stopped on the roof long enough to tuck the pouch and letter into her tunic then went on down the stairs.

She wondered where she might find the old man. Since the cave was being cleaned, she was sure he was no longer staying there. Not positive how she might find out, she decided to ask one of the kitchen staff.

"The old goat? He's up in the silver room. Living it up, too, I bet." The woman grinned. "I think the Administrator wanted him close by, so she could make sure he didn't get himself into any more trouble."

"Thanks."

Making her way somewhat hesitantly to the fourth floor, Talia headed toward the silver-covered door. She glanced around to make sure no one was looking, then rapped lightly on the door.

A minute later, Nertak opened it. "Well, well, isn't this a surprise." He gave her one of his disrobing looks. "Didn't expect to have any visitors, and definitely not you."

She sighed softly, reminding herself all she was going to do was deliver the letter and go. "Here, I was asked to give you this." She took the letter out and handed it to him.

Nertak's brow rose as he took the letter in hand. "Hmm, interesting. Did you read it?"

"What?" She felt her indignation rise. "No, of course not!"

"Pity." He gazed at her seriously. "You should never pass up an opportunity to get information if you can help it. You don't know when it might come in handy."

She could only stare, realizing he was serious.

"Come on in."

"But..."

"What, afraid I'll bite?" He laughed at her expression. "You think I'd be fool enough to dare incur the wrath of that young man again?" He was still chuckling softly to himself as Talia hurried on in and he closed the door.

As with the Administrator's apartment, the door led into a hallway with three other rooms. Nertak opened the letter and walked into what should be the office, leaving her to follow.

"This is interesting," Nertak said as he read through the one-page letter. "Could have sworn he didn't have it in him."

"Didn't have what?" She asked this, half distracted, the office's contents surprising her. Rather than looking bare and holding someone temporarily, the room appeared to have been in use for some time. Papers, parchments, books, all covered several tall bookshelves. File cabinets filled to overflowing covered all of one wall.

"Why the mettle to admit he's wrong, that's what." He gave her a half grin. "I don't know if you've noticed, but our friend here is just a bit on the hardheaded side. Heck, you'd have to be to put up with what he does, just to keep trying to prove he's right. Not that Clarence is any less stubborn, mind you." He tapped the envelope softly against his chin. "Seems like he's finally realized he's been pushing too hard. Must admit he's not shown it before. We took all his hard work for granted, if you know what I mean. Guess even he's got limits, though he'd never admit it. Wait," he said grinning and holding up the letter, "I guess he just did."

Talia shook her head not understanding the old man at all. "So you're not angry?"

"Angry? What for? I've needed something to pump some adrenaline through me for a while. This backwater is occasionally a little too sedate for me. Not enough challenge, but still nice enough in its way. Lareen does keep me amused on occasion. Finding out what she's up to is harder than discovering most countries' best-kept secrets." He laughed. "She has her plans for Kel and Clarence. This much I know. We all try to help as we can, and I like the boy. He has potential. Shoot, if he'd been even half-inclined, I'd have made him part of my guild. But he's too honest for his own good really." He laughed again and plopped down on the chair behind the loaded desk. Digging through a couple of drawers, he finally found a blank sheet of paper. Dipping a pen in a half-dried inkwell, he swiftly wrote down a few lines.

While he did so, Talia continued to look around the room and all the papers strewn about. "The silver and bronze positions aren't really empty as they say, are they?"

Nertak looked up, a bright gleam in his eye. "Ah, caught that did you? Well, let's just say it's more beneficial not to have it advertised. Besides, Lareen works hard as a mule, though anyone not in the know wouldn't think so." He left her to think about this as he finished his letter.

She just couldn't understand how so many things were not as they seemed. Almost as if everything here were backward.

"Ah, here you go. If you wouldn't mind delivering this to him next time you see him I'd be much obliged." He took a ring from a hidden pocket and placed it over the overlap of the folded paper. After a moment, he lifted it off, leaving a thin wax seal on the letter. "Just in case you do decide to get curious." He smiled. "Think you can find a way around it?"

She shook her head. "I wouldn't think of trying to open it."

Nertak's head drooped, looking disappointed. "Why she's perpetually picking honest ones to be taught here is beyond me."

Chapter Twelve

TALIA LEFT NERTAK'S office, her mind full of questions and half-troubling thoughts. Was what Nertak said true? That Lareen picked the students to be taught at the school? Though a number of guilds did test prospective apprentices before signing the final paperwork, nothing akin to that happened for her to come here. If anything, she was only tested once all that was done. She'd assumed part of it was due to the fact they had all sorts of positions to fill, but Nertak's words seemed to imply otherwise. But if this was true, how or what did Lareen do to decide she was worthy to come here? More magic?

Not getting many answers and only more questions, she entered her room and closed the door. She put the pouch of jewels Kel gave her in a drawer, not looking at the contents inside. She set the sealed letter on top of her dresser.

When Talia reached Clarence's stall the next morning

with his breakfast, the dragon barely stirred. By the time she returned with the second barrel, however, the first was empty. As she set the second one down, Clarence roused himself enough to unenthusiastically reach over and consume its contents after bidding her good morning.

As the dragon ate and she fixed the dolly to the empty barrel, she peeked through the slats of the stall door to get a look inside. Against the far corner, she spotted four massive chests made of dark wood and bound in iron. Three shelves sat a few feet above them, holding big jugs as well as five or six jars and folded cloths. Rather than inquire about them, she said nothing, deciding for the time being to keep to herself the knowledge of the task she'd agreed to. Leaving the dragon, she took the barrel back to where it belonged.

She dropped off Nertak's letter to Kel with his breakfast. Though she was curious as to what it said, she didn't linger other than to note his look of shock as she handed it to him.

As on the day before, her class took the ten o'clock shift to clean Nertak's cave. Being there reminded her again of the things Clarence told her about the old man. She still found it hard to reconcile the information with what she'd seen of the man himself, though the visit the night before revealed a side of him she was sure most never saw. Maybe it was part of what made him good at his job.

Walking into the cave with buckets, mops, and brushes, it was immediately obvious the place was cleaner than when they left it the day before. She was only too glad to see it. By the time they were done, it was cleaner still.

Lunchtime came and went, and she rushed through it

to go feed her charges. Though she half hoped he would, Kel didn't mention the contents of his letter, though he did seem in high spirits. In the evening, she took Kel and Clarence their dinners then returned to the dragon dormitory to fulfill her promise to Kel.

Globe lights lit the spacious interior, making it seem as bright as day. Quietly walking down the hay-strewn path, she hoped Kel was right and Clarence would let her help him.

"Good evening, Clarence," she said.

Surprised by her voice, the cross-eyed dragon lifted his head and stared at her curiously.

Talia?

"Are you ready to get your skin oiled?" she asked him. She made no move to open the stall door, knowing it wouldn't be up to her.

What? His large eyes blinked at her several times. She'd not seen the dragon caught so off guard before. *How would you know about that? You've not been here long enough for those lessons.*

It was hard to keep from smiling. "I do have a scroll the Administrator gave me during my entry interview, and Kel told me as well. He asked if I would do this for him."

He did, did he? An undercurrent of doubt colored his tone.

"Yes," she told him. "He was very concerned about it. He also said you were too full of pride to ask for it to be done."

Humph! Dark smoke snorted out of his nostrils. *I wouldn't go quite so far. If anyone here is full of pride, he'd do well to look at himself. I'm actually quite astounded he'd ask anyone for help.* His askew gaze sharpened. *He is compensating you for this, yes?*

She thought of telling him no, but from his tone, she

could tell he'd be offended if Kel hadn't. "I told him he didn't have to, but he insisted."

Clarence nodded with satisfaction. *Good.*

"Is it all right for me to do it then?" She found herself a little excited at the prospect.

Yes, by all means. Please do come in. With one large, taloned claw, Clarence opened the gate to his stall so she could slip inside. *I presume you haven't done this before.*

Talia was forced to look up, not having been this close to the dragon in some time. It was amazing, and a little frightening, that he could be so large. "No, I haven't. But I learn fast."

All right. If you go to the shelves in the back, you'll find a stack of cloths. Beneath them, you'll find a strange looking mitten. You'll want to take it. He pointed at the shelves then at the chest on the far left. *In that chest, you'll find a rose-colored bottle. There should also be a shallow metal basin there. You'll need to pour some of the contents of the bottle into the basin then dip the mitten into it. It's not the typical oil I use, but I deserve a treat.*

Nodding, she hurried to the back of the stall and retrieved everything he mentioned. The rose-colored bottle sat in the chest, surrounded by other strange looking bottles. It was large and heavy, but at the same time appeared delicate. With great care, she poured some of its contents into the basin. The soft scent of wildflowers tickled her nose as a dense liquid poured out.

After setting the bottle back and closing the chest, she grabbed the mitten and dipped it into the sweet-smelling liquid. Though the outside of the glove absorbed the scented oil, her hand stayed dry inside it.

All right, start with my left and work your way up. Clarence stretched out his front left claw and placed it out before her. *What you want to do is lift each scale, carefully, and apply the oil from the root over the skin, covering everything thoroughly before going on to the next.*

She nodded; the procedure sounded simple enough, and it coincided nicely with what she'd read in her paper. Stepping forward, she studied his relaxed claws and gently touched the cuticle of one of them with the mitten. After thoroughly covering them all with the oil, she gingerly lifted the small scales around each deadly nail and worked on the skin beneath.

Though he stared at her work intently, Clarence said nothing as she toiled on. As she lifted some of the larger scales, she saw that what Kel said was true—Clarence's skin did look incredibly dry. In many places, she found it had the texture of old parchment and drank up whatever oil she spread on it like wood. She wondered why it would be this way, and even more what had the dragons done about it before their pact with the humans, but didn't dare ask.

After she finished with his left forearm, Clarence presented his right without a word. By the time she finished it, as well as his two back legs, the dragon was no longer watching her but instead set his head down in the hay, his eyes closed.

Talia decided to take it as a good sign.

While resoaking the mitten, she rested for a minute before carefully scrambling onto Clarence's back. The work was slow and tiring, but it excited her all the same. She was helping a dragon. Not only that, she was helping a friend, one whom she'd done wrong but who didn't hold it against her.

Out of nowhere, a memory of her mother and how she hummed whenever she knit or did certain chores came to her.

Her chest tightened. She missed her mother terribly. Before she knew it, Talia was humming, too, enjoying the bittersweet emotion of the recollection.

She faltered a few minutes later when an unexpected thrum rumbled beneath her. Startled, she took hold of a couple of Clarence's scales, not sure what was happening. The thrumming rose and fell with Clarence's breathing. After a few moments, she smiled as she realized this must be a dragon's version of a cat's contented purr. The thrumming coursed into her, vibrating through her body into her bones. Her smile grew bigger as she hummed to herself again and got back to work.

By the time she was through, her body ached everywhere, but she felt strangely at ease and satisfied. Briefly, she wondered if Kel felt this way when he did this for Clarence. Slipping quietly off the scaled body, she cleaned up as silently as she could then tiptoed out of the stall, leaving the dragon sleeping.

Talia stretched with a yawn as she made it outdoors, incredibly sleepy all of a sudden. The night sky was clear, the stars shining brightly within it. She watched them for a minute or two before going on her way.

She was heading for the entrance on the far right of the school when she realized the balconies above her were all dark. Frowning, she tried to guess what time it was, not having thought of it until now. It was probably quite late. How long had she been out here?

She quickened her pace, sure it was past curfew. She hoped they hadn't locked the doors and she could still sneak back inside. If she was fortunate, maybe she could even make it to her room without being seen.

She was reaching for the door, not sure what she'd do if she found it locked, when a cowled figure stepped out of the shadows. Before she could say anything, a pale and bony hand reached out from within the deep folds of the dark robe, the palm up as if wanting something.

Talia stared at the silent figure with rising apprehension. This rapidly turned to fear as she realized the hand wasn't just unnaturally thin but had no flesh at all. She took an astonished step back, tripped, and fell.

The cowled figure said nothing even as it took a step forward, its hand outstretched.

Her chest tight and breathing ragged, she fought to make her brain work so she could attempt to figure out what the creature wanted. Was this the reason they instituted curfew here? But surely if it were dangerous to be outside after dark, someone would have mentioned it. Wouldn't they?

The figure took another step, towering over her.

Going with the first thing which popped into her head, Talia reached inside her pouch and took out one of her gems.

Shakily, she tossed it toward the outstretched hand.

Her aim was off, but the hand reached out for it. Before the thin fingers could close over it, however, the jewel bounced off the bones and fell into the grass.

"Damn, I never could grab anything with this thing."

Talia felt goosebumps roll through her even as she felt suddenly giddy. She recognized the disgruntled voice.

Stooping to pick up the fallen gem, the figure pulled back the cloak's deep cowl to reveal the Administrator's face. Lareen glanced over at her and grinned. "Got you good, didn't I?"

All Talia could do was nod. Her heart was still thumping as if a rushing waterfall were inside her.

After Lareen retrieved the fallen gem, she reached down to help Talia to her feet. "You do realize it's past curfew, don't you?" Lareen asked her.

"Uh, yes, ma'am," Talia answered, her gaze on the skeletal hand, which was connected to a set of wires the

Administrator could manipulate to give it the semblance of life. "I got caught up in something and didn't realize how late it was. It won't happen again."

Lareen nodded. "How are things going for you? Any problems with Clarence or Kel?"

"Everything's fine." She hoped Lareen wouldn't notice how she answered her just a bit too fast. She still felt she needed to keep the matter of the bribe over Kel's food to herself.

"I'm glad to hear it." Lareen pulled the cowl back over her head. It hid her face completely. "Well, you've paid, so you can go on in. I have other targets to hit tonight."

Talia shivered, not envying others the experience. "Good night." Without another word, she opened the door and hurried inside. It wasn't until she rushed upstairs, and her room was in sight, that it occurred to her to wonder who else the Administrator might be expecting to have stayed out past curfew.

Luckily, she met no one else. Taking a quick bath in the dark, she changed and went immediately to bed.

The next morning, she was satisfied to note both Clarence and Kel seemed in high spirits. It probably meant her efforts last night were at least satisfactory. She decided not to mention to either of them her strange encounter with the Administrator.

Nertak's cave was almost shining clean when her class finished their shift. The old man came inside as they were getting ready to file out, and after some serious scrutiny, gave them all a pleased, boyish smile. Unfortunately, this somewhat soured things for Yllin. She wasn't happy something she'd done made the letch happy. Mandee teased her about it all through lunch.

Overall, things were working out well. Or so Talia thought until she reached the stairwell leading from the roof on her way back from delivering Kel's dinner. The narrow-faced youth who'd questioned her a few days before was back.

"Evening." The student stood in the middle of the stairwell making it plain he wasn't going to let her go past.

She slowed to a stop on the stairs, not wanting to get too close. "Evening."

Smiling a thin smile, the boy nodded at her greeting then pulled out a small bag from his vest. "I've come to get your answer on my question of the other night."

Talia tensed, knowing what her answer was but not sure what he'd do once he heard it. Fervently, she reminded herself if he tried to come near her, she could throw the tray in his face and possibly shove him down after it, or at least be able to pull out her dagger.

"I won't do it." She hoped she didn't sound as frightened as she felt.

The student's face sobered. "I'm so very sorry to hear you say so."

Her grip on the tray turned her knuckles white. "I've given you my answer, now please get out of my way or I'll have to call for a watcher."

The student stared at her face, her stance, then slowly nodded. "You're a gutsy one, aren't you?" He shrugged. "I'll move. But this isn't over yet." His thin-lipped grin grew nasty. With a slight bow in her direction, he turned around and headed back down the stairs.

She stared after him until he was out of sight, then sat down heavily on the stairs where she stood, her legs giving out from under her. Things went better than she could have ever wished. It'd been too easy. She sighed, hoping, though she knew it was futile, the student's last words were more out of bravado than anything else. She was sure he wouldn't let go of this quite yet.

After she was sure her legs would hold her again, Talia gingerly got up and went back to the kitchen. When she met Mandee and Yllin not long after, she decided not to mention what happened.

By the next morning, she'd almost managed to put the incident behind her. After a couple of more days, she barely thought about it. She'd had some luck after all.

She fed Clarence for the morning then finished her own breakfast. Telling her friends goodbye, she made her way to the kitchen to pick up Kel's tray.

On her way back through the dining hall to the main hallway and the stairs, she took the shortest route between the tables as she normally did. She wove her way between students and watchers, trying her best to keep the tray out of harm's way.

She made it halfway down the second set of tables when a booted foot abruptly shot out in front of her. Seeing it too late to stop, she tripped and went down. Her tray clattered to the floor with a loud crash. Stinging pain rose up her palms as she tried to keep her face from smacking the marble floor. Warm gruel rained around her even as laughter and startled cries overrode the usual din.

"Are you all right?" One of the watchers knelt down beside her to help her up.

She winced, her knees and hands smarting from where they'd hit the floor. Embarrassed, she stammered out an answer. "I'm-I'm all right, ma'am." She felt warm goo slide down the back of her neck.

Two more watchers converged on her and stooped to gather up the fallen tray and bowl as well as clean up the mess around them. People from the two tables to either side looked on in curiosity or annoyance as they cleaned off splatters of goo from their clothes.

Talia's embarrassment turned to anger though, as she

suddenly glimpsed a grinning face she recognized not far from where she stood. It was the boy from the stairwell. So this was what he meant. Well, he would have to do better than that if he thought he would stop her from delivering Kel his meal.

As she glared at the grinning student, one of the watchers tried to wipe off some of the gruel splattered on her hair and shirt. She was half tempted to point an accusing finger at the fiend and tell the watchers she'd been tripped on purpose, but didn't. Though she was sure he was behind it, she had no way of proving it. It'd be her word against his.

Smoldering inside, she retrieved her things from the watchers and returned to the kitchen to get Kel more food. It only made her more angry as she realized the delay would also make her late to class for sure.

Her elbow twinged as she set the tray back into its usual spot. Massaging it, she looked around wondering whom she should ask for more gruel for Kel. As she looked around, she noticed several of the kitchen staff stop working and stare openly at her. Great. The one closest to her turned and called out toward the back of the room. "Tula! You're needed over here."

This made things even more wonderful. Pretty soon everyone in the school would know what happened today. Her anger rose another notch.

"Aleere, what are you—" Tula's question stumbled to a halt as she caught sight of Talia. "What in the world happened to you?"

She felt her face grow hot even as she felt the eyes of everyone in the kitchen studying her. "I tripped." She didn't look Tula in the eye.

"Did you now?"

"Yes. I'm sorry." Her mouth tasted foul.

"Don't trouble yourself about it," Tula said. "We can fix this soon enough." She pointed at a couple of the women standing about and issued orders for clean dishes and more food. Her piercing gaze then returned to Talia. "Did you hurt yourself? Do you need to go see LaSeren?"

She speedily shook her head no, no longer trusting herself to speak. She must keep this fiasco to a minimum of fuss. Already she dreaded the number of questions she was likely to get from her friends once it got around that she'd provided this morning's entertainment.

Tula nodded slowly, studying her up and down. "Here, let me get a rag so we can clean the rest of this mess off you."

Talia put up quietly with the older woman's ministrations, wondering how bad she really looked. It was all that idiot's fault. It was so *stupid*.

Five minutes later, she was cleaner and held a reloaded tray. Thanking Tula, but still not looking her in the eye, she stepped back out into the dining hall. She gave the table with the boy who'd tripped her a wide berth, as she rushed out of the room.

By the time she made her way to the roof, her knees were complaining angrily. The palms of her hands were still red and stung.

Kel opened the door after she knocked, but his welcoming smile faltered as he took a good look at her. "Talia?"

Not wanting to talk about it, she sighed and cut past him. "I just had an accident. No big deal. I'm not hurt, just embarrassed." She could have added a few other bits but kept them to herself. She set his tray on the table and immediately picked up the one from the night before. She headed back toward the open door, barely sparing him a glance. "I'm running late. I'll see you at lunch."

On her way back, she made a detour to her room and changed clothes and applied salve to her aching parts. She then hurried down to the kitchen and after that ran most of the way to class.

Helyn raised an eyebrow as she rushed in and sat down, but said nothing. Talia was quite happy with that.

Much to her relief, it seemed her classmates hadn't heard of the incident, or if they had, didn't think enough of it to make much of it. No one asked her any questions as they made their way to Nertak's cave for their shift. Since the cave was now clean, the work groups were drafted to recreate the shelving for the place. In this, at least, she possessed some experience thanks to her father and did better at it than a lot of the others.

For the next three days, whenever she took food to Kel and while people were still in the dining hall, she made sure to take a different route each time. She kept her eyes peeled for the boy she knew, not wanting a repeat performance of the tumble she'd taken thanks to him.

On the fourth morning, however, her luck ran out. She'd almost reached the end of the last table before the doors when she was hit from the side. She bounced off the back of a rising student as she tried desperately to keep her balance, and crashed to the floor.

"Oh, gosh! I'm so sorry!" A girl Talia didn't recognize stood up. "Let me help you." She reached down for her and grabbed Talia's arm.

Talia snapped her head around as the girl squeezed until it hurt. "You're hurting me."

The blond-haired girl bent down close. "I know," she whispered, a gleeful look on her face. "But you brought it on yourself." She half yanked her to her feet.

Talia tore her arm from her grip as soon as she could

stand and stared. She was one of them. One of the ones wanting to hurt Kel. "You witch!" She shook where she stood, rage welling up inside her. Warm gruel dripped from her arms and back.

"Is everyone all right?" Two watchers hurried over to them.

The blonde's face changed as if a lever were pulled. Gone was the gleeful, menacing look—all they could see was an embarrassed older student. "It's all my fault. I wasn't watching where I was going and bumped into her."

The only thing Talia could do was glare at her in anger. She knew if she said anything now, she'd look spiteful. Oh, how they'd planned this. She glanced around and noticed a sprinkling of older students at the tables at this end of the room. It wasn't normal. The age groups tended to cluster, not pepper the area like this. Most of those she saw were looking in her direction, barely hidden grins on their faces. She even spotted the one who initially offered her the bribe in the stairwell, and he was grinning from ear to ear. Who did they think they were?

Feeling as if she might explode, Talia forced herself to look away and got down on her hands and knees to clean up the mess they helped her make.

"I really am sorry."

She didn't give the girl the satisfaction of even glancing up. If people like her made up the guild, what was the point? The dishes clattered on the tray as she dumped them onto it. The two watchers helped her with the mess and she soon was on her way back to the kitchen. She kept her gaze centered on the floor even as she felt the burning gazes of other students stick to her as they saw her food-covered form walk past. No way the story wouldn't make it around this time. She was positive her tormentors would make sure of it. It made her want to scream.

Talia looked at no one as she entered the kitchen and set the tray back in its niche. She waited patiently for the inevitable. It didn't take long.

"Tula!"

"Yes, what is it now?" The thickly accented voice carried over from the back. "By the gods!"

Talia's hands coiled into fists at her side. "I'm sorry. But I had another accident." She didn't glance up to look at the older woman though she could feel her presence nearby.

"Again, you say?" Tula's voice was low.

She gritted her teeth as she forced herself to lie. "Yes."

"Still, I have a problem believing you could be so clumsy," Tula remarked.

Talia said nothing.

"Well, let's get you cleaned up as best we can then." Her voice rose as she sent out orders to those closest to them in the room.

With quiet sufferance, Talia stood still as Tula wiped Kel's breakfast from her hair and clothes.

"You know, child, if you have troubles, there are those who would help you." Tula's whisper was very close.

By this point, her anger had cooled a little. "I—I know." Though she would appreciate the help, she wasn't sure it would make any difference. She could prove nothing. It was still her word against theirs. How did you even go about stopping people from hating another for no reason? She'd thought those belonging to the guild would be better than this. It was a miracle they'd lasted this long since they weren't. But some were worthwhile, she reminded herself. Still, how would the guild guard against those who didn't hold its best interests at heart?

No, she would do this on her own. She just needed to

try harder. She knew what she was up against now.

Luckily, Tula said nothing else. As soon as the tray was readied again, Talia thanked her then went on her way. She was still trying to figure out some kind of strategy to outsmart those other students when she reached Kel's door.

"Good morning."

Despite herself, she looked up at his cheery greeting and saw his expression sour from a ready smile to a deep frown.

Frowning herself as she saw it, she brushed on past him. "What happened to you?" Kel's concerned question followed after her even as the rattle of chains echoed in the room.

"I was clumsy. I fell down." She set the tray down a little too hard on the table.

"But didn't this—"

She cut him off. "I'm *very* clumsy." She didn't look at him as she shifted to pick up last night's tray. Grabbing it, she turned to go.

Kel blocked her path. "Are you sure that's all it was?" His bright eyes searched her face for an answer.

Talia looked away. "Sure. What else could it be?" She risked a glance at him and saw his expression fill with doubt, but he said nothing. She wondered if he was aware there were people who disliked him. She decided to leave before she was tempted to ask. "I'll see you later." He didn't try to stop her this time.

She was extremely late for class, having stopped by her room to change before returning to the kitchen, but Helyn made no comment. When the group was released to go work on Nertak's cave, however, she was immediately surrounded by several of her classmates on the way there.

"What happened to you this morning?" Sonsan asked eagerly. "We all saw you going back to the kitchen covered in goo."

"You weren't hurt, were you?" Daltan's quiet voice whispered to her from the back.

Talia felt some of her previous anger returning but tried her best to hold it back. "I had an accident. That's all. It was quite embarrassing and I'd really rather not talk about it."

"Yes, but someone told us this wasn't the first time."

She usually liked Sonsan well enough, but at the moment she wished she'd just shut up. "It's not easy carrying a heavy tray with people in your way." She walked a little faster.

The questions came at her again as Mandee and Yllin joined her at the cave. She repeated her excuses. She saw Mandee frown, her face less cheerful than usual. When they split off into groups, Mandee made sure to steer theirs far to the back.

"Talia, it's going around that this is the second time this has happened to you in less than a week," Yllin spoke softly as if afraid someone else might still overhear them.

"Does this have something to do with the guy on the stairs?" Mandee stared at her worriedly.

Talia bit the inside of her cheek, not expecting them to put the incidents together. "It—it doesn't matter. Don't worry about me, please."

"But this is serious!" Mandee insisted.

She shook her head. "No, it's just embarrassing and annoying. They'll figure out sooner or later they're not going to win."

"Either that or they'll come up with something more drastic," Yllin added.

Talia shuddered. She couldn't afford to think that way.

"I'll be fine."

Mandee grabbed her arm. "Look, if anything worse happens, promise me you'll tell us. Promise me you'll let someone help." Her eyes implored her to do it.

She shuddered again. "I—I promise." Though what anyone could do if things got worse, she didn't know.

She was still worrying about it, turning it in her mind, when she took Clarence his midday meal.

Ah, there you are.

"Hi, Clarence." She gave him a small smile as she set the barrel before his stall.

Is all well with you? He asked as he reached for his lunch.

"Sure." Her brow furrowed, wondering what prompted him to ask.

Clarence's askew eyes stared at her where she stood. *It would seem Kel is concerned about your welfare. And since he brought it up, it does seem rather strange to me you've scented yourself with food twice in a week's time.*

She looked away. "I-I told him it was nothing. I tripped, that's all."

I see.

Talia got the feeling maybe he did, and it worried her. "I'd better go get the rest of your meal."

The dragon's mouth pulled back with a look of distaste. *If you must.*

She was grateful when Clarence didn't bring the subject back up on her return.

Chapter Thirteen

THE FOLLOWING MORNING, Talia stepped into the kitchen to pick up Kel's tray. She chose a way to leave the dining hall at random and ambled past the tables, looking for any unfriendly faces in the crowd. Most of all, she kept her attention on the floor and kept an eye on people's feet as she went past.

On the last table, on her left, she spotted an older student sitting amidst a group of younger ones. She saw him turn to look in her direction then swiftly glance away. She slowed. She could turn back and choose to go another way, but it might bring up unwanted questions later. She'd go on ahead, and if he were stupid enough to try for her, he would be the one wearing Kel's breakfast this morning, not her.

She started forward, moving to keep as far away from him as possible when a watcher showed up beside the boy. "I believe you forgot to eat some of this." The short man dumped a large serving of hotcakes on the startled student's plate.

"What? But I—"

Talia slipped on past. She couldn't believe her luck.

Happily, she hurried out the door and continued on her way.

When two watchers just happened to be strolling by her side as she walked past a suspicious table the next morning, however, she got the idea something more than luck was at work. Even while she ate her own meals, she noticed the watchers seemed to be concentrating around certain individuals and making them eat more than was their wont.

When these seeming incongruities repeated themselves on the third morning, she was sure it was deliberate. But she didn't understand it. Did Mandee and Yllin tell someone she was in trouble? Surely they would have told her if they did, wouldn't they? The only other people she thought even suspected something were Clarence, Tula, and Kel. The dragon and his rider were in isolation so it couldn't have been them. This only left the head cook. Did she put the watchers up to this? The thought was disturbing though at the same time somewhat reassuring. Lareen previously told her Tula possessed many skills. Talia found her spirits lightening for the rest of the day.

ᚱᚷᚱᚱᚷᚱᚱᚷᚱ

"GOOD EVENING, CLARENCE. Ready to be oiled today?" She approached the dragon's stall, having come there directly after delivering Kel's meal.

Oh, yes. If you'd be so kind. Clarence flicked his tail and popped the stall door open.

"Which oil do you want this time?"

The dragon raised a claw and tapped his nose

thoughtfully as he considered the matter. *Oh, let's do the evergreen one today. It's the large jug there at the end.*

Nodding, she retrieved the thick bottle as well as the other things she'd need.

Clarence stretched out in his stall in delighted anticipation.

As she started her work on his left side, he let out a

contented sigh. Talia found a small grin tugging at the corner of her mouth as he wallowed in the sensations. She could really come to enjoy doing this for him.

Almost two hours later, she had worked her way up on to his back. His pleased thrumming waxed and waned as he breathed. She'd just reached the high ridge on his back when Clarence's whole body shifted abruptly. With a yelp, she grabbed hold of the nearest set of scales as she felt herself slipping. The dragon's head snapped up and was staring off in the direction of the main building.

"Clarence, wha—?" She saw the dragon's eyes narrow to mere slits while several puffs of smoke cleared his nostrils in annoyance.

The damn fool! He puffed smoke one last time, then settled back down.

She scrambled off his back, confused by the outburst. "What happened? Did I hurt you?"

Clarence opened up one dark eye to look at her. *No. You've done nothing.* He suddenly flinched. It made no sense to her. *It's the idiotic human I was a fool ever to agree to partner myself with.*

"You mean Kel?" She felt her heart grow cold dread. "Is something wrong?"

He winced. *Oh, yes, though you wouldn't think so from his tone.* The dragon sighed with disgust. *I volunteered to come to his aid, and he refused me. Tells me I would be breaking the ruling set by the tribunal if I were to go to him. He insists the consequences would be direr than the beating if I did. He's a fool, and I am twice that for listening to him.*

Clarence flinched again.

"Kel's being beaten?" The satisfaction she felt earlier at having thwarted the older students turned to bile in her throat. "You might not be able to leave, but I can." She threw the soaked glove on the floor and reached for her knife. Yllin was right; since they were thwarted, the bullies had gone on to worse things. This was all her fault.

No! Clarence's tail moved to block her path. *You mustn't.*

"But—" She turned around to stare at him, not understanding how he could just sit there and let Kel be hurt when he was quite capable of trying to do something about it.

No. If you thought he overreacted at what Nertak did, what do you think he will do if one of those incompetents hurts you when you come to try and rescue him?

His words gave her pause. "Surely, surely he, he wouldn't—" But she wasn't sure what he would do. Even now, she still didn't entirely understand Kel's previous actions. Yet if she did nothing ... "Then you have to go. Help him, please!"

I will not. The dragon looked away. *Let him learn from his own foolishness, from his stubborn pride.*

She stared at the dragon, not sure she heard him right. Clarence was refusing to help him? Only because Kel asked him not to and he was angry with him for it? They were both insane. She turned away, leaped over Clarence's tail, and rushed for the stall door.

Faster than she thought possible, Clarence twisted in the stall and grabbed her with one of his massive claws. *You mustn't.* He lifted her off the ground.

"Clarence, let me go! Let me go!" Angry and anxious,

she pounded on his scales to no avail. Her hands tingled with pain as they slammed into the smooth, green surfaces. The giant claw didn't hold her too tightly, but she still wasn't able to wiggle free.

Talia, I'm sorry. But I can't let you. Please understand.

"I don't!" She struggled in his grip until the rest of her strength was gone. Tears of frustration and fury rose hot in her eyes. She averted her face so he wouldn't see them.

They were mad, mad.

Many long minutes later, Clarence gently set her down. *They're gone. You can go see him now. Help him if he'll let you. He's in pain.* The dragon didn't look at her.

She ran from the stall with all the speed she could muster. She sprinted into the main building and headed up the closest set of stairs. Her side ached, and her lungs felt on fire by the time she reached the roof. Barely pausing to catch her breath, she stumbled into the squire's room.

"Kel?" Her voice rose in near panic as she saw the state of the place. Dishes, books, and clothes were strewn everywhere, not all of them intact. Her gaze scoured the room for him, yet she didn't see him. She started across to go to the area in the back.

A soft moan whispered from the other side of the low table. She made for it instead. "Kel!"

The squire lay crumpled on the floor, his shirt torn and his face bloody. His body was bruised as well as his face, one eye already starting to swell shut. Wincing at the painful sight before her, Talia knelt down beside him.

"How could they do this?" A flare of fury rose inside her, but she tried to push it back. Kel needed her now. There'd be time for the other later.

She gently reached out to touch him, hoping he wasn't even more hurt than he seemed. "Kel, can you hear me?"

Gingerly, she turned him onto his back. His face grimaced in pain, his one good eye fluttered open.

"Ta—Talia?" His gaze looked glazed and unfocused.

"Yes, it's me. Can you stay awake? I've got to go for some help." She studied his face, not sure he understood her and felt reluctant to leave him though she knew she'd have no choice.

"No." He reached out for her as she moved to stand. "Please don't." He looked at her, his eye pleading, even as his face shone with pain.

"You're hurt. You could be bleeding inside." She tried to stand again, but he kept his hold on her. She froze as the movement made him gasp. "Please, Kel, you need help!"

"No."

"Clarence is right—you are a fool!"

Instead of making him angry, he gave her a small smile. It made his bruised face appear even more grisly than before.

She didn't know whether to laugh or cry.

"Will you help me to the bed?" he asked her quietly.

Talia glanced over to the rumpled bed then back at Kel. "I could just leave you here and forget about you." She was annoyed at him. It was stupid, but she was anyway. Why wouldn't he let her fetch LaSeren? Why did he have to be so stubborn about everything?

He let her go. "If you want..."

She looked down at him and scowled, realizing he was serious. He was insane! He could die if she left him.

Cursing silently at mad squires and stubborn dragons, she got up and righted the mattress on the bed before coming back and carefully grabbing his arm and putting it around her neck. Slowly, she helped him stand.

Kel gasped in pain as she accidentally bumped his side.

She glanced at his pale face, her worry back full force, but said nothing. The sound of his rattling chains echoed about them as she helped him shuffle over to the bed. She felt her anger rising again as she heard them, knowing the manacles would have been a significant impediment for him during the struggle.

Kel sighed with relief as she set him down on the soft mattress.

She didn't like the ashen look on his face beneath the growing bruises. "Kel, I really should—"

"No!" His gaze darted to her, catching her where she stood. "Please. It would only make things worse." She could tell he was having a hard time breathing. "I'll be all right."

Talia studied him, not believing him at all. How could things get worse? She was tempted to go get help whether he wanted it or not. Once Lareen found out about what'd been done to him, those idiots would be made to pay.

His eye focused on the set look on her face. "You can't— tell anyone about this."

"I have to. They can't be allowed to get away with this!" She scowled down at him.

Kel slowly shook his head. "It'll only make things worse."

"You're not making any sense! How would it do that? They should pay for what they've done!"

"Many already resent me," he said as a matter of fact. "And my actions lately haven't helped." He struggled to speak clearly. "Accusing them of attacking me wouldn't improve anything. Besides, most would think I deserved it." His eye closed. "Maybe I do."

She stared at him in shock. How could he say that? No one deserved this. Not him, not even those who'd done this to him. "You're wrong."

He opened his eye to look at her again. "Please, it's what I want. And this should have satisfied them. They won't try it again."

She wasn't so sure.

Half-heartedly, Kel wiped away some of the blood drying at the edge of his mouth. "Curfew will be here soon. You should go."

Talia didn't move.

"You can—check on me in the morning. I won't be going anywhere." He tried hard to smile.

It hurt to see it. "I should at least clean you up a little." It was the only thing she could come up with to say.

He stared at her for a long moment then finally nodded.

Talia turned away, looking around for anything she could use. Eventually, she spotted a washcloth in a corner and after filling up one of his buckets with water from the tub, she brought both back and set them down next to the narrow bed. Sitting on the edge of it, she dipped the washcloth in the clean, warm water then gently used it to wipe his face.

Kel closed his eye under her ministrations, and his breathing eased a little. "Thank you."

She said nothing just curiously studied his face as she washed it. Why did so many things about him make such little sense to her? Was he trying to punish himself for what he did to Nertak? Didn't he feel the Administrator's punishment was enough? Lareen thought he was isolated due to his strange situation, but what if he was doing it on purpose? Would she grow to resent him as the others did because of it? Would she think he was putting on airs? The idea felt alien to her yet at the same time it felt right. She just didn't understand it.

By the time she finished with his face, she could tell

Kel had fallen asleep. She got up quietly and covered him with one of the discarded blankets. As silently as she could, she cleaned up his blood from the floor and tried to straighten his room.

It was getting late, and she knew it, but she couldn't bring herself to leave. She looked at his sleeping face—his cuts and bruises swollen and angry. If she left, she knew she would betray him and go get help, even if it meant getting caught after curfew. There was no option for her but to stay.

Kel's light globes dimmed but didn't go out, so she kept working. Not too many of his things were damaged and only one or two broken; most were just scattered everywhere. She was amazed at the number of books Kel seemed to own, yet more so at the large variety of topics they covered—dragon maintenance, law, the seven general rules of magic, architecture, politics, a little bit of almost everything. Was all this part of what made Lareen think Kel would make a good Judge? Or was it more due to the fact he kept himself so isolated?

As she put his clothes back into the drawers, she ran across a jar which resembled the one Yllin and Mandee gave her for her aches and pains. Opening it, she took a sniff of the contents inside and knew from the pungent odor they were the same.

She glanced back in Kel's direction and frowned. This would help his wounds, wouldn't it? Should she wake him so he could use it or dare she apply it to him on her own? After some thought, she decided to let him rest and do it herself. Since he didn't bring up the salve before, it was possible that if she asked him, he would refuse to use it. She wasn't going to take the chance.

Sitting down on the edge of the bed, she dipped her fingers into the thick mixture and gently spread it over his bruised face. His brow furrowed as her fingers touched his cheek, but almost instantly relaxed again.

After making sure she covered his face, especially around his swollen eye, she slowly pulled back his blanket and exposed his chest and the torn shirt barely covering it. Knowing it was beyond repair, she removed her knife and carefully cut out what was left of it.

She inhaled sharply as she spotted the rapidly darkening bruises on his right side. Were they so cruel as to kick him? She spread the salve carefully there working her way inwards. She felt Kel stiffen beneath her hand a couple of times. Each time she held her breath waiting to see if he would awaken, not sure what he'd make of her ministrations and not really wanting to find out. Luckily, he never did.

Once she was through, Talia covered him again. She studied his face and thought his color looked better. Maybe Kel was right; maybe he would be okay.

Suddenly bone-weary, she sat down on the floor after she put everything away and leaned her head on her arms against the bed. Her intention was just to watch him for a few minutes to make sure he was fine then make her way downstairs to try and sneak back into her room without being caught. She never got that far.

Chapter Fourteen

TALIA'S EYES FLUTTERED open as her hand reached back to rub at her neck. A dull ache rose into her head and formed a faint headache. She supposed it's what you got when you let yourself sleep propped up through the night.

Through the night...

With a jerk, she sat up straight and glanced around her. Oh, no. She'd fallen asleep. She didn't leave Kel's room last night as she planned. The globes were on at full power so she knew it was morning. Kel...

Her head snapped around to look in the bed. Kel lay there just as she'd left him, covered and unmoving. As she saw his chest gently rise and fall in sleep, she allowed herself to believe he was all right. His eye had turned purple and black but didn't look as swollen as the night before.

She started to relax, then felt another jolt of panic. What time was it? How long had she slept? She looked at the niche on the wall for his clock, then remembered it was one of the few things Kel's attackers had actually destroyed. She sucked in a breath through her teeth, making a thin, hissing sound, and jumped to her feet. If she'd overslept, if she'd missed breakfast, people would start wondering where she was. If Mandee or Yllin got worried enough, it would all quickly get out of hand.

Casting a darting glance at Kel to reassure herself he was still okay, she ran for the door. Oh, please, please, of all the mornings she could have chosen to oversleep!

As she came out onto the roof, she gazed to the east and saw the sun was definitely above the horizon. It was later than first light, so she was without a doubt running behind, but by how much?

She took the stairwell almost recklessly to make her way to the fourth floor. She instantly slowed as she came to the landing, spotting people walking about. Most of them looked to be on their way downstairs. She dared breathe a little easier, realizing that while she was late, she was not horribly so. Relieved, she followed them to the nearest stairwell and went down to her room.

Checking the time once she got there, she took a super quick bath then redressed. She almost flew down the stairs to make her way to the dining hall. She stopped at the large doors to catch her breath then calmly walked inside. A watcher on the other side raised a brow as she slipped in. Talia gave the woman her best "oops" smile then headed toward the nearest table.

"Talia!"

Heads turned at the frantic call two rows over. Grimacing, she changed directions and hurried to join her friends.

"Where have you been?" Mandee's worried gaze clung to her as she sat down. Yllin only stared at her silently with a deep frown. "Did you have trouble?"

"No, no." She shook her head, aware of the other ears around them. "I just worked too hard last night. I overslept. Sorry I worried you."

One of the watchers set a full plate before her. She picked up her fork to eat. "I've got to hurry. I'm really late." Not looking at either of them, she shoved her food into her mouth. She'd have to make this up to them later.

When she was finally able to put enough away to satisfy the watchers, she bid her friends goodbye and almost ran on her way to the kitchen. She was way behind. Helyn would not be pleased with her today. But she also wanted to hurry and check on Kel again.

Returning the greetings thrown in her direction as she dashed through the kitchen, she went out the back door. She barely paused for breath before she grabbed the dolly from its resting place and hitched it to one of the barrels then heaved it as quickly as she could over the uneven terrain.

With beads of perspiration running down the side of her face, Talia stopped in front of Clarence's stall, almost dumping the barrel over in her hurry.

You're late.

"I know!" She didn't even spare the dragon a glance as she pulled the dolly out from beneath the barrel and rocketed with it back out of the dormitory.

She frowned halfway back to the kitchen, thinking Clarence's words weren't exactly what she would have hoped for. As she came back, she remembered how angry and frustrated she'd been with him the night before. Clarence's attitude wasn't what she would have expected from what little she knew about the dragon's partnership. She was honestly hard-pressed to say whether she thought Clarence cared for Kel at all.

As she wheeled the second barrel in and moved to pick up the first, she hesitated a moment, waiting to see if he'd say anything, but he didn't. With a kernel of ire rising inside her, she hefted the empty barrel up on the dolly and left.

When she returned, she found Clarence playing with the second barrel, twirling it lightly in his claws. As soon as she came to a stop, he set it down on the dolly for her. *So...* He said amiably. *Am I to expect you this evening to finish oiling my skin?*

Talia closed her mouth hard to keep in the retort which popped into her mind. Didn't he care one bit about Kel? "Aren't you even going to *ask me*?" She almost shook as she struggled to keep her voice level.

Ask you what? The dragon's skewed eyes turned to gaze at her, an arched brow raised high.

She forced herself to take a couple of deep breaths, so she could resist the urge to yell at him. "About your partner. About Kel."

Oh. Clarence's tail flicked hay into the air even as he turned from her. *I sense he's alive. It's all I really need to know.*

"You!" Why were the two of them so thoroughly exasperating? "You're no better than he is." Angry, and not trusting herself not to say something she'd later regret, she roughly grabbed the dolly and its cargo and left.

Still steaming when she got back to the rear of the kitchen, she smacked the barrel against the stone wall. Why'd she ever bother to help either of them? They deserved each other. The stubborn idiots. She stomped through the kitchen, not looking at anyone, and picked up Kel's tray. The dining hall beyond was empty except for a few stragglers. She was only too glad of it. If she'd seen the face of one of those bullies just then, she would have...

When she reached the roof, she didn't knock on Kel's door, but instead hooked the tray against her hip and used her loose hand to open it quietly. Glancing toward his bed, she saw he was still sleeping. She considered waking him, and forcing him to eat, just to spite him and his dragon, but as she came closer and studied his tranquil face her anger evaporated. Looking at his bruises and the peace he carried in sleep, she couldn't bring herself to do it. The rest would probably be better for him anyway.

As quietly as she could, she set the tray of food on the table then picked up the dishes from the night before. Luckily, none of them were broken, which at least meant she wouldn't have to come up with a lie for the kitchen staff.

With a last, worried glance in his direction, she left him, closing the door softly behind her.

As fast as she could, she made her way to the kitchen to drop off the dishes, then made her way to class.

ฅฅฅฅฅ

"SOMETHING'S HAPPENED, HASN'T it?" Mandee stuck close to Talia as she and Yllin followed her to their work area in Nertak's cave.

Talia found it suddenly hard to swallow. This moment had lain heavily in her mind for most of the morning. "I can't go into it, but yes. And I need your help."

"What did they do?" Yllin's eyes flashed fire.

She shook her head. "I can't tell you. But don't worry; it wasn't to me. And I do really need your help."

Mandee and Yllin glanced at one another. "What do

you need us to do?"

Talia stared at them fondly, her heart telling her she didn't deserve them, while at the same time it filled with joy at the fact they were there. "I've got to finish a favor for Clarence, so I'm going to be tied up tonight. What I... what I'd like for you to do for me, if you can, is to stick around the staircase leading to the roof. And if... and if anyone tries to go up there, inform a watcher and have them go up there with you."

Mandee and Yllin traded glances again.

She could see the questions building up inside them. "Please don't ask me. I don't want to lie to you. But will you do this for me?" She implored them with her eyes, needing this badly. She just couldn't take the chance the bullies who'd hurt Kel might return. She hoped with her friends being there as possible witnesses, it would dissuade anyone from trying anything.

Mandee gave her a sudden, bright smile. "We'll do it." Yllin nodded her assent. "Sooner or later though, we expect you to tell us what this is all about."

Their ready acceptance made her feel warm all over. "I will, I swear it. This means a lot and I won't forget it. Thank you!" It was all she could do to stop herself from giving each of them a heartfelt hug.

ᚱᚷᛏᚱᚷᛏᚱᚷᛏ

THE WARM FEELING Mandee and Yllin gave Talia stayed with her all through lunch. With a light heart, she grabbed the dolly and its barrel to trundle over to the dragon dormitory. Without a word, she set the barrel down before Clarence's stall and left to retrieve the second one.

I hope I didn't offend you this morning. It wasn't my intention to do so.

She stopped and glanced over her shoulder at the dragon, who was eyeing her shyly over the closed stall door. She sighed lightly. "No, no offense was taken."

Clarence nodded. *He's been awake for about an hour. Thanks to your ministrations, he's in better health than he would have been otherwise.* His mental tone changed slightly. *Though it would have been no better than he deserved.*

She frowned at his words, her ire rising despite herself. "Why do you say such things?"

A puff of smoke curled up from Clarence's nostrils. *Because he is a stubborn fool.*

"Then why did you pair yourself to him? It was your choice, wasn't it?"

Clarence's askew eyes focused on her for a long moment then looked away. *Perhaps I'm as big a fool as he is.*

She waited to see if he would say more, but he didn't. After another moment, she turned around and went back the way she came.

When she returned, the dragon said nothing, but took the second barrel and emptied its contents into his mouth. After returning from taking back the first, she found Clarence with his back to her and his eyes closed as if he were asleep.

She tried to be as quiet as possible as she retrieved the last barrel and left.

Disposing of the barrel and dolly, she went through the kitchen and picked up Kel's meal. She took the stairs quickly, finding herself eager to see him since he was awake. Depending on his condition, she was already bracing herself to bring up the subject of getting LaSeren to come to see him and the arguments he was inevitably going to bring up against it.

When she reached his door, she quietly let herself in. She hesitated halfway in the doorway at the unexpected sight which greeted her.

Kel was half sitting up on his bed, one hand over his bruised side. A strange light emanated from his palm and spread out over his skin. She stared at this in wonder.

After almost a full minute, the light dimmed. The bruises which were so dark and prominent on his ribs appeared less severe than before. Breathing heavily, Kel fell back onto the bed.

She continued standing at the door and blinked several times, not sure if she should believe what she just saw or not. "How...?"

He glanced over in surprise. "Talia."

"How did you? What did you?" She took a few steps into the room then stopped. "Are you all right?"

His cheeks were flushed and perspiration covered a lot of him. Still, his color was better and both his eyes were open, the bruising on the swollen one almost gone. He sat up, but not without effort. "It was just a healing spell. They're not difficult, just draining."

A healing spell? Was Kel a wizard as well as a squire? She felt a shiver course down her spine.

"I really could use something to eat." His clear gaze locked onto her own as if unsure of what she would do next.

She glanced away, and after taking a hard swallow, forced herself to come closer. As she spotted the dishes she'd left there in the morning, she noticed they were all empty. She frowned slightly, remembering Clarence saying Kel hadn't been up long. Did magic take so much energy, or was it the healing itself? How badly was he hurt? Her worry overrode her uneasiness. "Are you really all right?"

He gave her a half smile. "Don't let it trouble you." His chains rattled as he swung his legs out of the bed.

Talia set the tray on the table then pulled it closer so he could easily reach it. As soon as it was close enough, he grabbed the bowl of gruel and shoved in spoonful after spoonful as if he were starving.

She watched this with a strange fascination, even as she picked up the morning's tray. "Are... are you a wizard?" She remembered the strange, cowled men who'd come to rid the school of the worms. Goosebumps rose on her arms.

Kel stopped in mid swallow, looked up at her then laughed. The sound was clean and free. She was inwardly glad to hear it, even if it was at her expense.

He shook his head. "No, I'm not a wizard. Though I've been told I've got the aptitude for it." He studied her, his eyes amused. "Simple spells are part of the fourth year's curriculum. I've dabbled in it some since then, but not enough to be considered a true mage." He gave her another half smile.

"Oh."

As Kel resumed eating, she turned to go. She almost made it to the door when he spoke again.

"By the way, thank you."

She didn't turn around, but only nodded, her cheeks feeling warm.

ᚱᚲᚱᚲᚱᚲ

WHEN SHE RETURNED with his dinner in the evening, she found almost all trace of his injuries gone.

"Good evening."

"Good evening." Talia stared at her charge from the corner of her eye, marveling at his recovery. If she hadn't been there after the others had left and seen his condition with her own eyes, she wouldn't have guessed anything untoward had ever happened to him.

"Any trouble today?"

The question caught her off guard. "No. Should there have been?"

Kel looked away from her questioning stare and shook his head. "No. Just curious."

She felt momentarily tempted to press him on why he expected her to have trouble but didn't.

"I think Clarence is worried about you for some reason." Though his tone was light as he said this, his expression was deadly serious.

"He said something to you about it?" she asked.

"No, but every once in a while I can pick up things. You seem to have been on his mind an awful lot today."

Talia looked away, sure worry for her had nothing to do with what Clarence might have been thinking. "Is this something you get as part of the bonding?" What little she knew about the subject from Clarence went through her mind. Hadn't the dragon said the two of them didn't share a true joining?

"Yes."

She detected something hidden in his soft reply but couldn't quite identify it.

"It's the reason some people don't enter the lottery," he added.

"What do you mean?" She found herself suddenly curious. She glanced over at him, but he wasn't looking at her anymore.

"To win the lottery means you will be bound to a

dragon. This bonding is more than just being together. It's... a sharing of minds, of everything that makes you who you are. It's a commitment you make for life." His blue eyes turned to look at her. "Some people don't want to share so much of themselves with another."

"Did you?" The question was out of her mouth before she could stop herself.

He looked away again. "Actually, no. I didn't contemplate participating once I found out everything that was involved. I—" Whatever he'd been about to say died away. "I'm pretty sure Clarence didn't intend to participate, either. But Lareen can be quite persuasive when she puts her mind to it." He gave her a sad smile. "She honestly thought the bond would overcome Clarence's handicaps. She thinks there's more to him than meets the eye, and I agree."

"But something happened?" She didn't dare breathe as she waited to see if he would answer.

Kel's reply was almost too soft to be heard. "It... didn't work out like it was supposed to. Our minds didn't fully open themselves to one another as they should have. No one knows what went wrong. So we practice, we struggle, hoping we can somehow overcome whatever's in the way and make it work." He gave a long, tired sigh. "If we could merge, truly merge, Clarence would be able to use my eyes to fly, use my own equilibrium. But though I think at him until I'm sure my brain will explode, nothing changes."

Memories flashed through her mind of the different times she'd seen Kel after he'd been riding with Clarence. So often he'd looked flushed as if he'd been exerting himself. Before, she'd assumed it was just part of surviving Clarence's erratic flights. Now it seemed as if it might be due to something else. No wonder he'd snapped. Who could constantly live under that kind of pressure? Even as she realized this, another memory surfaced, one of Kel and Clarence leaping over Lareen in a precise and graceful arc. "But, but you have done it."

He stared back at her in confusion. "What are you talking about?"

Talia glanced away from his intense gaze. "On... on the day of the attack. When you were chasing Nertak. The Administrator got in your way. Yet you and Clarence leaped right over her. It was a clean jump, a perfect landing. Cl— Clarence told me your anger caught him off guard so he wasn't been able to stop himself from doing what you wanted."

Kel stared past her, his brow furrowing with concentration. "I don't remember. Everything was happening so fast at that point." His face suddenly cleared, and he smiled brightly at her. "Maybe there's still hope."

She found herself mirroring his smile, though in the end, she wasn't really sure how her revelation would help them. But she did enjoy seeing him happy. Maybe, just maybe, it would mean the episode with Nertak might have a positive side. "I hope so." She truly did. "I've got to go."

A small grin still on his face, Kel nodded to her, his gaze far away. Talia left.

The rest of the day passed by swiftly. On her way back from taking Kel his evening meal, she spotted Mandee and Yllin waiting for her at the bottom of the roof's stairwell.

"Thank you for coming." She gave both of them a shy smile.

"No problem." Mandee grinned back. "We're happy to help."

"There's a teacher in the room three doors down, so we won't have any problems getting help if we need it." Yllin looked even more somber than usual.

"I owe you both for this," Talia said, her heart full of emotion. "I won't forget it."

"Don't worry about it. Just go do what you need to get done and leave this to us," Mandee told her. Yllin concurred.

Staring at them gratefully one last time, she turned away and headed off toward the kitchen. Once she dropped off Kel's dishes, she headed out the back to make her way over to the dragons' habitat.

Talia walked up to Clarence's stall, where she was sure the dragon was waiting for her eagerly. She couldn't have been more wrong. As she opened the door to the stall, she found Clarence lying on the ground, his eyes closed, thin streams of smoke rising from his nostrils. From the tense posture of his shoulders and flank, she knew he wasn't sleeping. Had something else happened? "Clarence?"

Please, just get on with it. I'm not in the mood for conversation.

Troubled by the irritation which came across in his thoughts, she walked softly over to the chests to retrieve what she would need. "Have I... have I done something wrong?" Clarence seemed fine when she brought him his dinner. She'd rushed through as usual but promised him she'd come back to finish rubbing his skin. He'd seemed quite happy at the prospect. What changed?

You told him. His tone was heavy and accusing as if those three words should have cleared up everything. A large puff of smoke rose from his snout.

She stared at him, having no idea what he was talking about. "I don't understand."

One of his purple eyes opened and stared at her

accusingly. *You told him of the leap.*

Was that all? What was wrong with that? "I thought you'd be happy about it. Doesn't it mean you and Kel might still be able to make this work? That you might get your joining to be complete and pass the final test?"

Clarence closed his eye and turned his face away. He said nothing.

She waited, but he didn't say anything else. Frowning, she decided not to press him further, though she still didn't understand. Quietly, she dipped the mitten in the oil and picked up where she left off the day before.

Though she could tell he enjoyed her ministrations, he didn't relax beneath her as he'd done before. She didn't dare hum and disturb the silence he wove about them.

After she was finished, she wished Clarence good night but got no response.

Did Kel realize Clarence didn't want the joining to succeed? Had the dragon changed his mind after being talked into it by Lareen? If so, why didn't he just say so? There was so much she didn't know about the subject; she wasn't sure what to think.

As she was about to reenter the main building, a form stepped out of the shadows. Not sure if this was yet another plan of the older classmen, Talia instinctively reached for her dagger. She relaxed, however, as she saw it was only the Administrator. "Evening, ma'am."

"Evening. Did I startle you?" Lareen asked.

"Just a little," she admitted sheepishly.

"How is Kel today?"

Her heart thumped a little harder at the question, but she speedily told herself it didn't mean anything. No one knew what had happened except for those involved, and none of them were talking. "He's fine."

Lareen's gaze locked with her own. "His wounds are

healed?" she asked quietly.

It took a moment for Talia to be able to answer. "Yes... He took care of them himself."

The Administrator nodded, satisfied. "I would have preferred for LaSeren to have looked after him right away, but I suppose this way keeps things quiet. I applaud you for your discretion these last few weeks."

Talia felt cold. "How did you...?"

Lareen smiled. "Know?" Her eyes grew serious. "There's very little which happens in this school I don't know about. Nertak's not the only one who's an expert at gathering information. Those involved have had notations put on their records. It will make a difference later when they are placed."

Talia shook her head, not sure she understood. "Why didn't you stop them? Punish them? Wasn't what they did wrong?"

Lareen half turned from her, her expression veiled. "No matter how much we may want to protect our children from harm or keep them from seeing the harsh ways of the world, we can't. In the long run, it would hurt them more than help. They have to learn to cope. They have to learn to grow. We can only watch them, guide them if we can. We interfere when we must, but some things must play out on their own.

And we learn a lot more about them this way." She turned to face her again. "Can you understand?"

Talia stood dumbstruck, not sure what to say.

"Think about it. It might be important one day." Then, the Administrator stepped back into the shadows and disappeared.

Talia stared toward where she'd gone for several minutes, before finally shaking her head and heading back inside.

Reentering the main building, she hurried to the top floor where she'd left her friends. She found Mandee and Yllin sitting on the bottom steps of the stairwell leading to the roof, reading.

"Any problems?" She studied them minutely, more worried about them doing this than she was willing to admit. She couldn't help but wonder if the Administrator knew she'd asked them to be here. Why wouldn't she? She seemed to know so much already.

Both girls looked up as she spoke. "No, everything's been quiet." Mandee yawned then stretched where she sat.

Talia heard herself exhale with relief. "I'm glad."

"So are we," Yllin told her.

Mandee laughed. "Yllin's been just a little nervous about this."

The somber girl sent her friend a scathing look. "As if I've been the only one."

"I didn't say I wasn't," Mandee countered with a grin.

"And I'm more than happy nothing happened at all."

"Do we need to do this again tomorrow?" Yllin asked.

"No," Talia said. "I've finished what I needed to do, so I can handle it until next week."

"What? You mean you're going to sit here every day alone?" Mandee's expression turned serious.

She looked away. "No. Ah, Kel offered once to help me with my studies. I-I thought I'd take him up on it. I doubt anyone would try anything if he's not alone."

Both of her friends didn't look too sure about her logic but they didn't argue.

CLARENCE TREATED TALIA civilly though a little coldly the next day, making no mention of what they'd talked about the day before. She was tempted to ask questions anyway, but held back, not wanting to alienate herself any further. Whatever was going on between him and Kel really wasn't any of her business anyway. They were free to keep things from each other as they pleased.

She was still trying to convince herself of this when she picked up her books in the evening and made her way to the roof. A little nervous, not only from the possibility of another attack but mostly because she'd never gathered the courage to tell him she was coming, she hesitated in front of Kel's door before finally working herself up enough to knock.

Unlike other times, Kel's door didn't fly open before her. Instead, she heard the muted sounds of his chains rattling as he made his way to the door.

"Who's there?" he asked from the other side.

It made her feel strangely better the squire was being cautious. "It's Talia."

She heard something scrape behind the door and after a few seconds, it swung inwards. Kel's surprised face greeted her from the other side.

"Hi. Um, you said you'd be willing to help me with my studies?" she said tentatively. "Is the offer still open?" Though she didn't understand it, she felt her heart started beating faster.

Kel's expression instantly brightened. "Sure! Please, come on in." He stepped out of the way of the door. As soon as she came inside, he closed it and placed a large bar across it.

She almost smiled. With it there, it was doubtful the

bullies would be able to make their way in here unwanted or unnoticed.

"Take a seat." Kel pointed toward one of the cushions in the room. "What do you need help with?"

She pulled out several papers with math problems they wrote down in class. "I'm not entirely sure what our teacher wants us to do here."

"All right." He nodded and took the pages from her. After looking them over, he explained what she already knew was required. To her surprise, though, he double-checked her answers once she did them, and even found a couple of errors for her. He didn't press or push her as she worked, seemingly content just to sit there and watch her. She wasn't so sure she could have been as accommodating.

"Kel, can I ask you a question?"

The squire looked up at her. "Sure."

She glanced away, not able to meet his trusting, blue-eyed gaze. "You mentioned before you thought Clarence was more than he seemed. What did you mean?"

It was his turn to look away. "It's a lot of little details, really. Things which don't add up." He shrugged. "At first I thought I was making too much of things until I found out Lareen thought the same thing."

Talia sat still, waiting for him to go on. Kel distractedly pushed away the hair from his face before speaking again.

She thought he looked tense.

"From talking to some of the staff, I learned Clarence has been here at the school as long as anyone can remember.

"Due to the pact drawn between humans and dragons, dragons have to give part of their time to the guild but otherwise spend their time with their own kind. Yet Clarence was here—even before he volunteered to become part of the lottery, which is usually the only time they come here. Plus he's here alone." He shifted where he sat.

"When other dragons are here, he's pleasant enough to them, but he doesn't seem to care one way or the other whether he spends any time with them or not.

"At first I thought he was an outcast and was here for refuge due to his infirmities, but most dragons don't treat him any differently than they do any others."

He shook his head. "It got me more and more curious. So, I sneaked in a few times to the dragon dormitory and spoke to him; I found Clarence incredibly intelligent and learned. Once, I couldn't stand not knowing anymore and asked him why he was here, and all he'd say was that he found humans intriguing."

Kel sighed. "His coloring is of a young dragon's, one barely fifty years old, but his skin says he's much older. Then there's the fact most dragons with a handicap don't hatch." He sent her a sideways glance as if to gauge how she was taking all this. "A hatchling has to fight his way out of the egg on his own. The process does something to them, something necessary for them to stay alive. Though many have tried, no one has been able to determine whether it's a chemical, or magical process, or both. The guild has attempted to help dragons before who couldn't break through the shell, but though they got them out, they all died anyway. There was nothing they could do. In the histories, they mention all the different things they've tried to overcome this, but they've not come close to keeping one from dying. It's a battle the hatchlings have to fight on their own, and despite his unusual handicaps, Clarence won and lived."

Kel stood up and slowly paced before her, his chains rattling in the silence. "As you can see, there isn't much there. But still..."

Talia nodded to herself. What the squire said made sense. She'd also noticed the fact about Clarence's skin but didn't know enough about dragons to realize what it told her. Did Clarence have something to hide? It would definitely explain some of his strange reactions to her telling Kel about the jump. But it still didn't clarify everything. He'd agreed to the joining after all. Surely he'd known what it would mean.

"It's getting late." He turned to face her. "You should probably get back before I get you into trouble."

She watched him and wondered at the strange, intent way he was looking at her. Talia quickly stood and looked elsewhere. "Okay. Thanks." She gathered her things.

Kel walked with her to the door. Quietly, he removed the bar and opened the door only a crack to take a look outside. Satisfied it was safe, he opened the door wide. "If you need any more help, I'll be happy to lend a hand." The words came easily, his expression normal. Whatever was bothering him about her was gone.

"I appreciate it. Thanks." Giving him a half smile, she took her leave.

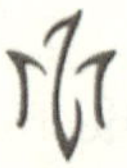

Chapter Fifteen

OVER THE NEXT several days, things returned to their normal routine. Goods started to arrive seemingly from nowhere to restock Nertak's rebuilt store. Construction of the shelves was finished, so the different shifts were put to work learning about inventory management and placement as Nertak bossed them around so everything could be arranged correctly.

Three days later, most of the student body was settling down to dinner when the Administrator's voice boomed across the hall.

"Listen up, everyone. I have good news!" Lareen climbed nimbly up on her chair so she could be seen. "Nertak's shop is about finished. So as a reward for all your hard work, classes will be suspended next week for a six-day carnival." She threw her arms wide. "There'll be free games and fun for everyone!"

A roaring cheer broke like a wave across the room. Students hammered their fists on the table as hoot calls filled the air.

Lareen flashed the assembly a brilliant smile before

moving to reseat herself and resume her dinner.

After a couple of minutes, the furor died down to a loud buzz, excitement filling the air.

"A carnival." Mandee's face glowed. "I've heard some of the other students talk about them before. Supposedly they're like nothing we've ever experienced. They're supposed to make the festivals back at our homes amount to nothing at all."

Talia felt her own excitement flashing through her. She enjoyed the carnivals every year—the games, the food, the contests. If this was going to be even better...

A grin was tugging at the edge of her mouth when a sobering thought came to mind. This carnival was a reward for all their hard work, yet the work wouldn't have been necessary if not for what Kel and Clarence had done. So in a way, they had them to thank for this. Yet she doubted very much anyone would. Worse, she realized their penance wouldn't be over until after the carnival itself was done. So the two of them wouldn't get to participate at all. She didn't feel quite so excited anymore.

Over the next two days, as the time for the carnival approached, a thrum seemed to fill any room where students gathered together. Everyone's mood was lighter. The air felt as if a much-needed storm were gathering.

Through it all, though, Talia couldn't bring herself to mention the fact the carnival was coming to either Clarence or Kel. She didn't have the heart to do it. She figured their punishment was hard enough as it was.

On the school's free day, in the late afternoon, she was in her room writing a letter to her parents when excited shouts drifted in from outside. Hurrying to her balcony to see what was going on, she saw several students out on the lawn pointing skyward. Taking a look, she gasped at what she saw. The sky—it was filled with dragons. Dragons of every size and color, and they were coming closer.

Hesitating only an instant, she ran from her room, heading for the stairs. Merging with a mass of other students, she hurried outside toward the landing strip on the south side of the school.

The dragons circled overhead then headed toward the landing area one by one. The first to land was a bright red dragon with strange flaps flaring from his ears. Six people were saddled on top of him and a large pack sat behind them. With sweeping grace, the dragon came down mere handspans from the ground and glided daintily to a smooth stop on the runway. Talia stared at the amazing display in awe.

Watchers poured out seemingly from nowhere and were instantly at the dragon's side, greeting the riders and helping them bring down the load on the dragon's back. A blue dragon soon landed behind the first. This one only held one passenger, but a huge bundle was strapped on its back instead. Akin to ants, the watchers rushed over and took the package apart and scurried off with its contents.

As each dragon landed and was freed of its burden, it meandered down to the lake on the other side of the runway for a drink. Most returned to the air not long after, but a few made their leisurely way to the dragon habitat.

As the number of passengers disembarking grew, they grabbed up some of the packs set aside by the watchers and headed off in different directions. Those who came with the dragons were as varied and different from one another as the dragons themselves. Talia recognized a couple as having come from her country, while others wore styles of hair and dress she didn't recognize at all and appeared to her to be incredibly exotic.

Away from the runway, tents started going up, spreading across the grassy plain. Wooden frames were speedily put together and were covered over with tarps to make frontend stalls. At the pace they were going up, within hours, they would surround the entire school.

Smiling graciously, Lareen sauntered outside to greet a man dressed even more outlandishly than she was. His hard features smiled at her ingratiatingly, colorful and many-layered robes covering him from head to toe. Laughing, the two of them locked arms and wandered off inside.

That evening, for the first time, Talia saw the dining hall filled close to capacity. The din in the room was almost overwhelming as the visitors picked random places to sit amidst clumps of students and were immediately bombarded with a million questions.

"Everyone, your attention, please." Lareen's voice boomed out across the room. "First, let's give a shout of welcome to our visitors."

The ensuing roar was deafening. Lareen grinned from ear to ear at the loud, enthusiastic greeting.

"We welcome all of you to our humble school. We hope your stay here will be as enjoyable as it will be for us to have you here."

Shouts rang out again, this time from both sets of diners. With infinite, good-natured patience, she waited for the din to die down before going on.

"Starting tomorrow, the carnival will begin." Lareen was forced to wait again as more shouts rang across the room. "To make things simpler for everyone, bread, meat, cheese, and fruit will be available here throughout the day so meals can be taken as time permits. However, there should be enough treats provided by our guests to possibly make this not even necessary." Her smile was infectious. "All games and contests are free and many will have rewards for those with skill. So please, make sure to play hard and often. This is a reward from me to you. Enjoy!"

The dining hall exploded with cheers. Even Yllin looked excited at the prospect of what they could expect tomorrow.

Finishing her dinner, Talia excused herself to take care of her chores. Her absence was hardly noticed, most of her friends still talking eagerly about the carnival and their guests. As she went into the kitchen, even the cooking staff appeared thrilled at the coming days. Tula stood on her stool in the back, shouting orders as usual, but she had a bright grin on her face. Shaking her head in wonder, Talia slipped outside.

As she placed the first barrel on her dolly, she stared at the changed landscape about her. Tents could be seen everywhere—almost no piece of open land seemed to have escaped them. Her route to the dragon habitat was long and convoluted as she was forced to zigzag between the tents and packages in her way.

She rolled the dolly into the dormitory then stopped in surprise. The usual semi-lit gloom was gone, overridden by dozens of globes all turned on as brightly as possible. Voices, snarls, and grunts filled the air as did the heavy animal scent of dragons. Almost every stall was occupied by one of the massive creatures. Their many-colored scales seemed to shimmer in the light as they lounged about and spoke to one another.

The strange feeling of inconsequentiality she'd felt once or twice at the school returned to murmur through her as she stared at the scaled giants. Almost in awe, she stepped forward, wheeling her burden on. Suddenly self-conscious, she looked only at the path as she made her way across the dormitory to Clarence's stall. She felt the hackles on her neck rise, feeling alien eyes glancing curiously at her as she walked past. She wanted nothing more than to stare back at them yet was afraid she would seem rude.

"Good evening, Clarence." She kept her voice low, not wanting to attract the other dragons' attention any more than she'd done already.

Good evening. Clarence lay coiled about himself, seemingly ignoring the fact other dragons were there. Even his thoughts seemed subdued.

Talia set the barrel down, embarrassed for him. It occurred to her this situation would be very awkward. Not only did he have to deal with the other dragons seeing his disability—though she possessed no real idea how they were about such things—any conversations between them would inevitably bring up the fact he was imprisoned in his room. This in itself would likely result in a tremendous number of horribly deflating and embarrassing questions. The excitement she felt before for the coming carnival cooled and twisted into guilt. As she left Clarence still coiled in his stall, she swore she'd find some way to make things better for him.

When she took Kel's tray to his room, he met her at the door. His smile was bright, but his eyes seemed troubled. He said nothing as she came in, yet once she set the tray on the table, his voice reached out to her from across the room. "How did Clarence seem to you today?"

She didn't quite meet his expectant gaze when she answered. "He was very quiet this evening. I ... I think he might be a little depressed."

He nodded as if she only confirmed something he already knew. "Why are all those dragons here? Do you know?"

She looked away. "The Administrator asked them here. For the next six days we're to have a carnival. It's a reward for all the work everyone's done because of the fire..." There, she'd finally told him. It would've only been a matter of time before Clarence informed him of it anyway.

"Oh! Those are a lot of fun." His cheery tone wasn't what she expected. "Lareen is really being generous. Carnivals usually only last a couple of days."

Though she was still listening for it, she didn't hear any disappointment in his voice at all. "You really need to make sure to try as many of the games as you can," he said.

His words threw her off balance. "I—I wasn't really sure I should go." When she saw his pained expression at her words, she felt even more off balance.

"Why would you say that?" he asked her. A number of emotions she couldn't entirely read flashed across his face.

Talia turned away from him. "It just wouldn't be fair."

"Why not?" he insisted. "You've worked as hard as any of them. You've actually done more than any of them." He said this with conviction as if he really knew all she'd done.

Talia slowly shook her head in denial. "That has nothing to do with it. I played a part in this mess and I wasn't made to pay like you and Clarence. So now I should take a reward?" In a way, it almost felt as if she was benefiting from their misery.

"You're wrong."

She glanced over her shoulder, startled by the intense emotion in Kel's voice.

His intense blue gaze met hers for a moment before

he looked suddenly away. "You had nothing to do with what I did, with what I made Clarence do. You were a victim, not an instigator. None of it was your fault at all. You had nothing to do with it." His eyes met hers once again. "You've already paid more than you ever should have."

Talia stared at the floor. He honestly thought her innocent. He didn't blame her for any of it. She felt wonder course through her, not sure how it was possible. If she'd never shown him the gem...

"Don't. I was the one who overreacted," he said. "You didn't even know what it was or what it did when you gave it to me. How could anyone think to hold you accountable? The fault was entirely mine."

She still wouldn't look at him, though at some level she knew he was right. Yet so much of it made no sense. A question left her lips before she took the time to think about it. "Why were you so angry, though?" She pushed out the rest of the words before her courage failed her. "You knew what the gem was. You knew he'd done this before. So why did it make you so furious?"

She kept her back to him, not sure he would answer. She heard the rattle of his chains echo about her as he walked away.

"I've-I've asked myself the same question almost every day since it happened." Kel sighed heavily. "I still don't understand it myself. But when you were standing there, when I realized what it was you'd put in my hand—it was as if a dam broke inside me, like all the hidden, pent-up frustrations of the last three years suddenly burst through."

Talia turned around, hearing the torment in his voice. Her gaze sought him, even as his fists clenched and unclenched as he battled to express himself. He sat forward on his bed, his elbows on his knees, staring intently at the floor as if the answers were written there.

"I couldn't control it. I didn't want to control it. All I knew was Nertak must pay and I was the one who would make him." Kel frowned, his face furrowed, and went on. "Clarence believes I've just been pushing too hard for too long. I know he's right, that Lareen is right." He laughed sadly. "In a way, this thing has been good for me. It's forced me not to push so hard, to relax. And I do feel better for it. So maybe it was for the best. I swear I won't ever let it get so bad again." He looked up at her. "Promise me you'll go."

"What?" She stared at him, momentarily not knowing what he was talking about.

Kel stood up, his face clear and set. "Promise me you'll go to the carnival and enjoy yourself." He watched her earnestly. "Please? If not because I ask, do it for yourself. You've gone through a lot and you deserve it. Plus, it would also make me feel better about things if I knew you were having a good time because of it."

"I—" Not trusting herself to speak, she finally just nodded.

Feeling strange and awkward when he smiled at her in return, she picked up the empty tray and left, bidding Kel goodnight.

Chapter Sixteen

THE CARNIVAL WOULD begin today. Talia hadn't yet decided what she would do about it, despite her half promise to Kel. She got up without much enthusiasm and chose not to worry about it until after breakfast.

When she reached the dining hall, she found a lot more students there than was usual for that time of the morning. Smiles shone everywhere and the expectant excitement from the night before was almost palpable now. The doors leading out to the garden path were already open, letting in the bright sunshine from the outside. As they were told the night before, the tables were laden with baskets of fruits as well as platters of bread and cheese. Students were coming into the room, grabbing a few things off the closest table then heading directly for the open doors.

Talia ate standing beside her table, feeling a little uncomfortable as no one but she stayed in the room. As soon as she finished eating, she grabbed several pears then headed to the kitchen.

A wave of heat washed over her as she opened the

door and she gasped, for once not having expected it. She'd assumed the place would be quiet and empty. Instead, it was jammed with people, and the heat was more overwhelming than ever before.

Talia stepped hesitantly inside, sweat breaking on her brow, as she watched unfamiliar men and women stride back and forth between the kitchen tables. Weaving her way past them, unknown sweet smells thickened the air, almost stifling in their intensity. Here and there she saw a cook or two she knew, but on the whole, they were outnumbered by those she didn't. The buzz of conversation was thick and more than once she passed by an excited discussion over culinary techniques.

With grateful relief, she was finally able to push her way out the kitchen's back door. She stared down at her pears, which looked to be a little worse for the experience, then stuffed them into the barrel with Clarence's oats.

As she fitted the dolly to the barrel and started on her way, she gawked at the changes in the area since she was there last. It appeared that all the tents she'd spotted the night before had spawned even more of them. Colorful streamers hung on most, as well as signs, banners, and miniature stages.

The front of many of the tents were extended to form storefronts or stalls. Exotic scents teased her senses— perfumes, paints, food, and who knew what else. Snatches of songs, as well as the sounds of instruments being tuned, drifted about, escaping from tent flaps as she walked past, almost like promises of the entertainment she could expect later.

When she reached the dragon's habitat, Talia noticed it had changed as well. Streamers were tied high on the outer façade with long banners hung from the windows.

Glancing back toward the school, she saw it was decorated, too. From the lowest balconies, streamers hung like waterfalls and curled ribbons floated gently in the wind. Paper flowers dotted everything as if there'd been a late explosion of spring.

Talia felt both excited and guilty as the urge to just walk around and look passed through her. Telling herself she'd have time later, she turned the dolly in the direction of the dormitory's door. To her surprise, she found two watchers stationed outside the large doors. They nodded to her pleasantly and said good morning before one of them opened the door for her. She responded to their greetings and went on in.

The lights inside were bright, most of the dragons within awake and moving about at the early hour. A number of their partners were in there with them. She pushed the dolly silently, trying to stay out of everyone's way. With a sudden start, she stopped for a moment to watch a shapely woman covered from head to toe in veils gently scratching the chin of a silver dragon. She was a dragon knight?

Talia frowned even as she started forward again before anyone noticed her scrutiny. She'd assumed, at least until now, that if you won the lottery and got a dragon, you would have to become a knight—a soldier. Could it be this wasn't true? Could you still be a cook? A farmer? Even a dancer, perhaps?

Puzzled by her own thoughts, she reached Clarence's stall. Unlike all the other dragons, he was still curled up on his hay, seemingly asleep. With as much activity as was going on around him, she didn't see how he could manage it. Rather than disturb him, though, she set the barrel down and left to go get the next one.

When she returned, the first barrel was empty, though

to all appearances Clarence had never moved.

Good morning, Talia. Even as he spoke into her mind, the dragon gave no outer indication he was awake.

"Good morning." She made sure to keep her voice low.

Thank you for the fruit. It was very kind.

"I was happy to do it," she said, glad he'd enjoyed them.

"I'll try to get some more for lunch. Do you like cheese?"

Please, he said gently, *do not go to any trouble on my account.* His tone subtly implied otherwise.

She almost smiled as she removed the dolly from the new barrel and hooked it up to the empty one. When she returned for the other, it too was empty, though Clarence still looked as if he hadn't moved. Not wanting to disturb him further, she said nothing as she picked up the barrel and left.

Setting the barrel and dolly against the outside wall of the kitchen, Talia took a deep breath before plunging into the chaos awaiting her inside. Some of the earlier crowd in the kitchen was gone, but the activity within was still fast and furious. She wove her way toward the front, dodging elbows, pots, and trays as she went.

"Hold on there, you!"

A hand fell on her arm bringing her up short. She glanced behind her wondering if she'd done something wrong.

A broad face smiled down at her, a sharp brown gaze locking with her own. "Missy, would you be kind enough to taste this for me? I'd be much obliged."

"Me? But I don't—"

The portly woman cut her off. "You'd be doing me an awful favor. These others here are competing with me for business so I can't trust them to give me a truthful answer. And the cooks," she said, throwing a half-glare in the direction of one of the school's regulars, "don't quite seem to believe in what I'm makin' and so they can't be trusted, either. You're the closest thing to a neutral party I've run across so far." She thrust a wooden spoon close to Talia's face. "Please?"

She stared at the spoon and the dark red mixture on it with slight misgivings, then at the hopeful face before her. "Okay, sure." She took a taste. Sweet tartness exploded in her mouth followed by a dash of cinnamon. Delicious!

"Does it need a little something?" The woman looked at her, worry on her face.

Talia couldn't understand why. "No, it doesn't need anything. It's perfect."

The portly woman beamed. "Ah, thank you so much. Come by my stall on the far side of the landing field and I'll happily give you some of the finished product in gratitude."

"I will." She nodded eagerly, speculating about what the woman might do with the strange mixture and finding herself looking forward to finding out. Thanking her, she turned away to continue on her way.

She didn't get far, however, before others of those cooking begged her for her opinion as well. It was as if having done it once, she sent a signal to everyone else she was willing. By the time she was able to make it to Kel's tray, her mouth was almost numb from all the exotic tastes thrust upon it even as her head buzzed with all the promises of free finished products. She grabbed the tray before anyone else could decide they needed her, and made her escape.

The dining hall was virtually empty, though signs of others having been by were evident, marked by half-emptied baskets and platters. Making sure no one was looking she set her tray down on one of the tables and added things to it from the food sitting there. As soon as she was done, she made her way out the door and to the stairs.

Talia reached the school's roof without seeing anyone about. Voices whispered to her from below, so, curious, she approached the edge and took a peek. Students were everywhere. It was as if someone had gone to a giant anthill or beehive and given it a good whack. Instrumental music as well as snatches of singing mixed in with the voices. A cheer tore through the crowd nearest her as two acrobats vaulted onto a small stage. The carnival had begun.

"It looks fun doesn't it?"

She jumped back, almost dropping her tray, startled by the voice behind her. Snapping around, she found Kel standing not far from her, a big grin on his face as he took his own peek over the edge. Her heart hammering, she stared at his feet and saw the chain was still in place. How in the world did he sneak up on her?

"Sorry if I startled you," he said, stepping away from the edge. "I just heard the music from inside and couldn't resist taking a look." He gave her a mischievous smile.

"I better put this inside." Talia turned away from him and headed toward his room, hoping he'd follow. If anyone spotted the squire, she knew there were those who would take great delight getting him in trouble over it. "I brought some extra things for you today."

Kel rattled along behind her. She frowned, hearing the chain distinctly, and wondered again how he'd been able to sneak up on her without her being aware of it.

"I appreciate it. Thanks." His voice was cheery and bright.

Setting his tray on the table, she picked up the other waiting there for her. "I'll try to get some more for you later." She started toward the door.

"Don't forget your promise." Kel sounded suddenly serious.

Not looking back, she only nodded and left. She'd hoped he'd forgotten about it. As it was, she'd yet to make up her mind on whether she was going to go or not.

"There you are!"

She was just entering the dining hall when a familiar voice called out to her. Turning around, she spotted both Mandee and Yllin heading swiftly in her direction.

"I'm glad we found you," Yllin said. "We were hoping the three of us could enjoy the carnival together."

"It's too bad you still have to do this, though." Mandee pointed at the tray in her hands.

Talia shrugged. "I don't mind. It really doesn't take long."

"They still shouldn't make you do it," Yllin insisted. "It makes you miss out on the fun, and you've worked just as hard as anyone else."

She said nothing as she recalled Kel saying something very similar not too long ago.

"Come on, hurry and get rid of those," Mandee implored her. "We're missing who knows what while we stand here talking."

Talia hesitated a moment longer then nodded. "It'll just take me a second." She left her friends and walked to the kitchen to drop off Kel's tray. As soon as she made it back, Yllin and Mandee grabbed her by the arms and made a dash for the garden so their day could begin.

Roaring laughter greeted them. A large crowd had gathered by a small stage to observe a man in white makeup trying to do simple acrobatic acts; he was botching them utterly, much to the amusement of those watching.

"What should we do first?" Mandee stared at them, her face radiant with barely restrained excitement.

"Whatever you two decide is fine by me," Talia told them. She had no idea what kind of amusements the carnival offered.

"Now you've done it," Yllin groaned.

Mandee's smile grew huge. "Well, since Yllin already gave me her usual 'I don't care' shrug and you'll do whatever we pick—I've decided we'll start on the left side of the carnival then work our way in. We're going to do it *all*."

Yllin groaned again, giving Talia a pitying look as Mandee grabbed their hands and led the way through the crowd. She kept on, even after the throng thinned, until they reached the farthest tent on the carnival grounds, feet away from Nertak's cave.

"Ladies! Come here, come here." A man dressed in red and bright yellow waved at them to come and join him at the booth. A table sat at the tent's entrance, bundles of darts set neatly on its top. In the back of the open-faced tent, caricatures were drawn on a large board with cushions growing from each of them. The cushions were part of the art and represented large noses, buttocks, fruits, and other more personal things. The vendor grinned from ear to ear as they came close. "How about trying out your skills, ladies? The rewards for success will be great!"

Mandee's eyes shone. "What do we need to do?"

"It is simplicity itself. Grab up three darts and aim at the cushions." He held a dramatic pose. "For just trying to hit them, you get a prize. If you show fortitude and strike one cushion, you will not go away wanting. If you hit two, as well as pride a reward will be yours. And if you hit three, humbling the rest of us with your skill, a treasure awaits such fortune."

His bright smile was infectious. "Will you try?"

Mandee giggled with delight. "Oh, yes. We all will." She instantly grabbed three of the darts.

Talia stepped to Mandee's right and Yllin to her left, and each took up three darts of their own. Back home, she had played this kind of game before. The small fairs which came through every year usually put up one of these booths. They too boasted of great prizes, but it was incredibly hard to win. Her father explained to her once the darts were of unusually low quality and weren't balanced, thus cutting down the chances for success. It was how the owner made his money and how he could boast the large, tempting prizes he did. Though how they would make money here, when all the games were free and they gave prizes away just for trying them, she wasn't sure.

She readied her first dart for a throw and grew more puzzled still. She didn't know much about darts, but these felt different from the ones she'd handled before. Suddenly eager to try, she aimed at the cartoon of a stooped-over grandmother working in a garden and let fly. She hit the woman's back and not what she'd been aiming for. She was successful on her second try though and almost got another on her third. Mandee did about the same, though Yllin was totally unsuccessful.

"That was wonderful, ladies!" He handed Yllin a piece of paper for free food at a nearby stand. He gave Mandee and Talia the same, but they each received two. "The prizes do get better with more successes. Care to try again?"

Mandee already held her next set of darts in hand. "Yes!"

Talia fared no better the second time than she did the first, but it was better than she ever achieved at home. Yllin got one cushion with her final dart, momentarily brightening her usually sour features. Mandee punctured two.

"Well done," the vendor said with feeling. "More coupons for the two of you, but as for you, miss..." He turned his hand and presented to her a yellow gem. It seemed to appear out of nowhere.

"Thank you!" Mandee was delighted. She took her prize and tucked it away.

Talia frowned at this, wondering how they could afford to give such things away.

"Care to try your luck a third time?"

"Oh, could we?" Mandee looked hopefully at the two of them.

Yllin gave her a scowl. "I think we should go try something else."

"We can always come back later," Talia added quickly. "We have all week."

"Oh, all right." Mandee didn't look as disappointed as Talia thought she would. "Let's go!" She dragged them off to next closest game.

By the time the morning was over, the three of them had joined a mock sword fight, sung in a singing contest, and even volunteered to hold small parts in a short comedic play. The three of them used what coupons they won to get food from the stalls scattered everywhere. Talia found not all vendors needed to use the school's kitchen to create their wares. Many brought with them their own small stoves or grills, which they set inside the tents or just outside them to cook. Others sold fruit or pre-made goods and didn't need to cook at all.

Even stuffed as they were after their third or fourth snack, it was hard not to get more as the mouthwatering scents drifted out to them as they walked on. Tired and full, the three of them finally stopped to rest on some benches set beside one of the eating stalls. Talia looked up at the sky, speculating what the time might be. She couldn't see the clock face at the top of the school from there, but she could see the sun had moved past its zenith in the sky.

"I'm late!" She jumped to her feet, mentally kicking herself for having lost track of time.

"Where are you going?" Yllin asked her, even as she licked her fingers of the last of the powdered sugar from one of her latest snacks.

"I've got to take Clarence and Kel their lunch," she answered distractedly, wondering how really late she was.

"Did you need us to help?" Mandee asked her.

Talia considered the offer for a moment then shook her head. "Thanks anyway. Did you want me to look for you when I'm done?"

Yllin gave a satisfied sigh. "We'll be here I think. I need to give some of this food time to digest."

She nodded. "I'll be back as fast as I can."

On the way to the dining hall, she spotted a food vendor without a line and purchased a couple of meat rolls as well as a sweet tart. Trying not to drop them, she hurried into the hall to pick up a chunk of cheese as well as some fruit. She then headed for the kitchen.

The pandemonium of the morning was no longer evident, though a few people still lingered by vats of strange concoctions. Making her way outside, she hid one of the rolls and the tart behind the second barrel and put the other roll as well as the cheese and fruits inside the other. She hitched up the dolly to the latter and went on her way.

Getting to the dragon habitat proved difficult if not slightly perilous. She was forced to dodge students, watchers, teachers, and others as they clogged the narrow byways between the tents. By the time she made it to the relative safety of the dormitory, she was covered in a thin sheen of sweat from having to come to abrupt stops, dodging and taking off at a moment's notice to get past the living flood unscathed.

The sun-protected habitat was a little cooler than the outdoors and she gave a sigh of relief. As she went on to Clarence's stall, she found the hum of voices outside intruded even this far. She was sure it wouldn't be pleasant to listen to the merriment all day, especially when one could take no part in it.

"I was able to get you a few things," Talia whispered in case any of the other current tenants were listening. Clarence lay curled on the floor, much as he was that morning, but this time actually opened an eye when he heard her speak.

Not waiting, she unloaded the barrel off her dolly and went back to get the next. After she was done with him, she picked up Kel's tray. She pushed herself to hurry, only too aware of how late she was. She was panting by the time she reached the roof.

Kel opened the door as soon as she knocked, and she rushed inside, apologizing for being late. "I brought some extra stuff, I hope it's okay."

"It'll be wonderful," he told her with a smile.

"Again, I'm sorry I was late. I won't do it again, but I have to go." She quickly retrieved his tray and left. She zoomed from the room, barely glancing at him.

Dumping the tray in the kitchen then hurrying outside,

she stopped in a relatively quiet passage to get her breath back. Hands over her knees as she took great gulps of air, she looked up and found her attention trapped as she spotted a watcher intently studying a boy getting ready to throw a knife at a target. Talia shifted to watch him as well and saw him hit the bull's eye. His second throw struck there as well. His third wasn't far off. Straightening up to go on her way, she glanced at the watcher again; he made notes in a small notebook then nonchalantly put it away.

As Talia walked on to join her friends, she mulled over the watcher's actions but then dismissed them.

"Hi!" She found Yllin and Mandee where she'd left them. "I hope I didn't keep you waiting too long."

"Nope," Mandee told her cheerily. "I hadn't even gotten terribly impatient yet." She gave her a wide grin. "I've been keeping busy trying to figure out what we should go do next."

"You'll love this." Yllin didn't sound thrilled.

"Come on!" Mandee grabbed Talia's hand and dragged her off.

The afternoon passed rapidly. First, they entered a pottery contest and learned the rudimentary skills of how to use a pottery wheel. Of the three of them, Yllin actually seemed to have quite a flair for the craft. She didn't seem to mind it much, either.

They'd just finished a speed-painting contest when Yllin spotted an offering from one of the stalls nearby. "Cherries!"

Several students turned around at her excited shout even as she followed it with a delighted squeal. "I love cherries!"

Talia stared at her friend, not having seen her this excited about anything before. The exhilarated expression on the ordinarily sour face was a radical change and made her appear like an entirely different person. Yllin ran to the stand in question, almost as if afraid it would suddenly disappear.

"Well, this is new," Mandee said an amused smile playing on her face. "I didn't know she had it in her."

"She never mentioned she liked cherries before?" Talia asked her.

"Yeah, but..." Mandee shrugged.

By the time they caught up with their friend, Yllin had already gulped down half of the two servings she'd bought. She grinned as she spotted them, her teeth stained red. "They're fresh and pitted. You've got to get some!" She herded them to the front of the booth.

As Talia bought herself a cupful, her eyes widened a little as she remembered something. "Excuse me, but do you have enough of these that you might consider selling me a bushel?"

The young man behind the counter raised an eyebrow. "Actually miss, we have tons of cherries. They're pretty popular with the dragons, so we made sure to bring quite a few."

"The pits are dangerous to them though, isn't that right?" she asked.

Mandee came to stand beside her, staring at her curiously.

"Only if they eat too many," the vendor told her. "A small amount is not bad for them. It makes them slightly intoxicated actually." He grinned.

Talia's brow furrowed. Would Clarence enjoy them? She decided to take the chance. "How much?"

The young man turned away then returned with a large basket filled to the brim with cherries. He set it on the counter with a slight thump. "One small gem, miss."

"Talia, what are you doing?" Mandee asked her this in a whisper as though already suspecting the answer.

"Just buying some cherries." She dug in her bag for one of her gems.

"Yes," Mandee hissed in her ear, "but for *whom*?"

The vendor took her money then pulled a lid out for the basket. Before he set it on, he sprinkled a layer of unpitted cherries over the top. "Here you go."

"Thank you very much," Talia said with feeling. She was delighted Yllin had found this place. She grabbed the basket by the handles and pulled it off the counter only to almost drop it. It was heavier than it looked.

"Talia!" Mandee stared at her, concern openly staining her face.

Yllin came over, all of her cherries gone, and looked with admiration at her purchase. "I should have thought of that."

"Yllin, this is serious! Those aren't for her." Mandee still kept her voice low even as she chastised her friend. "Don't you remember what they told us about cherries in class?"

Yllin hesitated, not immediately recollecting what Mandee was talking about. Then her eyes grew large and she turned to Talia. "You'll get in trouble!"

Talia set the heavy basket on the ground after moving several steps over into the small alley formed by the cherry vendor's stall and the one next to it. She put a determined look on her face. "Look, I'm going to do this. I need to do this. I wasn't told I couldn't, and it's the least I can do. If it weren't for them, we wouldn't even be having this carnival.

"Don't they have the right to get something out of it, too?"

Her two friends stared at her, neither knowing what to

say.

She plunged on. "It won't take me long, and you don't have to wait for me. I really need to do this."

"You can barely lift it," Mandee pointed out. "How are you planning on getting it there?"

Talia already knew of a solution. "I'll leave it with the storekeeper and go get the dolly from the kitchen. No one will think much about it."

"That'll take too long," Yllin told her. "We'll help you with it." Her expression was set. "With all the other dragons there, no one will know who it is we're taking it to."

Mandee's wrinkled brow suddenly smoothed. "Yes, that should work."

Talia stared back and forth from one to the other. "I appreciate it, but I can't let you. There's still a risk."

"But we want to," Mandee said. Yllin nodded in agreement. "Besides, you have permission to go into the dormitory, and if we're with you, we might be able to get in, too, and take a closer look at all those dragons."

"That's right." Yllin leaned over to grab one of the handles on the basket. "It'll be a good learning experience. So lead the way."

Hesitating only a moment longer, she gave in and nodded. Mandee took hold of the other handle and with Yllin's help followed Talia into the crowd. She led them off the main thoroughfare and went the long way around to the dragon habitat. Watchers still stood by the doors turning away students trying to get in for a peek at the visiting dragons.

Nervous, but trying not to let it show, she walked right up to the doors, paying them no attention. Yllin and Mandee followed close behind. The watchers didn't interfere with them in any way.

"I was sure they were going to stop us," Yllin whispered once they were safely inside.

Mandee preened. "I told you she'd get us inside."

Talia glanced back at them, getting the impression the two of them had had a discussion about this before she ever brought it up. Had she inadvertently come up with an excellent excuse to get them in here when it was something they actually wanted all along? She supposed she couldn't blame them. In their place, she would have wanted very badly to get a closer look at the dragons herself. "This way."

As she led them down the center of the aisle, Mandee and Yllin both gawked about them as they caught glimpses of the dormitory's occupants.

Talia? Is something wrong? She reached Clarence's stall, and the dragon raised his head just enough to look over it at her. *I didn't expect you again until this evening.*

"Everything's fine. I, we, just came to bring you some dessert."

Mandee and Yllin froze as his gaze turned to them.
Dessert?

Talia opened the stall door and waved her friends to go inside. Hesitantly, their eyes never leaving the towering dragon, they scooted in and set the basket on the ground before rushing back out.

Clarence reached down and with one carefully placed claw, flipped the lid off the basket. *Cherries!*

Talia almost burst out laughing at the dragon's reaction, the glee and amazement in his tone too closely resembling Yllin's. "I was hoping they would be all right."

Clarence's tongue rolled out like a snake and snatched a single cherry from the pile. His eyes shone as he swiftly brought it back to his mouth. *You've just made this whole ordeal almost worthwhile.*

She smiled and stepped out of the stall, knowing this was going exactly as she hoped. It felt good to have been able to find something to make the dragon happy. In turn, it would make Kel happy as well.

"Excuse me, miss." A gravelly voice trickled to her from the right. "Could I speak to you for a moment?"

Not having thought anyone else was there, she turned around, as did Mandee and Yllin. To her surprise, she didn't find a guest or even a watcher but instead found herself looking into the long-snouted face of the red dragon from three stalls down.

Glancing at her friends for a moment then at Clarence's closed stall door, Talia stepped over toward him. "What can I do for you, sir?" She hoped she guessed the gender correctly, not having any idea how a female dragon would sound. Other than for Clarence, this was her first experience speaking to a dragon. Nervous but simultaneously excited, she waited for what he would say next.

As she came near, she noticed the dragon's red scales looked faded, a few of those around his face almost discolored to white. Clarence's scales were bright and deeply green. This matched what she'd seen of most of the other dragons visiting there. Could the discoloration be a sign of age?

"Pardon my intrusion, but I couldn't help but overhear part of your conversation." Dark brown eyes with orange rims studied her intently. "By any chance, were those *cherries*?" He said the word as if it were a cherished treasure.

Talia sobered, not sure what she was about to get herself into. "Yes, as a matter of fact, they were." She thought she saw the old dragon's mouth water. In the stalls around them, several heads popped up from behind the stalls, their eyes shining with interest.

"Talia!" Mandee and Yllin came close, as all the dragons in the dormitory raised their heads to stare at them except for Clarence.

The old dragon's head drew closer, his hot breath washing over her. "If you wouldn't find it too inconvenient, might I impose on you for a favor?"

"What do you need, sir?" She fought to keep her voice steady, the staring dragons and the old one's piercing attention proving a little overwhelming.

"As you might imagine, it's difficult for us to roam about with all the students loose on the premises. So since we are not able, would you mind purchasing cherries for us so we may all partake of them as well?" he asked.

Talia glanced back at her friends, who nodded rapidly, staring nervously at the hungrily watching dragons around them. "Yes, we'd be happy to."

"How kind of you!" Agreement rang out throughout the dormitory, some vocal and others not. The old dragon disappeared behind his stall for a moment then returned with a medium-sized purse. He dropped it on the ground. "We'll need nineteen servings, please. That's a bushel per. There should be more than sufficient funds there. Whatever is left, please split amongst you as my thanks for your services."

She lifted the heavy purse from the ground. From the weight of it, she could almost guarantee it contained more than they would need. "No payment is necessary, sir. We'd be happy to do it."

"Of course it is!" the dragon said imperiously. "A payment for a service. It does not matter how large or small, each act deserves recompense."

Talia decided it might be in her best interest not to

argue the point. "Thank you, sir." She gave him a small bow. "We'll return shortly." Mandee and Yllin nodded, looking eager to be gone.

She led the way out, her two friends sticking very close. They were watched every step of the way by eager, reptilian faces.

"They, they talked to us!" Mandee laughed out loud as soon as they got outside and were out of hearing range of the watchers keeping guard. Her voice was full of a mix of fear and awe. "And Yllin, they seemed as crazy about cherries as you! Though they are much scarier looking."

Yllin threw her a sour look. "It won't be much fun traipsing nineteen bushels around. Why didn't they get their partners to do this?"

"Maybe they are," Talia said, a sudden amusing thought flashing through. "This way though, they might get twice as much, especially if they don't mention to anyone we've already done it for them."

"That's evil," Mandee exclaimed. "I love it. And if Yllin could get away with it, she'd do it, too!" She deftly dodged a grab by the dark-faced girl.

"We can get the dolly I use to bring Clarence's meals. It should make this easier," Talia suggested.

"Sounds good." Yllin tried to grab Mandee again as she spoke but was once more unsuccessful.

After retrieving the dolly, the three of them made their way over to the fruit seller's stall. Weirdly enough, he didn't seem surprised to see them. He didn't even raise a brow when she gave him their request. "Yeah, I'd a feeling you'd be back. That group never passes up a chance for these if they can help it." He gave them a wide grin. "Just glad it wasn't me. It's so hard to refuse a bunch of hungry dragons."

"Will you have enough?" Yllin asked as Talia took out

the payment.

"No problem," he told them. "More are on the way. Dragons just can't get enough of the stuff." He grinned. "Come around to the back and we can get started."

Mandee grabbed the dolly, and with Talia and Yllin following they walked over to the back of the tent. They could see stacks upon stacks of crates filling the interior as the proprietor lifted the flap up for them. Two men sat on the outside with a container open and a bushel basket next to each leg. Their fingers were stained red as each reached into the crate and pulled out cherries then took out the pits. The scent of the fruit was overpowering.

The proprietor looked over at the two busy men then winked at the girls. "Dor, Sti, our big order has arrived ahead of schedule."

They both looked up and over at him, their expressions not pleased. "That's not funny."

"Who said I was joking?" He gave them both a hard look.

The men's faces fell.

"You won't have to carry them though. For this round, we've got some help." He hooked a thumb in the girls' direction.

"Well, at least that's something..." Both of the men sighed.

As one, they pushed to work faster.

Talia guessed the carnival wasn't really fun and games for everyone involved.

"The stack over there is ready." The vendor indicated a stack of bushels just inside the tent.

"Thank you." She and Yllin grabbed the first one off the top and loaded it onto the dolly. Taking three more, they left with their first load. The girls took turns stacking and pulling. Each time they arrived at the dormitory, a silent cheer would ripple through the dragons waiting expectantly for them. By the time they finished bringing them over, the atmosphere inside was quite cheerful. The dragons were happily conversing with one another.

Much to her surprise and pleasure, Clarence rose from the back of his stall and even deigned to engage the old red dragon in conversation.

After about an hour, the three girls were finally done.

"That was almost as bad as bringing in the water," Yllin complained rubbing briskly at her arms.

"You think they might want us to do this again for them?" Mandee looked very excited at the prospect as she asked.

"It's likely." Talia couldn't help an amused smile. Remembering the leftover gems, she pulled them out. She gave Yllin and Mandee four a piece and kept the last three for herself.

"What should we do now?" Yllin asked glancing at the games around them.

"I know just the thing." Mandee headed off to the right, not waiting for them.

"Here we go again." With a groan, Yllin took off after her.

Grinning, Talia rapidly followed as well.

A couple of hours later, she left her friends watching a puppet show so she could go take care of her evening chores. On the way, she bought Kel and Clarence some sweets with her winnings for the day as well as more fruit and cheese from the dining hall tables.

When she arrived at the dragon's dormitory, she found Clarence and the old dragon still in deep conversation. They were keeping it quiet, not that Clarence ever spoke out loud, but from what she could overhear from the red dragon's side of the conversation it sounded extremely involved and perhaps a little heated.

Though she wasn't quite sure how she could tell, Clarence seemed incredibly content. She was still pondering on it when she arrived at Kel's room. He opened the door and stood there grinning at her from ear to ear.

"Welcome!" He stepped out of the way so she could come inside. "I owe you a great debt of thanks," he said as she placed his tray on the table. When she turned around, she found him down on one knee. He bowed as he spoke. "I thank you for your efforts from the bottom of my heart."

She took a step back, astonished by the display. "It was no big thing. It's just a few sweets."

Kel looked up, his clear blue gaze trapping her own. "It's not for those, but for what you've done for Clarence. His spirits are much higher than they've been of late and it's all due to your efforts. *Thank you.*"

Talia felt herself blush. He really shouldn't be making such a big deal out of this. "It-it was the least I could do. I was happy to."

"You'll forever have my thanks. If there's anything I could ever do for you..." He stood up, making her feel a little better. She didn't see how she warranted being knelt down to.

"Have you been enjoying the carnival so far?" he asked her.

She turned away from his piercing stare and picked up the afternoon's tray. "Yes, very much."

"I'm glad."

She could hear he meant it, and weirdly it made her happy she went after all.

"I'll bet there will be a fireworks display on one of the nights," Kel told her. "They're not to be missed." He grinned.

Talia recalled the rare occasions when their own festivals were graced by such displays. If it proved to be as grand as the carnival was compared to those at home, the fireworks display would be phenomenal.

"Feel free to watch it from up here when they do," he added. "The view would be perfect."

"Thanks." She left not much later, returning the empty tray to the kitchen. Rather than leaving the dining hall and rejoining the massive throng outside, she sat down at one of the tables and enjoyed the quiet solitude for a while. It'd been an exhilarating and strange day.

"Talia."

Her head snapped to the right, not having noticed anyone coming in. Yllin and Mandee were storming over toward her.

"What are you doing here? We've got hours to go before curfew." Mandee waved for her to get up even as Yllin gave her a pitying look. "Let's go."

Chapter Seventeen

TALIA FINISHED DELIVERING Kel's and Clarence's lunches and started back toward where Mandee and Yllin had agreed to meet. When she arrived, her two friends weren't there. Not really concerned, she decided to take the opportunity to grab a short break. Standing between two of the tents to be out of the way, she watched some of the students as they played the nearby games. As her gaze drifted randomly up and down the thoroughfare, she spotted watchers in the crowd. After several minutes, she realized while they were frequenting the food vendors, none seemed to be taking advantage of any of the free games. As she pondered the question, she also noticed a few of them, while not participating in the games, they did seem to be keenly interested in the students playing them. Could it be—?

"Hey, sorry we're late." Yllin bobbed into Talia's line of sight. "I had a bad craving for some of those cherry tarts from yesterday. Have you been waiting long?"

Mandee stood beside her, saying nothing because her mouth was full of sticky sweets.

"No, just a few minutes," she told them.

"Well, unfortunately, Mandee's already chosen the next torture for us."

Mandee stomped her foot on the ground, her mouth still too full of food for her to be able to protest.

Yllin grinned. "Speechless, are we?"

Mandee swallowed hard. "Yllin! Just for that, you're going first." She grabbed her friend with her free hand and cut through the crowd. Talia followed after them, hiding a smile with her hand, her previous thoughts forgotten.

About mid-afternoon, a lance throwing contest and a juggling lesson behind them, she pulled her friends aside. "I forgot to tell you. Stal, the red dragon from yesterday, asked if we wouldn't mind helping out again today. He's already given me the money. From what you said before I didn't figure you'd mind?"

Both Mandee and Yllin grinned. "I'm still pinching myself wondering if yesterday was just a dream. If Sonsan and some of the others only knew we'd been allowed in there..." Her grin turned into a mischievous smile.

Yllin nodded. "Besides, it means I get more cherries."

Mandee rolled her eyes then burst out laughing. Grinning, the three of them went to retrieve the dolly before going to the fruit seller's stall. Talia couldn't help notice that, after a couple of trips, her two friends seemed much more at ease in the dormitory than the day before.

By the next day, Mandee's irrepressible nature reasserted itself. She introduced herself to all the dragons and happily greeted them and chatted with them as if they were all old friends.

"They really are the same as people," Mandee told Yllin and Talia after they said their goodbyes for the day. "They've just got bigger bodies is all."

"It's all a little scary if you ask me," Yllin admitted. "I can see why people almost killed them off, but I can also see why the first Dragon Knights made the treaty with them, too."

Talia saw both sides herself. With their long lifespans, their brute strength, breath weapons, plus their ability to fly, it would be easy to fear them if you didn't look past that. But they were intelligent, they had skills and knowledge they passed down from generation to generation, things which could be of great benefit to mankind. She was glad some humans back then saw past the superficial to what lay beneath.

Later in the day, she left her friends so she could deliver Clarence's and Kel's dinner but promised to return. She made good time, so she leisurely made her way back. She watched some of the students playing and smiled at the way the vendors encouraged even those without much skill. As she strolled by, she noticed once more how intently some of the watchers seemed to be studying the students as they played. She was sure she'd seen at least a couple of them taking notes. She surprisingly got the distinct impression that while all the students were here partying and playing the watchers were actually working. Frowning at the thought, she stepped over between two tents and paid strict attention to the watchers.

They were mixed in with the students, some appearing to be following particular ones while others hung around specific booths. Even the vendors seemed incredibly watchful, now that she was looking for it. But why? What were they hoping to learn? Still, as she continued to stand there and watch, an idea started forming in her mind. This carnival boasted a hundred different types of games and contests—more than she'd ever heard of being in a festival before. Some of the games were outright strange, things she wouldn't have thought would be included. What did cooking contests, sleight of hand tricks done by the audience, pottery, improvisation, and short storytelling ever have to do with a carnival? Yet looking at them another way, each could be said to promote or represent a particular type of skill or talent. If that was true, and if you let a group of unknowing students participate, might you not then be able to ascertain what they were good at without...

"Your mouth is hanging open. It's not an appealing look, don't you agree?"

Talia whirled to her left, snapping her mouth closed, only to find the Administrator standing beside her with an amused look on her face.

"I take it you've just had a revelation?" Lareen smiled knowingly.

"No. I mean, I—" Talia stared at her, out to the moving crowd and back again.

The Administrator's smile grew. "You may not believe this, but we don't try to hide what we do. Still—you'd be surprised at the number of students who never even suspect." Her expression grew sly.

"But—" Talia glanced out once more at the river of people, not sure how to put all she felt into words. "Are... are they being tested for other guilds then?" The realization of all she'd seen seemed almost too much to take.

"Sub-guilds. The Dragon Knight Guild is mostly self-sufficient. Because of this, it needs all sorts of skills. These are handled through sub-guilds," Lareen explained. "We have a job for everyone."

"Then the vendors...?" She couldn't bring herself to say it out loud.

"Yes, they represent most of our sub-guilds. And while this is not a usual recruiting period, it does make them as well as us aware of potential candidates."

"Oh." It was the only thing she could find to say. The vendors were here to look for likely candidates for their guilds. The watchers would see what sorts of things the students enjoyed and liked as well as which things they were actually good at. Did it mean they tried to not only give them jobs they could do but jobs they might enjoy as well?

"I assume I can trust you not to spoil this discovery for the others?" Lareen asked her quietly.

Talia nodded. Now that she knew the truth, she could see evidence of it everywhere. It almost shouted out it was happening, yet no one could see it. How could this be? But, until only just then, she hadn't seen it herself. Was nothing in this place ever what it seemed?

Lareen smiled at her again, almost as if she knew what was running through her mind. "Don't let the truth keep you from enjoying the carnival or from participating. I'm counting on you to try your best." With a wink, the Administrator walked out into the crowd.

Talia could only stare after her.

After a moment or two, she snapped out of her stupor and headed off to rejoin her waiting friends.

Since she knew the truth, she found herself watching everyone more closely. Each game, each effort was more serious to her than before. The future of a lot of the people around her might be being decided as she watched.

That night, she didn't sleep well. When she got up in the morning, she felt more tired than when she went to bed.

Clarence was awake and waiting for her, but most of

the other dragons were still asleep. She greeted him quietly as he gazed at her sleepily, but said nothing else.

When she made it upstairs, Kel smiled at her as he usually did when he saw her. She didn't see his smile falter as she walked on past.

"Is everything all right?" Kel asked her.

Talia nodded absently, setting his tray down. "Everything's fine. I'm just a little tired this morning."

He said nothing at her answer, instead picking up one of the tarts she'd added to his breakfast. "You don't have to keep bringing me treats, you know. I don't want you to deplete your funds on my account."

She shook her head. "I've been getting those with the food coupons I've won. I've gotten more than I can possibly eat on my own." Even as she said so, she realized the coupons and prizes were being used as incentives for the students to test themselves. They were being paid to categorize themselves for the school. She looked away, her brow creasing.

"You've figured it out, haven't you."

Talia looked over at him in surprise, caught off guard by his words. How did he guess? For that matter, how had Lareen known? Was it so obvious?

"I had a feeling you would, sooner or later," Kel stated brightly.

She frowned. He'd known about it all along, even as he encouraged her to go. "It ... it doesn't bother you?"

He shrugged. "Why should it?"

She couldn't come up with anything definite just thought that it should. She realized what they were doing might help her make up her mind as to what field to choose, but...

"It's fun," he said. "Enjoy it. In the end, it's for our benefit as well as the guild's. And regardless of what else it is, it's still a carnival."

"What... what if they find out you're especially good at...say, cooking? Does that mean you'll be made to join the kitchen staff? Would you have a choice?"

Kel gave her a grin, pleased by her questions. "No one is forced to join a sub-guild unless they want to. You might be gently prodded in a particular direction, but nothing will be forced. And just because you have skills as a cook doesn't mean your other talents might not make it better for you to join the thieves' sub-guild instead."

"I don't understand," she admitted.

He nodded. "Okay, you'll admit our cooks here are pretty good, wouldn't you?"

"Yes, their food is wonderful," she agreed, not sure where he was going with this.

"Yet cooking wasn't the primary mission Tula and a number of the others were on before they were assigned here. Several of them worked for years for a foreign lord who was maneuvering for a chance to advance into his neighbor's lands. Though Tula and the others were hired there as cooks, the main reason they went there in the first place was because they worked for the guild as spies. While they cooked for the lord, they gathered evidence to prove his underhanded actions and got him stripped of power before he really got away with anything. They did a wonderful job."

Talia stared at the squire, not sure she could believe what he was telling her.

"When they got sent here, it was as a reward for service to their sub-guild. Though I have my suspicions that Lareen also arranged it so she would have help in keeping Nertak in check."

"You... you're joking, right?" Surely he must be.

"No." Every line on his face told her he was sincere.

"What about becoming a Dragon Knight?" she asked.

"Any member of any of the sub-guilds can opt to enter the lottery. You can even try as many times as you want. Most don't, though. For if you do win, there would be some jobs you'd no longer be able to do. And there're other reasons." He didn't elaborate, and she was too overwhelmed to ask.

"But as to what you're good at, Lareen will have a file on you before too long. She keeps a file on everyone," he told her. "All the data the watchers and vendors accumulate will be added to it. I have one and so does Clarence. Knowing her, she probably has one on everyone living here, not just the students." He gave her a lopsided smile.

She wasn't sure she wanted to hear any more. "I—I probably should get going." She turned to go.

"Talia."

She stopped, still not sure what to make of everything. "Yes?" She didn't turn back around.

"I'm sorry if I said something wrong. I didn't mean to upset you."

She shook her head. "It's not you. I'm just not used to all this." She took her leave before the squire could say anything else.

By the time she reached the kitchen to drop off Kel's tray, she had a slight headache. Kel had been here a long time, so of course he knew how things worked—but why did she feel more lost because of it? Did other people really see so little? If not for the strange events she'd been involved in since she came here, would she have realized anything at all? Life would be simpler if she was oblivious to all this. But would she prefer that? Did she want to be ignorant of what she knew? Would she want to be steered toward a sub-guild without consciously making her own choice? She didn't really know.

The questions were still nagging at her when Yllin and Mandee showed up in the dining hall looking for her. Before long, the three of them were back outside, with Mandee searching for their next adventure. Talia couldn't help but question whether her friend's exuberance at the games and contests would be less if she knew the truth about them.

It surprised her a little when she realized it probably wouldn't. Perhaps it would be better if she just forgot about what she knew as best she could and tried to enjoy herself. By the end of the afternoon, she was feeling much better.

In the evening, she excused herself to go take care of her chores. "I won't be joining you when I'm done, though," she told them.

"Oh?" Both girls looked at her, momentarily forgetting their current argument about what they'd be doing later.

"I need to oil Clarence's skin."

Mandee's eyes lit up. "Can we help?"

Talia tried hard not to smile. "Thanks, but no. He's particular about how this gets done and who does it."

"This will be your last time, won't it?" Yllin asked.

Talia blinked, realizing she was right. Amidst everything, she'd forgotten Kel's and Clarence's punishment was almost over. "Yes."

"Only three more days and you'll have your freedom again! You'll actually be able to sit down and enjoy your food at mealtime." Mandee grinned.

Talia tried to smile in return though she felt a weight settling over her heart. It indeed was almost over.

With mixed feelings, she left her friends to feed those in her charge. The realization this would be one of the last times she'd get to do so tasted a little bitter. But it was for the best, wasn't it? Clarence and Kel would be free. Yet she couldn't quite shake the feeling that with their freedom, she would lose something in the bargain.

Talia approached the dragon dormitory after serving Kel, to spread oil over Clarence's skin for probably the last time.

As she poured the oil into the basin, Clarence stretched out across the stall, his crossed eyes watching her intently with anticipation.

"Where would you like me to start today?" she asked him.

Clarence took a moment to consider the question then held out his right claw. As she spread the oil over his cuticles, Clarence closed his eyes, sighing with pleasure. She couldn't help but smile as he soon thrummed with contentment. She felt a small ache tug at her, knowing she would miss this. She wondered if she ever did decide to try for the lottery and somehow got a dragon, whether he or she would enjoy this as much as Clarence did.

"Say now, surely you're a little young to have been paired with a dragon."

Talia glanced over her shoulder from where she sat on Clarence's back, surprised at the voice. A handsome man, somewhere in his late twenties and dressed from head to toe in green and black, was leaning against Clarence's stall door. He was looking her way with amused interest. A couple of dragons in adjoining stalls were also staring her way.

She frowned, momentarily wondering how long they'd been watching her work. "Ah, no, I'm just doing a favor for a friend."

The man smiled. It was a secret, amused kind of smile. "You seem to have the touch though. He really appears to be enjoying himself."

She looked away, not sure what to say.

"Maybe she could give you some pointers, Alos." A gravelly voice came from a blue dragon two stalls down.

Alos rolled his eyes and made a dismissing gesture with his hand. "My dragon companion is hard pressed to appreciate my endless efforts—fool that he is."

"You wish!"

Alos grinned. "I hope your friend appreciates *your* efforts. True gratitude can be such a rare thing." He sent the last more in the dragon's direction than hers. "What's your name by the way?"

"T—Talia."

He nodded. "And as you've already heard, mine is Alos. My at times rude companion's is Bynian."

"Less rude than you!"

Alos ignored his friend's additional comment. "Say, you wouldn't happen to be the same Talia who rumor has it has been spoiling our scaled friends here, would it?" He gave her a mischievous smile.

Most of the dragons around them suddenly looked or ducked away, pretending they'd not heard. She saw their evasion and wondered if she should do the same. Still, it wasn't as if she'd ever made a secret of the purchases. More than likely Alos heard about the cherries from the vendor himself. The dragons paid for the fruit, so surely nothing was wrong with it. "I wouldn't exactly say I was spoiling them..."

Alos shrugged. "You're probably right," he said. "But they do so enjoy getting away with things." He said the last very softly, his eyes bright. "I'll keep your secret for you, don't worry."

She wondered what it was he thought she was worried about. He was just teasing her. Right?

"Well, I guess I should let you get back to your work.

It was nice meeting you, Talia." Alos tipped his feathered cap her way, then went off in the direction of Bynian's stall.

She watched him go, a little perplexed at the strange meeting. After a moment, she shook her head and got back to work.

Time passed but she kept working, wanting to finish the job as thoroughly as possible since this would be the last time she might be doing this for Kel. Her back ached a little when she was finally finished, her arms sore. She sighed contentedly though, sure she'd done her utmost. Taking her time, she put away the oil, bowl, and glove. She then turned to take a long look at Clarence.

The dragon seemed as huge as ever, his chest rising and falling with his relaxed breaths. But as she watched, she also found herself feeling fondness for him, fondness rather than the fear which had played inside her on their first meeting. He was a person to her now, just as Lareen said he should be. They all were. She would miss her times with him, with the others, she really would.

Smiling sadly, she sat down, leaning against one of Clarence's chests, intending to rest for a bit before going to her room. She yawned loud and long, the day catching up to her. Before she realized what was happening, she fell into a light doze.

Talia sat up with a start, realizing she'd fallen asleep. She looked about her, a little disoriented, but not frightened. Clarence had shifted in the stall, his tail coiled in a ring about her. She frowned, seeing she wasn't where she'd been sitting last. Her frown deepened as she looked down and found not only had she been moved but someone scavenged a blanket and covered her up with it. Did Clarence do this? She wondered why he didn't wake her instead.

Rising to her feet, she glanced toward one of the high-set windows, wondering at the time. A touch of light was lessening the darkness outside, heralding that dawn was near.

Combing her hands through her hair to dislodge the straw which stubbornly decided to take residence there, she silently made her way to the stall's gate. Leaving the blanket draped over it, she sent Clarence a grateful glance then slipped out of the stall. Tiptoeing past the other sleeping dragons, she opened the main doors just enough to sneak outside.

Dew dampened her boots and trousers as she wove between the field of tents and shops to go into the main building. Signs of life already flickered here and there, the carnival once more reviving for another full day of games and testing.

Trying to call as little attention to herself as possible, she made it to the end of the garden path and the door leading into the dining hall. Hurrying to her room, she took a quick bath and got redressed before going back downstairs.

She snatched a small slice of cheese then munched on it as she made her way through the kitchen. The guest cooks already there sent her hopeful looks as she made her way out. As happened to her every morning since the carnival began, she knew on her way back she would be accosted by requests to taste their wares. Talia was surprised she hadn't gained ten pounds from it already.

As she loaded the first of Clarence's barrels, she realized one side benefit of the carnival was all the talk about Clarence, Kel, and Nertak looked to have ceased. With their sentence almost over, she was only too glad of it. She wondered if the Administrator chose to do the carnival with this very side effect in mind. Whether she had or not, Talia was still grateful.

WITH THE FESTIVITIES down to their last two days, everyone seemed to be playing in earnest. As they'd done all week, Mandee and Yllin helped her bring the dragons their cherries. A number of them were gone from their stalls, and when Mandee asked, they were told it was because they were outside giving rides to students. With eyes lit, once they finished their deliveries, Mandee dragged her two friends out to the edge of the sea of tents so they could watch.

"They're so graceful!" Mandee said in awe.

Two dragons were currently in the air, riding the wind.

"It almost looks as if it'd be fun," Yllin said.

"You think so?" Mandee's eyes shone with mischief.

"Ah, when compared to Clarence," Yllin added quickly. "Not that I actually want to try it."

"Why not?" Mandee asked indignantly. "We came here to be part of the Dragon Knight Guild, right? And that means getting to ride dragons."

The three of them wandered closer to the end of the landing field.

"We're nowhere near having to deal with that yet and I still remember our ride here only too clearly." Yllin glowered at her friend. "Just because they seem more graceful doesn't mean the ride would actually be any better." She then pointed at the field's far end. "Besides, look at the size of the line. We'd be waiting hours for a turn for who knows what kind of horrid experience."

Mandee gave her an unhappy look followed by a pout.

"The line is long." Talia could see at least twenty students waiting. Each ride looked to be taking about thirty minutes apiece, and there were only three dragons on the field.

A large shadow engulfed the three of them from above, making them all look up. A gust of wind whooshed through them as a blue dragon roared past. His wings abruptly flared out and brought his body to a stop. He settled to the ground, making the earth tremble momentarily beneath them.

"Greetings, Talia."

She stared in surprise at the dragon's rider. It was the man she met the night before—Alos.

"Hi, Bynian!" Mandee waved at the dragon even as she swept her wind-blown hair out of her face.

"Greetings, fair maidens," Bynian said smoothly.

Mandee giggled, and Yllin greeted him back.

"What are you doing out here?" Though the answer was obvious, it was the only thing Talia could think of to say.

Alos smiled down at her. "We're here for our turn at giving rides to the students."

"Oh."

"The two of us discussed it, and we decided you three should get a ride while we're still fresh. Extra payment, if you will, for spoiling our mutual friend here." Alos gently patted Bynian's neck.

"Spoiling me is a good thing," Bynian said. "I prefer to encourage it whenever I can. Some people, though, don't seem to get the hint."

Alos went on as if he didn't hear. "So, ladies, how about it? I'm rigged to take on at least three passengers."

Talia felt nervous at the concept, not sure after her ride on Clarence whether flying was for her. Yllin looked as unwilling as she, but Mandee held no doubts whatsoever.

"Yes! We'll go!" Mandee said, almost bouncing. "It's most generous of both of you." She turned to face her two companions. "We've *got* to do this. We won't get another chance like this anytime soon. *Please?*"

Talia sighed quietly, still not feeling sure about this course. But Mandee had been there for her when she truly needed someone, and in all honesty, she didn't want to insult either Alos or Bynian by turning them down. "Okay."

"Yllin?" Mandee studied her friend expectantly.

The solemn member of their trio looked at the other two long and hard before finally admitting defeat. "Sure. Though I may live to regret it."

"Yes!" Mandee grabbed both of them and pulled them toward the dragon before they might change their minds.

Alos jumped down from his saddle even as Bynian crouched down on the ground. As they climbed astride the seats with Alos' help, Talia noticed Bynian wasn't as wide as Clarence and the blue dragon was longer.

Alos helped them all strap in, grinning at them the entire time. This didn't do a lot for her confidence. Once he was done, he nimbly climbed onto his own seat. "Are you ladies ready?" he asked them over his shoulder.

Mandee squealed in delight saying yes, while Talia only nodded behind her. Yllin did nothing, sitting in the rear.

"All right then." Alos' grin was still on full force. "Let's go!"

In one fluid motion, Bynian rose on all fours and started forward. His wings spread out on either side then began to flow up and down like waves on a beach. With a powerful jump, they suddenly found themselves in the air.

Talia held on to the front of her saddle with both

hands, even as Yllin gasped behind her.

The ground dropped away beneath them but it did so slowly and gently, not in the nightmarish chaos they were subjected to when Clarence took flight. Talia braced herself anyway, but Bynian's flight was smooth, flawless. The beat of his large wings was strong and steady. His path was straight, without effort. She could almost have believed they weren't moving, if it wasn't for the fact the terrain kept changing below them. After a few minutes, she started to relax.

Alos and Bynian took them along the mountains surrounding the school. At times he flew high amongst the clouds while at others he barely skimmed the tops of the trees.

Talia was slowly suffused with wondrous amazement. This, this was what Kel and Clarence were trying to achieve. This was the true joy of being a Dragon Knight. Pleasure bubbled inside her. She fervently hoped her friends were also sharing her feelings. This was utterly wonderful.

Sooner than she would have hoped, Alos and Bynian turned back to return to the landing strip. A slight shadow of her previous concern returned when she realized they were going to land. This part of the flight was typically the worst with Clarence. She'd seen him go astray too many times on his landings. Would it be difficult for Bynian or would this, also prove easier as well?

Bynian carefully slowed their descent. He flared his wings when he came very close to the ground and was able to set them onto land with minimum effort and no skidding at all.

"We're back, safe and sound." Alos stared back at them, his eyes bright. He undid his straps then started to help them with their own. "So, was it as bad as you feared, Talia?"

She glanced up at Alos, surprised he'd seen through her so easily. "No. Actually, it was quite marvelous. Thank you both very much."

"Yes, thank you!" Mandee piped in. "It was indescribable."

"It was definitely better than riding Clarence," was Yllin's cheery reply.

"Well we're both glad you enjoyed it."

"Yes, indeed," Bynian added.

Smiles passed all around.

Alos helped them down then climbed back into his saddle. "Perhaps we'll get a chance to do it again sometime. Though right now, the two of us better get back to work. Take care." With a wave, Alos and Bynian left them to saunter over to the line of eager students waiting for a ride.

The three girls waved after them enthusiastically. They watched from the sidelines as three students scrambled on to Bynian's back and after a couple of minutes the group launched into the air.

"I think I could really enjoy doing that," Mandee said.

Talia and Yllin nodded in silent agreement.

⁊ᚴ⁊⁊ᚴ⁊⁊ᚴ⁊

TALIA WOKE REFRESHED the next morning, her dreams filled with flying dragons and knights. For the rest of the previous afternoon, she'd had a hard time thinking of anything else. It'd been a fantastic experience. If only the dragons could all stay here to give them more rides.

But today would be the last day of the carnival. It would also be the last day of Kel and Clarence's imprisonment. After today, the two would be free at last. It was definitely something to be grateful for. Excited for them, while at the same time slightly saddened that so many things were coming to an end, she dressed and headed downstairs to grab breakfast.

The usual carnival chaos raged in the kitchen, though she did notice more of the regular staff were on hand. She traded cheery greetings with people from both groups. Yet this, too, would be something which would be gone as of tomorrow.

Clarence was awake as she wheeled the first barrel into the dormitory. *Good morning.*

"Good morning."

Isn't this a beautiful day? Clarence asked her.

She nodded.

Tomorrow it will be more beautiful still, the dragon said with feeling.

She nodded again, not sure what to say. It was good he was looking so forward to it.

When she took Kel his breakfast, she found the squire mirroring the dragon's quietly excited mood.

"Did you see the sunrise this morning?" Kel took the tray from her and shuffled to set it down on the table for her, his chains rattling as he moved. "I haven't seen one so crisp and beautiful in a while."

She smiled a secret smile, finding their excitement contagious. "I think you're right."

Kel gave her his brightest one. "We wouldn't have made it this far without you."

Embarrassed, she looked away. "I better be going. My friends will be waiting."

"Talia."

She hesitated. "Yes?"

"The fireworks display will definitely be tonight," Kel told her. "If you and your friends come up here, the view is bound to be the best in the entire school and a lot less crowded."

She didn't look at him. "Thanks. I'll think about it." She went on her way.

Once she joined Mandee and Yllin downstairs, she was dragged outside, as Mandee prodded them into a mad plunge to try to do all the things they'd been unable to get to so far.

By late afternoon, Talia was exhausted. She was amazed at how Mandee still seemed as full of energy now as when they started. She excused herself to take Clarence and Kel their meals, glad for the break. It was a good thing it would be a rest day tomorrow. Otherwise, most of the students would be in no shape to return to class, not if the frenzied activity she saw was any indication. Most looked to have Mandee's same goal in mind—to try to do *everything* before the day was over.

Kel and Clarence were both still in high spirits, and Kel even reminded her again about the fireworks. The school must really put on a show if he thought so much about it. She figured she'd find out tonight.

"Talia!" Mandee spotted her as she made her way back and ran up to her, almost jumping with excitement. "We just found out there are going to be fireworks tonight."

"I heard about it."

"You have?" Mandee looked surprised. Yllin stood up from where she was resting and joined them, slowly shaking her head.

"Sorry I didn't mention it earlier," Talia said. "But, if you want, we have permission to watch them from one of the best spots in the school."

"We do?" asked both girls simultaneously.

She nodded. "Kel said we could watch from the roof if we wanted."

"He did?"

The incredulity on their faces almost made her burst out laughing. "Yes. He said the carnival people really put on an amazing display and it wasn't to be missed." Now that she thought of it, this would also be a nice reward for her friends for all the help they'd given her over the last month. "Unless you don't want to get the best view?"

Mandee and Yllin glanced at each other then Yllin answered enthusiastically for both of them. "Let's do it!"

As the sun dropped toward the horizon after she taking care of her chores, the three of them split up and went to turn in their coupons at their favorite food stalls. With loaded arms, they joined up again and made their way indoors then as unobtrusively as possible threaded their way to the fourth floor and on to the stairs to the roof.

Talia stopped in surprise when they got there; a blanket already set out for them close to the edge. She quickly glanced toward Kel's door, but it was closed. Her friends didn't question their good fortune and sat down on the blanket making themselves comfortable.

The three of them ate with the last of the fading light, expectantly waiting for the show to begin.

Without warning, a white streak rose to the heavens then exploded in a resplendent shower of blue sparks. Talia and her two friends gasped as the light expanded and faded, seeming so close they could almost reach out and touch it.

Music poured up from below as another streak rose to the sky followed almost instantly by two more. The first burst into a dazzling red butterfly while the other two formed a curtain of green for it to fly above.

With her eyes full of wonder, she glanced back as she half rose, determined Kel should share in this, his punishment be damned. She didn't make it to her feet before she sat back down, chiding herself for having ever worried. Kel's doorway was open and he was sitting inside it, officially still in his quarters but yet able to get a view of the magnificent display.

After a moment, he noticed her gaze and waved at her, sending her a bright smile. She quickly returned it then turned back to enjoy the show.

Appreciative 'oohs' and 'ahs' drifted to them from below along with the timed music, but otherwise it was as if the show were for their eyes alone. Talia gazed at the display, totally enraptured by it, not having imagined such marvels possible.

Magic must have something to do with it. Surely they couldn't have gotten all the effects they saw purely from powder. The crystal waterfall made her heart sing with the beauty of it. She had never seen anything like it.

After almost an hour, a giant flurry of rockets launched into the sky and exploded in a kaleidoscope of colors so bright it seemed almost like day. Applause rang out from below even as the music softly wound to a close. Sadly, the wondrous display came to an end.

She glanced back over her shoulder but Kel was already gone, his door closed once more.

"That was fabulous!" Mandee exclaimed breathlessly.

Yllin nodded her agreement, her eyes still dazzled from the last of the fireworks.

"They were grand, weren't they?" Talia said, grateful Kel made such a point to get her to see them from here. It was a sight she'd not soon forget.

Chapter Eighteen

TALIA LEISURELY MADE her way downstairs. The games and contests had gone late into the night, but she hadn't stayed up for them. Many others had, however, trying to squeeze all they could into the time they had left. She grinned, doubting too many people would make it downstairs until much later in the morning.

As she entered the dining hall, she found she basically had the place to herself. Food was set out the same as on the days of the carnival, so she picked up a plate and served herself. She sat down and instantly dug into her meal, but after a minute forced herself to slow, reminding herself she had no reason to rush anymore. Today she was officially once more just one of the hundreds of students here—only having to deal with the typical chores of a rest day. She looked down at her plate and sighed. She was already missing them and it hadn't even been a few hours. Would they miss her as well? Probably not. She wouldn't in their place—she would just try to forget the whole unpleasant business and put it behind her. Things would now go back to the way they were before.

She sighed quietly again and ate her breakfast nowhere near as enthusiastically as before.

She saw no sign of the squire or dragon in the morning as she went back and forth with her filled buckets of water. Whenever she ventured outside, she looked up at the sky, wondering if they were out flying together, trying to make up for lost time. But there was no sign of them, only of the carnival people packing up their wares and loading their dragons so they could go home. She toyed with the idea of going into the dragon dormitory just to say hello, but didn't, knowing she had no right to be there anymore.

During lunch, her gaze kept gravitating to the Administrator's table, looking to see if Kel would show. The room grew pretty full, students and what carnival people still remained availing themselves of the noon meal and conversation. She was almost done with her own food when she finally spotted him.

Kel took his usual seat, his eyes downcast, not looking at or speaking to anyone. As she watched him, she suddenly understood the awkwardness he was feeling. Kel sat with teachers, not students, with people above him. Students would be below him. He possessed no real peers. Plus his offense had been against one of those above him. He'd not spoken to any of them in a month, and there was nowhere else he could go.

Her heart ached for him. She wished she could do something to help him. Even as the thought passed her mind, however, one of the teachers at the table turned to face him and cheerfully said hello. Kel looked up, appearing surprised, and returned the greeting, a shy smile momentarily flickering on his lips. He looked even more astonished, as a few moments later Nertak showed up and sat down next to him slapping him heartily on the shoulder. The old man didn't usually eat at the table.

"Talia, what are you looking at?"

She snapped her gaze in another direction as Sonsan asked her question. "Ah, nothing. Just trying to see how many of the carnival people are left." She felt her cheeks grow warm at the lie. She hoped those around her wouldn't notice.

"Hey, looks like the squire is back." Dyl half stood and pointed in the direction of the Administrator's table.

Talia grimaced, wishing they hadn't noticed it.

"Does it mean you're off the hook now, Talia?" Sonsan asked her.

She didn't look at her classmate directly as she answered. "Yes. My duties ended last night."

"So you can tell us all his secrets now?"

Talia glanced over at her, her face hard. "There's never been anything to tell. Would it really hurt so much just to leave him alone?"

Sonsan stared at her in amazement, a grin tugging at the edge of her mouth. "You sure do seem awfully concerned about him. Could it be there's something between the two of you? A prisoner and jailer dalliance? You have spent a lot of time alone with him."

Talia felt her ire at the brown-eyed girl rise, though she tried stubbornly to squelch it. "You can believe whatever you want."

Sonsan pouted at her reply, obviously disappointed. "I'm sure he'll get in trouble again," she said without much wind.

"Maybe it might be you instead," Daltan said quietly from across the table.

Sonsan stared at the dark-haired boy as if he'd suddenly grown fangs. "Well, that wasn't very nice."

"No, but you earned it." Yllin gave the other girl a

nasty grin.

Mandee hissed in a breath beside her, shocked by her friend's words. She wasn't the only one.

Sonsan glared at Yllin before rising to her feet. "I guess this table is just full of bad-mannered people today. I think I'll go sit with more appreciative company." Throwing them all a snooty look, she picked up her plate and moved farther down to another table. Talia felt a dull surprise as she saw Sonsan sit with a group of older students. One, whose face she knew well, was glaring in the direction of Kel and Nertak. Maybe all of Sonsan's prodding and questioning weren't mere curiosity after all.

Talia sighed. It was over though, Kel was free, and so they would no longer have any need of her. She was still somewhat startled at the unexpected turn of events ending with Sonsan's leave-taking. At least it gave those in her group something other than the squire to talk about.

Kel showed up at his usual place at dinner. Lareen made an appearance as well and seemed to pay the squire a lot of attention during the meal, purposely bringing him into conversations and asking his opinion on several matters. Even with the extra consideration, as was his usual wont, Kel left as soon as the door was opened out into the garden.

Talia watched him go, wishing she could find some excuse to go out there with him.

Classes restarted the next day, though enthusiasm amongst the student body was at an all-time low. She welcomed the work, however, wanting to keep busy rather than to spend her time as she had the day before, wondering what Kel and Clarence were up to.

Sonsan didn't deign to sit with them at breakfast, but by lunch, she joined their group again, acting as if nothing untoward had ever happened. Yllin didn't look excited to have her back. Talia didn't mind as much as she thought she would but planned to keep her eyes on her. She was just glad Sonsan was wise enough not to bring the topic of the squire up again.

In the evening, she noticed Kel as he rushed through his meal and left the dining hall by way of the kitchen. When the rest of them were released, she spotted him riding Clarence, the two of them twisting madly in the sky.

Talia stopped and stared as Clarence unexpectedly dived and dropped like a stone. She waited once he disappeared behind the building for him to reappear, but instead heard a cracking, crashing noise. Without thinking, she took off at a run. A number of people near her did the same.

Coming around the corner of the building, she skidded to a halt, not sure if she should believe what she was seeing. Past the landing strip, in the line of trees on the right side of the field, broken branches and dislocated leaves littered the ground. She could see Clarence past them, wedged between several trees. As she watched dumbfounded, Kel stumbled out from the trees and sat down with a plop on the ground, staring back at the dragon.

"Talia. Do you think they're all right?"

She started as Mandee put a hand on her arm. It was only then she realized her friends had followed her. "Kel, Kel should be. His armor is magicked." She didn't say more, not sure if the same would apply to Clarence.

"Well, it seems their month off didn't help their flying any."

Laughs sprang up all around at the comment. Talia turned to stare at Yllin, anger flaring up inside her. As their gazes met, Yllin looked away, for once appearing embarrassed—as if she didn't realize what she was saying until after she said it.

"I'm sorry, I didn't mean..."

Talia didn't wait for her to finish, but turned away and stomped off in Kel's direction. No one followed her. It was almost as if they were afraid to get too close. It only stoked her irritation. Kel and Clarence could have been seriously hurt out there; would they have just been left to die?

By the time she reached the trees, Kel was removing his helmet and critically studying the dragon's predicament. Clarence's neck was twisted up and over his back; he watched Talia as she came close.

"Are you both all right?" she asked them.

Kel glanced back in surprise, but quickly looked away, his cheeks flushed. "I'm fine. I'm just a little winded."

I'm in good health as well, except for this bit of trouble of course. Clarence sent an annoyed glance at the trees pining him where he'd fallen.

"He's stuck?" She was already pretty sure of the answer.

Kel sighed. "Afraid so."

"Do you need any help?" she asked. "Just tell me what you want me to do. If you prefer, I'm sure I can round up at least a few people to come over and give you a hand."

Kel slowly shook his head. "It's all right. Thanks anyway." His voice lowered to where she almost couldn't hear it. "This is all part of my punishment."

She frowned, not understanding what he meant.

"Punishment?"

Kel cocked his head in Clarence's direction. In a flash, she understood. None of this was an accident—Clarence had landed there deliberately, hoping to make Kel pay for all he went through in the past month. She shook her head, not wanting to believe this, but what the dragon said next took any doubts right out of her head.

Yes, thank you for your offer, but Kel will be able to deal with this on his own.

She blinked several times as she mentally stumbled for something to say. "I see."

At this time, two farmers came up carrying axes. Kel walked over and got between them and the dragon—thanking them for the tools and telling them to leave it all to him. Exchanging puzzled looks, the two men shrugged and gave him the axes then went back the way they came.

Kel removed his armor, setting each piece carefully out of the way. With only his under-tunic on, he sent Talia a sad half-smile and picked up one of the axes. Settling it over his shoulder, he approached the largest of the three trees pinning Clarence and got to work.

Talia slowly walked away, looking back as the echoes of Kel's ax biting into wood followed her. She didn't understand why Clarence felt the need to do this. She understood even less why Kel was willing to let him get away with it.

The crowd of spectators after the crash thinned and those remaining didn't look much interested anymore. Yllin stood against the corner of the building, her face grave. Mandee stood beside her. As Talia came close, Mandee waved her over, her eyes imploring her to please come.

"Clarence is all right, too," she told them softly. "But he's stuck between some trees. Kel is cutting him out."

Yllin looked up at her, her eyes miserable. "I'm really sorry for what I said, Talia. I swear I didn't mean anything."

She tried to give her a smile. "I know. I overreacted. I'm sorry. I guess I've just become a little protective about them."

"And so you should."

All three girls turned at the unexpected voice behind them. Lareen gave them a faint smile as she gazed at their astonished faces. She then looked out past them toward the line of trees. "They're both all right?"

"Yes, ma'am," Talia informed her. "But Clarence is stuck." Yllin and Mandee tried to make themselves as small as possible even as she spoke.

"Hmm, let me guess." Lareen's gaze locked with Talia's own. "Clarence wants Kel to get him out alone."

Talia nodded.

"And Kel is going to oblige him."

Talia nodded again.

Lareen sighed. "One day their stubbornness is going to be their undoing." The Administrator's face looked troubled for a moment but then cleared. "Well, it was nice talking to you. Perhaps in a couple of hours, you'd be kind enough to take Kel something to drink? I have a feeling he's going to be at this for quite a while."

"Yes, ma'am."

Giving her a soft smile, Lareen turned away and headed back indoors.

"I think she likes you," Mandee whispered beside her as all three watched the Administrator walk away.

"What?" She glanced at her friend, not understanding where she could have gotten such an impression.

"She actually spoke to you seriously, not in the usual, frivolous way she normally speaks to most people." Yllin nodded in agreement of Mandee's explanation. Talia didn't know what to make of it at all.

A COUPLE OF hours later, after unsuccessfully trying to finish her reading for the next day's assignments, Talia grabbed one of her buckets and left her room. She made her outside and followed the usual route to the small lake the students pulled their water from. After filling the bucket halfway, she started across the fields to where she left Clarence and Kel earlier.

The sound of steady chopping echoed toward her as she came near. The sky grew cloudy, deepening the night, but she could still see where they were by the light of a solitary lamp. Someone must have taken pity on Kel and brought it out so he wouldn't have to work in the dark. It hadn't occurred to her to do that.

As she came close, she saw Kel had already cut down three of the trees holding the dragon. Her brow furrowed, thinking Clarence looked more wedged in than he did before. She shook her head, trying not to think about what the dragon might be doing.

"Kel, I brought some water for you."

The young squire let the ax swing one more time then left it embedded in the thick trunk he was working on before looking up. The top half of his tunic lay nearby on the grass, leaving his exposed skin covered in sweat. His hair clung stubbornly to his head, and his face was heavily flushed. He gave her a grateful, tired smile as he tried to catch his breath. He stumbled over to where she stood by the lamp, which was sitting on an old stump. "Th— thanks."

Kel grabbed the bucket with slightly shaking hands and drank some of the water down with great heaving gulps. He then took what water was left and dumped it over his head.

She stepped back as the water splashed around him. Clarence watched from where he lay somewhat disinterestedly.

"Would you like some water, too, Clarence?" she asked the dragon. "I could bring you some in one of the barrels."

That would be incredibly nice, he said.

"No, I'll get it," Kel interjected. "I need a break anyway."

I should think not. Clarence's eyebrows arched high. *My situation has barely improved since you started working and I've no desire to remain out here all night.*

She saw Kel's fist clench at his side. "So you're not satisfied with just punishing me, you have to bring her into this as well?" A hard edge had crept into his voice. One Talia had never heard before.

I'm not doing anything of the kind, Clarence replied haughtily. *She offered to do it—I didn't ask her. If you'd gotten me out of here promptly, she wouldn't have even needed to do so. So in the end, her inconvenience is your fault as well.*

She stared from one to the other of them as their words escalated. "It's no one's fault. I offered. I wanted to."

You do not need to cover for his uncouth behavior, Talia. We all know who we're dealing with here. The dragon's tone was in no way kind.

"That's enough, you ungrateful lizard," Kel said heatedly. He took a step toward him. "You and I both know you've been wedging yourself in tighter whenever I've even come close to getting you free. And it's no secret you crash landed here on purpose in the first place!"

Clarence snorted, sending a thin stream of smoke flowing from his nostrils. *So you say.*

"You want out," Kel retorted, "I'll get you out. This is how I should have done things in the first place." He turned on his heel and snatched up the glass lamp.

"Kel what are you—?" She took several steps toward him, fearing what he might be about to do. Though she was loath to admit it, she was frightened of his temper, and of the extreme acts it drove him to before.

Kel glanced over at her, his eyes losing a bit of their fire as he saw the misgivings on her face. "Don't worry, I'm not going to hurt him. I'm just going to give him a little incentive to get out." With that said, he abruptly dashed forward.

Clarence spotted him and swung his tail hard in the squire's direction. Kel jumped over it as it came at him. Running headlong, he threw the lamp as hard as he could at one of the trees still holding the dragon prisoner.

The glass shattered on impact, smearing the tree's trunk with oil and a moment later with hungering flames.

Clarence hissed and tried to hit Kel again with his tail as the squire retreated. At the last moment, Kel rolled out of the way and getting back on his feet, rapidly ran out of the dragon's range.

The flames licked farther up the tree and down several small limbs, reaching out to caress Clarence's flank. The dragon gave a mental roar made up more of annoyance than pain.

"But the forest will catch on fire!" Talia looked from Kel back to the burning tree, still shocked by what he'd done.

He glanced over at her, shaking his head. "It won't. He won't let it."

As if to show her the squire's words were true, Clarence roared again, his tail lashing madly back and forth even as his back legs took hold on the trees to either side and pushed. Both trees snapped, the sound echoing about them, and he pulled his body free. Turning sideways, Clarence let out a mind-numbing roar before thrusting his body against the burning trunk. His claws dug into the dirt around him and brought it up to smear it on the wood as well.

When the flames died down, leaving only burning embers, strange, formless words echoed in her mind as a swirling cloud grew just above the cinders and thickened over them until they were smothered.

As soon as the embers were out and the danger was thwarted, the small cloud disappeared. The dragon turned to glare at his partner. *Human!*

Clarence slithered toward the squire, a roiling storm advancing on a lone skiff. Kel waited for him, his stance defiant and unafraid. "Lizard."

"Stop!" Talia rushed between them, not daring to think about what she was doing. She wasn't sure she would live through it. "You've got to stop. This is going too far. *Please.*"

Clarence came to a skidding halt, his hot breath mere inches from her face. She stared at him, her eyes pleading with him to listen to reason, even as she quivered inside at the type of damage her friend could do to both her and Kel if he so wished.

Clarence's crossed eyes focused first on her then on the squire. They came to rest on her again, his teeth bared. *As you wish.*

With a last flare of smoke from his nostrils, Clarence backed away and turned around before snaking out onto the landing strip and launching up into the air.

Talia's knees suddenly gave out on her. She fell to the ground, her breath quivering in relief.

"Are you all right?" Kel's worried query reached her as

he rushed forward to kneel before her. "He wouldn't have hurt you."

Talia nodded, not looking at him, not sharing his confidence at all.

"Do you need anything? Is there something I can do?" He sounded more concerned than before.

She shook her head emphatically then tried to get back on her feet. Kel reached out to help her, but she pulled her arm away before he could take it. "I'm all right!"

"Talia..." Kel hesitated as she continued to keep her gaze averted from his own.

"Curfew will be here soon. I've got to go. Excuse me." She took off at a run. Her eyes stung as she left the squire behind as swiftly as her legs would take her.

Reaching the deep shadows of the school's buttresses, she finally slowed. She wiped at her face, trying to catch her breath, and looked back the way she came. Other than for the darkened line of trees, she couldn't see much of anything.

They were such idiots—*both* of them! Why did she even care? Brushing her sleeve again over her eyes, she turned away and made her way inside.

THE NEXT MORNING, Talia spotted Kel as he came into the dining hall for breakfast. Seeing her, he waved shyly in her direction. She didn't return it. She still hadn't made up her mind as to exactly how she felt about what happened the night before. Clarence was childish in trying to punish Kel as he did, yet Kel had also been reckless. If she hadn't intervened, who knew how far the dragon would have gone in his anger. Without armor, Kel would have been totally at the dragon's mercy and in no way able to stop Clarence from doing something he might later regret. It was a good thing she was there, though she was also aware that if not for her arrival with the water, things might not have gone where they did.

Kel returned from the kitchen with his meal and sat down looking somewhat more subdued than usual. Yet it wasn't until he got up to leave that she realized something wasn't right. Instead of hanging on to his usual bounty of fruit, his hands were empty as he exited the room. Worse, he did so through the door other people used to come in rather than through the kitchen or the garden.

Talia frowned at this even as she tried telling herself she didn't care.

By lunchtime, the fact Clarence had crashed and been pinned between some trees made the rounds, and so did the fact while three of the trees were cut, two others were broken close to the base, and one of those was burned. Whispers full of speculation flowed back and forth.

She said nothing about any of it and gladly saw Yllin and Mandee do the same with what they knew. She tried to listen to as little of the conjecture as she could get away with.

Later, she found herself out on her balcony. After some time, she realized Kel and Clarence wouldn't be practicing. A dull sadness reached for her at the realization, but she squelched it, telling herself the two of them were probably just being fools again. After a month of being locked away from each other, one would have thought they'd have treated one another better. Obviously, this wasn't going to be the case.

The following morning, she found herself anxiously waiting for Kel to show. When he did, she waited for him to look over and wave, not entirely sure if she'd allow herself to return it. Instead, he kept his gaze on the floor and not once even glanced in her direction. She tried to tell herself this was only payback for her ignoring him the previous day, but as she watched him walk by, deep down, she didn't really think that was it. Kel looked drained, his expression was blank and hidden. His hair was half mussed, his clothes untidy. Surely he didn't take her rebuff as more than it meant, did he? Why was it he and Clarence seemed able to live only for extremes?

Again Kel carried no fruit and left the hall through its main entryway.

When she saw they didn't practice yet again that night, she started to worry. How long were the two of them planning on letting this go on? The longer they waited to resolve it, the worse it would be.

The next morning, she fidgeted in her seat as she waited for Kel to show before her friends did. When she finally spotted him, she stood up, but again he didn't look her way.

"Kel!" She yelled across the room to get his attention.

The squire glanced over in surprise, dark circles standing prominently beneath his eyes.

She waved enthusiastically.

He only stared, stunned for a moment. Then his features softened and a soft smile tugged suddenly at the side of his mouth. He waved back tentatively, before going on his way to the kitchen with a lighter step.

Talia sat back down, watching him go with some satisfaction, and deep down a touch of fear. Kel's reaction only proved she'd been right in her original guess. Still, how was it she could have such an effect on him? The two of them didn't really know each other. Kel shouldn't really have cared very much about how she felt about him one way or the other. Aside from Clarence, though, could she be the closest thing he had to a friend? If she had only two and both of them were unhappy with her, wouldn't it make her feel terrible? The questions passed back and forth in her mind for the rest of the day.

When they were released from lunch, she slowed as she made her way out of the garden when she spotted Kel and the Administrator standing together outside of the dragon dormitory. Kel was staring at the ground, his face blank as Lareen spoke to him with a grave expression.

Talia's brow furrowed. Had Lareen also noticed the squire and the dragon's strange behavior? She hoped whatever she was saying to Kel would help bring their strange quarrel to an end, but didn't hold much faith it would.

That night, Kel didn't show up for dinner. Lareen looked far from her usual jovial mood. Whisperings filled the hall as even more speculation made the rounds.

"You won't believe this!" A third-year student who occasionally played swapball with some of their group on freeday slipped over to their table from the one across the way. He shoved his wiry body between Dyl and Jarel, his face excited. Several of those seated there, especially Sonsan, looked over at him expectantly.

"The Administrator gave the squire an errand to run this morning and he wouldn't do it. They're saying he and Clarence had a falling out since the dragon got stuck in those trees a few days ago."

Talia glanced up, interested in what he was saying despite herself. It seemed to fit with what she saw earlier.

"Well, the Administrator insisted they go anyway. Clarence wasn't happy. Some guys saw them when they came back and said the dragon was flying ten times worse than normal, doing flips and twirls and all sorts of other stomach-turning acrobatics." The student scanned his audience, obviously happy to be spreading the news. "To add insult to injury, Clarence slipped sideways when he landed and buried the squire beneath him, dragging him halfway down the field. When they finally came to a stop, Clarence took his sweet time getting off him, too."

Talia frowned even as those around her started speculating at the odd news.

ᚱᚵᛏᚱᚵᛏᚱᚵᛏ

WHEN SHE SAW Kel and Clarence weren't going to practice again, Talia closed the book she was reading with a slam and left her room.

Enough was enough. If the two of them weren't going to do something about this, maybe she'd have to. With a determined look on her face, she stomped downstairs to make her way to the dragon habitat.

Once she got there, she slowed and slipped quietly inside, not entirely sure how she was going to go about this. When she reached Clarence's stall, she stood before it silently for a moment then, trying to sound more cheerful than she felt, she made her presence known. "Good evening, Clarence."

The dragon looked up at her from where he was leisurely batting a large crystal ball back and forth between his huge claws. *Good evening.* He looked away.

She waited to see if he'd say anything else, but he didn't. She was sure he wasn't going to make this easy. "I haven't seen you for a few days. I've missed that."

The dragon said nothing, still gently batting the ball

across the hay-strewn floor.

"I've noticed you and Kel haven't been practicing. Rumor has it the two of you are still mad at one another," she said.

Clarence humphed lightly, sending a thin trail of smoke rising into the air.

She steeled herself and said what she came to ask. "How long do you plan on staying mad at him? Wasn't a month long enough?"

The dragon continued playing as if she hadn't spoken.

"You pushed Kel too far," she said, trying hard to keep her voice level. "We both know it. You were being unreasonable and only got mad because he wouldn't put up with it anymore."

None of this concerns you.

She felt a spark of anger flare inside her at the bored tone in his words. She scrounged for something to say—anything to make the dragon pay attention. "Would it be because I'm an annoying human or only because you're enjoying this self-chosen path of destruction you're on?"

Clarence glanced up at her, a brow raised high on his scaly face. *Path of destruction?*

"What else would you call it? You know, if you wanted out of your contract with Kel so badly, there are probably easier and less hurtful ways to go about it."

I'm doing no such thing. Clarence reached out with his tail to retrieve his ball, which had gotten away from him.

She pushed on. "Aren't you? Are you sure? Because the way you're acting, it looks as if you'd like nothing better. Didn't you imply you were tricked into this arrangement in the first place?" Even as she said it, she realized how right her words were. What did Clarence really want?

You are mistaken. His tone didn't hold the conviction

behind it one might have expected.

"Then explain to me why you're alienating him," she demanded.

I'm doing no such thing. He's the one who's stopped coming to see me.

"So if I went to him right now and got him to come, you'd welcome him in? Or would you, through your partial bond, send him your anger and scorn so he'd stay away without your having to say anything?" What she said was a gamble, a half-formed suspicion, but from the way the dragon suddenly looked away, she could see she guessed right. Kel's anger might burn hot when finally driven to it, but it didn't linger.

Clarence's on the other hand...

You are mistaken. His tone held even less conviction than before.

She decided to press on. "You're holding a grudge. How else can you explain the fact your flying has gotten worse or how you purposely landed on Kel today instead of trying to protect him and the cargo from the worst of it as you normally do?"

She saw the dragon flinch.

It wasn't like that.

"We both know Kel is very sorry for what he did a month ago, for the punishment he dragged you into. Wasn't he the one who asked you not to come to help him when those bullies beat him up just so you wouldn't get into any further trouble? Isn't he the one who's too proud to ask others for help yet he almost begged me to oil your skin in his stead so you wouldn't suffer unduly?"

Clarence didn't look at her.

Talia took a deep breath, having saved the worst for last. "Or could it be this started out as only annoyance and stubbornness but turned into something more when

Kel forced your hand and set fire to the trees making you use your strength and hidden skills in magic? Are you so afraid of people finding out you're not as weak and helpless as you seem? Should I go discuss these things with Lareen and others at the school?"

Clarence shifted and stared at her through veiled eyes. He said nothing for a long time. *You seem more perceptive than I previously gave you credit for.*

She paid no attention to the barbed compliment. "I don't know why you feel the way you do, and frankly I don't care. Your secrets are safe. I won't talk, so you have nothing to worry about. But please, stop punishing him and yourself. It's getting you nowhere, and it's for no good reason."

Clarence stretched out, looking away from her as if getting ready for sleep. So softly as to be almost imperceptible, his voice rang inside her head. *I will consider what you've said.*

He closed his eyes and didn't look at her again.

Talia was sure she would get nothing more from him. She hoped this would be enough. "Thank you."

Without saying anything else, she left him to his thoughts.

As she stepped out into the cool night, she did admit something to herself—she'd lied to Clarence about one thing. She did indeed care about the reasons the dragon felt he must hide his powers. Sure he really was doing it, her curiosity ate at her as to why. What was the point? She knew though that if she'd let on, if she'd dared ask, he would have refused to speak to her entirely. She sighed. With any luck, things would work out for the best anyway.

A SMALL SMILE lighted on Talia's face the next morning as she spotted Kel coming out from the kitchen. His expression was clear, his steps light, and a basket of fruit hung from his arm as he made his way to his table. She waved at him as he spotted her and he returned the greeting with a bright smile.

It seemed everything would be all right after all—for now.

Her schoolwork seemed to increase exponentially and so other than for greeting Kel in the morning or watching him with Clarence as they practiced at night, she saw little of the dragon or squire during the week. On freeday, however, she made a point of going to the dormitory. As she'd hoped, she had no trouble getting inside. She found Kel there with Clarence, the squire oiling the dragon's skin.

Not sure how Clarence would feel about her presence, she shyly greeted them. "Morning."

"Talia!" Kel looked up from his work, looking pleasantly surprised.

Clarence glanced over as well. *Good morning.*

She couldn't read the dragon's tone but decided to take the fact he was speaking to her as a good sign. "I only stopped by to see if you were both doing all right." Now that she was here, she didn't have any idea how to proceed.

We're doing tolerably well.

"I'm glad to hear it." She looked away not sure what else to say, yet not wanting to leave since she just got there. "Well..."

"You know, Clarence's been complaining I don't do as good a job as you did on his skin," Kel said. "If you're not too busy, would you consider showing me your technique?"

Her face lit up before she could stop herself. She glanced at Clarence then looked away. "I'm caught up on my work, but..." She left the rest unsaid not sure how Clarence felt about it.

I would be most grateful if you would. You have the touch, and it would do him good to learn of it.

A swell of happiness cut through her at the dragon's words. Her hands itched to help again. "I can!"

Kel opened the gate for her to come inside. She couldn't help smiling.

For the next month, on every freeday, she went straight to the dormitory as soon as she was able and spent one to two hours with the dragon and the squire. She helped oil Clarence's skin, and in turn, Kel and Clarence would converse with her and even help her with things she was having problems grasping in class. Clarence was exceptionally well versed in history for both human and dragon kind. Neither seemed to mind her bouts of endless questions, looking more amused by her curiosity, or her simple, inexperienced point of view than anything else.

She was quite pleased with the arrangement.

Chapter Nineteen

"LISTEN UP, EVERYONE!"

The students were about to be dismissed from breakfast when the booming voice cut through the dining hall. All heads turned toward the Administrator's table as Lareen appeared in a flash on top of it. The room grew abruptly silent, Lareen's unusual appearance—in armor no less—and the seriousness in her tone, trapping everyone's attention.

"An emergency has arisen and our help is needed." The Administrator's eyes gleamed intently.

"Maeloon have attacked a village a few hours flight from here. It's not only one, but a group of them."

Gasps rang all around. Talia felt a shiver make its way unwanted down her back. Maeloon. In a pack.

"It gets worse. This is not the first village they've attacked, and a group of ruffians is following behind them pillaging in their wake. The Fifty-eighth Squadron has been dispatched to deal with the matter, but they need help caring for the wounded, distributing supplies, and protecting the camp while they divert the maeloon and take care of the bandits.

"I've pledged the school's help since we're close to the devastated area and we have plenty of stored supplies. As for personnel, this will be on a purely volunteer basis. We'll need people helping both here and there to move the materials, run errands, keep watch and whatever else might come up. The chances of danger are slim, but there are no guarantees. Maeloon and humans working together is an unprecedented event, and until we're able to better ascertain how this has been managed, the true extent of the threat will not be known.

"Classes are suspended. Anyone wishing to volunteer, please report in armor to Nertak's cave in an hour. We'll be using his transportation circle to get there so we can start assisting as soon as possible. I'll see you there." Lareen disappeared as abruptly as she came.

The room erupted with voices as everyone started asking questions and speculating at once.

"It sounds horrible," Dyl said. "Maeloon of all things. I saw a caged one once. It gave me nightmares for weeks." His eyes were round. "It snarled and slobbered, biting itself trying to get out." He spoke fast as if unable to stop now that he'd started. "It didn't seem to care. It was big, as big as a miniature horse, though its back legs were shaped funny. Its tail had a strange pointed barb. The way it smiled all the time." He shuddered.

"Its teeth, they reminded me of a mesh of wires, and those eyes..." He covered his face as if it would protect him from the memory.

"How many volunteers do you think they're looking for?" Mandee asked no one in particular.

"Surely they wouldn't take first-year students as volunteers." Jarel looked at the others with unease.

"I've never seen the Administrator look so serious. It

must be pretty awful," added Yllin. Her quiet remark brought home the truth of the situation more than anything else so far.

The watchers started herding everyone outside. Clumps of people stuck together discussing the present situation.

"Talia, are you going to volunteer?" Mandee asked very quietly as they went back into the building.

She glanced at her friend then looked away. "I—I thought I might." Bumps ran up her arms even as she considered it. "If maeloon were running all over my village, I'd hope someone would volunteer to help us." Old stories told in the night about the creatures made a kernel of fear form hard inside her. It was every villager's worst nightmare to think of finding themselves confronted by one of the misshapen maeloon.

"That's true...," Mandee said pensively. "I hadn't thought of it that way."

"Just because you volunteer doesn't mean someone else would if they were in your place," Yllin added cynically. "Not that I'm saying you shouldn't," she said quickly as Talia and Mandee stared at her in surprise. "I'm going to do it, so don't get me wrong. I'm hoping to get a chance to see LaSeren at work."

"Oh, and maybe Wulan, too?" Mandee giggled, though it did sound a little frayed.

"Besides," Yllin pointed out, "it's not likely they'll have us, so there's not much to worry about. Even if they do take us up on it, you can bet we'll be put as far from the danger as possible. They'll probably make us stay here and move supplies around."

"You're probably right," Talia said. "The more experienced students are probably the ones they're really hoping will volunteer." She felt her previous trepidation ease a bit. It was highly probable she could volunteer, help out, and yet not come anywhere near the maeloon. That would suit her just fine.

The three of them parted at the stairs and each headed toward their own rooms to don their armor. Talia had almost reached hers when she spotted Kel pacing just outside her door. The moment he saw her, he rushed over, relief and a few other emotions she couldn't place flashing in his face.

"Talia!"

"Is something wrong?" Worry nipped at her, knowing Kel didn't usually seek her out.

His light gaze locked with her own for a moment then looked away. "No, no, everything's fine." He hesitated. "I just needed to talk to you."

She frowned feeling confused. "What about?"

Kel's blue-eyed gaze met her own again. "Are you planning on volunteering?"

"Yes. Why?"

He nodded. "We'd figured as much. Come with me. I need your help."

"What?" Talia asked.

Rather than responding, Kel took her hand and started off down the corridor. She was left with no choice but to follow.

"Where are we going?"

Kel didn't answer, instead increasing his pace. He took her to the nearest stairwell then rose to the fourth floor. Once there, he took the stairs to the roof. She grew more confused by the moment. Why would he be taking her up there?

She was forced to cover her eyes as they stepped out into the bright sunshine and it blinded her. A moment later, a large shadow blocked out the sun as Clarence stepped across the roof.

Kel released her hand and nimbly climbed onto the dragon's back.

"Kel, what's this about?" she asked, worry and annoyance warring inside her.

The squire stared down at her shyly from his lofty perch. "Clarence and I have already volunteered to help on this mission. We both also figured you'd do the same."

Yet it is not right you should go, Clarence told her.

Kel nodded. "Yes, for once, we totally agree."

She stared at the two of them, not entirely believing what she was hearing. Did they know something she didn't? "There's no guarantee they'll even take me as a volunteer, not if enough of the older students, teachers, and watchers do it."

"We don't want to take the chance," Kel told her. "I was in Lareen's office picking up our delivery for today when the messenger popped in. I saw and heard everything." His expression was grim. "The maeloon and those mercenaries following them aren't just looting and doing wanton destruction."

She felt a chill wriggle through her as Kel said nothing more. Her mind had no trouble imagining what those worse things might be. She shook her head to try to dispel the fear trying to crowd around her. "It—it doesn't matter. I have to be willing to do my share. I thought this was what the guild was all about."

Kel and Clarence's gazes didn't quite meet her own. "Yes. But for us to do what we have to, we can't afford to be worrying about you, wondering if something horrible has happened to you. And we'd be nowhere near to help if something did. It's best for all concerned if you were somewhere safe until all this is over."

"What?" She stared in astonishment at the two of

them. "I appreciate the sentiment, but I'm quite capable of taking care of myself, thank you. I'll volunteer if I want to."

And she thinks we're stubborn. Clarence's amusement was clear.

Talia didn't find it comical at all. "This conversation is over." She turned around to storm down the stairs.

She'd almost reached the doorway when Clarence's long claws wound themselves about her waist and lifted her effortlessly off her feet. "What are you doing? Let go of me!"

"I'm sorry, we just can't take the chance," Kel said softly behind her.

She glanced over her shoulder, fury filling her eyes. How could they do this? Who did they think they *were*? "Let me go this instant!"

Clarence spread his wings wide then leaped upwards.

She gasped as she was unexpectedly jerked up.

"Don't do this!" Her protest was ripped from her lips by the wind as the three of them rose high into the sky. Talia clung hard to the claws about her, her dangling legs making her feel she would fall through the dragon's grip. "Take me back!"

Neither rider nor dragon heeded her commands, the school rapidly growing smaller behind them.

Clarence flew on, his progress occasionally dipping to one side or the other though not as drastically as was usual for him. While a part of her noticed this, most of her was too incensed to care. The farther they went, the hotter her anger became. Who did they think they *were*? If they could volunteer, why couldn't she?

Clarence's altitude dropped as they approached one of the mountains close to the school. A lush forest covered its side, except for patches of open ground where the trees had been cleared for lumber. Clarence headed toward one of these spots located halfway up the mountain. A small cabin sat on the clearing's edge. Clarence came to hover next to it then suddenly dropped to the ground.

Talia's teeth rattled in her head at the impact. It took her a moment to realize the dragon had let her go and she was standing on her own.

"There's food in the cabin, and anything else you should need," Kel told her. "We should be back for you no later than a couple of days."

She snapped around to glare at them, realizing what it was they meant to do. "Don't you dare leave me here. You have no right to do this to me! Take me back *now.*"

The pained look she saw in Kel's eyes at her fury did nothing to assuage her raging temper. "I can't," he said. "Please try to understand. It's essential for us to know you're safe."

Clarence spread his wings. *This is for the best.*

"*No!*" She ran at them as Clarence leaped, hoping to grab hold of him so she wouldn't be left there. The dragon saw her coming and with a hard beat of his wings flew out of her reach. "Take me back!"

Kel's troubled gaze looked down at her even as she cursed them with every oath she knew. She shook her fist at them as they turned away and rapidly flew out of sight.

"Damn you." Fuming, her body shaking, Talia turned to face the cabin and with a yell kicked at the closest wall. Imagining the logs were their faces, she kicked at it until her sides hurt and her breathing grew ragged. Then she kicked it a few times more just for good measure. "How dare you? *How dare you!*"

Finally, sighing, she dropped to the ground to rest. What was wrong with them? Did they really think she was just going to let them get away with this? And what about the school? Not for the first time, she told herself the squire and the dragon were totally insane. She would be missed. People would worry and ask questions. She was sure having her students kidnapped would not sit well with the Administrator. Why were the two of them such morons? Why were they so afraid for her? She shook her head slowly, their actions making no more sense than they usually did.

Still, she wouldn't let them get away with this. She wouldn't give up. The only one who would make decisions for her would be her—even if there were things she couldn't make up her mind about. She looked up across the clearing and could clearly see the mesa and the top where the school sat. Those two had eaten too many cherries if they thought she would just meekly sit here and wait for them to pick her up.

Rising to her feet, her anger spent for the moment, she walked over to the cabin door and opened it. After going in and finding anything which might prove useful, she held every intention of starting back toward the school.

ᚱᚳᛏᚱᚳᛏᚱᚳᛏ

HOURS LATER, TALIA rested beneath the shade of a tall fir, able to make out the mesa through the widespread foliage. She scowled, thinking back on the cabin and what she found there. When Kel said there would be food and other things, she'd figured they'd be some staples left there by the woodsmen for when they might return. Instead, she found fresh bread, fruits, meat, and cheese as if they'd just been brought there that morning. Even the linen on the bed was new. Kel and Clarence *planned* to kidnap her. How long had they known about the trouble before Lareen announced it? She stood up, shoving the question aside. Those things didn't matter now; her only concern was getting back to the school.

The large trees loomed, the fresh scent of pine and fir strong in her nostrils. She felt a slight shiver as she gazed at their long limbs and thick foliage. There'd been so many changes in her life, what she saw around her being but one of many. Forests were something she'd heard of in stories, yet here she was, amidst one in an adventure of her own. At home, the most she ever ran across were clumps of trees, most of the fertile land converted to farmland. Yet here, on this mountain, the trees ran as far as she could see. If not for the fact she could see the mesa in the distance, she might have found herself inextricably lost. Trying not to dwell on it, she plodded on.

As the sun sank in the horizon, she sighed, the mesa looming a little closer but nowhere near as close as she'd hoped. That a few minutes in the air could have taken her so far was amazing. Though at the moment it was more bothersome than anything else—she was making her way back on foot after all. Glad she'd thought to bring one of the blankets from the cabin as well as food, she nestled down against a large tree, and after eating a cold supper, tried to rest.

She didn't sleep well. The strange night sounds kept bringing her awake, and when she did sleep, her dreams were filled with the indistinct forms of maeloon.

Talia woke in the early morning hours, her back sore and her body stiff. She stretched, feeling in a foul mood, and tallied her discomforts as one more thing she would make the squire and dragon pay for once she got her hands on them. Her temper didn't get better as she looked up at the sky and noticed the thick dark clouds gathering overhead. If it rained...

A light shower did catch her about midday, but she was able to find sufficient cover beneath the canopy of some thick trees and only became mildly damp. The scent of decaying leaves and wood doubled in strength around her as the air became very humid. She stared unhappily at the mesa, wondering if anyone had missed her yet. With all the magic at the school's disposal, surely they could use some of it to find her if everything else failed. She could already picture the bombardment of questions and the rumors that would be flying from all this. She shook her head. Maybe she could make it back before it got nasty, though a part of her heavily doubted it.

By late afternoon, she was almost to the base of the mesa. Staring at its steep rising sides, she started to question whether her course was the best to take after all. She didn't want to stay at the cabin and wait for Kel to come to get her, but she wasn't sure how she was going to make her way up the mesa's side and up to the school on her own.

She was still trying to puzzle out her problem when a loud crash startled her from behind. She was spinning around to find out what caused it when she suddenly found herself enveloped by cold metal arms.

"Thank the *gods*. You're all right." Kel's relieved voice poured into her ear even as she spotted Clarence pulling himself out of the ruins of a toppled tree. The dragon disgustedly spit out a branch from his mouth. Kel's helmet, with its dilapidated feathers, sat looking forlorn on the ground.

Hello, Talia. Glad to see you are well.

Kel pulled back, holding her by the shoulders, his gaze eagerly searching her face to reassure himself she really was all right. "Why did you leave the cabin? I told you we'd be back for you. I was sure something horrible happened to you."

Talia saw heartfelt concern and relief washing over his face. She felt her heart trying to soften toward him, but her day's foul mood, the rough night, and her previous anger at both of them wouldn't let it. With a shrug, she stepped back out of his reach. "How dare you? Did you really just expect me to meekly wait for you after you dragged me off somewhere against my will? Who do you think you are that you can make my decisions for me?"

Kel stared at her, shock staining his features. "I—"

She cut him off. "Forget it! I'm in no mood to hear your excuses." She knew she was harshly unfair, but at the moment couldn't stop herself. "If you don't mind, I'll be on my way now. I've got a long way to go before reaching the school."

Kel frowned, the pain at her words still lingering in his eyes. "But, it's almost nightfall. And the cliffs..."

Her eyes flashed. "What about them?" she demanded.

The squire glanced back at Clarence, but the dragon only stared off to the side, as though not wanting to get involved.

"We'll take you back," Kel said softly. "We did bring you here after all." He seemed unsure of himself.

"It doesn't matter," she told him. A part of her kept insisting she was an idiot, that she was being as stubborn as she frequently accused them of. It wasn't as if she honestly had any clue how she was going to get back. It made no difference though—her anger was in control.

"I'll get back on my own." She started to turn away.

"No! Talia..." Kel reached out to grab her by the shoulder. As his gauntlet touched her, she jerked roughly away. Her shirt caught in one of the gauntlet's folds and she heard the fabric rip.

"Now look what you've done!" She glared at the squire, even more annoyed than before.

Kel stared from his hand and where the bit of cloth still hung to her and back again. Then suddenly his eyes grew wide with something akin to horror. "No!"

He lunged at her, driving her down even as a dark form crashed into him from the other side. Talia landed hard, the breath knocked out of her, as Kel and the intruder rolled away. As soon as she got a look at the attacker, her blood turned cold. The five-fingered claws, the barbed tail, the insane looking smile—it was a maeloon. It was more ghastly than she ever imagined. "Kel!"

The two continued thrashing on the ground. She heard Clarence cracking more trees as he struggled to get closer.

It had lunged at her and Kel had saved her. But what was it doing *here*? Kel said he and Clarence were taking her somewhere far from the fighting. Was it one of the reasons he seemed so worried about her? Because they'd found out there were more than the ones they'd been told of? Before she knew it, her dagger was in her hand. Even as she struggled to get back on her feet, her gaze swept the darkening area looking for others. Seeing none, her attention turned back to Kel and the creature he was still struggling to keep from tearing his unprotected throat.

Talia, stay back.

She didn't listen. Clarence slithered forward, both of them trying to find an opening to help Kel.

Laughing snarls filled the air. The maeloon suddenly disengaged from Kel, leaping gracefully backward. Its human looking gaze locked on her. She shuddered as she stared into the face of madness. She was suddenly unsure her small dagger would be enough.

"Get back here!" Kel lunged desperately at the maeloon, having noticed where it was aiming its attention. The maeloon avoided him easily, making for her.

Talia felt her breath come in harsh gasps, even as she brought her dagger forward to meet it. The maeloon leaped.

No, you don't. Clarence's head snaked out, his massive jaws clamping on the creature's body, snatching it from midair. A scream of pain filled the air for a moment, then ceased. Clarence spit out the maeloon's body, which was almost split in three, onto the ground.

Talia barely spared it a glance, running instead toward Kel.

The squire was doing the same thing and met her halfway.

"Are you all right?" they asked one another at the same time.

She laughed, tears rising in her eyes in relief. It filled her with unexpected warmth to see him as relieved as she was.

A haunting howl cut through the trees from the direction the maeloon originally came from, killing the warmth and replacing it with dread. Another answered the first then a third.

"Are those more of them?" She was sure she wouldn't like the answer.

They're close.

"We've got to go." Kel held his hand out for hers. After a moment's hesitation, she took it. Together, they ran toward Clarence, skirting the cooling maeloon body.

Kel helped her up onto Clarence's back then followed after her. Strapping themselves in as quickly as possible, Clarence lifted off as several dark bodies appeared from the trees. Snarling, the maeloon jumped up, trying to clamp on to the fleeing dragon. Clarence batted one aside with his tail then was too high for them to reach him. Talia glanced down and watched in horror as four of them leaped onto the body of their dead comrade and tore it apart.

She forced herself to look away.

The three of them reached the school before long and Clarence brought them in for a landing. "Over there." Kel pointed in the direction of Nertak's cave, where lanterns were being lit one by one as darkness descended. Clarence rushed off the runway with her and Kel on board, heading for the lights.

Lareen is not here, but Nertak has returned to pick up supplies. He's inside.

Startled glances followed them as Clarence rushed up toward the entrance of the cave. Students dived to get out of his way. By the time he came to a stop, Kel had already released his restraints and leaped down to run into the cave's interior. Talia wasn't far behind him.

"Master Nertak!" Kel brushed brusquely past several students, wedging his way further into the cave. Moving in his wake, Talia noticed a lot of surprised faces as well as a few hostile ones as they realized who'd shoved them aside.

Kel headed toward the back, behind the newly rebuilt counter. The old man came out, the narrow-faced young man who'd asked her not to feed Kel close behind him. The student didn't look pleased to see him.

"Clarence told me you were coming. What's wrong?" Nertak waved the student aside as he tried putting himself menacingly between the Kel and the older man. Kel paid the boy no attention at all. Talia could tell neither made the student happy.

"An unknown number of maeloon are almost on top of the school," said Kel. "They're coming from the forest to the east. I didn't see any mercenaries, but they could be out there as well."

"You've got a lot of nerve," the narrow faced student said. "Why the heck should anyone listen to a stuck-up, murderous, loony like you?" Students crowded around to see what was going on.

"He's not lying. I saw them, too." She felt a flood of irritation trying to get the best of her.

"You're a first-year, what would you—"

"Billa, that's more than enough out of you." Nertak turned cold eyes on the student. "You might show a lot of promise for my guild, but in some areas, you have a *long* way to go." The young man stared at Nertak as if he'd been slapped.

"Sir?"

"Now make yourself useful and get to the camp and pass this information on to Lareen. Tell it as you heard it, without any extra commentary."

Billa hesitated a moment, but after throwing Kel an odd look, he turned around and ran back toward the back of the cave and the transportation circle there. Murmurs were springing up all around.

Nertak ducked down to search through a bin behind the counter. "Ah, thought I left it here." He brought up a scroll and unrolled it on the counter. It was a map of the school's intermediate area up to the border. He pointed to a place close to the line. "This is where the maeloon and the squadron were engaged. I thought things went a little too easy there. Where did you see the others?"

Kel pointed to the mountain on the east side of the mesa. "It was about here. We only spotted them because we were on the ground. The woods are so thick there you can't really see anything from the air. It didn't help the sun was going down, either."

Nertak frowned at the map, obviously not liking what he was seeing. "It would seem their intended target might be the school." Gasps rang all around.

"But how would they scale the mesa?" Talia thought the feat daunting at best.

"The creatures are five-fingered and have claws. Scaling the walls would be easier for them than most, and they're insane enough to try it in the dark."

Kel took off one of his gauntlets and reached inside his armor to scratch below his neck. "With our attention diverted and most of our people gone, if they sneaked up here at night, they could take the school before anyone was the wiser."

Talia felt a chill at the thought. If Kel hadn't kidnapped her, if she hadn't decided to come back on her own ... "What are we going to do?"

Nertak looked up, smiling. "Why, we're going to stop them, of course." He actually looked quite happy. "About now I expect the maeloon and the men at the village will have rallied and mounted some heavier resistance than up to this point. This would keep everyone busy and stop them from returning to the school. But, now that we know what they're up to, we won't be caught unprepared. We're going to show them even the students of the guild are to be reckoned with.

"Kel, I want for you and Clarence to be my eyes and ears out there. I need to know where they are and where they're coming from."

Kel nodded.

Nertak glanced out toward the other students. "As for the rest of you, listen up! I want each and every one of you to return to your quarters and put on your armor.

When you're done, take yourselves down to the armory. You'll be given a weapon there. Take something you can handle, this is no time for stupidity. If you see any watchers or teachers, tell them to come see me here. Once you're done, meet in the dining hall for further instructions. Now go."

A mass exodus headed for the cave entrance. Talia turned to go as well when she felt Kel's hand on her arm. "Talia, wait."

She felt her face grow hard. "You're not going to keep me out of it this time."

She saw Kel half glance in Nertak's direction before speaking. "I'm not." He let go of her arm. "If you're willing, I want you to come with Clarence and me. We're going to need the extra pair of eyes."

She saw the earnestness in his face but wasn't sure she should believe him. "If this is a trick..."

"No trick, I swear it. I was wrong before. I know it now." He scratched at his neck again.

"Is that all right?" she asked of Nertak.

The old man smiled. "The more eyes the better. This isn't going to be easy."

"I'll go then." The gods help him if this was some sort of bluff.

Talia ran to get her armor after agreeing to meet Kel by the armory. He, in turn, would go downstairs to get himself a new helmet and weapons for them both.

She was on her way down, trying hard to hurry and yet not fall when she suddenly found an armored person cutting off her path.

"Talia, where have you been?" An excited voice reached out to her from the closed helmet.

"Daltan?"

The boy reached up and opened his visor. "Are you all

right? We've all been so worried."

She looked away. "I can't explain right now. But I'm fine. Please tell everyone not to be concerned. I'll be helping the squire."

"Is that where you've been? With him?" His tone grew more insistent.

She didn't want to lie to him. "Not exactly. But I really can't explain it right now. He's waiting for me. I'll tell you what I can later." She hurried past him.

Five other students were in the armory as well as a few watchers handing out weapons. Kel was standing in a corner waiting for her. "There you are. Here." He handed her a quiver of bolts, a light crossbow, and a short sword. "The crossbow is easy to use. You just put one of the bolts here, then pull this crank to set the line in place. Then just aim and pull the trigger. The sword is just in case."

She had seen crossbows before but not used one. She hoped it'd be as easy to use as he said.

"Come on." Kel led the way out of the room and the growing press of armored bodies. The two of them rushed to the dragon habitat and found Clarence there, waiting for them.

"Kel, why would anyone want to attack the school?" She clambered with some difficulty up onto Clarence's back.

"There could be several reasons really," Kel said. "If they took over the school, they'd be messing up the guild's system for creating members, it'd show the guild is not infallible, and that by sending your children there, you might get them killed. They've probably also heard the rumor some of the schools also serve as treasuries for the guild. I don't know if the last is true, but since the schools are so inaccessible, it would make some sense to keep the guild's money there."

"But wouldn't attacking the school just bring the whole wrath of the guild on top of them?"

Certainly, Clarence responded. *But they would need to know who was responsible before they could do so. Also, the fact they have maeloon on their side speaks of the possibility that they possess great power.*

"Does the guild have that many enemies?" she asked.

Kel turned to glance at her as Clarence prepared to take flight. "It has almost as many enemies as it has friends. The guild does a lot of good, and helps keeps the peace. But there are those who'd rather not have peace dictated to them, or who would prefer to have the right to make war with their neighbors if that's what they want."

They took to the air. This cut off any further conversation. Clarence took them back toward the east, flying close to the trees so they could search for signs of the maeloon. The moon was out in the night sky, but the treetops still spread before them as a sea of darkness. Clarence swept dizzily back and forth, but none of them could see any signs of anything untoward. She was just glad Clarence seemed to be flying better than average.

After about an hour, Clarence turned back toward the school and flew around the perimeter of the mesa. Talia was slightly startled as his voice suddenly rang in her mind.

A messenger has returned from the Administrator. Things have abruptly intensified on their end. Luckily, the squadron was not yet gone, or the area set up by the teachers and students for the wounded would have been overrun.

Nertak was right. This was planned from the beginning. The village's plight, while terribly real, was still only a diversion. She shivered, trying not to think of how close they'd come to being unprepared.

Several hours later, they'd still spotted no signs of the enemy. She was beginning to wonder if perhaps there really was nothing to worry about when she saw movement at the edge of the trees. "Kel." She pulled on the squire's arm to get his attention then pointed toward the ground. Clarence changed direction and dove to take a closer look.

Crazed, human-like eyes turned to watch them as they swept by. Talia shuddered as she felt their gaze on them. She counted thirteen maeloon and more looked to be coming out farther on.

I've advised Nertak, Clarence sent to them. *Defenses have been set at the top of the mesa. We're to try and slow them down or stop as many of them as we can.*

Kel signaled her to get her crossbow ready even as he readied his. Clarence dove closer to the maeloon. She tried to aim at the dark masses as best she could then pulled the trigger. The crossbow jerked back against her shoulder, sending the bolt toward the ground. She heard a pained grunt, but couldn't see if she'd actually hit anything. Abruptly, Clarence tilted upwards as arrows shot toward them from the forest below. Talia yelped, struggling to hang on, almost losing her hold on the crossbow.

The maeloon are not alone. It will make things more difficult.

She saw Kel gesture at his friend but couldn't hear what was being said. Clarence turned, and she spotted a group of maeloon leaping up the side of the mesa. Clarence aimed toward the highest of them and let out a small burst from his mouth. A ball of flame shot from him and hit a maeloon square in the back. Screaming, the creature let go and tumbled down the side of the mesa. More arrows shot at them from below but fell short.

Talia watched as the lit maeloon bounced off the rocks to land amidst its brothers at the bottom, before going out. If he'd gone too much farther, Clarence's fire might have caught on the trees and caused a massive forest fire. She understood now why he hadn't used his flame before and even then not at full force.

Clarence followed the outside of the mesa, trying his best to hit what maeloons he could as they rose as one on all sides. Kel and Talia shot at them as well, but like Clarence, were tending to miss more than hit as the maeloon flickered from one spot to another every few seconds. With their human-like claws and prehensile tails, the maeloon were having little trouble scaling the almost vertical surface.

As the three of them made another pass, she spotted something cascading from the top of the mesa. Almost as if reading her thoughts, Clarence provided an explanation. *They're pouring oil. They're hoping it will make the rocks slick, and if worst comes to worst, they will light it.*

She hoped it wouldn't come to that.

If the school had had more dragons, they could have made short work of the intruders. As it was, the maeloon continued to gain more and more ground with only Clarence there to try and stop them.

Twice, she spotted a maeloon in the forefront reach the oiled areas of rock. The first one slipped and fell, the sound of breaking bones echoing in the night. The second didn't, using his claws to cling even harder to the mesa. Clarence swept by and Kel hit it with a bolt. Once it stopped writhing in pain, Clarence swept it off the mountain face with a sweep of his tail.

Talia tried to count the number of maeloon and was astounded to realize there were hundreds of them. Not even in the worst stories about them, had she heard of so many being together in one place. How were those strangers able to gather them like this? What could they have offered these weird creatures to get them to cooperate this way?

As more maeloon came close to the top, torches were dropped on the ground until a vast ring of fire covered the mesa. With the greater amount of light, she noticed a large trench dug out around the lip of the plateau filled with oil and pitch. It was a barrier of fire the maeloon would have to struggle through to get at the school.

Kel?

At the dragon's query, Talia tore her gaze from the ring below. She turned just in time to see Kel's crossbow drop from his hand to the darkness below, his body slumping forward. "Kel!"

Something is wrong. I did not notice it earlier, but something's been wrong.

She didn't question this but hurriedly tied her crossbow to one of the tethers then reached out for the squire. Pulling him up, she leaned his body back toward her. Fumbling with her gauntlets, she took them off then reached for his helmet. Removing it, she gasped as she saw his neck beneath it. It was swollen and red, tendrils of angry flesh reaching toward his face and below the armor. A point close to the edge was dark, full of puss, and gave off a faint, acrid smell. It appeared to be a small puncture. Only too clearly did she recall Kel hadn't been wearing a helmet when the maeloon attacked them in the forest. The point at the end of the maeloon's tail would make just such a wound. "No."

Kel's eyes roamed beneath closed lids, his lips moving in mumbled words she couldn't hear as they were taken by the wind. His skin was hot to the touch and almost burned in the areas of redness. "Clarence, we have to take him down."

The dragon's head turned to look at her as if he'd heard then began to descend. *I've already called for help.*

Clarence cleared the ring of fire and landed softly ten arm lengths from the school's main doors.

We've arrived, Clarence said. *Help will be here in a moment.*

Talia nodded, not sure how Clarence knew all this, but grateful all the same. She struggled to untie herself as quickly as possible and turned to start in on Kel's restraints when the front doors opened.

An older man and two women hurried over to Clarence's side with a stretcher and a lamp. The man clambered onto Clarence's back and helped Talia with the rest of Kel's restraints. Once they'd gotten him free, she helped the man hand Kel down to those waiting below.

"We'll take over from here." As soon as they put him on the stretcher, they carried the squire inside.

She was thinking of running after them when a pained howl rang from the edge of the fire. The maeloon had reached the top.

Talia watched the stretcher move away for a long moment then turned from the sight, pulling the short sword at her side. "They'll pay for ever having come here." Something wet and cold slid down her cheek but she paid it no attention. Her burning gaze met Clarence's. "You know what you need to do."

The dragon said nothing, instead taking to the air.

Talia ran toward the wall of fire.

A thin line of students and watchers were arrayed around the burning trench, swords, tools, and bows at the ready. She joined the line, the fire before her close to the sudden fire inside her. This was a school—they were its students. No one had the right to bring war to this place. No one had the right to hurt Kel, not this way, not after all he'd been through.

Clarence made a dive on the other side of the fire, spewing his hot flames on the maeloon there. Trapped between them, the maeloon laughed their snarling laugh and lunged through the cooler of the two fires toward the students.

Students and watchers fell back then surrounded the burning creatures and stabbed them with their weapons. Talia rushed forward when one cut in before her, and with a yell brought her sword down on its head even as others rushed forward to help. This monstrosity would not hurt anyone here.

Blood stained the grass beneath her feet, the cloying smell of wet fur and iron weaving around her.

She stared at the corpse, feeling nothing. She had just killed a living being but felt no remorse. These things were deadly; she could spare them no sympathy. She frowned as she noticed it wore several coils of rope about its neck, but had no time to wonder why as another maeloon broke through further down the line.

"Eggs, eggs." Its hair on fire, the creature seemed oblivious to its pain, its maddened gaze searching frantically about.

As students closed in on it, the barbed tail swished around dangerously. "Watch out for the tail, it's poison!" She yelled this at a couple of students who came in too close.

"Stay back!" This came from a watcher who deftly aimed her crossbow at the maeloon's head and shot it in the face.

The maeloon screamed, leaping over her, heading toward the dragon habitat. "Eggs, eggs."

Talia didn't chase it, turning back to hold the line, a shudder racking through her. Surely she hadn't heard right. It sounded so close to human speech, but it couldn't have been.

Could it?

ᚱᚴᚱᚱᚴᚱᚱᚴᚱ

TIME BECAME A BLUR and all was fighting, fire, and blood. Maeloon after maeloon leaped through the line, only to be killed by the waiting students. Talia didn't know how many she helped strike down. Yet throughout, she felt imbued with a sense of purpose and a protectiveness she'd not known before.

It is done.

She blinked, realizing it was Clarence's voice in her head. He sounded tired. She dropped to the ground as the meaning of his words sunk in, only then realizing how exhausted she was herself. The dragon landed nimbly beside her. Clarence gently nudged her with his snout until she opened her eyes again.

Are you all right?

"Yes, fine," she managed to whisper. Her throat felt raw. "Is it really over?"

Before Clarence could answer, Nertak's voice boomed over the field. "The enemy has retreated. Most of the maeloon are dead. The battle has also ended at the camp. Everyone will soon be coming home. We've also called for reinforcements. A fresh squadron is already here to scour the area for any maeloon that remain. Well done, everyone. Now go get some sleep."

Groans whispered through the grounds as students forced themselves to get up to drag their tired bodies inside. Talia wasn't sure she could so didn't bother to even try.

It looks like there are very few wounded.

Her mind was shutting down. "Good." Nertak's strategy was sound, and with their armor on, the maeloon weren't able to really hurt any of them. She shied away from thinking how the bloodbath would have been reversed if they'd had no prior warning. She then remembered the first casualty in the battle.

"Kel!" She sat up, her muscles protesting, and turned to stare at Clarence. "Have you heard anything about him?"

No. I believe LaSeren is with him now, however.

She could make nothing of his tone and was just too tired to try harder. "I'll go find out what's happening."

I'll wait for news in my stall. He slowly lumbered away toward the dragon habitat.

She watched him, achingly rising to her feet. Once the ground would stay still, she made her way toward the main building with as much speed as she could.

Asking directions of several tired-looking watchers, Talia headed downstairs toward the area she'd been taken to when she was ill. A large room with beds held eight students being helped out of their armor. Most just looked tired and scratched, only a few actually having cuts or broken bones. She shuffled through the room, looking left and right, but saw no sign of Kel. Her breath coming faster as she tried not to think the worst, she caught sight of a familiar face and rushed forward. "Yllin."

The sour-faced girl was sitting on the edge of one of the beds, cleaning out a nasty cut on a student's arm. Yllin looked up at the sound of her name, and her face broke into a wide smile as she realized who stood before her. "Talia, I'm so glad to see you. You disappeared then Daltan told us he'd seen you working with the squire. But when I heard he was brought in..."

"I'm fine. Really. But I'm trying to find Kel, do you know where he is?" She tried her best to keep the desperation out of her voice.

Yllin nodded. "He's in the small office, two doors down." Her expression grew troubled. "I hear it's bad."

Talia suddenly felt like crying. "I've got to go."

Rushing away, she found the room Yllin mentioned and wasn't surprised to discover it was the same one she'd been taken to before. Quietly, she pushed open the door and peered inside.

She spotted Kel in the cot in the corner. LaSeren leaned heavily on her cane watching over him.

"LaSeren?"

The old woman glanced back toward the door her face grave. "Come in child."

She did which gave her an unobstructed view of the patient. Kel's eyes were half-open and glazed. His lips were moving though no words came out of them. His armor had been removed so she could clearly see the ugly wound were the barb hit him. The angry redness she spotted before had spread to cover half of his face. Strips of cloth were tied from one side of the bed to the other to hold him in.

"No..." She felt her eyes grow unfocused.

"None of that now," LaSeren pushed a stool toward her. "Come, sit down." She gently pushed Talia onto it.

"Is he .. is he going to be all right?" She knew he wasn't, she could see it, but she needed to be told.

"It all depends."

"On what?" Talia removed her helmet so she could see the old woman better.

"The fact he isn't dead already shows he didn't get a full dose of the poison. The healing gem in his armor helped stave off the effects but wasn't able to counter it entirely, neither have any of the magical antidotes in my stores. Maeloon poison is not the same as other poisons. If I were made to guess, I would say it has magical properties. Wulan is getting a sample from the bodies outside, but time..."

LaSeren faced her squarely. "Cases of this kind are rare. Normally maeloon don't leave any victims alive. There have been some accounts of it, but none the guild has been involved in and what they've said..." The old woman shook her head as if the tales were too fantastical or horrible to believe. "We just don't know enough."

"Is there nothing you can do?" Had Talia gotten to finally know this stubborn man only to lose him?

"I've sent messages to the other guild healers, and Wulan will work to make what he can of the poison. There's always a chance he will come across an antidote or some way to delay what is happening. If the bond was whole, then perhaps we would have been able to learn more, maybe enough to try something..." LaSeren looked suddenly worn as if her years were weighing her down. "Ah, pay me no mind. We'll do all we can for him."

"Thank you for being honest with me."

"No need. I'm not sure I've done you a service." LaSeren gave her a half-hearted smile. "You look exhausted. Why don't you go rest? If anything changes, I will make sure you're told."

Talia nodded slowly, her fatigue clinging to her even more than before.

Thanking LaSeren again, she left and made her way upstairs. Once inside her room, she took off her armor and let it fall where it may. The scent of fur and smoke and blood clung to her, so she pushed the doors to the balcony open for some fresh air. Men and women drifted about the yard below picking up maeloon bodies as well as discarded weapons, buckets, and anything else left behind. The sun was just peeking over the horizon, as if unaware of the night's events. Shaking her head, she turned away, and still dressed in her pants and shift, crawled into bed.

Chapter Twenty

WIDE-EYED, TALIA STARED at her bed's ceiling. Free to try and get some sleep, she found it wouldn't come. Kel was going to die. He was going to die, and nothing she could do would change that. Her chest ached with helplessness.

Yet she couldn't even find the strength to cry.

There had to be something that could be done, there just had to be. Ever since she came to this school, it seemed as if she'd caused Kel nothing but trouble. This would be the time to make it up to him—if she could only figure out how. Her eyes burned.

LaSeren thought there might have been a chance if only Kel and Clarence's bonding had worked. But why hadn't it? From all she'd seen, she knew Clarence possessed powers she didn't understand. Could he have used these powers to make the bond not work? Couldn't he, if he wanted to, use them now to fix it? So he could do what he could to help Kel come back to them? She tensed. The bond, the bond was the key. Clarence needed to fix it. But what would it take to do it? She just didn't know enough about it to even guess.

With a rough jerk, she pulled her blanket off her body and sat up. She needed to know more. Ignoring her aches, she fumbled about for some clean clothes.

Leaving her room, Talia quietly made her way downstairs.

The school was silent, the previous night's exertions having taken their toll. She made her way to the far corner of the building to the immense library housed there. With any luck, it was here she hoped to find the answers she sought.

With sure steps, she crossed between the bookshelves and headed for an area on the left side of the library. It was there the books about dragons were kept. Cautiously, she approached the tall box set right outside the area. She stared at it with some slight trepidation, though Helyn had shown them all how to use it several weeks ago.

"Query: I'd like information on the human and dragon bonding." She whispered her request at the box.

After several moments, the top of the box shimmered and showed her a three-dimensional picture of the stacks. Three books in the picture glowed a faint blue. Two others glowed red. From what Helyn taught them, she knew the red choices were currently not in the library. Studying the picture intently, she set the location of the three blue books in her mind then went looking for them.

Walking toward the closest of the three, she spotted it glowing softly from the end of the third shelf up. Retrieving it, she went in search of the other two. As soon as she took each of them from the shelf, the blue glow subsided. Looking for a chair, she picked one a little out of the way to stay out of sight.

The first book she opened spoke about the history of the guild and contained one whole section devoted to the bonding ritual and its modifications over the centuries. After spending almost ten minutes glancing through what it said there, she set it regretfully aside, not finding what she was looking for.

The second book broke the bonding ritual out into its specific components and the mechanics of the different rites, including the spells generated for the bonding to occur. She understood little to nothing of what she was reading. After a half-hour, she despaired of finding what she sought in it, knowing even if she somehow stumbled over what she was looking for, she didn't know enough to realize it for what it was.

She set the book aside with a sigh, a light headache beating behind her eyes. She picked up the third book.

Almost at once her hopes rose, the text inside not technical but written more for the layman than the other two. She eagerly flipped to the back section on bonding and read what was there.

About an hour later, she closed the book and stood up. Picking up the other two, she took all three to the query box and set them on top. All three promptly disappeared. She stood there, looking at where they'd been, doing nothing. The suspicion growing inside her ever since she first started reading the last book slowly coalesced into certainty.

Clarence had *lied*.

Her thoughts rushing inside her almost too fast for her to keep up, she left the library and headed north.

Slipping outside into the warming day, she unerringly made her way over to the dragon dormitory. The large door opened without a sound and she crept inside. The interior of the vast place was dark except for two dimly lit globes at each entrance. Feeling her way, she moved forward, hope and anger warring inside her as she approached the dragon's stall.

"Clarence." She peeked into his stall, barely able to make out the dark blob nestled in the interior as she opened the gate.

A faint rustling sound issued from within.

"Clarence." She called his name out a little more forcefully.

She was suddenly blinded as the globes in the stall sprang to life.

Has something happened? Clarence's snout was almost in her face, his thoughts sounding anxious and worried.

She frowned, the dragon's feelings making what she knew less understandable. "No. Kel is still unconscious. I'm sorry to have startled you, but I need to talk to you."

The dragon eased his vast bulk back onto the hay-littered floor, his crossed eyes staring at her through half closed lids. *What is it you wish to talk to me about when sleep is what we should both be seeking?*

Talia ignored the light rebuke and pushed on. "I want to ask you why you aren't helping Kel."

The dragon studied her intently. *I can't help him. He's been poisoned. Healing is LaSeren's area of expertise, not mine.*

"I think you can." She pushed on. "LaSeren believes a full bonding might be able to reveal information which could be used to help him."

That is her opinion, Clarence said crossly. *I want him to be well as much as you do, and I would help him if I could.*

She felt a twinge of doubt at his words but didn't let go. "You say this, but I don't believe you. You could help Kel if you allowed the bonding to be complete. Her opinion or not, it would at least be something to try. But you won't, will you?"

He stared at her, his eyes hard. *I don't know what you're talking about.*

She sighed. "Clarence, I don't want to do this, I really don't. Yet from what I've seen, no one else can help Kel but you. I don't know why you're doing any of this, but Kel can't help himself and no one else can, either. There's nothing Lareen or LaSeren can do. That leaves only you. I would do it for you if I could, but I *can't*. The only thing I *can* do is to try and bring you to your senses."

Clarence turned away from her. *Nothing is so simple. You do not understand.*

"Then make me understand," she demanded. "Otherwise all I see is a selfish dragon, who treasures his secrets more than another's life and is willing to watch his friend die or become irrevocably mad because of it."

The dragon sighed, his whole body dragged down as if a great weight had just been placed on top of him. *You do not understand...*

Talia bit her lip, knowing this wasn't the way to get where she wanted to go, but not sure how else to get there. "I read some texts on the bonding. I understand why not as many people try for the lottery as one would expect. The bonding is literal, a connection from mind to mind so the dragons and humans back then could be sure of the honesty and intent of each other. A desperate means to prove each others' worth in a sad, terrible time."

She took a deep breath and pushed on. "From the beginning, I was told your joining with Kel didn't go as expected. That somehow the bond didn't go as far as it should have. But that's not actually true, is it? I've seen the effects of the full bonding working through you, I've seen the two of you work in perfect unison." The instance of Kel and Clarence's flawless leap over the Administrator was but the first hint that what she said was true.

"For your own reasons, I think you and maybe even Kel have been putting off the bonding—fighting against it, holding it back. If the only one doing it was Kel, he's in no position to stop it from being complete any longer. That would mean you should be able to use it to help, you should be able to see what's wrong. Unless I'm right and the one holding both of you back is you." She studied the dragon critically waiting to see what he would do.

Clarence said and did nothing.

Talia tried her best not to lose hope. "Clarence, you know Kel wouldn't hesitate to give his life for you. You don't have to go so far, but yet you do nothing. Isn't he worth helping? Are your reasons, are the powers you're trying so hard to hide, so precious they're worth his life? Do you not care for him at all?"

The dragon sighed again. The sigh sounded weary beyond measure. *Perhaps, perhaps there is another way to do this... But I can't do it alone. I might not—might not understand what I find.* She had never heard the dragon sound so unsure of himself. *I've studied humans for a long time and still comprehend them only a little.* He glanced at her as if to say she was one of those. *I'm afraid of doing more harm than good.*

"So you *can* do it! Please, you have to. Nothing you do could make things worse than they are now." She felt herself flush with hope.

I'll need an intermediary or a buffer, if you prefer. Someone who can rightly interpret the things we might see.

"I'm sure Lareen can find someone who can do that. She has to!" Talia prayed it was so, not totally understanding what it was Clarence was looking for.

That won't be necessary, he said. *You will do. Too many are involved already. Much of what you may discover will not necessarily be new to you.* He paused. *And I believe any additional knowledge you gain will be safe.*

She swallowed hard. "I swear it will." She put as much conviction into the statement as she could. "Just tell me what to do."

Clarence stared at her long and hard with his crooked eyes, then finally nodded. A large claw reached for one of the small chests in the back and brought it forward. Gingerly, he flicked the lock open with his sharp nail. Nestled inside was the crystal ball Clarence had played with before. He picked the ball up with his massive claw and brought it over to her. *Take this and go to Kel's side. Once you are there, hold the crystal in one hand and take his in the other. We will go from there.*

Talia nodded and took the ball. It felt strangely warm in her hands. It was the size of a large melon but light in weight. "I'll go there right away." She turned to go, then glanced behind her for a moment before leaving. "Thank you."

She left, the crystal ball held tightly in her arms.

Not wanting to have to answer any questions if she was seen holding the strange object, she headed for the concealment of the garden as soon as she got outside. Following the path the students traveled every day, she made her way to the dining room doors. As she'd hoped, they weren't locked. But before making her way in, she listened at them intently to make as sure as she could no one was inside. Hearing nothing, she sneaked on in.

She crossed the dining hall until she reached the doors leading out. Again she hesitated, trying her best to make sure no one was out there. Easing the door open, she peeked into the hallway then slipped out.

She rushed along as quietly as possible and headed for the stairs leading to the level below. The few patients still there were sound asleep. She hesitated at the closed door into LaSeren's healing room. Listening intently, she crept up close to the door then opened it slightly to take a look inside.

A lone globe lit the room, its light subdued. Kel was still in the bed across the way, his pale face in the half-light looking even more wan, except for the angry tendrils reaching out across it. Talia spotted no one else in the room. She went inside.

Once in, she closed the door. Grabbing LaSeren's stool, she placed it beside Kel's bed and sat down. The crystal ball warmed even more in her grip, though she only half noticed. Most of her attention was fixed on the young man on the bed.

Kel lay pretty much as she last saw him, his body covered over with a light blanket. His face was slack, his lips no longer moving, and his eyes were mercifully closed. Studying him, she felt a shudder course through her as she noticed the progression of the redness. With any luck, they might be able to do something about it soon.

Taking a deep breath, not knowing really what to expect, she held the warm crystal ball on her lap with one hand and took Kel's cold hand in the other. After a moment, the ball grew hotter, and she had a sudden bout of vertigo. Closing her eyes, trying hard not to be afraid, she hoped Clarence knew what he was doing.

When she opened her eyes again, she found she wasn't where she'd been. Rather than in LaSeren's small, comforting room, Talia found herself in a vast, gray plain which spread out in all directions as far as she could see. The crystal ball was glowing in her hand with a soft, green luminescence. She was sitting on nothing yet did not fall. She felt fear nipping at the edge of her consciousness. "Clarence?"

I am here.

She felt a weight settle on her shoulders and jumped a little even as she turned to look. She gasped quietly as she spotted a miniature replica of the dragon sitting there. His crossed eyes looked up into her startled face.

Shall we begin?

She couldn't read the dragon's tone and didn't trust herself to speak, so she just nodded.

Nothing happened immediately. Talia glanced at Clarence but saw the dragon had closed his eyes. After an interminable set of moments, the air before them changed. The gray landscape was gone. In its place, she found they were inside Kel's room, or something resembling it, for this one was misshapen, and the walls appeared to be breathing.

"What is this?" She hugged the crystal ball to herself, frightened by what she was seeing.

I believe it is where Kel feels the most at home, safe, but something or someone is changing it, was Clarence's response.

Talia stood up and took a step further into the room, trying not to look at the changing walls, but instead searching for the one they sought.

Over there.

Though he didn't point, she somehow knew which direction Clarence meant. Looking at the far corner, a figure was scrunched up next to a bookcase, partially hidden in shadow.

"Kel?" Talia took a step closer.

The figure moved, turning partially in their direction.

"Who's there?"

She took another step, relieved at seeing Kel's profile. "It's us, Talia and Clarence. We've come to try and help you."

"No." Kel cringed away. "It's a trick, a lie. None of this is real, none of this is real."

"We're real. Please believe me. Remember the maeloon?

"One of them poisoned you. Right now, you're in a bed at the school, its poison slowly killing you. Clarence and I have come to see if there's something that can be done. LaSeren says the poison can't be cured like others can, that there might be magical properties to it? She thought... she thought if you and Clarence could fix your bond, maybe we could learn enough to..." she left the rest unsaid.

Kel laughed. The mad tone twining through it made her hair stand on end. "It won't happen. Especially not now. I've found someone else to bond with. Whether I want to or not." He turned to face them fully, coming out partially into the light.

Talia took a step back, bile rising in her throat. While the right side of Kel's face and body was normal, in this other place, his left side—the side showing the signs of the poison—had turned into the features of a maeloon. Even as she watched, she could tell it was spreading. "I don't understand..."

Kel turned away from her, hiding once more in the shadows. "I do. It's all in here now." She saw his hand move to point at his head. "These, things, they don't breed the same way as other creatures. Instead, they make others into themselves. They take them over, drive them mad, then they change them, change them until they, too, are maeloon."

"No." Talia felt horror growing inside her. "How can they...?"

It must be the poison itself, the magic in it, Clarence said quietly. *I can feel the force of it from here. It's very powerful.*

"But how can no one know about this? There are hundreds of stories about maeloon, and none of them talk about this." It just couldn't be true.

"It's why they raid towns on occasion," Kel said in a

deceptively calm voice. "To make more of themselves. Not all the bodies are found when they do, and this is the reason. They're not killing humans just for sport, but because they need to make more of their own. And once started, the process can't be stopped."

"No, I won't believe that!"

Kel laughed again, the sound echoing in the room. "It won't make any difference what you believe. It will happen. I'm growing weaker—I can feel it. You can *see* it." He lunged out, showing her his face again, and just as quickly retreated back into the darkness. "In a true bonding, the minds are linked, awareness shared, but in this, it's mind takes over yours. It's not alone, either. All the others it has been are there as well. You can't resist them. Soon they will beat me and I will cease to exist altogether. This is why if you're truly here, if you're not just a hallucination, you will leave, and you will kill me before I am totally lost."

"No..." Talia fell to her knees, her last hope crushed by the truth she heard in his words. All of it had been for nothing.

She was too late.

"Clarence..." Kel hesitated for a moment. "I don't know who the men are, the maeloon don't care and don't think that way, but I thought you should know... They've promised them a reward for their work. They—" Kel suddenly gasped in pain. He fell out into the light, his hands holding onto either side of his head. One of them was normal, the other was a five-fingered claw.

"Kel!" Talia half stood, not sure what she could do, but willing to do anything. He waved her back.

"They gave them... they gave them people to change." His voice quivered with the effort. "But they also promised them a higher reward. Something they let them taste, something they now hunger for."

Her eyes grew wide. "Dragon eggs."

Kel laughed again, this time sounding close to the laughing snarl she'd heard at the forest, and went back into the shadows once more. "Delicious..."

Fury suddenly radiated from Clarence in waves. *They would dare?* Amidst the anger, she sensed a deep-running sadness, as if from something long ago, but it was swiftly tucked from view.

"Now go, go and kill me. And be free."

Talia didn't move. She knew he was only asking for a kindness, but she wasn't sure she could ever bring herself to do such a thing.

"Go!" Kel's voice was changing. "I can't hold on much longer."

We don't have much time.

"What?" She turned her head to look at the dragon on her shoulder, not believing he would just leave Kel like this.

You have done my kind a great service with your warning, though you had no reason to give it, and perhaps more not to bother. All deeds must be repaid. Clarence spoke almost in a monotone as if even more weight then ever before were heaped upon him. It held a note of resignation.

His crossed gaze locked with Talia's own. *I will now complete the joining. I will lend my strength to his. We will either both succumb, or the maeloon will be driven out. If purged, you will have to deal with it. I doubt we will have the strength to drive it out a second time if we succeed at all.*

Purged? Deal with it? "But how?" She tried her best not to feel her fear.

Here, reality can be what you make it. Use the truth of your feelings, your convictions to arm yourself. I will show you how.

The globe in her hands flashed. She reeled but

managed to stay on her feet. Her eyes grew round as the knowledge of what she needed to do blossomed prominently in her mind from his. Was this really possible?

It might be dangerous. We might lose. Or it might prove too strong for you. If you feel it necessary, you can escape purely by letting go of the orb. His decision made, Clarence's voice rang clear. *No dishonor would touch you for this. All I ask is that you pass the information you have learned about the enemy to the guild. The eggs must be protected. Only if you live will someone know. Therefore you must.*

Talia nodded, suddenly feeling the importance of all which might soon rest on her.

Our fates are in your hands. With that said, Clarence leaped from her shoulder toward a cowering Kel. His form grew to twice its size and pierced the squire's body like an arrow before disappearing within. Kel howled in pain and rage, his features twisting madly.

As she watched, the young man's face split into three distinct forms: human, maeloon, and dragon. A moment later, the dragon and human parts merged and seemed to grow. The maeloon screamed once more, struggling to injure itself even as Kel's human/dragon half fought to hold it at bay.

Talia watched the struggle and started to smile, her heart beating fast, as more and more of the body reverted back to Kel and the maeloon piece got smaller and smaller. As it was crowded toward the original entry point on Kel's neck, the wound began to ooze. The ooze soon became a stream and pooled on the floor. From it, a maeloon started to form.

It was Talia's turn. She wouldn't cower away. This was what she came to do. Using the knowledge Clarence gave her, she gathered her feelings for the two of them as well as her need to save them from the abomination before her. Molding these things to her will, she was suddenly encased in golden, shimmering armor. The crystal ball in her hand shifted and changed, covering her hand then elongating itself into a thin sword. She felt herself fill with strength and purpose.

The maeloon finished forming and turned, snarling, in Kel and Clarence's direction. Kel/Clarence held up an arm to try and protect himself, but she could see he was weak and could barely move. She knew if she did nothing, the creature would kill them since it could not take them.

"You will not have them." She lunged forward and stabbed the maeloon through the back. Snarling, it turned on the blade, injuring itself further, pure hatred coming from its maddened eyes.

Talia jumped back, freeing her blade, as the maeloon swept its talons at her. This thing would not hurt her, this thing would not wound her friends again. "You will not have them."

The maeloon jumped. She put one leg behind her but did not run. As the Maeloon came down, she partially turned, and with a calmness she didn't know she possessed, cut the maeloon in half even as he grazed past her, making sparks flare from her armor where it attempted to grab at her face.

The creature fell to the floor with a splat.

Kel's room coalesced immediately to more normal proportions. The body at her feet began to fizzle. Acrid smoke rose and dispersed around it, then both disappeared.

Talia breathed a sigh of relief, the sword turning back into a crystal ball and her armor disappearing as if it had never been. All her strength seemed to flow out with it. She suddenly felt drained and weak. Abruptly the world turned black, and she was gone.

ᚱᚷᚠᚱᚷᚠᚱᚷᚠ

TALIA SLOWLY OPENED her eyes. She still felt weak, but also strangely exultant. She looked around her, not sure where she was and not caring at the moment. The stone beneath her told her she was on the floor and on her side. The shelves filled with jars of powders and ointments told her she was still in LaSeren's room. Then her gaze lighted on the cot and the form lying there. With a gasp she sat up, remembering everything. Her sight swam from moving so fast, but she didn't let it stop her and rose to her feet.

Kel was still in the cot, tied as before, but everything else was changed. No longer did red, hungry marks reach across his face, no longer did the wound at his neck look raw and ugly. His expression was at peace.

Giddy, she wiped at her face, happy tears clouding her eyes. They did it. They really had!

She righted the turned over stool and sat down, her gaze not leaving Kel. Absently, she reached down for the crystal ball which helped make this possible. As if it were a cue, his eyes fluttered open. "Kel."

Without thinking, she reached forward and took his hand in hers. The ball glowed as it once more took her away from there.

After a moment, Talia found herself in the strange gray place she went with Clarence before. Kel stood before her and so did Clarence, though in a smaller version of his true self. Though now separate, unlike when Clarence joined with Kel to fight the maeloon poison, seven semi-transparent lines joined the two of them at consistent intervals from their head to their feet. Was this what the bonding looked like?

"Talia, I'm glad you're here." Kel smiled at her, and his pleasure not only showed on his face, but she could actually feel it coming from him. "I wanted to talk to the both of you, and I guess this is as private a place as we could ever get." The lines between squire and dragon lit between the two.

She found herself smiling back, just glad to see him acting normal, even as a touch of humor escaped from him at the words.

"First, I want to thank both of you for what you've done on my behalf." Kel's deep gratitude and sincerity poured into her, though it held an undercoating of sorrow. "It's not something I am sure I can ever repay. Though I will find ways to try." He gave her a small, grateful nod, his smile growing for a moment before he turned to lock his gaze with Clarence's. "I realize and understand many things now. Things I couldn't before.

"I don't know if it's possible, but for my part, I release you from our contract. I promise you I will use every resource I own and the guild's to find a way to reverse the ritual so you may be free again." Determination, sadness, and loss poured through with the words even as she felt Kel trying desperately to control the last two.

And if I do not wish it? Nothing came from Clarence but the words.

Talia felt a spike of hope in her breast though she knew they alone meant nothing. Yet this was Clarence's domain— this speaking of minds—even if he were now fully bonded with Kel, with his powers, he wouldn't reveal what he didn't wish, though it seemed she and Kel might have no choice.

"I'll abide by whatever you decide," Kel said honestly. "I will keep our contract or break it, whatever you wish. But either way, your secrets will be safe."

I will think on it.

Talia grinned, her certainty as bright as a beacon. She knew what those words meant.

Clarence sent her a disgusted, crooked look.

Before she could get herself into any more trouble, she set the crystal ball on the floor.

The gray realm around her instantly disappeared and she felt something slip away from inside her. LaSeren's healing room filled her view once more.

She immediately glanced at the cot and found Kel, his eyes open and staring at her. His hand was still nestled in hers. "Thank you."

Tears gathered in her eyes again. She wasn't able to help herself. Before the startled squire could do anything, Talia threw herself at him and hugged him hard. "Kel!"

She was still grinning, the two of them talking quietly, when LaSeren hobbled into the room, her face brightening with surprise at the sight of them.

Chapter Twenty One

AFTER CHECKING KEL over to make sure the poison was indeed gone, LaSeren made him take a brown draught and bid him rest. She gave Talia a cupful as well and told her to hurry off to bed. Cradling Clarence's crystal ball in one arm, she sent a last happy glance in Kel's direction and headed to her room. Her eyes felt incredibly heavy by the time she got there. Placing the crystal ball in a drawer to keep it out of harm's way, she crawled into bed and immediately fell into a deep, restful sleep.

A knock at her door brought her awake many hours later.

"Time to rise."

She blinked several times at the familiar call. It was still daylight when she came back to sleep, wasn't it? Did she sleep away the rest of the day and all night as well? LaSeren's draught must have been stronger than she realized.

Talia stretched and yawned, feeling much better than the day before. She got out of bed, washed and dressed, wondering if Kel would be released this morning. So far everything seemed like just another day, but she knew different. A lot had happened in the last few days, and for once, she was eager to get downstairs to see what the others might have to say about it.

She rushed down to the dining hall and was chided by one of the watchers and told to slow down. It made Talia's heart sing. She realized she loved this place. The thought made her skin tingle. She and the other students had fought to protect it and they'd succeeded. Somehow it also made the school feel more her own.

Reaching the dining hall, she made her way toward her group's regular table. She glanced in the direction of the teacher's area, looking for any sign of Kel. She wasn't too surprised not to find him there but was brought up short when she realized the table's gold-trimmed seat was for once actually occupied. Lareen was joining them for breakfast.

"Talia!" Mandee jumped up from her seat as she spotted her. Yllin, Daltan, and a few of the others got up as well, all smiling.

"Good morning." She smiled back glad to see they all appeared in good health. "Is everyone all right?"

"Everyone's fine," Mandee told her happily. "And Yllin told us the good news about Kel. She found out because she's gotten in on Wulan's good side with all the help she gave him and LaSeren after the battle."

"Mandee!" Yllin's cheeks grew a dark red, and for once she looked coy.

Talia laughed, but then forgot them as she spotted Nertak and LaSeren escorting a suddenly hesitant Kel toward the teachers' table. She was happy to see he seemed fine, though he walked as if still tired. As they approached, Lareen stood, a great smile on her face.

"Good morning everyone." Her voice boomed across

the hall. "We have much to be thankful for this morning. Not only were we able to help those relying on the guild for aid, but as most of you know by now, an attack on this school was also averted."

The hall went quiet, a sense of pressure building as everyone waited to see what she would say next.

"I want to commend all of you for your efforts to the guild and to this school," Lareen said. "Those who came with me to aid the Fifty-eighth Squadron, please stand."

The majority of the older students, watchers, and teachers stood.

"Everyone, give them a hand." The dining hall exploded with clapping and yelling.

Once the furor died down, Lareen signaled for them to sit again. Talia felt a knot of rising excitement growing inside her. She could see the same emotions reflected in her friends' faces as Lareen spoke again.

"Now, all those who fought for this school and gave that which was not expected of you, rise." The applause and yells were even more deafening than the time before.

Talia and her friends stood. As she gazed across the large room, she realized for the first time how small a number had actually been there at the time of the crisis. It seemed a miracle they'd pulled it off, but they had. They might be inexperienced children, but those teachers and watchers who were here with them made up for it with their wisdom and planning.

Talia glanced over at the teachers' table and saw Nertak smiling from ear to ear with the applause. Kel stood beside him, a small smile on his face as he clapped as hard as the rest.

The Administrator threw up her arms to call for silence.

They all sat down again.

"We won, yet it was a close thing. Only due to providence and the watchfulness and determination of a few were we able to find out the real goal of our enemy's attack in time to thwart them. Thus proving once and for all that despite their problems, their hearts are those of true Dragon Knights." Lareen's smile shone. "Not only did they warn us of the impending peril, but they fought with everything they had to save this school. We're very fortunate to have them. We owe this day to Clarence and Kel."

The room erupted. Talia leaped to her feet, clapping, even as dozens of others followed suit. Soon just about everyone in the room was standing and applauding in the squire's direction. She couldn't help but smile as she saw Kel trying to make himself as small as possible. True, the reason he had been out there to see the maeloon was personal and perhaps selfish, but he and Clarence had come through for everyone nevertheless. Lareen and Nertak didn't allow Kel to bow out; the two of them moving to stand to either side of him and kept him upright to receive the school's thanks.

Talia studied the faces applauding Kel and spotted a few she knew who'd thought little to nothing of him clapping along as hard as the rest. She felt her smile grow even bigger.

"There is one more who should not be forgotten." Lareen's voice boomed over all the applause. "For though she has only recently joined us, she, too, helped bring the threat to our attention and helped save one we thought beyond saving." The Administrator's gaze cut through the crowd straight to her. "Talia."

Talia's hands froze and fell to her side even as her friends seemed to turn almost as one to congratulate her. She didn't want the attention, yet it appeared today she would receive it whether she wanted it or not. She found herself staring at the ground.

"Ta-li-a. Ta-li-a." Mandee and Yllin took up the cry only loud enough for her to hear.

She would put up with this, for the good done was worth it. She brought her head up, her eyes seeking a particular face in the crowd. Kel's gaze met hers, his shy smile sharing her embarrassment, but glad for her as well.

This was her new home, and for the first time, she felt it to the core of her being. She would study hard and learn all the guild would teach her. She would share her mind and soul with a dragon if it was meant to be. Her heart filled to overflowing as another thought entered her head. A conviction for something she never thought she'd find. For foremost, she would devote her life to defend the guild and those it was created to protect in the first place. She finally knew what she wanted to do.

The End

ABOUT THE AUTHOR

Gloria Oliver lives in Texas making sure to stay away from rolling tumbleweeds while bowing to the never-ending wishes of her feline and canine masters. She works full time shoveling numbers around for an oil & gas company and squeezes in some writing time when she can.

Due for release in 2019 is "Alien Redemption." This is Gloria's first science fiction novel. This is also her eighth book to see publication. Her previous works have been fantasy, urban fantasy, and young adult fantasy novels. Several contain romantic and mystery elements. Her short stories of speculative fiction can be found in all manner of anthologies, covering things from the fantastic and strange to a Bubba Apocalypse.

Gloria is a member in good standing of BroadUniverse though she has yet to make the list for Cat Slaves R Us.

For some free reads, novel related short stories, sample chapters, appearance schedules and more information on her and her works, please drop by and visit her at www.gloriaoliver.com

In the Service of Samurai

CHAPTER 1

The sun dipped beneath the horizon, taking with it the last light of the day. Toshi crouched a little lower over his workbench as the light faded, knowing his master wouldn't want the lamps lit while a moment of daylight still remained.

Bought from his family while he was very young, he knew his master's ways well. Just as Master Shun didn't want any money wasted unnecessarily, he also precluded spending it on unneeded frivolities. Toshi ran his hand over his black hair, fingering the old, thin, stretched tie holding it in a ponytail. Though the last few months had seen a growth spurt for him, he knew he would not be receiving a new pair of knee-reaching breeches or a loose-fitting tunic for several moons yet.

Still, he was well-fed, and the skills he was learning would earn a better living than some. Aside from his not-so-common profession, he was the same as hundreds of others, a boy with the usual dark hair, brown eyes, slightly tinted skin, and almond-shaped eyes—characteristics which made it virtually impossible for a foreigner to pass as a native.

With precision gained from long practice, his brush slid smoothly over the thick rice paper as he diligently copied the curving meridian lines from the yellowing foreign parchment pinned on the desk beside him.

As he squinted, he dipped his brush in the small reservoir of ink built into the desk. Gently twirling the brush on the bowl's long lip, he bled off any excess. His steady hand guided the brush in another slow curve, marking the outline of his map. His attention didn't waver from the delicate work, even as he heard the shop's front door slide open.

"If you would please wait a moment, O-kyaku-sama, I'll be right with you," he said.

At an unhurried pace, Toshi came toward the end of his curving line. An unusually cool breeze made its way through the long shop, carrying with it the heavy scent of the sea. Like most shops in town, theirs was comprised of two stories, one in which to conduct business, the other for sleeping and eating. Master Shun believed in cleanliness, so a day did not pass during which Toshi didn't have to sweep the entrance or run a wet cloth across the floorboards. On days when it rained and prospective customers tracked in the mud with them, it was all he could do to keep up.

A large counter took up the left side of the front of the shop, while the rear held the working desk and wall-to-wall niches to hold their wares.

He rubbed his suddenly cold feet together, wondering why the customer hadn't bothered to close the door. His gaze snapped up as he realized the customer did shut the paper screen door, remembering the soft wood on wood sound as it had slid closed.

Yet the scent of salt and seaweed still crowded into his nostrils. It was strange the smell had come so far and was so strong since the shop was a distance from the port. Dismissing the oddity as he heard the late customer moving about, he set his brush carefully aside.

"O-kyaku-sama, I've finished." He bowed in the general direction of the visitor out of long-ingrained habit though he couldn't see him. "I apologize for the wait. How may I help you?"

He glanced at the shadow-enshrouded figure on the far side of the room, just as the last of the sun's light dwindled away. He quickly left the side of his workbench and its wooden platform. A small, unexplained chill coursed through him as the customer's ever deepening shadow came to loom over him. "Sir?"

He didn't receive an answer. Realizing Master Shun wasn't likely to make a sale if his customer remained in the dark, he shifted past the familiar surroundings and reached for the nearest paper lantern.

"I'll have some light for us in a moment, sir. I apologize for it being so dark." He removed the paper covering of the lamp and exposed the candle inside.

"Where's your master, boy?"

The unexpected voice made him jump. Though the customer was standing less than five arm lengths from him, the low, monotone voice sounded as if it had been issued from far away. Toshi glanced up to answer, but he hesitated as he saw a flash of greenish light issue from somewhere around the customer's face.

He rubbed at his eyes, feeling foolish, even as a tinge of unreasonable fear tried to crowd into his mind. Realizing his continued silence could be misunderstood as rudeness, he turned away from the figure and answered the question. At the same time, he reached to light the lamp. "Master Shun wasn't feeling well today, sir. He retired early. If you wish, you could leave a message for him. I'm sure he'll be feeling better tomorrow."

Warmth tickled his fingers as the wick caught fire. He placed the oval paper covering back over the candle. Its light gently spread over the room. He then carried the lantern to the main counter in the front of the shop, and turned to get his first good look at the waiting customer.

The man was facing away from him, so Toshi's gaze landed upon well cared for armor with its small steel plates hooked on lacquered leather. He wasn't surprised by what he saw, having already figured from the harsh and emotionless tone his customer was samurai—an elite, upper-class warrior.

Dressed as if for battle, the samurai wore the commanding rounded helmet with protruding strips of plate to guard the back of the neck. Fitted back plates and metal shoulder pads were attached to the toughened leather that made up the sleeves and the lower skirt. Strapped-on leather tubes protected the warrior's legs.

No, what made his eyes grow wide and his heart beat faster were the long tufts of wet seaweed hanging from the armor. Droplets of water reflected the lamp's light as they fell from the armor and the soaked clothes beneath to make a small puddle on the floor. His eyes followed the water trail leading from the samurai's feet back to the front door, his throat growing dry.

He took an unsteady step back, not sure what it all meant. His gaze traveled back to the armor and looked at the family crest painted there. The crest showed three white crescent moons facing each other within a thin circle. He didn't immediately recognize it. It wasn't one belonging to any of the prominent samurai families in town. Perhaps the man was a ronin, a masterless samurai, but the good condition of his armor and his kimono suggested otherwise.

Toshi watched with growing curiosity as the samurai slowly turned about to face him. His breath caught in his throat as a demonic scowl stared him in the face. He tried to still his racing heart as he realized the evil, horrifying expression before him was but a mask clipped to the front of the samurai's helmet, hiding the man's true face.

Taking another step back, he forced his eyes to leave the mask. Why would a samurai in full battle regalia come here to see Master Shun? He wondered what time it was and when the city watch would be coming by. Ever since the foreigners, the gaijin, had been allowed entry into the ports and even certain regions of the city itself, the curfews and patrols had become more stringent than before. If he ran out to look for them, would they cut him down before he could explain why he had broken curfew? Or worse, would he even make it out of the store if he decided to try?

His eyes fixed themselves on the sheathed swords, the long katana and shorter wakizashi, hanging from the samurai's side. He wasn't sure he could run past the strange customer to get help before the warrior could draw either blade and make its razor sharpness cut through his hide.

Glancing up into the warrior's masked face, he froze. He had seen it again—a flash of greenish light in the eye slits of the mask! Excitement and fear clutched at his breast and a thin sheen of perspiration rose on his brow. He stared hard at the samurai's metal mask, noticing for the first time how dark the area beyond the eye slits were and how the brown eyes that should have been there staring back at him were nowhere in sight.

"Sir, it…it's time for the shop to close. Is there a message you wish me to convey to Master Shun?" He tried not to look at the snarling, demonic mask, though his eyes were drawn toward the unnatural emptiness of its eye slits.

"Can you read gaijin maps, boy?"

Toshi felt surprised rush through him at the totally unexpected question.

"Yes, sir. A little. My…my master has had dealings with a number of gaijin to try to learn their ways of making and reading maps. I have studied this with him."

He hadn't meant to say so much. He didn't want to deal with the strange samurai. That was Master Shun's responsibility, but his frightened tongue hadn't known when to stop. With a long, silent shiver, he wished his master would come downstairs right then, even if it meant he would get a flogging.

"Do you have maps for the area with the chain of islands just to the north of here?"

The samurai's distant monotone slammed into him even as he tried to figure out what he should do. When he didn't immediately answer, the seaweed-covered samurai took a long step forward. Toshi took one back.

"Well, boy?" the samurai asked. His impatience was unmistakable; his voice sounded like it came from a deep well.

Not wanting the samurai to come any closer, Toshi tried to answer his question as quickly as possible.

"Yes, sir, we have many maps."

"Show me."

He scurried away to the shop's rear. Against the wall, on the right, racks of small square-shaped shelves were stacked upon each other almost to the ceiling. Ruffling through the carefully rolled parchments in a number of the squares, he grabbed what he was looking for and walked cautiously around the samurai to stand behind the safety of the shop's front counter. He laid the rolled parchment on the end of the counter closest to the unusual customer then backed away from it.

Without a word, the samurai stepped forward. Toshi watched as the man raised his arm to reach for the map. Filled with a bolt of sudden fear, he jumped back, smashing his head against one of the shop's wooden support beams as the hand he expected to see reaching for the map never appeared. With spots of color flying before his eyes, he stared in paralyzed horror as fleshless fingers reached instead to claim the waiting map.

"You're *obake*. A monster!" The boy clamped his hands over his mouth as he realized the accusing words were his. He stared at the samurai in cold terror, sure his words would be the end of him.

The samurai ignored him.

As his death didn't immediately manifest, Toshi's eyes shrank back to normal. He made no attempt, though, to remove his hands from his mouth. With dread-filled fascination, he watched the samurai's fleshless hand as the creature took the rolled map and, with another equally bare, undid the string holding it together. He observed the skeletal fingers as they spread the map out over the top of the counter.

All the old stories were true. Demons did walk the earth. But why was this demon here? He and Master Shun had done all Shinto prescribed in order to keep themselves out of the reach of evil or mischievous spirits.

Shinto—The Way of the Gods—made them aware of the spirits that inhabited every rock, tree, and mountain, and which spirits were best avoided and how. The two of them had exorcized the shop and its living quarters above on New Year's as they did every year, driving the evil spirits out and good luck in. They'd gone to the temple and made the prescribed offerings. The prayer strips were all in place. Had the gods decided not to protect them? What had Master Shun done to bring such evil to this place?

The samurai's voice interrupted his thoughts.

"Are all known reefs and other hazards of the area

contained within this map?"

Toshi nodded rapidly, his hands still clamped over his mouth. He tried crawling back into the beam behind him as the samurai's empty stare turned toward him, a flash of eerie green light momentarily filling the mask's slits. Sweat poured down the side of his face as he realized with a start the samurai hadn't seen his nod and was therefore still waiting for his answer. He forced his hands to move away from his mouth.

"Y-yes, sir." He could barely keep his words from stumbling over each other. "It's…it's all there, as far as I know. Master Shun has spent a lot of money getting the gaijin to help him make accurate maps."

He clamped his hands over his mouth again, knowing he'd just told more than he liked. The samurai's stare shifted away from him back to the map.

"You can read this map? The numbers, the words?"

Toshi hesitated a long moment before nodding when the samurai's eyes turned toward him again.

"Could you guide someone with it if you had the gaijin instruments?" he asked.

Toshi stared at the samurai, caught off-guard by the question. Should he lie? Very few people got the opportunity to meet gaijin, let alone learn their ways. The demon couldn't possibly know the gaijin merchant they'd contracted had taught him a lot more than required. Even Master Shun didn't know how much he'd learned. Despite being a demon, the samurai wouldn't sense a lie, would he?

"Well?"

The deep voice didn't sound happy to be kept waiting. Green fire flared in the snarling mask's eyes, and Toshi knew he couldn't take the risk. Although he had a horrible feeling he would regret his truthfulness, he nodded.

"Fetch me paper, ink, and brush."

He cringed against the wall, not understanding the reason for the request.

"Move!" The samurai's fleshless hand dropped to the hilt of his katana.

Driven by the commanding tone as well as the unspoken threat, Toshi bolted to the back of the store. Searching for the items requested, he hurried back, the skin on the nape of his neck prickling as he noticed the samurai stood between him and the door.

He almost dropped the wooden ink well on the counter as he tried to put the requested items down. Laying all the supplies within the samurai's reach, he scurried back to stand against his wooden beam.

The skeletal hand reached out and expertly took hold of the thin, longhandled brush. With frightened eyes, Toshi noted as each of the delicate bones in the hand moved with careless grace. Goosebumps covered his arms and back as he saw there was nothing holding them together.

With elegant fluidity, the samurai inked the brush and began to write. Despite himself, Toshi appreciated the evenness of the samurai's strokes. The writing was very clear, and he had no trouble understanding it despite the fact it was upside down to him. With morbid curiosity, he found himself reading the message the samurai was writing for Master Shun. Literacy had been one of the few unexpected gifts he'd gained since being sold as an apprentice.

His face drained of color as he realized the meaning of what he was reading.

"No! Sir, please don't do this," he pleaded. "Master Shun doesn't want to sell me. I've been his apprentice for too many years. You mustn't do this, sir. You mustn't do this!"

Fear overwhelming his sense, he leaped forward to grab the offensive piece of paper. Before his fingers could even brush its surface, the samurai's bony hand lashed out and caught his wrist.

Toshi stared in desperation at the glowing eye slits as an unearthly cold spread into his arm from the samurai's fleshless hand. The cold moved through him like a living thing, paralyzing him where he stood.

Never loosening his hold on the boy's arm, the samurai returned to completing his message.

As the grisly metal face looked elsewhere, Toshi found his eyes and numbed mind free again. He tried to scream so he could wake up Master Shun or attract the watch—anything that might get him away from this demon, but his vocal cords were as frozen as the rest of him.

He read the note again and again, noticing as the samurai finished that it lacked a signature. Who was this demon? Studying the family crest again, he thought he might have seen it somewhere before. Was it important?

The samurai reached inside and produced a hand-sized silk sack from within the lacquered armor. The jingle of coins echoed through the room as the samurai let the sack drop on the counter. He then reached into a small bag at his side and brought out a long bamboo tube. He carefully rolled up the map and placed it inside. Returning the tube to the bag, the samurai turned his burning green eyes in Toshi's direction.

"Come."

The intense cold that had kept him rooted to the spot lessened. Toshi walked hesitantly around the counter, the samurai pulling on his wrist.

His worried gaze swept around the shop, a heavy feeling in the pit of his stomach telling him this would be the last time he'd ever see the place he'd called home since he was six. With an overwhelming sense of loss, of leaving all he had ever known, he stopped and planted his feet on the floor, not willing to let it all go so easily.

Without looking back, the samurai yanked his arm, pitching him forward. Landing hard on his knees, Toshi felt his eyes fill with pain-induced tears as the samurai then dragged him toward the door. The snarling mask with its glowing eyes glared at him without the slightest sign of pity or mercy.

With a soft whoosh, the samurai slid open the shop's paneled front door and wrenched him to his feet.

"Now walk." The samurai's free hand landed on his sword's hilt once more, reminding the boy of its silent but deadly threat.

Toshi looked away, hating the way he felt as he realized he

had no choice. He slipped on his old sandals, sitting just outside the store entrance, and stepped out of his old life forever.

Keeping his gaze on the dirt road, he followed as the samurai set an easy pace away from the shop. As they walked, a thin fog sprang up around them. Toshi shivered, cold inside and out.

All he was being forced to leave behind flashed through his mind–Master Shun, quirky and strange though he was; the Kawa family next door and their gaggle of children; the sweet dumplings he always bought during festival nights from the old woman near the temple; his room and his few possessions; the friends he'd made from the gaijin ship. His heart ached.

Very few lights were on in the bottom floors of the many two-storied buildings surrounding them on either side. A number of the lights in the living quarters on the second floor had already gone dark as well. Only the howling wind and the lonely howl of a stray dog disturbed the silence as he was led down the street in the direction of the docks.

The scent of the demon's clinging seaweed wrapped about Toshi as they walked. He shuddered despite the warm night breeze as the samurai strolled on as if he were lord of everything around him. Toshi refused to look at him, to look at the monster that was ripping him away from all he knew.

The buildings changed as they approached the docks. The wood-and-paper homes grew smaller as they crowded in side-by-side. The wail of a hungry child or a quiet, lonely moan occasionally escaped into the street, the smell of human waste and rotting garbage growing ever thicker. The samurai appeared to be oblivious to it all, yet for Toshi, these scents and sounds only too sharply expressed the despair and unfairness welling up inside him.

At last, he slipped a hateful glance at the samurai. Of course, it wouldn't bother a demon if there was suffering and misery in the world or that he was about to add to it. After all, wasn't that what demons were for?

He quickly wiped at the tears threatening his eyes,

determined not to show any weakness to this demon. Although he hoped for it with every step, the samurai's cold grip never lessened on his wrist. If he could only get a chance to try to escape!

With unbelieving eyes, as they crossed the last street intersection before the docks he spotted two samurai of the watch. Hope sprang in his heart, and he tried to scream for their attention as the demon pulled him across the street. Yet although he tried and tried, no sound made it past his lips. The two men continued walking as he felt his last chance for freedom being swept away by fate.

While his soul wailed with despair, his eyes lighted on a rock on the dirt road less than two feet in front of him. He felt an urge to look at the demon beside him, to make sure he hadn't seen the rock. He forced himself to curb the impulse and kept his gaze glued to his one possible means of salvation.

Leaving himself no time for thought, he dropped to the ground and swung one of his legs hard, tripping the samurai. The armored figure fell.

Toshi lunged for the rock. Gasping, he felt the bitter cold from the fleshless hand that still held him pour greedily into his bones. He couldn't feel the rock as he wrapped his fingers around it. His body slowed as he fought with every ounce of his being to lift his arm so he could throw the stone to try and gain the attention of the watch.

Perspiration broke out all over his body from the effort as the flowing cold pierced him to the core. With a silent scream, he watched the two samurai disappear from sight as his raised arm froze at the top of the throwing arc.

Hot pain blossomed on the side of his face. Unable to move, he couldn't stop himself from toppling onto the dirt, the samurai's blow knocking him off his feet. A whispered hiss fell on his ear as his vision swam.

"Fool."

He would have cringed from the scorn in the samurai's voice, but he couldn't even do that. A hard yank brought him to his knees. He tried his best to ignore the grotesque mask and the glowing eyes before him.

"If you find someone willing to try to stop me from taking you, I'll kill them. Their death will be on your head."

The samurai's voice was cold. Toshi looked away. He knew the demon would do what he threatened.

Another rough yank brought him to his feet. He gasped in pain at the hard pull, the rock he had risked so much to grab falling forgotten from numb fingers. The samurai's words continued to reverberate in his mind as he was dragged forward once again.

Why would a demon be willing to kill to keep him? Why then pay Master Shun instead of just stealing him away? This wasn't the way demons did things.

Toshi offered no more resistance as the samurai pulled him onto the platform for the docks. He kept looking back, however, trying hard to engrave the memory of the home he was being torn from in his mind. He wiped at his face with his sleeve, his eyes burning.

The majority of the boats tied close to them were long and flat-bottomed, most of them fishing boats. On the dock's far side were the gaijin ships. Their tall masts and swollen bodies dwarfed all the other boats around them.

The samurai paid him no attention as he pulled him along and strolled down each of the platforms, gazing at all the ships gathered there. After several minutes, they came across a fishing boat with a small skiff tied to its side. Toshi was dragged toward it, and he wondered what the samurai was planning.

Moving through the fishing boat toward the single-oared dory, the samurai left three coins wrapped artistically in paper next to the ship's tiller. Toshi's eyes strayed to the small bundle, puzzled by the fact the coins had been prepared as a gift. It then dawned on him what they were being left for. His brow furrowed. Why would a demon have need of a skiff?

With his one free hand, the samurai pulled on the rope tied to the small craft and drew it closer to them.

"Get in." Flashing green eyes turned in Toshi's direction

with the barked command.

He tried to do as he'd been told. His legs, though, still filled with the samurai's unearthly cold, were numb and unresponsive. As he tried to crawl over the ship's rail, he shifted his weight too quickly and fell. Watching in startled fear as the boat rose up to meet his face, he felt his arm wrenched from behind. Pulled upward, he was kept from landing face-first into the boat. His legs continued to go down and smacked into the side of the craft as he dangled there by his arm, but he barely felt the impact. This bothered him more than the fact he could have been hurt.

The samurai pulled him up farther until he got his legs into the boat before suddenly letting go of his wrist. Toshi collapsed to his knees, the thread of cold pouring through his bones replaced by a jolt of warmth from his pumping heart.

The fog that had followed them on the streets slithered from the fishing boat down into the skiff as if it hungered for them. Toshi sat still in the bottom of the craft, trying to dispel the memory of the wooden deck rushing toward his face.

The samurai lowered himself into the skiff in a fluid drop, barely rocking the boat. Gazing down at Toshi for a moment, he slid his hand onto the shorter of his two swords before whipping it out of its sheath and slicing through the skiff's mooring line in one smooth motion.

"If you try to leave this craft, I will cut you in half before you can hit the water."

Toshi would have laughed at the irony if he hadn't thought the samurai would cut him down for that, too. His body felt so numb and slow he doubted he could even save himself if the boat suddenly tipped over, let alone try to escape.

He felt the samurai's green gaze staring at him again. He tried his best not to let his own cross its path.

"Take the oar and row us out to the middle of the bay." The samurai waved his hand toward the back of the boat.

He crawled to where he'd been ordered and stared at the long angled oar waiting there. Watching to make sure his hands got around it, since he still couldn't feel them, he moved it back and forth to get the craft moving.

As the small boat inched away from the docks to deeper water, he glanced back at the city one more time. His eyes grew moist as he stared at the dark silhouette, no hint showing in the darkness of the bustle and life that had made it so dear to him over the years.

The fog grew in intensity. It cut off his view of the city. In a way, it made it seem as if the city had never existed.

After a time, the skiff picked up speed. Toshi became ever more grateful for the task the demon had given him, as it loosened the numbness from his body. The heat of the work was exhilarating compared to the unearthly coldness that had gripped him before.

He stared at the samurai's armored back, seeing nothing but fog and sea beyond him. When he was feeling more like himself, he worked up the courage to speak.

"Sir, might I ask where we are going?"

The samurai didn't react to his question, just remained fixed, facing the prow of the boat. Toshi continued rowing and didn't speak again. He still had no idea as to their destination when his arms began to tire.

"Stop here." The samurai made a chopping motion with his hand.

Toshi stopped rowing, staring at the samurai in surprise, able to see nothing but the swirling fog around them. Keeping his gaze locked on the samurai, he waited to see what he would ask him to do next. An unwanted chill cut through him as he tried his best not to guess at what it might be.

His attention was drawn to the water as bubbles formed on its surface. The bubbles grew to a writhing mass, a soft glow coming from beneath them. The fog slithered away as if afraid of what was happening in the water. He watched the spot of light beneath the bubbles get larger and brighter.

His knuckles turned white as he gripped his oar in apprehension. The knocking of his pulse in his ears was the only sound he could hear as an eerily glowing rod broke through the surface of the frothing sea.

The rod rose higher. A crossbeam broke the surface beneath it, long strands of seaweed strung from its length. A tattered square sail followed, emblazoned with a gold-colored replica of the crest on the samurai's armor.

As terror welled within him, his gaze was inexorably drawn to the samurai. The warrior slowly turned to face him and stared at him with his burning green eyes. Toshi shook his head in helpless denial as the samurai stood up and pointed toward the still-rising ghost vessel.

"No! This is not my karma," he said. "I won't go to a cursed ship!"

The samurai stared at him impassively, the green light issuing from the demon mask's eyes brighter than before.

"Row.

Toshi shook his head again, forgetting whom he was denying in the grip of his horror. He let go of the oar as if it burned him. His gaze darted around, as he looked for a way to escape and saw his only option was to dive into the sea.

He turned, determined to leave the boat. Something solid struck the back of his knee, folding his leg under him. As he struggled not to fall, the samurai's lacquered scabbard flashed ahead of him just before it slammed into his stomach. He fell hard into the boat.

Panic drove him to ignore the flaring pain in his leg and stomach as he fought to throw himself overboard. He'd reached the side of the boat when his cotton tunic was wrenched from behind and he was yanked with it. He tried desperately to pull away, his fists flying, but a shot of unearthly cold wove down his spine, draining his resistance as fleshless fingers wrapped around the back of his neck.

He screamed.

His terror and desperation multiplied as the cold spread through him. Still screaming, he tried to pry the bony fingers from his neck, but his hands were slapped away. Soon he could no longer move. With a soundless cry of fear, he shut his eyes, not wanting to see what awaited him.

The flat-bottomed ship had come fully to the surface.

Indistinct shapes moving within it silently brought out long poles with hooks and snared the small boat. As the skiff was secured to the side of the larger vessel, a number of fleshless hands reached down toward it.

Toshi fought as half a dozen hands attached to his body and pulled him upward. The samurai's hand left the back of his neck. In panic, he snapped his eyes open to see why the demon had deserted him. He gazed straight into a grinning skull.

Empty eye sockets stared into his own, a reddish glow flaring for a moment in their depths. He opened his mouth to scream, but no sound passed his lips. The fleshless face came closer. The creature's eyes flared with bright-red light. Toshi tried to squirm away, but in vain. His heart threatened to burst from horror before that fleshless grin.

An arm thrust between them. Sudden hope flared within him as his frightened gaze shifted to seek the samurai's masked face. He didn't feel the samurai's hand as it latched onto his. His numbed body was turned around, and he glimpsed the rest of the crew. His mind wouldn't count them, it didn't want to see them. It shrieked in disbelief as he stared at the white gleaming skeletons before him.

They stood upright and wore clothes he would have seen on men on any common street. Some wore short pants and sleeveless shirts. Others only wore fudoshi–a long cloth coiled around the body that served to cover the genitals like a loincloth–and short vests.

Half-supporting, half-dragging him, the samurai took him toward a door set in the wall of the raised deck housing the tiller. His mind as numbed by terror as his body was by cold, he didn't resist as he was taken into the small hallway beyond.

Ignoring the ladder going below, the samurai pulled him forward, stopping before the second doorway on the right. Throwing the door open, he thrust Toshi inside.

Unable in his paralysis to break his fall, he slammed onto the glowing floor. The door was closed and bolted behind him.

The pain of the fall a very faint perception, Toshi gave in to his fear and despair. He scooted to a corner and hugged his knees to his chest. His wide eyes stared at the glow that permeated everything in the room.

Read Chapters 2 and 3 at www.gloriaoliver.com/samurai

www.ingramcontent.com/pod-product-compliance
Lightning Source LLC
Chambersburg PA
CBHW051553100726
47898CB00001B/82